THE SALTWATER CURSE

AVINA ST. GRAVES

The Saltwater Curse by Avina St. Graves

Published by Avina St. Graves

Contact the author at author@avinastgraves.com

Copyright © 2025 Avina St. Graves

Editing by the Fiction Fix

Proofreading by Nessa's Lair

Cover by Andrea Corsini

ISBN Print 978-0-473-73651-4

ISBN eBook 978-0-473-73653-8

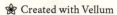 Created with Vellum

AUTHOR'S NOTE

To the FBI agent assigned to me,

THIS was why I was Googling all those shady things. I swear. I pinky promise I don't have a lab at home where I'm trying to make *that* stuff.

Plus, half of what I wanted to know wasn't even online, so I was left with no choice but to take liberties. If I *actually* made it, there's no way it would work.

Just trust me. You can take me off that list you put me on.

Now, to whom it's about to concern,

To avoid being placed on any more watchlists, please do not take the information contained in this book as fact. It is a work of fiction, in which a literal shape-shifting kraken exists.

If you somehow know the intricacies of mass manufacturing fake passports, I should warn you, I do not. Please know I failed high school physics, barely passed computer science, and no one on Reddit has asked this question before—that I could find.

Additionally, if you are a marine biologist, it might be in your best interest to reconsider reading this book, because I can promise you, I took a lot of ocean-related liberties. Kelp grows wherever I say kelp grows.

And as a PSA, out of respect, I am not touching on the myths, beliefs, or religions of my people. The kraken culture is entirely made-up, and any similarities with real-life religions are coincidental.

TRIGGERS

Stretching, sex, tentacles, unconsented voyeurism, cannibalism (depends how you look at it), murder, gore, death by tentacles, shark attack (kind of?), sad animals, kidnapping, nerve issues, toxic characters, death of parents and siblings (off-screen), death of a spouse, domestic abuse not by the MMC, reference to sexual assault, trauma, PTSD, racism (by krakens toward humans).

PLAYLIST

Angry Too - *Lola Blanc*
MILK OF THE SIREN - Melanie Martinez
Never Felt So Alone - *Labrinth*
Burn - *The Pretty Reckless*
Cross My Heart I Hope U Die - *Meg Smith*
The fruits - *Paris Paloma*
Which Witch - *Florence + The Machine*
Freak - *Sub Urban, REI AMI*
Wasteland - *Royal & the Serpent*
The Night We Met - *Lord Hurton*
Atlantis - *Seafret*
Cinnamon Girl - *Lana Del Rey*
To Be Alone - *Hozier*
Ophelia - *The Lumineers*
Again - *Noah Cyrus ft. XXXTENTACION*
Satu Bulan - *Bernadya*
All I Want – *Kodaline*
I Found - *Amber Run*
Romantic Homicide - *d4vd*

PLAYLIST (UNOFFICIAL)

Going Under – *Evanescence*
Cake By The Ocean – *DNCE*
Waterfalls - *TLC*
Waves - *Dean Lewis*
Hoist The Colours - *The Wellermen*
My Heart Will Go On - *Céline Dion*
Rain Over Me - *Pitbull, Marc Anthony*
Riptide - *Vance Joy*
Ocean eyes - *Billie Eilish*
High Water - *Sleep Token*
Sailor Song - *Gigi Perez*
The Beach - *The Neighbourhood*
West Coast - *Lana Del Rey*
Wellerman - Sea Shanty - *Nathan Evans*
Soaked - *Shy Smith*
Siren - *Kailee Morgue*
Swim - *Chase Atlantic*
Waterloo - *ABBA*

To those who always knew that "three-in-one" has an entirely different meaning in romance books.

PROLOGUE

How would I sleep at night if I killed him right now?

Peacefully, I think.

I would only regret I didn't do it sooner.

The pristine marble floor and the clean, white cupboard doors go in and out of focus. Tears trickle from the corners of my eyes, twining with the crimson trickle of blood leaking from the gash on my forehead, blazing a path onto the cold floor. If I move, he might kick me again.

It's my fault.

I should have known better than to bring my emotions home.

Tommy is particular. He has certain expectations of his fiancée, and being upset over the third anniversary of my father's death isn't one of them. I should have been dolled up, head bowed, with dinner served on the table the moment he stepped through the imposing wooden door.

I should have done better.

The pain in my side is a faint ache, the bruise along my cheek a distant thought.

All I wanted was to visit the beach where I had spread his

ashes, then spend the rest of the day wallowing and choking on my grief over the man who raised me.

I was foolish. I should have seen this punishment coming.

I should have *known* better.

If I had known the type of person Tommy really was, or what the Gallaghers were up to in the dark of night, I would've never applied for the job at his family's tech company. I wouldn't have fallen for his charming smile, nor would I have said "yes" when he pulled out a huge diamond ring, asking me—without words—to be his indentured servant. I wish I had seen through the fancy dresses and jewelry he showered me with, all the times he convinced me to stay home with him instead of seeing my friends or my dad.

I should have run the second I laid eyes on him four years ago.

But here I am, regretting every move I made since I met him.

I'm so tired.

"Get the fuck up." A hand wraps around my arm, yanking me to my feet and adding another bruise to his battered canvas.

He shoves me back, and the corner of the kitchen counter hits the small of my back, sending a piercing jolt up my spine. My hand flies out to support myself against the marble. My wrist brace lands in a pool of water, soaking through the thick fabric as I slide along the counter, fingers grazing the edge of the chopping board I was using when Tommy came barreling in.

I'm not a fan of what I was making. If he didn't enjoy eating my country's cuisine, I wasn't allowed to make it. But he likes tonight's meal, and what he likes, I like.

And I like... I don't know what I enjoy anymore.

If Dad were here, he'd stand up for me.

The thought lodges a boulder in my throat. I force myself to suppress a sob so I don't anger Tommy more. Why didn't I listen when Dad warned me this man meant trouble? It was the only thing we ever argued about. I wish I could apologize to him now. Dad was the only person I had, and I fought him tooth and nail under the misguided pretense that Tommy was *different*—special. A man of his word, someone who loved me. I fell for his façade.

Nothing is worth the heated floors, indoor swimming pool, or stupid fucking six-car garage filled with vehicles I'm not allowed to touch.

"Do you think I want to come home to find you looking like shit? Huh?"

I keep my gaze averted. Meeting his eyes never bodes well, at least not anymore.

Silent tears stream down my face as a glint catches my eye, and I try to ignore the light reflecting off the silver blade just inches away from my fingers.

I thought if I did the steak *just* right, my mood would be forgiven. If the roasted sweet potatoes, broccoli, and carrots were seasoned *just right*, my appearance would be quickly forgotten.

But again, I knew better.

I'm so sorry for disappointing you, Dad.

"I was nice enough to let you have a day off. Maybe I shouldn't have if you can't appreciate everything I do for you."

Do for me? What the fuck do you do for me, Tommy? Because I'd absolutely love to know.

I was given a credit card I'm not allowed to use. If I get groceries, I have to show him the receipt. If I need a dress for an event, his assistant gets it for me. If I want to visit Dad's memorial, I need permission—and he always says no. If I breathe too loud, I get yelled at. If I blink too much, I'm glared at.

The only thing Tommy has ever done for me is hate every single aspect of my existence.

I stare blankly to the side, the knife's plastic handle taunting me, orange carrot residue pebbled along the serrated edge.

Speak when spoken to. Bend over when told. Spread my legs when he wants.

He doesn't want a wife. He wants a servant.

Dad would be disappointed to see what I've become.

3

I clench my jaw, trying to stop my body from trembling.

"Do you know how many girls want to be in your position? I could have my pick from a hundred of them, but I chose *you* to be my wife. And you've been nothing but ungrateful."

Then why did you do it, Tommy? Was it the brightness in my eyes when you found me fresh from university? Or did you decide I would make the perfect victim when you discovered I had the skills required to elevate your business?

I had dreams, Tommy. Hope. Real talent. I could have made a difference, saved lives. I was meant to soar.

I would have been everything without you.

But you killed me, Thomas Gallagher.

You and your brother, John, buried me alive.

He slaps my cheek, and my head whips to the side as the sound of skin colliding with skin ripples through the plain room. Red blossoms along my cheek, burning a path straight to my still-beating heart. "You would be nothing without me, Kristy."

I despise hearing those two syllables on his lips.

Kristy.

That name used to hold such fond memories—how my father used to say it, the way the etching of "Misty" gleamed on his bike's gas tank. Now, I hate it. I never want to hear it again.

"*Nothing,*" he yells.

Tommy is a piece of shit in an expensive suit. His whole family is—criminals with deep pockets and an even deeper hold on the police. Everyone turns a blind eye to the heinous acts carried out within their *enterprise*—gang, group, organization, whatever they want to call themselves. The effect is the same.

I could kill Tommy, and I wouldn't shed a tear. His entire family could drop dead at my feet, and I wouldn't bat an eye. They're all monsters, the worst dregs of society, hidden behind diamonds and gold.

My lips twitch, and I have to fight back a sneer. I just wanted to mourn my dad today. Was that really too much to ask?

His fingers wrap around my throat, cutting off my oxygen. Pain swells around my neck, worse where his skin touches mine. My flesh is still raw from when he did this two nights ago. It pales in comparison to the rest of my injuries.

I don't struggle or fight. He prefers it when I do. The last thing I want is to bring him more pleasure from my suffering.

My watery stare flicks up to his putrid green eyes. His pupils are blown out, the corners of his eyes are creased. His mouth is curled down. There's a rosy tint to his tanned cheeks. The tendons in his neck strain, but not from exertion.

I know what will happen next. It's what always happens when Tommy looks at me this way. He'll turn me around and take me. If I'm lucky, I'll be able to sit tomorrow.

I hate him.

I hate him. I hate him. I hate him.

God, I fucking *hate* him.

Dots scatter across my vision, everything going blurry. I sputter and cough despite how hard I try to hide my desperation for air. Both my hands hit the counter behind me, flailing around for some semblance of reprieve, as if touching stone might stop my lungs from burning. Agonizing pain slices up the arm he injured earlier. My braced hand catches on an object, and the chopping board clatters to the floor, the vegetables a rainbow mess across sparkling marble.

Tommy doesn't react, too lost to whatever sick fantasy is playing out in his head. My stomach drops like a boulder in a landslide.

I'd rather die than live through this again.

He and his family have taken so much from me when I've given them everything. All they've left is a faint glimmer of the person I was before he swept me off my feet and made me feel like a princess, only to then throw me in the dungeons, a crown of poisoned thorns on my head.

His heated breath skitters across my skin, sticky and cloying.

He shoves my sweats down my legs before he fumbles with his belt, undoing his zip. "No one will love you like I do."

I hold his stare as I rasp, "Thank God."

His eyes widen when I raise my arm. Scarlet bursts from his skin, crimson dots splatter onto my top and part of his favorite meal.

Oxygen slams into my lungs, making my knees buckle. Hot tears stream down my face as I watch the man who made me believe the devil exists stumble back, gripping the knife protruding from his neck. My hand trembles in my wrist brace as I relive the feel of skin and tendon parting under the blade.

"You were always pathetic," I croak, voice raw, body shaking. Fury has found a home in my heart. I want to scream. Riot. Take the knife out just to plunge it into him ten more times.

But I'm better than that. Stronger. *Smarter.* Violent men aren't violent because they lost their temper—they're violent because they know they can get away with it. If it was an issue of emotional control, his entire family would have met his fists as frequently as I do.

No, I'll bottle this rage up and use it to survive. *That's* how I'll make my father proud.

"You made me do this," I whisper.

Those moldy green eyes widen when I echo the words he has used on me more times than I can count. He hip checks the kitchen island and tips sideways, smearing red around the once-pristine kitchen, making this place as rotten as it is on the inside.

It's fitting this way. White was never his color.

"You..." He tries to speak through the blood sputtering from his mouth.

"Learn to enunciate," I mock, itching to grab the knife.

He backhanded me while saying that once.

Tommy slumps to the floor in a tangled mess of limbs, sight still fixed on me. I want to imprint the image of the life draining from him into my memory. It'll be the picture I fall asleep to at night, my first thought when I wake in the morning.

"You killed me, Tommy," I whisper. Tears trickle down my cheeks as I recall everything I've endured the past four years. "And, in return, I'm killing you. A corpse is *killing* you. Isn't it funny how that works? A bit ironic, no?"

My entire body trembles as I stare at him, his blood threading through the pattern of my skin, drying into a crust.

I feel nothing.

Regret nothing.

He had it coming.

My sock-covered feet step back across the slippery tile floor. "Goodbye, Tommy," I rasp. "I'll see you in hell."

They'll come for me. His brother, his parents. They won't rest until I pay for taking Tommy away from them. From this day until I take my last breath, I will never be free, a tagged bird forever flying faster than the wind. But I'll take that over a gilded cage. I'll paint the trees with blood if I have to.

This isn't just an escape. It's retribution.

My murder made me silent. All that's left for them to do is put me in the dirt. But Tommy made one grave mistake: he forged me into a weapon.

A tarnished blade can still cut.

1

CINDI

Fifteen months later

The tweezers clatter onto the table from the sudden piercing pain from my elbow down.

"Fuck," I hiss under my breath.

I stretch my fingers and wiggle them to ease the tension. It does jack shit. Over a year later, and I'm still paying for the crap Tommy put me through. Huffing, I snatch my wrist brace off the nearby shelf and strap it on before pushing away from the workbench.

Whatever. I'll fix the speakers later. It's not important. I need to get ready for my meeting.

Distracting myself does very little to stop my fingers from tingling. I need medical attention—surgery, injection, physio— but it's not an option. What would be the point? There's only so much someone can endure when their ex breaks the same hand three times and forces them to work through the agony. Plus, that means letting someone touch me, and... No, not an option.

A wave of vertigo hits me when I stand, hands flying onto the bench to stabilize myself. My eyes screw shut, and I breathe against the sudden blow of exhaustion. It slowly ebbs away as the seconds pass, until I can walk. It's been getting worse over the past six months. My own body is giving out on me.

Grumbling under my breath, I step out of my air-conditioned workroom into the living area, suppressing a grimace at the dip in temperature. The faintest scent of the sea breeze permeates the humid air over notes of Dad's favorite *pad kra pao moo* recipe I had for lunch—not as good as how my grandma made it, but it'll do.

I eyeball the many in-process repairs lying around the room and amble over to the clean laundry pile on the couch, where my keys stick out from between the cracks in the cushions—proof I haven't left the house in, what? A week?

My little two-bedroom cabin is nothing fancy. There's an old water stain on the ceiling in the bathroom. The water pressure can be more accurately described as a trickle. A couple of the living room tiles have hairline cracks in them—one of them is actually starting to chip. Half the wallpaper in my bedroom is peeling, and one of the wooden boards on the stairs leading to the front door is rotten.

The place is free from blood money, devoid of walls I've been thrown against, corners I've huddled in. This little shack by the ocean is *mine*, a slice of Earth untouched by the Gallaghers.

The two girls who got me fake passports changed my name to Cindi—it's close enough to Kristy that I'd remember—and brought me into their fold, Deedee and Nat, helped me put a fresh coat of paint on the rest of the house, organized for an AC unit to be installed in my bedroom, and got the bathroom redone so I wasn't stuck with a squatting toilet.

The cabin is close enough to Kuta and Ubud in Bali that I can make drops and pick up supplies for the microchip lab without having to drive for hours. Plus, there are a bunch of trees between me and my neighbors and next to no foot traffic to make it easier to survey my area.

Being close to the beach and the cheaper rent are bonuses.

I grab the gun hidden beneath the coffee table and stuff it in my backpack, mentally tallying the supplies I'll need to order for next month's shipment so we can meet rising demand for our fake passports. Maybe I can convince Deedee to overstock so we don't have to stress about that every month.

She'll probably fight me on it, but it's not my business, so I can't fully complain.

The Velcro of my brace catches on the shoulder straps of my backpack when I tug it on, and pain darts up my arm. It's just one thing after another.

Get over it, I chastise myself.

My good hand hovers over the door handle. Paranoia and fear skitter down my spine at the thought of leaving the safety of my house. What if a pirate is tracking me to find our lab? What if I run into a Gallagher? What if Tommy's family catches me and—

The muscle in my jaw pulses. Tommy does *not* control me anymore. I refuse to be stuck behind bars of my own making.

The moment I step outside, damp air slaps me in the face, and I almost turn right back around. I want to be either in the water or lying beneath the AC, not spending the next hour or so on the road to meet with a man-child.

The door automatically locks behind me, the alarm system engaged with a couple of taps on my phone, beginning a countdown on my laptop to self-destruct if someone tries to break in.

If someone told me I'd be using my engineering degree for home security, I would've laughed. Yet, here we are.

Blowing out a breath, I squint against the sun as I round the house to the garage. Unlocking and rolling up the door, I falter at the engine conveniently sitting *outside* the car—Dad would've had my car up and running in a matter of days. He would've made it an all-hands-on-deck situation at the shop. But all this shit is my problem now, and my problem alone.

I hang my head back and suppress a groan. A spike of pain tears through my arm, and I glare at the stupid brace, then at the even stupider Honda Civic with the shitty transmission. If my car is out of commission, I'm bearing the full wrath of Satan on a bike.

Pulling the roller door shut, I curse Tommy under my breath for the millionth time as I head for the motorbike, fishing out a pair of sunglasses from my backpack. I clip on a helmet before settling on the seat. The engine rumbles alive beneath me, soothing my soul—but it's not nearly enough to calm the paranoia rearing its ugly head.

Clenching my eyes shut, I count to three.

Tommy's family doesn't know I'm here.

I stretch my fingers out one last time before gripping the throttle. The wheels skid across the ground, kicking up a cloud of dirt that follows my wake, and I'm off, tearing down the long driveway before making it onto a gravel road. I switch between main streets and side ones, one eye always out for any vehicles that might be tailing me.

Sweat drips down my forehead and spine, and the harsh fabric of my shorts chafes painfully against my skin.

Fuck you, Tommy.

The anxiety curdling low in my stomach worsens the closer I get to the meeting site in Denpasar. The heavy bag of passports sitting on my shoulder acts as a constant reminder that one wrong move, and I could be worse than dead. I've seen and heard what he and his family were capable of—all the lives lost over slight inconveniences, all the rumors about what they've done to people who pissed them off.

After emptying out Tommy's safe, I went to his company's office building, made a copy of the microchip research I did, patented it, then systematically deleted everything from the server and every single one of their backup servers.

The last thing I did was hop on a plane and got my ass out of the country.

Overnight, the Gallagher family lost millions of dollars' of information, and it felt fucking good.

Tommy's family almost found me when I was hiding out in China, and then when I stupidly thought it would be smart to hide in Dad's hometown in Thailand. Indonesia is by far the best location for me to be utterly forgettable. With so many tourists around, no one blinks twice about the fact I can't speak a lick of *Bahasa*, even if I might physically pass as a local.

A car suddenly pulls out in front of me, and I squeeze my brakes hard, giving myself whiplash. *Asshole.* I hit the horn and yell a string of profanities at them before continuing like nothing happened.

Driving here isn't for the faint of heart. I've almost died at least fifty times trying to navigate the nonexistent road rules and reckless drivers.

With traffic, it takes a little over an hour to get to the stall where I'm meeting Budi, a guy who's been working with Deedee and Natalie long before I got here. He's a fencer of sorts. We aren't friends, but if I die, he dies too. It doesn't make us BFFs or anything, but mutual trust is important.

The heat hunkers down on me as I come to a stop in front of a food stall on the side of the street. I tug the helmet off. The rush of air is absolutely heavenly. The thick coat of sweat makes my hair stick to my scalp and across my face. Summer in San Diego was barely tolerable; this makes drowning in the cool sea water sound like a dream.

My knees threaten to buckle when I drop to my feet, and the world tips slightly as dizziness rushes through me. It's gone as quickly as it comes.

Fanning myself, I bend beneath the tarpaulin awning to

approach the man behind the portable kitchen, scanning the area to make sure no one is watching me. His attention snaps up to mine, and he wipes his hands on his jeans.

"*Apa kabar, ibu,*" he greets without smiling, brows pinched against the blaring sun.

"*Baik.*" I offer him a curt nod, unclipping my backpack to wear it in front of me to fish out my wallet. "*Enam sate ayam sama Badak, donk?*"

Six chicken kebabs, and the drink that's a million times better than Coke, please. The extent of my Indonesian vocabulary is ordering food.

Deedee introduced me to this place. According to her, it's rare to find *Badak* on this side of the country, so snagging a bottle during these meetings is like microdosing happiness. I consider it a little treat for not getting murdered or dying from a stress-induced heart attack.

Awareness prickles at the back of my neck. I whip around to the busy street, eyes darting between passing motorbikes, tourists walking in and out of shops, patrons and vendors around the street. No one pays me any mind.

You're imagining it. Get your ass out of the open.

He takes the cash and hands me the change from his pocket. Another thing I love about this place: cash is the main currency. I flew into Jakarta with a fake passport and a couple grand—both thanks to Deedee—took a bunch of different trains and buses to get to Bali, and then we sourced a place for me to stay using that accepted cash.

I grab a seat on one of the plastic chairs under the shade and place the helmet on the narrow table. Nobody gives me more than a cursory glance as I check my phone for messages, the cameras at home, the microchip lab, and the factory where we print the books.

The biggest thing with a heartbeat near my property is a stray dog. In the factory, Deedee checks paper stock while Nat operates one of the machines at the lab, wearing a pristine white coat, hairnet, and mask as she works her artistic magic.

I tap my thumb on the table, periodically stopping to check my surroundings before going back to the footage of my cabin, flicking between frames so I don't miss a thing. A text pops up on the screen from my group chat—I see both girls check their phones on camera.

> Deedee: Tell Budi he still hasn't paid up for losing that bet last week.

> Nat: OMG, he has to pay me too. The guy gambles too much lol. It's always stupid bets too.

> Deedee: He's single handedly making me richer. U kno he bet 100ribu he can do a backflip.

> Nat: Well, can he?

> Deedee: Guess.

> Nat: *Laughing face emoji*

I'm too wired to joke around with them, and like hell am I about to tell Budi any of that and prolong our conversation more than necessary.

My spine snaps to attention the second our fencer steps in, my grip tightening around my phone like it's a weapon. Flip-flops, shorts, a sweat-stained T-shirt.

Potential threat, my brain registers.

"Sup," Budi says.

I flinch when he holds his hand up for a fist bump. It's a harmless gesture, but the thought of skin-on-skin makes me want to puke. *Just suck it up and do it.* I quickly tap his hand with mine, feeling another layer of sweat building along my forehead.

He drops down across from me, half-heartedly casting his dark eyes around the little food joint. The only person left is a guy chipping away at his noodles while watching a video on his phone with the volume all the way up. *Probably not a threat*, my brain registers.

"How's it?" Budi raps his knuckles on the table.

Carefully pulling the tote bag out of my backpack, I slide it across to him. "Turkish, German, and Canadian are in there. You can tell Harta twenty Australians and thirty Americans will be ready in a month. A machine broke, so we're slow going."

Budi quickly shoves the product into his own bag without bothering to check the contents—it's idiotic on his part. I could've lied about the number of passports in there, then come knocking on his door asking for payment.

Any artist with the right printing facilities can make the passport book. The hardest aspect isn't perfecting the paper weight or the nuances within the designs.

The real art is in the RFID chip.

A fake passport is only good if you don't get caught.

The microchip was the one part the Gallagher's shady company couldn't nail down until I came along. My degree and naivety made me the perfect employee who could be easily controlled.

Tommy wanted a microchip that would pass all the tests to better establish their family, and I cracked the code three days before I killed him, though I never reported my discovery.

Now, all the information is with me.

The lab manufacturing process isn't perfect, but with more time, resources, and research, it could be.

Nat and Deedee already had an established gig going before I stepped in to improve their product with the research I stole from the Gallaghers.

After Deedee finishes printing, Nat and I step in to add the microchip. She works on production while I deal with the serial number and placing it into the book—on my good hand days.

Budi's job is to distribute the product to another fencer, who will get it to the consumer—the ones at the end of the line, taking the pictures and interacting with the gangs, filthy rich, or a random person willing to put every cent they own into getting free.

Once it's out of his hands, we all split the cut, with Deedee and Nat taking a higher percentage. We could've grown a lot more if I were smart enough to get the production process down pat.

"Cool, cool," Budi says. "I've got a bro in Singapore wanting to know if you'd do a batch of Armenians."

My brows hike up my forehead. "I'll have to check with Deedee if she can do it. We'll need more research and an original sample." The shape and weight of every country's chip is different. "Are they planning on paying more?"

He shrugs. "She might."

I stare at him blankly. I know Nat and Deedee have been working with him since they started their operation five years ago, but he's not the brightest person I've ever met. Loyalty trumps intelligence, I guess.

My skin prickles, and I do a quick sweep of my surroundings, three times for good measure. Someone could come out at any second—*especially* since I'm in the open.

The Gallaghers aren't the only people trying to track me down. Deedee and Nat's passport manufacturing operation caught the eye of a gang—*pirates*, they call themselves. They have it out for us, but I can't bring myself to leave when I know I should. I like it here too much.

I lower my voice, foot tapping the ground. "Any updates on the pirates?"

Budi scratches his head. I can't tell whether he's concerned or unbothered. From what I've gathered, they've always been a problem, but it's only getting worse. Nat's slightly panicked, but Deedee couldn't give two shits about it, blissfully ignorant as she tinkers away in the factory.

"Nah. Nothing. All quiet."

My forehead wrinkles. "Are you sure?"

"Yeah, man, we good. They're no big deal—stop stressing."

I get the same answer every time I ask, yet I've had supplies intercepted, finished products stolen and sold by them, and customers who switched sides—all of which started after we incorporated my findings.

I flinch when Budi leans over the narrow table to stand. Panic flares, and my muscles brace for an impact that never comes. My lungs squeeze, unable to pull in oxygen as the man before me morphs into Tommy.

My knuckles go white around the backpack strap. *It's just Budi.* He doesn't have a violent bone in his body. Or an observant one, since he's oblivious to my turmoil, double-tapping his earbuds far too casually for the highly illegal exchange we're having.

He nods toward the kitchen, and I turn just as the clerk holds up a bag with a Styrofoam container and a plastic bag with a straw poking out the top.

"*Sate?*" Budi asks, and I stiffen.

It's not Tommy. It's not John. It's not any of the Gallaghers.

Pull. Yourself. Together.

"Yeah," I mutter, scrambling to my feet as the world roars louder, a fist around my lungs.

"Good shit." He grins, motioning for the clerk to make one for him as well.

I snatch the helmet off the table, grab my order, and unceremoniously shove it into my pack—forgetting I should probably offer him a tight-lipped smile. "Yup. See you next week," I say, inching backward. My nerves are haywire, convinced a member of the Gallagher syndicate is standing on the other side of the tarpaulin with a gun pointed at my head.

Heart stuck in my throat, I duck beneath the shade and hurry to my bike. The engine barely has a second to start before I'm peeling off the sidewalk onto the busy road.

My attention keeps flicking to my side mirrors as I tear down the street like I'm being chased by hell's army. I'm convinced I'll turn to see Tommy sitting behind a wheel, alive and well, back to make me wish it was me who bled out on the kitchen floor.

I tighten my grip around the throttle. It's fine. I'm fine. Everything *will be* fine as long as I focus on my work. If we keep selling and saving, it'll be easier for me to run. I can lay low for longer without worrying about how I'll secure a roof over my head.

Stopping myself from becoming roadkill is the only thing that keeps me from slipping off the tightrope and falling into full-fledged panic.

My harsh breaths are forced. I focus on my surroundings; the honking, yelling, the hum of engines, the wind in my hair, the heat of the motor beneath my legs.

The minutes tick by and the hour drives into two as I take more back roads and side streets, twisting and U-turning, going around in circles in case anyone is following me, until I finally reach my destination.

The sun has long begun its descent by the time I come to a stop, certain I'm not being followed. The salty sea breeze fills my lungs, coating my fraying nerves in familiarity. There's nothing but miles of sand and water each way, not a soul in sight.

No Tommy. No Gallagher. No pirate.

I hope.

Swallowing, I take my helmet off and pocket my keys before climbing down the dunes to get to the beach, parking myself a few feet from the shoreline.

There's a resort a mile to the left, and another a mile to the right. This is the sweet spot tourists never make it to because there are prettier things to see in the other direction.

Even Dad's death, heavy as it is, feels small when faced with nothing but miles upon miles of blue. The existential crisis of being insignificant is a welcome reprieve to the horrors of the echo chamber I've landed in.

My legs stretch out in front of me, and I dig my toes into the cool, damp sand. The waves roll in, only a foot away from where I stand. The tension slowly unwinds from my muscles as I stare into the vermillion sky, ears constantly straining to hear incoming cars or people.

Grabbing my dinner from my bag, I clean my hands with the sanitizer, then double-check the gun is still there—my safety blanket. My stomach sings the desperate song of its people as my energy saps into the sand from the adrenaline rush.

The bone-deep itch between my shoulder blades from a still-healing tattoo prickles, a nagging irritant that keeps me constantly on edge and makes my dinner taste sour when it isn't.

My eyes drift shut of their own accord, absorbing the sound of the waves crashing against the shore, the cool wind kissing my sweat-stained skin, the salty air filling my lungs.

At least, after everything, it's cathartic knowing that even though Tommy killed me, my corpse is slowly coming back alive, battered and bruised, with a heartbeat he doesn't have.

His ghost still haunts me. Wounds still fester. What was broken will never be whole.

2

ORDUS

The reef sways with the ocean's current, shifting colors to the rhythm of my family's dead hearts. Blue and yellow for my sister's burial site. Brown and white for my brother. The Curse took the life from the graves of the queens and kings before them long ago.

It should be me becoming one with the sea floor. It's what everyone would prefer. I should be feeding the coral with my mortal flesh until the ocean dries.

But my people would never give me the honor of burying me with my family.

I should have never became king.

My oldest sibling, Queen Chlaena, was small but mighty, feared and revered by every creature in and out of the ocean, capable of killing a fleet of humans with a single release of her venom.

Yannig was an exemplary king. My brother understood how

other species worked and was able to convince any foe they were one and the same. A true diplomat. The smoothest of talkers.

Me? I am nothing. A fool who can hide. A cuttlefish blending in with my surroundings. A joke of a king who still lives out of sheer desperation.

My claws dig into my palm. This is why I never visit their graves. I can barely stay upright through the regret. The grief. The exhaustion of spending every waking moment hiding from my own subjects. That is no king—that is a coward.

I should have died in the wars, a soldier meant to perish in my family's name. Yet, I am all that remains of the royal line, the abomination amongst krakens.

One of my many long arms reaches out, threading through the coral in the hopes I may feel my sister's soul. Chlaena died many decades ago in battle, yet not a day passes that I do not wish for her return.

The reef atop my siblings' graves and the small patch of land near it are the only vegetation left in my territory. The Curse destroyed everything else.

I move to Yannig's burial reef that's diminishing as the Curse chips away at the last vestiges of sea life. My hearts twist together as I tip my head in respect. Twenty years have passed since he died fighting those who wished to take our land, and in the end, his death will be meaningless.

Even in death, rotting at the bottom of the ocean, the Witch will be the only victor. Chlaena killed the Witch after she murdered our mother and cast the Curse over our territory—a blight that poisons the water and takes all life.

I grunt from an impact to the back of my head. I whip around, chest expanding and tentacles rising, ready to strike my attacker. Vasz swings around, suddenly pawing at the sand casually, avoiding eye contact just as the offending coconut floats down to the coral beside me.

"Vasz," I growl.

The annoying pup innocently lifts his snout, sniffing the air before digging at the sand. His big ears worked fine earlier when I asked if he wanted to go to the mainland.

Like me, Vasz is a violation of nature, a cross between three different species, another witch's sick experiment.

The elders have never seen such a thing—hence their inclination to kill him when he was first seen with me.

Two fins line his back, elongating into a tail. If he swims close to the surface, he could be mistaken for a shark if not for his brownish-red coloring and yellow-tipped ears. From the side, his four legs are visible, his body shaped like a dog with his shoulders and knees. White suckers dot the back of his front legs and along his chest and stomach. His face is somewhere between a shark and canine, with the yellow coloring of the native octopus species around his eyes, ears, and feet.

Able to walk on land and cross the sea, he's a hunter far more intelligent than any I've ever encountered. He is one of the few lesser beings krakens can properly communicate with. My only companion.

A tentacle wraps around the offending coconut to crush it into pieces. His head whips my way, and he bares his sharp teeth at me for desecrating his precious toy.

Serves him right.

It's rare for the currents to carry such fruit this deep into my territory. They are aplenty on the mainland—much to Vasz's utter joy and my displeasure. I can't stand it. My den is littered with husks.

I hold his stare, crushing the coconut until it splinters in my grip. He snaps his maw at me, and I release it. The last time I didn't heed the crazy mutt's warning, I almost lost a limb, and I'm rather fond of my limbs. Regrowing one is much too tedious.

Sand clouds around me as I shoot upward, siphoning water

before contracting the muscles in my tentacles to blast it. I propel forward without waiting for Vasz to follow.

"Wanker," I catch him muttering, scurrying for his toy. The human tongue is rubbing off on him.

I scowl, leaving him behind. I may be faster than the creature, but there is nowhere I can go where he won't sniff me out.

An odd sensation starts in my chest. It's the barest tug, like an itch. I head toward the mainland to hunt, reverting to my instincts. Scents. Changes in temperature. The flow of tides. As I pass empty homes and deserted seas, the only color comes from the offerings of the Sea Goddess, Edea. The quiet festers, burrowing deeper into my bones.

My territory used to be revered. We were attacked from all sides because others wanted our bountiful lands for themselves. Many sentries died protecting our land from those who wished to take it. My siblings led many into battle. But after the Curse, the attacks slowly lessened until eventually, they stopped altogether. All that remains is waste from the humans and the husk of our once-bountiful lands. I can't remember the last time I had to fight creatures off at the border.

Why would anyone want unviable land? Land that leaves its people starved and sick from the poor water quality.

The Kingdom of Aletia. That's the official name. Now, it is known as the Dead Lands.

If any of my family rose from the dead, they'd be so disappointed in the state of it. The Curse sped up after Yannig died twenty years ago.

It is the reason why the passing stones are arid; they were once brightly covered with corals of every color. Fish would swim between arches, scattering when a predator came too close. Sharks used to hunt these lands. Eels, manta rays, turtles, octopuses—it was impossible to leave my den without seeing life.

The Curse the Witch cast was to destroy all kraken territory by pushing out game and turning the water sickly so kraken may die from either starvation or illness.

My suckers bristle, on alert for any shift in the current that might indicate disturbance from another kraken. The darkest recesses of my being are pleased the Curse is reaching its peak. That alone is proof it was me who should have died in my brother's place.

Kraken-kind used to hunt in these lands. Without game in the area, krakens have had no choice but to risk their lives to travel close to the mainland or rely on the few strong hunters remaining to travel far to bring back food.

They can no longer rely on Krokant for game. It's the one parcel of my territory with vegetation, and it's shrinking by the day. Many krakens have left in an attempt to find sanctuary, but I have heard no news as to whether they've succeeded, or perished by foe or incompatible climates.

Others have risked moving closer to where there is game at the risk of bandits and exposure to humans, but the majority of krakens have little choice when they are neither good hunters nor strong enough to make the swim to the mainland and back. I, however, am strong enough, leaving me alone in my corner of the territory.

It's...freeing.

My people are starving, and I...I couldn't care less for their suffering. They deserve it.

With fewer creatures in the area, the chances of seeing one of my kind are growing slimmer, and the whispers of my unsavory crossbreeding have minimized to zero.

It has been years since anyone dared comment on the human influence on my appearance; hair, claws, an extra finger, no webbing between my arms and ribs. It sets me apart from every kraken in existence.

I speed up when I reach a patrol path, cautious not to intercept any of my subjects, lest I want to add to the kraken death toll.

Some have left simply because they would rather live without protection than be ruled by an abomination they've failed to kill.

My lungs and ribs ache at the reminder. My mother and my siblings were the only ones who did not care about my appearance—they saw me as family, not as a monstrosity. They were my only friends. And now, they're dead.

Many mutinies formed following my brother's death and my ascension to the throne. My reign, and continued existence, remains only due to the royal blood in my veins, giving us a fighting chance to break the Curse. It allows me to shift into two legs and walk amongst the humans, as well as stay above land for more than a handful of minutes.

They can protest and seethe all they wish; I am the only hope they have of ending the blight that plagues our land.

My mother died because of the Witch. Chlaena killed herself and utilized every resource we had to bring an end to the Curse. When Yannig died, the last words he spoke to me were his wish I return life to our sea.

As much as I loathe krakens, their deaths cannot be for nothing. My territory will be restored in my family's honor if it is the last thing I do.

For Chlaena. For Yannig.

For my future bride.

If not for my family's sacrifice, I question the level of devotion I would have to bonding myself with whomever I am *destined* to be with, as the Witch said this is required to bring an end to the Curse and save those who find me deplorable.

Chlaena took a husband, and the first kraken died from the Waste.

Yannig took a bride, and half the territory became a graveyard.

The only person I will marry is my fated mate. *That* is who I believe will be the one to end the Curse. My *destined bride*, as she called it.

I have prayed to the Sea Goddess for my mate since I learned such a thing existed—a being created to be perfectly compatible in body, mind, and soul.

My siblings and the Council called me foolish for falling for the *make believe*. They claim it is a tale told to children to help them sleep at night, but some elders believe such a thing exists. It has been written into our tomes many times.

I rub at my chest where the subtle itch has turned into a tug. I navigate through stone arches, thinking about the empty den I'll return to after my hunt. No mate, no cubs, no one who will look at me without disgust.

I've dreamt of finding my mate since I was a cub, longed for it with every part of my being, because my mate would not hate me for having hair instead of a mantle. She would never leave or ignore me, or call me unworthy for my appearance. My mate would love me. She would pick me.

Mates have to be real.

I'm certain it's the only way to end the Curse.

Vegetation and life begins to sprinkle the land once I cross the border until the ocean is bursting with it. It's a different route than I normally take, further away from my den. There's plenty of game around to make for a successful hunt, but I can't bring myself to stop. Instinct forces me to keep going, getting closer to the mainland than I normally would.

Yannig and I would come up onto the mainland so he would *mingle* with the locals before he became king, but it has been years since I've made it this far from the main city.

I slow down, surveying the area, but something innate continues pulling me forward, closer than I've been in many moons and even further away from my island, to a beach I've never cared to approach.

I come to a halt, rubbing my chest, staying there. There's no reason for me to swim this far out from my territory. It'd only make the trip home all the longer, and my energy will have waned from a full day of swimming.

I must hesitate for so long, I feel a nip at one of my tentacles. I spin just as Vasz darts off, charging ahead of me—to avoid my wrath or to hunt for coconuts. Likely both. He never misses an opportunity to go near land. The mutt insists on bringing back a tacky souvenir every time. It's hardly valuable, only a mere eyesore.

Until he throws them at my head.

Or hides them under the bed so they poke into my back.

Or leaves them lying around to crack under my weight.

"So far," Vasz complains, panting and swooping around me to herd me forward. I'm surprised he caught up so quickly. I mustn't have been going that fast.

"Silence." The tugging has grown uncomfortable, an incessant ache. The sun is setting, and I'd prefer to be in the comforts of my own home before the sea becomes too still.

There's a shark in the distance, one large enough to keep me fed for several days. I turn toward the mainland, where the rope around my chest seems to be connected.

I cave to the need to keep swimming. The pull grows stronger the more I swim, until the beach comes into view. The only time I come this close is if I plan on shifting into human form to search for treasure—or maybe, perhaps, possibly find my fated mate.

I will not get a second chance. Once I see her, I will recognize her as my mate, my destined bride who will end the Curse. I am certain of it. There is no other choice.

A lifetime, I've prayed. Twenty years, I've searched. Twenty years, I've come up empty. Soon, before the last reef in Krokant withers to nothing, I will have to marry the first kraken the Council sacrifices to me in an attempt to break the Curse. If that doesn't work, I will have failed my family.

The tug turns into a vicious, near-painful, yank. I swim harder. Desperation claws at my ribs. I cannot fail. I *will* find her. My lands *will* be saved. My family's deaths will not be in vain.

I breach the surface of the water. I need to rip the gnawing ache out of my chest. It's all-consuming. The magic in my veins thrums and twists. This wretched, foreign feeling between my ribs twists my mind into a disoriented mess of torment and—

Air crashes into my lungs.

Sitting on the shore is a little female.

The vermilion glow of the setting sun kisses her bronze skin. Tendrils of dark hair flutter around her soft face with the afternoon breeze. Her fingers are splayed into the sand, head tipped back as the waves caress the tips of her toes. She's the most beautiful creature I've ever seen.

My hearts still. For a moment, they stop beating all together before they collide in a frenzy. My soul vibrates and sings, pushing the female to the forefront of my mind until there's no other thought.

It's *her*.

She's the one. I've been waiting for her all my life. My *mate*. My bride. The one to end the Curse. And she's…human?

The Council will be up in arms over this. A member of the royal line hasn't bonded to a human in over two hundred years, and my grandmother was made a pariah for tainting the bloodline, even though she ate him after they mated.

No matter. I will kill anyone who questions my decision. Food is scarce in my land. I'll turn kraken into dinner. I don't care what any of them think.

The fates made her for me. She is my mate.

There is nothing further to discuss.

It is the rarest treasure to find a mate. Most krakens live their long life never finding one.

But I, Ordus, King of the Dead Lands, am one lucky kraken.

If I moved closer, I wonder if I could taste her in the water.

Humans are delicate little things with weak minds. I fear how she may react if she sees me out here. It is forbidden for krakens to go near them or otherwise make our existence known. History has proven her species to be unkind to what they do not understand, brutal when they do not wish to learn. It was the fate my sire succumbed to before I was born.

But my mate will be different. She will accept me as soon as I show her I can provide for her. I will prove I am worthy, and she will be ecstatic to bond with me.

I wish she would open her eyes, look at me so I can watch the moment she recognizes me as her mate. She'll leap into the water into my arms, guiding me into her sex so we may begin the marriage ritual, and she'll leave her bonding mark on my skin.

My breeding limb hardens at the thought, halted by a flurry of concern.

But she is so small, maybe half the size of me.

Everything about her is little: tiny head, short arms, small hands, the cutest little nose so small, I'm worried she does not get enough oxygen through. One of my limbs is bigger than both her legs. I could crush her without thought. Humans bruise easily. Their bones can snap from a short fall.

What if I harm my human?

I could accidentally kill her with my size.

No, that will not happen. I'll be delicate—the most delicate of all krakens. I may be a bad king, but I will be a good husband. The best mate. Any marks will be from my suckers. And my teeth, too, should she wish. Our size difference will be of no hindrance. The Goddess made her to be my other half. She chose her for me.

Yes. It is decided. She will be my bride—not that it was ever a doubt.

The Witch's Curse requires the bride be willing. My mate will be. Fate has deemed it so.

My loneliness will end. My den will no longer be empty, my

bed warm. I will have a companion other than Vasz. I will be able to speak to another without fear of judgment or scrutiny over matters given to me before birth.

The Goddess listened to my prayers. I finally have a mate.

My beautiful, perfect female opens her eyes and stares at the threads of foam bubbling along the shore. Without much thought, I risk exposing myself by moving closer to the shore. The water laps at my face, splashing into my eyes as I lower myself to keep from being caught. She'll see me if she focuses on the waves.

What else did the tomes say? Such things were rarely mentioned the few years I attended Temple and School.

Right—scents.

My nostrils flare, breathing in the salty air. It's...interesting. The mate pull is not as the scriptures described. I've read it a hundred times so there would be no mistaking my mate. This feeling is similar to what was noted, yet somehow different.

The magical current through my body is there, as is the need to twine my body with hers, to bring her back to my den and pump her full of my seed. My desperation for her is turning me into a creature running on pure instinct, as the scribes detailed.

Her scent... It is delectable, but it is not making me resort to my baser instincts. I could become addicted to her smell, but it isn't sweet and all-consuming, not like those who claim to have met their mates report.

The Witch must be trying to fool me so I never break the Curse. Alas, I would recognize my mate anywhere.

My heightened vision allows me to see her clearly without closing the distance. Her eyes are blank, empty. She is but a life-less shell. It's a look I would recognize anywhere. The silence becomes deafening, and every breath sounds like a roar, but inside? Nothing, like the sudden bout of quiet after a snap of a twig in a singing forest.

Every instinct yells at me to take her sadness away.

What troubles my little mate? I will fix it for her, make her the happiest human to ever have existed. Her sadness is unacceptable.

I breathe her in, use my suckers to try to taste her, ingraining her scent into my memory. I must learn everything possible about my mate before bringing her to our den. All her likes, dislikes, passions. That way, I can prepare our home, and she will be impressed and immediately fall in love with me. Then, we will marry, my kingdom will be prosperous once more, my mate will carry my cub, and I will never have to endure the silence ever again.

Dipping back beneath the water, I yank Vasz away from the crab he's terrorizing and drag him close to the surface. I point in my mate's direction. "Memorize her smell."

The pup rolls his eyes, wriggling in my grip. "Ugh. Do I have to?" His snout leaves the water for a second too short. "She smells bad."

"Do it," I growl, staring into his beady brown eyes so he knows I am ordering him as his king.

He tips his head in a total lack of regard for my authority. "What do I get out of it?"

I grit my teeth. Must everything be so difficult? "I will bring home a coconut for you." He can only hold one in his mouth. My offer is more than generous, since the creature brings nothing but clutter into my den.

He holds up his four webbed toes. "Five."

"Two."

He considers for a moment. "Fine."

I'll bring it back, but who's to say I will not destroy it once there? After all, I must prepare our nest for my mate.

Vasz grumbles under his breath and then collapses onto his back. "Pats as payment."

I huff and lightly tap his stomach a couple of times, scrutinizing my mate's den. It's too small, too cramped to be deserving of her.

Her scent hangs heavy in the air, unbearably heady. My weak human knees almost buckle from the knowledge the smell belongs to the female the Goddess deemed to be my perfect other. Our fate was written in the foam threading through every wave, every star that pierces through the surface of the water.

I have a mate.

A mate.

Someone to share my life with. A bride who will end the Curse and make me worthy of the love my family gave so freely when I've been nothing but undeserving. Everything will finally be right.

Vasz smacks my hand when I stop petting him and gives me a pointed look.

I quietly hiss, "You are testing me, creature."

He huffs. "Your mate is not lost because of me. Keep patting."

I bare my teeth at him, doing as he demands, rubbing Vasz's stomach until his tongue rolls out the side of his mouth. The pup is acting far too brave today. Goddess knows, he'll be exploiting my weakness as much as possible now that I have one.

It wasn't long after I found my sea-sent mate that she rose up on two feet and left me behind in the water without so much as a backward glance. It was hard not to be disappointed she never noticed me, and it was impossible to track where she disappeared to on her bike.

If not for Vasz's unnervingly good nose, I could have spent months searching for her. The few hours we were apart were torturous enough as it was. I felt like I was succumbing to the Waste when she was out of my sight, the poison eating my mind until reality was no longer a concept I recognized.

Not a full day, and my mate is already driving me crazy.

How long is one meant to wait before approaching their fated human? An hour? A week? A month? No, that's too long.

The sooner we marry, the better. Before Krokant succumbs to the Curse, and there is no more viable land in my territory. There's no telling if it will be possible to break the curse if that occurs.

Vasz slaps me again, and I gnash my teeth at him. The threat of my venom perfumes the humid air.

He rolls his eyes, sits back on his hind legs, and holds up one webbed toe. "Six coconuts as payment for my service, like we agreed," he reminds me before pointing at the three on the ground.

I blink at him. "We agreed on two."

Vasz's finned tail hits a nearby tree as he trots back toward the beach. "Nine, or I bite your mate."

Perhaps I should have sent him to School to learn numeracy when I found him—*before* he became prone to biting.

Shaking my head, I return my focus to my mate's home. Droplets of water trickle from my hair, down my torso and two legs. Dust and dry dirt stick to my skin as I circle the property from a distance, keeping to the shadows, letting my skin pulse and shift to blend into my surroundings.

Beneath the moonlight, it is difficult to tell what colors paint the walls of the old house raised off the ground. There's only the tinge of orange in the bricks on the roof.

It's unlike the new, grand buildings appearing around the island the past few decades. *Villas*, I believe the humans call them. The ones with bright white walls, a pool, and too many windows.

They offer no protection against the elements or predators. Anyone could see through the windows. A single stone to the glass would rupture her security. When the rainy season hits, she'll be better suited to withstanding any floods.

My mate's house is not like that.

A bug lands on my neck. I slap a tentacle over my neck, killing the pest in a clean strike.

I study the house; its height, the number of piles it sits on, the spacing between shuttered windows, the distance between the wall and the edges of the roof. No light seeps through the drawn curtains to give away what room she might be in. It looks sturdy —not quite perfectly straight, but it's solid. A smart choice of den.

It tells me nothing about my mate.

What's her name? What does she do during the day? Does she work? How long has she lived here? Is she a local? What does her voice sound like? What does she taste like? Her favorite gemstone? Necklaces or rings? Does she prefer gold or silver—I'll need to know how to decorate our nest.

The questions are endless. I'll know in time.

I creep closer to the house, hoping to catch sight of her through the shutters.

Magic hums to life in my veins as I shift my ears back into my normal form. The wooden wall brushes my webbed ear as I focus on what lies beyond. The faint thrum of electricity, gurgle of plumbing, a low whine from one of my mates' machines, but nothing from her. Her scent and the bike are the only indication she's home.

My eyes drift shut, listening to the sounds within the den, my feet faltering beneath a window when soft snores seep through. My instincts run rampant. I need to see my mate. I must find out if my suckers would leave marks on her supple human flesh. I yearn to lay my eyes on her and memorize every curve.

I summon my magic to the surface to partially shift, tentacles unfurling, raising me higher to peer through the window, but I can't see anything through the shutters.

A frustrated growl builds in the back of my throat. My mate's intelligence is a hindrance to me.

An ant begins crawling up my arm, and I squash it before it can make it any higher. *Vermin.*

I slide my fingers along the corners of the shutter, nails elongating into claws as I shed my human form. The tips dig beneath the old wood. It slowly lifts away from the wall with a loud groan that silences the creatures of the forest.

I shift back to two legs. Excitement purrs to life at the prospect of interacting with my future bride. My hand flattens against the rough wall to listen to any sounds coming from inside. The elation dwindles away with the passing minutes.

She's not coming out.

It's for the best. Our den should be prepared before she realizes I am her mate and she leaves the island to spend the rest of her days with me. A few days is nothing to a lifetime.

I continue my perusal of the house. Blades of grass rustle beneath my feet before changing to wood. The steps leading up to the front door creak. I falter, but no sounds follow from inside.

My molars grind together. Any predator could come to harm my mate, and she wouldn't wake at their approach.

That is not acceptable.

As long as she is home, I will be here, protecting her. It is my duty. I will never leave her side.

My hand wraps around the door handle, and my head tips to the side. How odd. I've never seen such technology before. There is no hole where a key is inserted to unlock it. Instead, it's... What is the term? Digital?

I push the handle down. A loud, sudden beeping blares through the forest, and I jump back, shifting in an instant to destroy the threat. Yet the area remains desolate save for the sounds of frantic footsteps coming from inside the—

I leap from the porch, darting past the line of trees until I'm certain her human eyes will not see me in the distance. My skin morphs, shifting colors to blend into my surroundings.

The front door never opens. The curtains behind the shutters never flicker. The beeping stops after several long minutes.

A purr rumbles to life in my chest. I was wrong to doubt my smart mate. She wouldn't leave herself exposed to predators— not that it matters anymore.

From this day forth, I vow she will never again worry about her safety. She is my mate. My bride. She belongs to me.

3

Cindi

Fuck. Fuck. Fuck. Fuck.

    The gun trembles in my grip.

    They're here.

    The Gallaghers are here.

    They're at my door. They've come to kill me.

    If not the Gallaghers, then the pirates.

    "Come on. Come on," I whisper, willing my phone to work faster as the alarm blares.

    I dart my eyes between the locked workshop door and my device, my trembling fingers flying across the screen to enter the password for the security camera. My injured hand screams at me, louder with each swipe.

    I flatten myself against the wall, hoping and praying I'll make it to the hatch on the other side of the room before they knock down the door. He'll have men outside. It won't matter how quickly I make it beneath the house. Someone will see me running.

3

Fuck, why didn't I hide an emergency pack in the forest in case I needed to make a quick escape?

The alarm continues blaring through the house, pounding against my head as viciously as the Gallaghers will once they get their hands on me. They'll want to keep me alive for what I've done, to exact their pound of flesh and the data I store in my mind.

I turn off the gun's safety and point it at the door.

The application finally loads. Sixteen surveillance videos blink into view. A cold sweat skates down my spine as I click through each footage. Once. Twice.

Four more times.

Nothing.

No Tommy. No Gallaghers. No pirates.

No one inside or outside.

That can't be right. The alarm wouldn't go off by itself.

Maybe it was an animal, or a random thinking they could rob me while I'm asleep, or maybe a glitch caused during the assembly process because of my limitations.

The empty screens don't make me breathe any easier. The Gallaghers are out there. I know it. They're watching, waiting, playing me for their own sick game.

I hit Rewind on the security tapes, muscles bunched, ready to see the ghost of the man who haunts my dreams.

I killed him. I know I did.

I think.

There was no social media covering his funeral, but he was removed from the company register. That's all I have to go off.

That, and the lack of a heartbeat when I left him on the floor.

Someone's out there. I can feel it. My short breaths make my head swim as I navigate the shitty, user-unfriendly app Deedee's friend made.

A figure appears in the camera installed on the porch. I hit Pause, frowning. What the... I rewind the footage, watching him or her—or *it*—move in reverse, from the front of my house to the windows by my bedroom, circling my place before retreating into the woods.

The figure is nothing more than a giant blob of darkness that doubles in size in front of my bedroom window.

I scroll back, earlier into the night when the sun set and I had just gotten back home. On the screen, my face is as clear as day, as is the fly that landed on my leg and the puff of fumes from the exhaust.

How could anyone pull something like this off? This is far more advanced than anything I know exists. What would turn a person into a black blob on screen? At least two feet around them is blurred and distorted.

I scramble to the safety of my hiding spot to grab my laptop off the bench before scuttling back beneath the desk. With the gun in my clammy hand, and the device in my other, I pull up the tapes. Maybe there's an issue with the app on my phone.

But no. All sixteen camera angles show the same thing.

I silently tap my foot on the floor. I don't feel safe stepping foot outside to do an in-person check. I don't feel safe inside either.

Cold sweat trickles down my back. I gnaw on the inside of my cheek, debating whether to wake Deedee up to send out an SOS.

It was probably a fucking poltergeist. Tommy's *actual* ghost, not a figment of my imagination.

Whatever it was, it can wait until morning. Until then, the Glock is never leaving my hand.

I lower the laptop to the floor, rise to my feet, then tiptoe to the door. According to my security cameras, the living room is empty. Still, I hesitate, a scream lodged in my throat, ready for any sudden movement.

Fuck. Here goes nothing. I throw the door open and dash for my bedroom, slamming it shut behind me before locking it and shoving the deadbolt in place.

I clamber for my bedside table, whipping it open and faltering at the sight that greets me. Maybe putting a hunting knife next to my monster dildos wasn't the best idea.

Shoving the toys aside, I grab the mini taser then change into a practical pair of shorts before locking myself back in my workroom.

It's going to be a long night.

I'm seeing triple.

My blood sugar is shot from the adrenaline rush I've been riding for the last fifteen hours.

I'm on three hours of sleep.

Every time I turn my head, I'm hit with a wave of exhaustion.

I'm convinced Tommy is sitting in the back seat of the car.

My painkillers have made me drowsy, but it's done fuck all to get rid of the pins and needles assaulting half my arm—not to mention the near-agonizing pain every time I move my elbow.

To top it off, I'm stuck in rush-hour traffic because my fucking supplier thought five o'clock in the middle of Seminyak was a good time to do a drop.

I spent the whole day messing around with my cameras to figure out if the anomaly was intentional or a fault on my part. When I couldn't get to the bottom of it, I installed a couple of sensors that link to a silent alarm in my bedroom.

Droplets of sweat trickle down my spine, burning the inflamed, still-healing tattoo rubbing painfully against my cotton tank top.

The AC in Nat's car isn't strong enough. I feel like I need to throw myself into the water just to wake up—and Jesus fucking *Christ*, this weather is going to be the death of me if Tommy's family doesn't kill me first.

I pull up into a free parking spot on the side of the road and say a silent prayer before stepping out of the car. My equilibrium shifts, and I nearly trip over my feet while doing a 360 check of my surroundings.

Balancing myself on the dirty car, I avoid a near collision with a motorbike and hustle to the sidewalk. I scrub my clammy face, willing myself to wake up so I can pay proper attention. But the world is too loud. Too busy. There's too much *everything*.

Too many people want to kill me. I'm in a constant state of fatigue. I need a twenty-four-hour nap. I like my life here—or, at least, I *liked* it better when the only soul who visited me was Deedee.

I considered booking a hotel room tonight so I can sleep without fear, but I figured if I'm going on the run, I need to save all the money I can. There's no point wasting it for a single night of reprieve.

Tourists and locals mingle in the street, getting from point A to B or sitting back, taking drags of a cigarette. As always, nobody pays me any mind, but it still feels like I have a thousand pairs of eyes trained on me.

I keep my head down, fighting the ripples of fatigue as I keep my eyes peeled, passing a few more stores before crossing the road into an air-conditioned smoothie joint. Once I have my order in hand, I settle in the seat near the back of the store with a clear view out the front window, waiting for Wayan. If I spot one of the Gallaghers, I'll have a few second head start to make a run for it.

Deedee may have vouched for Wayan, but I don't trust him as far as I can throw him. The guy rubs me the wrong way.

The pressure in my head grows with the ever-present feeling of doom. The dread doesn't pair well with my smoothie, but I force myself to polish it off, swallowing down the bile. I need all the energy I can get. Forgetting to eat all day was also a bad move on my part.

My gaze flicks in the direction of the beach. It's been days since I've been out in the water. If I live to see tomorrow, I'll go.

Maybe for the last time.

My leg shakes restlessly. I check my phone at five o'clock on the dot to see a text come in from Wayan that he's going to be forty minutes late.

Fucking prick.

That's another forty minutes of me being out in the open.

I shift in my seat, pushing myself up against the wall, flinching whenever someone walks in or when there's a loud noise. Even though it's not my place, I send a frustrated message to Deedee about her supplier. They might be friends, but I don't care at this point. It's plain rude and disrespectful to send that type of text at the exact time you're meant to meet.

Wayan doesn't pull up across the street from the smoothie joint until an hour and half later. I would've gone straight home if I didn't need the supplies to make more chips and fix one of the machines at the factory.

I sway as I jump to my feet. The world is vibrating with colors and sounds I swear I can smell. I blink back the exhaustion from my eyes and storm across the street, narrowly avoiding a collision as I slip into the front seat of his car. The plan was to meet inside, but fuck it. I'll get in. I can't sit in there for any longer.

I have a gun in my bag, a switchblade in my boot, and a modified taser in my pocket. If Wayan wants to fuck around, he'll find out.

The car unlocks as I approach. The constant state of anxiety has strung me so tight, I'm about to snap.

"What the fuck do you call this time?" I fume, slamming the door behind me. Cigarette smoke and BO slams into me, and I almost swing the door back open to escape it.

My brows spear into my hairline when he holds a hand up to my face without looking at me.

You know what? I might kill him too.

Wayan prattles off a string of words in Bahasa, throwing his hands up in annoyance before pointing angrily at the tourists in front of the car as if they're the ones on the other end of the phone. He says his goodbye in the form of an aggressive tap before chucking his phone on top of the four others sitting in the center console.

Oh, good. It looks like we're both in a splendid mood.

"Let's make this quick, ya?" he mutters, scowling. "I have things to do."

"So do I," I snap. "I don't appreciate being told you're late at the time you're meant to be here."

He glowers at me, and I return the glare tenfold. I flinch when he reaches behind me, and I quickly right myself to pretend it never happened. He unceremoniously drops a box onto my lap.

"Careful," I hiss. Gripping the container, I send a scathing sneer his way.

His shrug sends a bolt of irritation through me. I grit my teeth and focus on checking the wafers. If he broke *any* of them with that little stunt, I'm ripping his head off.

Attempting to ignore the low throbbing in my arm and my blurring vision, I unlatch the box to check it.

What kind of sick joke is this? "Where the fuck is it?" I'm not in the mood for any of this bullshit—or any bullshit, for that matter.

He doesn't look at me. He just takes a deep drag of his cigarette. "Pirates," is all he offers as an explanation.

My stomach sinks. "Tell me everything," I demand.

Wayan shrugs, rolling down the window to flick the ash out onto the sidewalk. "Got there, and it was already empty."

I stare at his side profile. *"And?"*

"The courier said it was pirates. That's all I know."

It's fine.

It's fine.

Fuck.

It's not fine. We need those wafers to make the next batch.

"And the parts I ordered for the machine?"

Wayan nods at the empty container. "Gone."

I gawk at him, dipping into my energy reserves to stop myself from blowing up at him. "And you couldn't have *called me* about this so I didn't come out all this way for nothing?"

An hour and half, I waited, and for what? The time I could've spent dealing with my security breach could've been the difference between life and death.

I feel like I'm about to lose my mind. I want to smack him upside the head, or maybe just hit someone in general.

Tears spring to my eyes. I'm so exhausted. I'm tired of looking over my shoulder, tired of seeing Tommy hidden behind every corner.

I can't deal with this right now. I want to go home, back to the garage I was raised in, back into Dad's arms whenever he'd do his weekly reminders of how proud he was of me.

I grit my teeth. *Pull yourself together.* This is the shit I've been dealt, so deal with it.

I've been in far worse situations. This is nothing. We have enough for the current batch, which means I have time to figure out an alternative. If I can't find a supplier in Indonesia, then Malaysia. We'll look at rescaling, or focus on just printing in the meantime while we try to find a solution. Maybe we'll expand the factory to make the wafers too. Or maybe the pirates will wipe us off the map.

Or it could be a Nat and Deedee problem if Tommy or whoever was at my place last night kills me.

Who knows.

The possibilities are endless.

I scrub my face, fighting back the tears.

Tomorrow. I can't think when I'm running on fumes. I need to sleep, even for a couple hours. Everything else can wait until I can regroup and talk to the girls about what we should do.

Taking a deep breath, I fix my stare on the beach at the end of the street. *Survive the night, and tomorrow, I can go.* "Fix it." The words fall without infliction.

Wayan scoffs. "What do you expect me to—"

"I don't give a shit what you have to do, you *fix. It.* You have one job. *One.* I don't care if you're busy. I don't give a shit if your kid has her first fucking school play. You get paid to do a job, so *do it.*"

I'm out of the car, slamming the door behind me without waiting for his response.

Nausea churns in my stomach. I sounded like Tommy. He had the means to back up his threat, but there's nothing I can do to Wayan. No one will back me up.

My thumb taps an erratic rhythm against my thigh as I will the memories to fade. I try to blink away my blurring vision. My eyes dart from person to person, swinging my attention behind me then to the side into each store. Every person begins looking like they have *his* moldy green eyes, *his* dirty blond hair.

Tommy's laughing at me. I'm nothing, just like he said. No one wants me. No one's there for me. It's just me. I'm nothing.

Oxygen burns a path down my lungs as the sound of motors and chatter grows louder, the smell of garbage and fumes stronger, and the moonlight bears down on me like a tangible weight. Each flickering light is the spark of a bullet, every movement a threat.

He's here. He's everywhere.

My throat starts to close. I can't breathe. I've got to get out of here—

The air whooshes out of me when I collide with a brick wall. Strong hands steady me, keeping me close as I blink away the shock to get my bearings.

"I caught you."

"Get your hands—" My attention snaps up to the man with the deep, melodic voice, and for a moment, I'm completely transfixed. The words are dead on my tongue. His scent engulfs me, so potent that my knees threaten to give out beneath me. It's like I'm stepping straight onto a beach untouched by humankind—where the salty air tastes fresher with the scent of rain and the breeze feels freer.

I've never seen someone so...beautiful. He's almost ethereal with the way his tanned skin glows beneath the fluorescent lights from the nearby stores. It catches on his deep blue eyes, the shadows dipping beneath his cheekbones before cutting into a lethally sharp jaw paired with sinfully soft lips.

Raven black hair spills over his broad shoulders and onto his burly chest, grazing the bottom of his ribs. For a second, I want to reach out to touch the silky strands to see if it's as soft as it looks, but my thoughts fizzle out when my attention lands on his naked torso.

The muscles of his pectorals and shoulders tighten as he pulls me closer to his orbit. I'm helpless to drop my gaze to the hard expense of his abdomen, every dip kissed by shadows to accentuate his Greek God–like appearance only amplified by his towering height. He must be over 6'6", maybe taller.

Something molten heats my core as I follow the prominent lines down to the deep V that trails below a pair of shorts to a massive bulge. My stomach quivers at the thought of what he'd look like without a single string of thread to cover him.

My slow perusal lands on the strong hands around my shoulder.

The realization makes me leap out of his hold with a snarl. My skin burns where he touched me. Panic rises in my throat.

"Don't touch me," I hiss.

He can't be touching me. No one can touch me.

"Mate," he whispers.

Blue eyes flicker to green. Long, black hair shortens to dirty blond.

The man morphs into Tommy right before my eyes.

It doesn't matter how many times I tell myself it can't be him. My mind is certain it is.

It's him.

4

ORDUS

My mate is distressed. I must fix it.

Her chest rises and falls with panicked breaths, dark eyes wide with panic as she stumbles away, fists trembling at her side.

Claws protrude from my nails as I search the street for danger. My sights land on a nearby man smoking a cigarette as he stares at a square device in his hand.

Shall I kill him? Will that make her feel better?

"What is wrong? Speak to me." My attention catches on the black brace wrapped around her wrist. Fury explodes through me, white and searing. Someone harmed her after she left her den. She wasn't wearing it at the beach yesterday, or during the brief moment I was blessed enough to catch her departing her cabin.

I had to barter with Vasz again to convince him to locate her. It was not my intention to have this interaction, but I could not resist the urge to come near her.

It's fortunate I did, because my mate needs me.

I step forward, raising my arms to touch her. My fingers still tingle from the memory of her soft flesh beneath my skin. It was an effort not to shift to my true form to taste her with my suckers.

Even now, I'm fighting my primal instincts not to act on my urges. I want to nuzzle my face into her neck, lick her frantic pulse, memorize every inch of her small human body with my limbs.

My fate-sent mate flinches away from me, staring up with her arm poised in defense, as if I'm a monster. Daggers pierce my hearts. She's looking at me like the others do, which can't be right. That's not how mates are.

I will kill whoever made her upset. Man. Woman. Another kraken. They'll die.

I will thread shells into his entrails and gift them to her so she may decorate our nest.

Yes. That is an excellent courting present.

It will prove I am a strong mate, capable of protecting and avenging her. My mate will be the one thing I do right in my life. I failed to protect my siblings, failed to save the waters. *This*, I will prosper at. I must.

"Your hand. Tell me who harmed you," I demand, speaking in the tongue both visitors and locals often speak.

The fear slips from her face, and she blinks up at me in wonder.

My mate is even more beautiful up close, with big brown eyes framed by long, curling lashes that kiss her sharp cheeks every time she blinks. Her tapered jaw ends in a point I want to press my lips to. I could spend years staring at her, and I would never be bored.

I am the luckiest male to have ever existed to have found such a perfect mate. I am certain, without a shadow of a doubt, she will be the one to end the blight over my lands.

There is no other option. She is the one. She *must* be the one, or else no creature will survive the Dead Lands.

Her sweet face contorts and her scent burns, directed at me. My claws recede into human form, and my stomach twists with unease. Is my mate...angry at me? That cannot be right. She should be feeling joy, excitement, elation, all good emotions at discovering I am her mate. Is she unwell?

Just moments ago, her arousal scented the air as she took in my small human form. I even puffed my chest for her. My human had found me worthy. She wished to mate me, have my children, become my bride.

But now, I am...confused. She does not want me? That's not possible. The Goddess chose me to be her mate.

There must be a threat I am not seeing.

"You're asking a lot of questions for someone who has no business asking me anything," she snaps. Her voice is better than a siren's song. I want her to keep talking and never stop.

Yet, her eyes harden, and her lips curl into a sneer. At...*me*?

How would my brother, Yannig, navigate this? He was smoother with his tongue, able to bend anyone to his will. He would know how to calm my—

No. She is *my* mate. I do not need another male to tell me what my mate needs.

I extend my hand toward her, and she flinches, stumbling back. A flare of panic goes through me. Did I hurt her before? I tried to be gentle, but maybe I held her too tightly. I must fix it. "You're hurt."

"It's nothing." She hides her hand behind her, eyeing me warily.

I frown. "It very obviously isn't nothing. Show me your hand."

My mate gapes at me, taking a step back. "No, I—*No.* You can't just tell me to do something. I don't know you. You're a random stranger off the street," she says, more to herself.

"I am no stranger," I assure her, reaching for her once more. "Please—"

"Excuse me." She shoves past me, storming in the opposite direction of the beach.

I stand there, staring at the tiny female running away from me. I did something wrong. I clench my fists, playing back the interaction. Was there a human greeting I forgot to do? Did I say something offensive? Bile curdles up my throat at the thought I might have harmed her.

This was not how our first meeting was meant to go.

She is angry at me. She hates me. No. Mates do not hate each other. She *must* know our souls have chosen one another. Her injury must be severe if she has not registered who I am to her.

She exited the black, wheeled vessel upset—the one still parked in front of the shop she was in. The urge to follow is strong, but the need to defend my mate is stronger.

No one gets to upset her. No one gets to lay a hand on her.

My sister was a lethal killer. My brother was a mastermind with charm. I will be both.

Somehow. For my mate.

I can take another's life easily—it's the only thing I excel at— but I am unsure how to be as eloquent with my words as Yannig. My interactions with others have been limited to Vasz and the occasional Counselor.

But I can woo my mate. Of that, I am certain.

My claws dig into my palm. I *have* to be certain.

I'm forced to watch my own mate from afar as she enters a vehicle and takes off. As soon as she is on the road, I stalk toward the vessel she exited moments before colliding with me. The pores of my skin undulate, blending me into my surroundings, turning me invisible to all creatures until I can be identified by scent alone.

It's impossible to see the male through the blackened windows, but I can smell him clearly when I open the door and slide into the seat behind him. I've never been in this type of vessel. It's smaller than I thought, dirtier.

And the windows… Fascinating. I can see outside clearly, but those outside cannot look in. I'll need to find this type of glass to keep in my cave. I'm not yet sure what I could make with it, but my mate would like it, since she enjoys her privacy.

Before the male can react, I summon my magic to the surface, shifting parts of my body to allow a few tentacles to unfurl. I have the door shut and the man subdued in a single breath.

My kingdom's main laws are that we must never reveal ourselves to humans or kill them. But what is the point of being king if I cannot break my own rules?

His fear scent explodes into the small space. His battle roar turns into a stunned cry when my limbs wrap around his waist, arms, and legs. I can see his wide eyes in the middle mirror as he stares down in horror at my tentacles. No one can see inside the car, and his screams are pointless against the blaring of horns and the thump of music playing up and down the street.

A rectangular device clatters to the floor as a searing pain hits my tentacle. I snarl and whip the cigarette off my limb. "Stupid human," I snarl.

I circle my fingers around his neck, and his cries vibrate against my palm. It's more satisfying to feel their life drain from my hand, being able to choose who meets their end and who can continue plaguing the Earth with their presence. It's a surge of power forever unmatched.

He uselessly attempts to thrash against me, wiggling his arms in a pathetic attempt to dislodge my hold on him. It's a truly useless endeavor. Five of him couldn't fend me off. Humans are weak. They always were and always will be.

I tighten my grip, and his screams cut off entirely. Nothing but the radio can be heard. "You upset my mate."

"Who?" he chokes. At least, it sounds like the word *who*.

This imbecile dares play stupid about my beloved?

He jolts when I snarl. "Do not act stupid with me, *human*." I could make his bones splinter out of his skin in a blink of an eye.

The male sputters with his attempt to speak. As much as I would rather take his pathetic life now, my curiosity wins over. I loosen my grip. "I don't know—"

"You are testing my patience," I snap, tightening my limbs around him to drive my point. The first bone cracks, and I smile. "The precious treasure who was in this death contraption with you earlier."

I adjust my hold enough for him to speak. "Cindi?" he coughs and sobs at the same time.

That is my mate's name? It's perfect.

"*Cindi*," I say, rolling my tongue around each letter as if I may be able to taste her. I repeat her name several more times, enjoying the way it sounds.

Queen Cindi of Aletia, breaker of the Curse upon the Dead Lands.

Yes. I like that a lot.

The slimy human's nails dig into my tentacle. "Cindi is—"

Crimson sears my vision. How dare he speak *my* mate's name on *his* tongue. I crush his throat in my hand. Tendon and bone mince together. He has no need for speech or breath. No *human* is going to educate me about my own female. He has lived long enough. He must suffer for what he's done to Cindi.

A delighted sound rumbles through my chest.

My mate, *Cindi*.

I repeat her name in my mind, over and over, as I squeeze my limbs around the human until his bones have flattened against the seat, stabbing into me. Blood pours over my tentacles, soaking into the fabric of the vehicle, but I pay none of it any mind.

"Cindi," I say again, a slow smile spreading across my face. "Cindi, bride of Ordus." A purr rumbles through me, and one of my tentacles wags side to side on the floor. I lean my chin against the headrest, picturing the way her eyes heated when I was holding her.

Cindi wanted me.

My *mate* wants me.

I avenged her. She will want me now.

5

VASZ

Rock.

Rock.

Rock.

Ro—not a rock. It's moving.

I peer closer. Since when do rocks move—? A pincer clips onto my paw. I yelp, flinging my arm to the side. The crab goes soaring through the water and scuttles away from our battle. It's too late. The damage is done. I bare my teeth at the cruel world, blue liquid trickling from the deep gash splitting my paw pad open.

"Bad crab," I growl. It disappeared behind the reef, too afraid to face me again.

Hmph. That's what I thought.

I curl my arm so I can lick the grievous wound. I could've died. I am so brave for surviving such a heinous attack. I was a warrior in my last life, and in this. Ordus will build a shrine in my name for protecting him from a vicious foe.

I glance toward him, holding my head high to receive his gratitude. He dragged me to the mainland to see the human last night, made us sleep in the woods around her house. Now, he's making me wait around so he can watch his boring female. Is this my prize for my loyalty?

Agony slices up my arm when I place my paw flat against the sand. I choke back my whimper. A mighty warrior stands tall, even at the risk of bleeding out.

I stay still, about to die from blood loss, patiently waiting to be showered with praise.

He doesn't even look at me.

My ears flatten against my head. How dare he not acknowledge me when I have just gone into battle for him? The humans call a third of me *man's best friend*. Am I not his best friend? The one and only companion of the king?

Yes.

Yes, I am.

And he will thank me.

That human he's been watching is not more important than me.

Leaping up toward the warmer water, I wriggle my tail to gain momentum. The suckers along the backs of my limbs pulse as I tuck my legs up against my chest, staying small to swim easily, using the fins along my back, stomach, and sides to steer.

A low growl starts in my chest. Ordus still isn't looking at me. My eyes narrow on one of his floating arms. It sways and wiggles, threading through the water to keep him afloat. My jaw loosens, and I oh-so-carefully swim closer. Maybe he won't notice if I take one little nibble—

"Vasz," he warns. "Think very carefully about whether you want to bite me right now."

I snap my mouth and avert my gaze to the side. Nope, not looking at him. I wasn't about to bite him. I don't know what he's talking about.

"We must catch crabs to keep in the den for my mate."

I blanch, haunted by the memories.

"Snapper too."

This, I approve. What was I here for?

Oh, yes. That's right.

Untucking my arm, I show him the gaping wound on my paw pad. "I was injured in your name."

Ordus leans forward, and I put on my brave face. I am a mighty warrior. Scars are a symbol of my prowess.

"Where?"

My ears fall, pointing down to the sea floor. Is he blind? I push my snout into the cut and almost die from the pain. "*There*."

Ordus grabs my arm to take a closer look. His eyes narrow, and he tips his head to the side. "I don't see it."

The wound is half the size of one of those land ants and as thick as a strand of his hair. How can he not see it? That he would dismiss me after everything we've been through—

Is that a coconut?

I snatch my arm and swim away.

Oh my.

Oh *yes*.

Look at her. She's beautiful, the *most* beautiful thing I've ever seen. I have never seen a coconut so amazing. It's green with a patch of yellow the same shade as the skin around my eyes.

There's a spot in my quarters where it would—

Not a coconut.

Crab. Crab. Crab. Retreat.

Spinning around, I move my tail as quickly as I can, darting back to Ordus before the crab can wound me again. I've won one war today; I must heal before going into another.

I circle Ordus, enjoying the clean water. I don't know why we can't live out here. I could have a coconut farm, and I'd never need to travel so far to get a snack. The water doesn't taste yucky, and I can listen to the humans talk and play music and dance.

But all Ordus wants to do now is watch his boring human.

I huff, sigh, then huff again, staring at his tentacle, debating how fast I can run away if I bite it.

"I'm bored," I declare.

He ignores me.

I snap at him, and then I dive down to the sand to sniff around for treasure before going back up.

Exploring the sea is no fun when we've been in the same place all morning.

His human's seven legs—I can't count—dangle over the edge of a board, and my ears perk up, my mouth watering. I've hunted her eighty-five times in the past twenty-one days. I deserve a reward after Ordus brought only nine coconuts back to the lair. Her nice, thick thigh bone will be good.

I swim up to Ordus. "Can I eat her?"

"No."

I lick my lips. "A nibble? Please."

"*No*," he growls, showing me his teeth.

Ugh. "Okay."

I wait for her to start flapping her arms in the water, and then I fly through a wave like I do back at the island. Eventually, her three legs come back into the water.

"What about now?" I ask.

Ordus' arm snaps out, and I dart away before he can catch me. My tail moves fast as a light noon—or light thing? Or...lighter? What did I hear the human song say?

My head shakes. It doesn't matter.

I am a lone creature. I do not need Ordus. If I want to eat a—

Legs.

I sniff the water.

Legs that don't belong to Ordus' female. I scrunch my nose. Legs of a smelly human.

My tail slumps. A male with dirty feet. I suppose I must find another meal.

The creature moves to lie flat on his board to give me a clear view of the coconut painted on the bottom of his toy.

I've found lunch.

6
_____

CINDI

The morning sun kisses every inch of my exposed skin and warms me to my core. The mildew and mist that hung in the air and on the grass is long gone, but everything is always crisp out here. I think I could live out here—in the ocean, where no one can find me. Maybe a secluded island with a house right along the beach where the water is at my fingertips, where the freshness of the salty breeze fills my lungs.

Most of all, pain doesn't exist out here. My wrist isn't aching. My fingers aren't on fire. The slight throb in my neck is gone.

The waves gently rock me and my surfboard side to side, lulling me like I'm being swung in a cradle. With each sway, a little bit of my anxiety trickles into the water. Not enough to make me forget about last night's panic attack or the alarm tripped in the late hours of the morning, but just enough for me to unclench my jaw and relax my shoulders.

Sorrow twists in my stomach at the memory of weekends spent with my father—his laughter echoing over the waves, his hands steady as he helped me onto a surfboard for the first time. I'd twisted my ankle that day, but he just grinned, nudging me back up, saying, "No pain, no gain." Back then, I believed him.

Every Sunday, we'd be up at the ass crack of dawn. We either went surfing or hopped on a Harley, riding to some quiet place to reconnect with nature. It was our favorite thing in the world.

At least, that's how it was before I met Tommy.

Dad ate healthy and was the fittest man on Earth—I thought he was going to live forever. He was still in his fifties and went through life acting like he was going to survive well into his nineties. But in the end, carbon monoxide poisoning got to him first, something entirely avoidable.

Tears sting my eyes. I know it's not rational; the *what-ifs* and *had-Is* might change the outcome of that weekend. But it feels like his death could be my fault. If I saw through Tommy sooner, if I broke up with him and didn't engage in the argument about my "prioritizing Dad over him," Dad would never have died. I would've seen him that weekend. He would still be alive, and I wouldn't be running from ghosts and men with guns. If I had just listened to Dad's warning, none of this would've happened.

This morning when I checked the feed, all I could spot was a dog—or at least, I think it was a dog. The dark blob looked about the same size as a midsized one, and it trotted around the same way a canine would. It rubbed itself along my cabin, took pee breaks on the trees and posts, and pawed at the back door.

Whatever it was, it ate all the kibble I left out for the stray animals in the area. Either way, it's time for me to move on. I've already been here too long.

"*Sialan*," Deedee curses in Indonesian—actually, my vocabulary also extends to swear words. "I'm pruning like a bitch."

I peel my eyes open to glance at Deedee as she grimaces at her hands before resuming her fidgeting with the bracelet, staring out at the horizon.

I snort. She's been out here for almost an hour and half. I've already doubled that, because I got out here well before she did. I crane my neck back to check if Nat is still sunbathing on the shore—sleeping off a hangover, apparently—then scan the streets to make sure no one has decided to join us at our secret spot.

The hair on the back of my neck prickles, and I survey the streets one more time to be safe. I can't hear anyone drive further out than this.

My focus returns to Deedee, the feeling of being watched as strong as it always is. She has an unnatural sort of beauty, the kind where you look twice because her deep golden tanned skin glows without a drop of makeup, and she seems to wash her shiny hair with the Elixir of Life.

Her long, black braid is partially undone. Chunks of hair stick out at odd ends. Dark strands frame her face and catch the light every time she moves. Her plait reaches the tattoo on her ribs—it's the same matching one I have on my upper back.

The woman is well above her thirties—or so she claims—but she doesn't look a day over twenty-five. The one time I asked for her skincare routine, she laughed and said, "The blood of virgin men and Neutrogena." It wasn't very helpful, but I figured I'd need more than an oil cleanser to wash away signs of four years' worth of trauma.

"I don't want to look at the state of my hands." I chuckle, cutting myself off at the frown she casts toward the open sea. Her fingers stall on the golden bracelet. "You good?"

She makes a noncommittal noise. "Just memories. You know how it is." She offers me a weak, placating smile.

Don't I know it?

"Want to talk about it?" Sometimes, it's nice to get things off my chest when the world feels too much. I've confided in Deedee before—brief stuff, mostly, but she has a very generalized idea of the type of demons I've got under my bed.

She hasn't told me much either, beyond losing her family and changing her name to feel like she's taking back control of her life.

My stomach sours as I watch the corners of her eyes crinkle with pain and a haunted look passes over her. Seeing her like this makes me feel hopeless. She lost her sister decades ago, and she still hasn't gotten over her grief.

I doubt I'll ever stop feeling like I'm being torn in two whenever I think about Dad.

Deedee nods to our right. "There's a beach a couple kilometers that way where me and Ni Luh used to swim. My mother used to yell at us every time she found out we snuck away—beat us with the broom a few times." She snorts. "Those straw ones that sting like a bitch? *That.*"

I grimace. Dad's form of punishment was only letting me have one scoop of ice cream instead of two—but I was allowed to have some of his.

"Did she surf too?"

Deedee shakes her head. "I didn't get into it until recent years. I was too chickenshit." She laughs.

My lips tip up at the corners as I cast a glance at the street. "I'm pretty sure my dad would've insisted on a water birth if he knew what it was."

"And mine would've loved an epidural if she knew about it." She sighs, turning her bracelet around her wrist. "If she knew what I got up to now…"

The phantom sound of a car soaring past makes me flinch. I clear my throat. "We really need to figure out what we're going to do about the pirates." Even though I'm getting out of here, I don't want to leave them in the lurch after she got me set up and settled.

Deedee pioneered the whole gig. She's the one who began the factory, made the connections, built the clientele. Nat came on board later to do the tech side of things. Then, I injected myself into their operation.

"I think you should reach out to your contacts in—"

She waves me off. "Shit like this happens all the time. Don't worry about it. Give it a week or two, and it'll sort itself out."

Tension returns to my muscles.

It's hard enough that only fifty percent of the chips can be used—for the life of me, I can't figure out why—and we're producing more books than usable chips. Although the quality of our stock is better, Nat and Deedee had to scale back on how many passports we ended up selling because of my many shortcomings.

It hasn't impacted profit margins by much, but the wastage is bound to catch up on us—if the pirates don't screw us over first.

The latest stunt by the pirates is going to screw us big-time unless we act.

"I don't think crossing our fingers and hoping for the best is the best course of action. We need to be proactive." In Tommy's world, that meant either doing something legal, or something *very* illegal that even I wanted nothing to do with it. "They've never taken a whole shipment before. At most, they've stolen half. In a few weeks, we won't be able to operate."

She rolls her eyes, and *boy*, does it make me want to scream.

"Just trust me. You've been doing this for about a year. I've been running this for a lot longer."

I feel like pulling my hair out. She saved my life by getting me a new passport back when I was searching dark web-forums, and we got to chatting. She made Bali sound like the right place for me, so she helped get me here, found me a place to stay, trusted me with her business, and let me into her fold. I owe her everything I have, but sometimes, her laid-back attitude pisses me the hell off.

How can anyone run a factory without a backup plan? She might be a phenomenal artist, and I know the printing side of things is her domain, but without the microchips, we're just another subpar passport manufacturer.

I take a deep breath. After losing Dad and living under Tommy's boot, I've learned my survival depends on knowing how to react to things going tits-up.

"At the very least, I think we should put contingency plans in place in case it doesn't *sort itself out*." Surely, that's a reasonable compromise instead of doing nothing. "Without the parts Wayan was meant to give me last night, I can't fix the machine. We're operating at—"

"Cindi," she says, voice soft but firm.

I almost flinch at the sound of my new name.

"Just breathe. It'll all work out. I'm sure it'll show up in a couple of weeks."

For fuck's sake. I'm talking to a brick wall.

Deedee grins. "I know what will fix this."

I hold my breath, waiting for her to continue. I'm not going to like whatever idea she has.

"We'll get you blackout drunk tonight so you forget all about it."

Don't roll your eyes. Don't roll your eyes.

My teacher once said if I can't say anything nice, I shouldn't say anything at all. But I think my silence might be taken as an act of violence right now.

"My stomach's been uneasy. I don't think drinking is on the cards for me." It's not entirely a lie. The cause of it is purely from anxiety.

Deedee was born and raised in Bali. Hitting the town with her is an experience like no other—I assume so, anyway. I've only been out of the house past dinnertime three times in the past year, and I didn't dare have more than two drinks. The one time I made it to the third, I was hyperventilating in the bathroom because I thought the guy who wanted to dance with me was Tommy.

With what happened with the pirates, this feels like the worst possible time to go out drinking in public.

But what I *really* want is to sleep for two days straight.

"Come *on*." She drags the single syllable out.

After I got out, I promised myself no one would be able to pressure me into doing things I don't want to do anymore. I'll have to make an exception. This will probably be the last time I hang out with them. I'll wrap some things up at the lab, then head out within a few days. It might be months, or even years, before I get the chance to surf again, so I'll take advantage of it while I can.

"We'll see how I feel tonight."

Deedee gives me a look that says, "I see right through your bullshit." I ignore it the same way she's ignoring our problems.

My complacency sure as shit didn't make Tommy any less abusive. Doing nothing will only make our issues with the pirates worse, and I feel like I'm the only goddamn person who cares whether or not this business fails.

It might not be my problem in a couple of days, but I neither want to burn bridges *nor* watch them burn. Nat and Deedee are good people.

I lower my chest onto the board and start paddling closer to the incoming wave before she can say more. I speed up my strokes, preparing to move to my feet at the right moment. This usually relaxes me—makes me feel invincible—but my mind is elsewhere, jumping from Tommy to passports to Wayan's lack of response on when our next shipment might be, and...rows of firm abs, silky black hair, hypnotic blue eyes, and his scent—*Gods*, I'm out in the open, breathing in the real thing, and I swear, he still smelled better.

I push to my feet as the wave catches me. I know the second before I lose my balance that I'm going under. Pressure forces the nose of my board upward, my feet with it. Oxygen is yanked right out of my lungs from the force of the collision against the water's surface. Bubbles and the roar of the sea explodes all around me. My arms flail, trying to get to my board, or at least get some kind of stability. But it keeps coming, coming, coming, turning my body upside down, contorting me to the sea's wish.

Panic, raw and debilitating, tears through me. None of the tricks I was taught work. Instinct isn't saving me.

My leg slams into a stone. Bubbles explode around my muted cry, and my lungs burn from the lack of oxygen.

I shouldn't panic, but shit, I'm going to drown. Something hard hits my head, sending me into a stunned daze muffled by the surge of adrenaline. I twist my body to try to fight the water's drag, using every ounce of my power to claw out. Every time I get a glimpse of the surface, I'm yanked back under.

Something wraps around my legs just as my body curls from the force of another wave. It stops me from being pulled further from the shore. A scream tears through my throat and bubbles around me from the faint puckering against my bare skin. Through my blurry vision, I just make out a huge, reddish-brown *thing* curling around my arm toward my board.

Is that a fucking tentacle?

Oh, fuck no.

I whip around, trying to dislodge whatever the hell it is. I *swear* it lifts me toward the surface, because the next thing I know, oxygen slams into me at once with a choked gasp. My board bobs beside me, and I scramble onto it, hoping and praying it doesn't take my desperation for escape as an act of aggression. It isn't until my body is plastered on top of the board that I'm certain I'm not becoming octopus chow.

"Jesus Christ," I gasp, lying on my stomach to catch my breath. The shore has to be four-hundred yards away. I can just make out Nat and Deedee's ant-sized frames watching me from the distance, oblivious to my near-death experience.

Paddling back to shore, I try *very* hard not to think about what might be in the water. If that thing latches onto me again, I'm going to pass out.

The next wave carries me along the water to make it back in

half the time it would've taken me to paddle. There's none of the familiar joy or euphoria I'd usually get, only stone-cold relief. I know I said I could die happy out here, but I wanted to go peacefully—not by getting mauled. Drowning, on the other hand? I wouldn't hate it, I don't think.

"Holy shit. I think a fucking octopus just touched me," I pant as I use the last of my energy reserves to jog over to our area on the beach, surveying the surroundings.

Nat cocks a brow, looking at me from above her book. Her blond hair is splayed out on the towel like a halo. "Did it now?"

"It was *giant*." I shove my surfboard into the sand and drop onto my ass, lightheaded from the lack of oxygen. My body succumbs to the fatigue, and I collapse onto the sand. "It wrapped around my leg and my stomach, and I thought I was going to get strangled—or eaten."

I narrow my eyes at Deedee as she laughs. "Cindi, zero. Seaweed, one." She rummages through her bag and throws a few things onto my lap.

"What's this for?" I croak. Shielding my eyes from the harsh sun, I lift my head to inspect the painkillers, medicine bottle, and metal tube. "Are we drug dealers now?"

"Hold up. I think I've got a condom in my car to add," Nat teases.

"*Anjing.*" I call her *dog* in Bahasa.

Deedee snickers. "The ointment is for your back. My doctor friend said it's an antibacterial or antifungal cream—I can't remember. Actually, it might be an antihistamine. Just try it. The rest are from Nat."

I resist the urge to glare at her. This is all her fault. Maybe trusting a non-tattoo artist to do my first tattoo was a bad idea. Slightly inebriated me was sure it was a great idea to get one at the time. Tommy *hated* them on women, and I thought it was a good *fuck you* to Tommy and a symbol of my freedom. It's a cross between a motif design with a plant-leaf thing—I'm not really sure, honestly. I let Deedee decide, and apparently, she chose to give me the exact same tattoo she has.

Hindsight is a beautiful thing. Had I known I'd have a reaction to red ink, I would never have used so much of it. It's been over six months, and it still hasn't healed.

Nat points at the painkillers. "That's what I took when I had a back injury." She winks when she points at the bottle. "And the vitamins are for your hangover tomorrow. But I should be giving you my condolences."

"What? Why?" My brows flatten.

"Because we're eating calamari tonight."

Ugh. "It was an octopus, not a squid."

Can my day be over already?

Kill me now.

I'm getting too old for this shit. Or maybe I'm too cynical. Or altogether an angry, hateful woman.

My migraine is in full force from the loud, thumping, bad music and the screeching men and women alike. I'm not sure what the science behind it is, but I feel two seconds away from a heart attack from all the flashing lights.

How I enjoyed these things when I was in college is beyond me. I used to be out every Friday or Saturday night—before Tommy, of course. As per his *expectations*, a proper woman wouldn't have more than a glass of wine, and God forbid she do anything to enjoy herself.

I bounce the heels of my wedges against the floor. I grip my drink, using the cold to numb the ache in my wrist. I keep close to the bar and dart my eyes around the room, studying every new face. I can just spot Natalie dancing with another woman I've met several times, but I can't remember her name. Deedee isn't that far away either, happily getting felt up by some guy—probably a tourist. They're the most fun, apparently.

They'd both always had a carefree air around them, even though our line of business could land us in a ditch or in prison.

My second cocktail isn't doing shit to stop me from grinding my molars. My mind isn't registering the taste. The lack of food and water is making the alcohol go straight to my head—I don't feel even remotely *laid-back*. The atmosphere sure as hell isn't any more tolerable.

Even if I wanted to drink more to prove to myself Tommy's rules hold no bearing on me, the fear his family has ingrained in me is still there.

If I'm drunk, that means I can't think straight.

If I'm hungover, I'm slower.

Anything could happen at any moment, and I need to be prepared to run. I won't become a victim just because I decided to indulge in a Sex on the Beach.

For what must be the thousandth time tonight, I check my cabin's security footage. I glance at the cameras in the corners of the room as I tap my fingers against my phone. I'm so exposed out here. What if someone is watching me from those cameras?

The Gallaghers have the means to hack into security footage. What if they have access to facial recognition software I'm not aware of? Does that even exist?

They could track me to this very spot and drag me out.

I blow out a breath, focusing on calming the fuck down before every person in this bar starts looking like Tommy. Unshed tears threaten to spill as I fight the urge to bolt.

The cheesy pop tune hammers against my eardrums. I pretend not to hear Nat calling me over to dance. I'll lose my grip on my sanity if I do.

A hand curves around my lower back, and I jump away, breathing hard and trembling at the stranger who touched me.

Goosebumps rain over my flesh, and my stomach ties into a hundred knots that threaten to empty the contents of my stomach. Every nerve ending in my body locks up, prepared to be struck. A faint ringing sounds in my ear, and suddenly I'm back in the cold, white mansion, cooking dinner, terrified he had a less than savory day and he knows about a misstep I've taken that I'm unaware of.

No, I'm not there anymore.

My knuckles are bleached white on my purse. I'm half tempted to pull out my taser to use it on the tourist just trying to make the most out of his holiday.

"You're looking a little lonely over here," he slurs.

"That's intentional," I mumble under my breath so he can't hear. I flinch, ready to be slapped for talking back, even though the rational part of my brain is aware I won't be. A year and a half ago, I would have been beaten black and blue for—

I dig my long nails into my palm, focusing on the pain. *Stop thinking about him, Krist—Cindi.*

Fuck. Mey name is Cindi, not Kristy.

I step back when he sways forward. "How about you and I go for a little dance?" He touches my hand, and my fist flies before I can think better of it, hitting him square in the gut.

Holy shit. What did I just do?

The man buckles over with a grunt.

"I'm so sorry." I stagger back, pulse racing. My heart races. Do I run? Make amends?

God, I'm fucked in the head. I need to leave.

I spin on my heels and come to a complete stop in front of a wall of muscle. Sea breeze trickles into my lungs, and warmth seeps through my bloodstream. Something fizzles to life in my soul, a struck match in the darkest recesses. My gaze collides with a pair of endless ocean blues. For one brief, fleeting second, all my terrors, all my worries, disappear, and I finally remember what it means to be content. *Safe.*

But it's a fallacy. Reality comes crashing down as the man's appearance takes shape: his long, black hair, sharp jawline, and chiseled chest made by the Greek gods themselves. The man from last night.

He's following me.

"Why are you here?" I gasp.

"Did this man touch you?" His rage sends a bolt of shivers down my spine. The initial shudder comes from the forbidden allure of hearing someone be protective of me. Then, it's the realization his anger might be directed toward me.

To Tommy, it was always my fault if someone got handsy, never theirs.

Panic chokes me. The man's ocean-blue eyes morph into mold green, and I find myself nodding as survival instincts in.

I don't stick around for follow-up questions. I turn tail and run. It's the only thing I know how to do.

7

This human made three mistakes.

The first was looking at my mate.

The second was approaching her.

The third, and most unforgivable, act was thinking he could touch my beloved Cindi.

The disgusting, pungent male struggles uselessly, if at all. He's too intoxicated to realize the danger he's in. The crowd parts for me, casting curious looks at the human hanging over my shoulder.

No one attempts to stop me. A few pat my back and cheer. The guards step aside to let me pass.

Humans are confusing.

A purr rumbles to life at the memory of Cindi in the teal dress draped across her from one shoulder, hanging loose around her other. It hugged every delicious curve of her body before splitting midway up one thigh to expose her smooth leg. And her face?

Dark charcoal lined her eyes, garnet swept across her lips, her cheeks a pretty pink. I did not think it was possible for my mate to be more beautiful. I was barely able to contain myself from grabbing her the moment I saw her.

I had no choice but to stay back to figure out what had her on edge.

The residue of Cindi's fear lingers in the air, following her like a trail that can be seen to the naked eye. I do not understand why she is always in distress every time I see her, or why her scent soured a second after it sweetened when she looked at me.

She's a mystery to me.

That will change soon enough.

I barrel through the crowd, stalking in the same direction she went, growing increasingly restless with each passing second she isn't in my line of sight. Anyone could approach her, and I would be too far away to know.

The streets are packed with humans laughing and singing along to the music pouring from the open doors of the many buildings. Cars and motorbikes zoom by, blaring their horns, carrying passengers whom I'm sure will congregate with the masses. Unnatural lights flash in an array of colors, making my skin itch with the need to morph, so I blend in with my surroundings.

I avoid the mainland at this time of night for this reason. Humans give me a headache during the day. At night, I want to tear my brain out.

A woman offers me a saccharine smile I return by baring my teeth in a snarl. I am loyal to Cindi and only Cindi.

I will my short human legs to move faster. I don't slow until I turn down the first empty alleyway I find and drop the human onto his feet—at least, that was my intention. The male crumples, slating sideways like a newborn cub without muscles.

He touched my treasure. For that, he must pay. I cannot allow a precedent to be set on account of his insobriety.

Cindi's nearby scent isn't strong enough to combat the putrid smell of trash and urine in the space. No one spares a glance our way. It is human nature to avoid looking into the darkness, blissfully unaware of what lurks in the shadows.

The male points a crooked finger at me and slurs a string of words I can't make out in any of the languages I know. He stares at me through half-parted lids, using a nearby broom to help him to his feet. It wobbles against his weight, and it takes him four pitiful tries to get off the ground.

I step forward, watching his unseeing eyes. "Do you know why you are here?"

He answers.

I'm not sure what precisely he answers with.

I can't make out a single word from his tangent.

Unfortunately, avenging my mate will not be as satisfying as it was yesterday. Magic crackles as I shift, transforming two legs into eight tentacles. I can taste the rancid alley with my suckers, along with the faintest, almost discernable scent of my frightened mate.

A flicker of sobriety flashes through the male's widening eyes, and the air turns acrid. "What the fuck?"

Ah, finally, he's making sense.

There's no need to further delay the inevitable. Cindi has spent too long out of my reach, and this pathetic human will be no fun to play with.

The human shrinks beneath me as my muscles contract, lifting me higher until I'm nearly double his height. The lower half of my body expands twice the width of my shoulders, spilling onto the ground and crawling up the walls. I open the beak hidden in the middle of my tentacles as wide as possible, then lunge for him before he can scream or run.

Two of my limbs wrap around his lithe frame and shove him beneath me to force him into my maw.

The first bite makes me gag. This human tastes positively foul.

Too much sugar, high cholesterol, and a dash of plastic. It isn't a good combination.

Never mind. My message has been sent. There's no need to finish the whole human. A third of his body is more than sufficient.

I will never understand why humans were considered a delicacy centuries ago.

He should be thanking Cindi he is being granted a quick death. He'd be suffering far more if she hadn't hit him with her cute little arm. I wish I had been closer to see it more clearly, but the simple act of recalling it fills me with delight.

I release him and shift back onto two legs. Copper and sulfur mixes with urine and garbage. My stomach turns, and I feel slightly queasy. I blow out a breath and almost reach for the wall to stop myself from falling. It feels like I'm letting the sea carry me, floating freely on the water's surface.

I think the human is making me...

Oh, alcohol, old friend.

Back when the prospect of Yannig and I wearing a crown was just a funny joke, Yannig would drag me with him to go hunting for the squid that would give krakens a high from its venom. When we got older, he'd force me to try the human liquor.

A heavy weight eases onto my chest. It has been many years since I've consumed such toxins. The only person I've ever been around in this state is Yannig. It's been...what? Two decades since I've had a positive experience with another kraken—longer since I had any type of *fun*, because he was occupied, attempting to end the Curse.

My life of solitude—with Vasz—is over. I have Cindi now, and I will keep her safe, protect her from her own nightmares.

My nostrils flare as I break into a run on shaky legs, tearing through the streets to follow her scent. Too much time and people have passed for there to be a clear trail.

AVINA ST. GRAVES

Did she use her own vehicle to get here? Where would she have parked—

My hearts stop beating when a cry rips through the air.

Cindi.

I force my human legs to move as fast as they can, and I frown at the sound of a very *male* cry. I cover the distance within a matter of seconds, rounding a corner before skidding to a stop.

There's a male groaning and rolling around the ground, cupping his sex. My attention snaps up toward the sound of shuffling, and red explodes across my vision. One man has his hand in Cindi's hair while the other tries yanking her backward by her arms as she kicks.

Rage bursts through my chest. A vicious snarl renders the night still. Four pairs of eyes swing my way, but all I see is red.

My hold on this form vanishes. A rare burst of magic explodes from me, crashing into my surroundings as I roar. A cacophony of blaring car horns sends my anger to new heights. Three of my arms shoot out, sending the men holding my Cindi crashing against the wall.

I grab the one who had his hand in her hair and crush both arms in my tentacles. White splinters stick out of his thin skin. I do his legs next before moving to the other male to rip his limbs from his shoulders. Crimson squirts from the gaping sockets, spraying the dirty walls with his filth.

Cindi stands there frozen, fear scent strong, staring at me with her deep brown eyes like I truly am the monster she's been made to fear. Her mortification breaks through my bloodlust, and I hold my breath, waiting for her to start screaming at my appearance.

My grandmother procreated with a land dweller, but I am the only one in my family who held markings that proved our tainted bloodline. I was deemed an abomination the moment I was born without webbing between my arms and chest, with five fingers instead of four.

The whispers worsened as I grew older. The upper half of my body began to resemble the two-legged kind: claws, some straight teeth, *hair*. My own mother's eyes would crinkle with guilt when her sights landed on me, like she regretted birthing me and subjecting me to this life.

Cindi is looking at me like the other krakens do: as if I am a plague.

The smell of her horror permeates the air. It...it must be because she's never seen my kind before, not that she believes there is something inherently wrong with me—that can't be the reason.

A warning growl rips from me when she looks away to the two unconscious bodies. I don't want her to stop looking at me. I want to see her. I want her to see *me*.

My head snaps toward the spare human, who lets out a shrill scream, jumping to his feet to run for it. I snarl and grab him by the ankle to slam him against the ground, cracking his skull in two.

When I look up, my mate is nowhere to be seen; there's only the harsh echo of her shoes slapping the ground. She's running from me. I need to catch her before she escapes my grasp, before I can no longer protect her.

Every instinct in my body thrums with raw, primal energy. My muscles prime and contract, ready to give chase. Each of my senses sharpen until all I can hear and smell is my fleeing treasure. The excitement of the hunt is quickly washed away by the bitter scent of her terror—like ash and acid.

I curl my hands into fists, staring in the direction she ran. Maybe I was wrong.

Not even the Goddess could create someone who could want me.

8

CINDI

What the actual fuck was that?

I'm going insane.

Absolutely fucking insane.

There's no way that was real. I'm imagining things. I drank too much. I've been drugged.

Or I have a concussion from hitting my head when those guys tried to capture me.

This is like that time Tommy threw me into our basement and locked me in there for three weeks. There was no light, no window for me to look out of, no sound. Just my thoughts and the one time a day he'd visit to feed me.

I heard voices—Dad's. Thought I saw my mother too. They spoke to me, kept me company, and checked on me when no one else did.

Maybe I've just lost the plot, because there is no universe in which an eight-legged tentacle creature just saved my life.

An eight-legged tentacle creature changed from two legs in a second flat. One I've run into twice in two days. One who I thought was the most attractive man I've ever seen.

He's an alien. He has to be. There's all that shit on the news about how they live in the ocean and can shapeshift to pass off as us or whatever. I haven't got a clue what else he could be.

Scrubbing my hand over my face and looking around my bedroom, a wave of fatigue has me tripping over my feet and leaning against the wall to catch my breath.

I need to leave. *Tonight.*

Once is an accident. Twice is a coincidence. Three times is a pattern. I'll be damned if I stick around to see that *thing* a fourth time. The shit that's gone on with my alarm and the pirates is reason enough. Tonight's events are expediting my departure.

Those men are a mystery to me. One of them was European, and the other might have been Indonesian—I don't know. It was dark, I was scared, and I couldn't make out their faces. I didn't understand a word of what they were saying or whether they were complete strangers or pirates or Gallagher connections.

Tears spill down my cheek. God, I hate that I liked it here. I liked my cabin. The two friends I made. The beach. The food. The smell of the fresh air in the morning. The whistle of the wind between the trees during a storm.

I shouldn't have gotten attached.

Furiously swiping at my cheeks, I run around the house, shoving everything I can into my luggage—laptop, burner phone, cash I'll strap to my body later, more fake passports, more fake IDs, disguises, toiletries. My go bag already has everything I need, but it's better to have more, since I still have the work car to run away with.

It was only a matter of time before the Gallaghers followed me here. It's a miracle I've even lasted this long.

The *thing* that killed those men could be connected to either of the people who have it out for me, or maybe someone else I've inadvertently pissed off without realizing.

My best bet would be to find a quiet area in the middle of nowhere, far from civilization and cameras, and lay low. Go radio silent. Maybe try going back to Thailand to hide out on a secluded island.

As I shove my things into my bag, I decide I'll stick with my initial plan. I'll drive to Bandung to hide out for a bit and keep minimal contact with Nat and Deedee. Once the heat dies down, I'll leave Indonesia. I'm not sure where to yet, but I'll figure it out.

I scramble to my dresser and yank a drawer out, sending it clattering onto the tile floor. Its contents spill around the room, and I drop to my knees and run my fingers around the wood to feel for the false bottom. I turn my nails into a makeshift crowbar and pry the wood off before chucking it aside.

My hand hovers over the drawer. These are the most important items I have, priceless beyond reason and completely irreplaceable.

Choking back a sob, the tears fall harder down my cheeks, onto my dress. More blotches of darkness bloom across the darkness with each tear. My trembling fingers trace the picture of Dad holding up a child-sized me and beaming with pride over my first solo surf.

I remember the joy in his voice as he called up my uncle and one of his buddies to tell them all about how well I did. He boasted about the size of the wave, my form, and how I kept my two little feet stable. He went on and on like I was a legend in the making.

He carried me on his shoulders to get my favorite treat, and we both went crazy from the sugar high. I can still recall the different ice cream flavors we got, how terribly I failed at devouring the six scoops.

Clutching the bundle of photos to my chest, I squeeze my eyes shut to try and focus on my breathing.

I miss him so much.

I slip a chain around my neck and hide the ring Mom gifted

him beneath my dress. It doesn't make me feel any closer to him, but wearing it makes it seem like he's watching over me.

What would he say about where I ended up? Hell, what would Mom say if she knew the daughter she gave her life to birth is running from both the law and outlaws?

Sniffling, I pull myself back onto my feet and carefully tuck the pictures away in my handbag. It's all I have left of my dad.

The front porch groans, and I freeze, pulse skyrocketing. A *bang* shakes the house. Self-preservation kicks in, and I'm on my feet, bolting out of the bedroom.

The smell of rain wafts through the house, carrying traces of the sea and the intoxicating warmth of *him*. That—that *thing*.

My heart stalls when I catch the vision before me. It's straight out of a horror movie. The top of his dipped head and broad shoulders brush the doorway—fills it. The moon backlights the man standing at the door, illuminating his hard edges like he's the devil himself. A harbinger of death.

The faint light coming through my bathroom catches on the water droplets dripping from his hair down his bare chest, rippling over each curve of his abs. A shudder works down my spine. An odd, almost animalistic sound rumbles from him, pulling me from my stupor and bringing me firmly back to the present, where I'm meant to be running from my life after seeing a man transform into a tentacled monster.

The same monster standing at the door.

My pulse roars in my ears, and my feet move before my head catches up. I dive across the living room for the back door.

Footsteps bound behind me, and a cry tears from my lips when something lashes out at me.

Why the fuck didn't I get a weapon first?

It wraps around my waist and hauls me back against his chest. "I caught you." His deep voice rolls through my veins. *"Mate."*

No, no, no, no, no. I'm meant to be getting away.

My eyes fall to the tentacle around me, and I *lose it*. I scream at the top of my lungs. I fight, throw my head back, try to kick my legs out, hit the fucking *tentacles* curving around me. Nothing works. It's like it barely inconveniences him.

A tentacle wraps around my shoulders so my body stays upright, but my injured elbows can swing free.

He's going to kill me. He's going to take me to the Gallaghers, and they're going to torture me.

"Let me go!"

"Only in death," he promises.

I suck in a shocked breath, momentarily disarmed by the declaration.

His suckers pucker along my skin, and a ripple of fatigue rolls up my spine. No, not fatigue—something similar, where my muscles feel like they're going limp, but not quite.

Soft fingers trail over my exposed arm, and when his sharp nails graze my skin, I flinch, bucking against him to break free— but all I can think about are how his hands are on me.

The monster's smooth, almost gentle touch is so unlike Tommy. His grip is firm but not painful. Tight, just enough to keep me pressed up to him.

It's not the same blinding terror of having regular hands on me, just a different kind. My skin doesn't crawl, and I'm not nauseated imagining myself standing in the white mansion, waiting to be struck.

Every inhale drags more of his scent into my lungs, spreading warmth through my veins from feeling like I'm out on the beach when there isn't a single soul in sight. It's messing with my brain.

He's messing with my brain.

Something's not right.

"No!" I throw my head back in the hopes it collides with his nose—if monster-him has one of those—but it has the exact *opposite* of my intended effect. He nuzzles his face against mine. His warm breath fans my cheek, holding me in place. Vibrations start up my back, an odd sound that warms my stomach and sends soft tingles down my spine.

Is he… Is that a *purr*?

"We will go home now."

What does he mean by—

Movement at the door catches my eyes.

"What the fuck is that?" I screech, thrashing harder to get away.

The shark-dog peels its lips back around the coconut in its mouth, continuing his trot into my living room.

"His name is Vasz," the voice comes from behind me.

It—*Vasz*—lowers his ass to the rug, swishing his shark-shaped tail behind him, giving me what can only be described as a nod of confirmation.

I swing my gaze from the shark-dog to the tentacles feeling me up, then backward to the open suitcase on my bedroom floor. Laughter bubbles up my throat. This is actually happening. "Oh, God. I've gone insane. I have fully, completely, and utterly lost it." Wave after wave of hysteria hits me.

"I do not understand." I can hear his frown. "What is funny, Cindi?"

Oh my God, he speaks.

The tentacle monster thing fucking speaks.

And he knows my name.

Of course, he does. I obviously widely advertise it. The whole country *definitely* knows who I am. So why *wouldn't* the ten-foot-tall, clawed, eight-tentacled monster with pointed ears know my name?

Laughter turns into heaving. Tremors rack my body. This is happening. It's actually happening. My lungs scream with desperation as I try to suck in oxygen.

"She is not crazy," the man-monster thing hisses. "She's perfect."

And he talks to himself too.

This is great. Amazing. Splendid.

"It's okay." The words come out gentle, like I'm a delicate thing he's trying to appease. And the—the *purr* deepens.

The tentacles dip beneath my dress, winding around my legs, writhing in an almost...exploratory motion.

I shake my head. *No, no, no.* This *can't* be happening.

"Please don't take me to them. *Please.* I'll give you whatever you want," I beg.

I know what the Gallaghers are capable of—the level of hell they'd inflict on me. But maybe this monster will do me the kindness of killing me quickly.

My back snaps straight when his hand skims the line of my jaw. His scent changes from fresh sea breeze to the oaky cologne Tommy always wore. I suppress a whimper, stilling, because maybe then, he won't feel as compelled to strike out. Maybe it'll hurt less.

His purring grows louder as he turns me in his arms and tucks me against his chest, legs curled bridal style as he moves us to the door. "Once we bond to each other, there will be no more reason for you to feel fear."

Bond to each other?

"The Goddess chose you for me. The Curse will finally be ended, and it will all be because of you. My family can rest in peace, and we can enjoy our time together. I will protect you as any mate should."

He's not making any sense. I can't move, can't run, can't speak. I'm back there, in the cold mansion, sitting on the floor, huddled against the wall, hoping and praying he doesn't break a bone and it'll all be over quick.

Staying rigid in his hold, I choke back a sob. No one likes the sound of crying. It aggravates people.

Rain hails down on me and yanks me out of my frozen state. "No!" I cry, using every ounce of energy I have to break free. I squint against the pelting drops to make out the trees flying by.

My fist slams down onto his tentacle. Blinding agony ruptures through my wrist, and I cry out, cradling my hand to my chest as the pain radiates up my arm. I can hardly breathe from the agony of a thousand knives stabbing into my elbow down to the tips of my fingers. Tears stream from my eyes unbidden. I can't stop them, no matter how hard I try.

"Do not cry, my little mate," he purrs, squeezing me like he's genuinely trying to comfort me. "All will be right soon."

The smell of the sea grows stronger, the crashing waves louder. Panic claws through my throat. Where is he taking me? The road is in the other direction—the *Gallaghers* are in the other direction.

"Please," I beg. "Take me back." Whimpers tear from me at the flash of pain. It worsens every time I move, a million pinpricks to my skin as the dagger pierces bone. "Please," I moan, squeezing my eyes shut against the pain.

Kill me. Drown me. Throw me over a cliff. I don't care right now. Make the pain stop.

"Do not worry, my Cindi. I'm here now."

The suckers pucker hard against my skin, and the same ripple of fatigue wavers through my bones.

I can't do more than squirm as the tears pour down my eyes. Each time I move to fight him off, it feels like my arm is getting torn off, and it's now a limp hunk of flesh. I try to focus on anything else but the pain, telling myself it doesn't exist. My arm is fine and it's all in my head. I can *just* feel his hand against my skin, but it's all dull against the mind-numbing pain rendering me paralyzed.

I'm vaguely aware we've reached the bank of the beach. The distance closes faster than I can process. Sprays of water splatter me, soaking my dress as he carries me further and further away from my house.

A wave crashes into my side, and I clamp my jaw against

another sob. The cold bite of the sea sinks its teeth into my organs, and my teeth chatter despite the humidity.

"What are you doing?" I croak, screaming at myself to fight, to get over the pain and throw my weight so I can run.

But I can't move.

Fuck you, Tommy. *Fuck you.* I killed you, and you're still controlling me from the grave.

Half my body submerges underwater. Panic slaps me into consciousness. I push the monster. Shove him. Elbow him. Anything I can do as he shifts me from his tentacles to his arms.

"I'll drown." I clamor up his body to keep from going under, squinting against the rain and the endless darkness ahead.

Finally, I look up and falter, momentarily disarmed by my first good look at him. Beneath the night sky, he doesn't look so monstrous, more a fallen angel with shadows across his face and the faintest glow from the moonlight. He still has the same striking features of the heaven-made Adonis I stumbled into yesterday.

A sharp jaw, a strong nose, deep cheekbones, gills along his neck, raven hair that looks smoother than silk. Except, in this form, he has faint dots around his eyes and arms, threads of blue in his skin, and big ears shaped like a spiny dorsal.

The monster's eyes brighten when they land on me. "I told you—I am bringing you home." His voice holds an excited yet hesitant lilt. "I will take care of you. You will always be safe as long as I'm here."

The waves climb up my body. Panic overtakes pain. I claw at him, feeling nothing. "*No, no, no, no.* I can't! Stop! Sto—"

Saltwater floods my mouth. Every ounce of my fear manifests into pure energy. I push against him with all my might, sinking my nails into skin, hitting any surface my fists will meet, until oxygen slams back into my lungs.

I sputter, coughing up the harsh liquid. The sound of rushing water comes from all around me. I quickly peel my eyes open. It isn't the sprawling sea or stormy skies that come into view. Beneath the dull, muted glimmer of moonlight, all I can make out is the faint outline of the creature who stole me and the barest glow of bubbles curling around my head like...a glass dome. A fish bowl.

Lifting my good hand up to my face, I squint, gasping at the feel of water trickling down my arm. My eyes widen when the beast's chest rattles. Is he...chuckling? Purring?

My jaw clenches as I swallow back a whimper. "How?"

If he responds, I can't hear it.

The cold current wraps around my body, heightening the pain. I have no way to tell how fast we're going or *where* he's taking me. My fruitless attempts only last a couple more minutes until the agony and the hopelessness win out.

What would be the point? He's far stronger than I am. If I manage to break free from his hold, do I seriously expect to outswim him? How far from land would I even be? If a shark doesn't kill me, the storm will. What about the *thing* chewing a coconut? I didn't come all this way to die because of my own stupidity.

What does this monster want from me? Is he planning on killing me? Forcing himself on me? *Eating me?*

I need to run the second I get the chance. Scream like hell, find a weapon, increase my kill count to two if necessary. The monster knows where I live, so I'll need to head straight to the factory, get myself a new passport, and catch the first flight out of this country without turning back.

I don't bother trying to suppress my sob. I wish my dad were here. I wish he was never taken from me so I didn't have to suffer through all this bullshit alone. If the monster wants to kill me for crying, drowning isn't the worst way to go.

I lost my father, killed Tommy, ran from the Gallaghers, made and sold fake passports, all to be captured by a monster. What am I even fighting for anymore? I have no one. Nothing. Deedee and

Nat are my friends, but I doubt they'd do more than shed a tear for me at my funeral.

The cold makes it feel like my arm is being sawed through. Whimpers fall from the worsening pain. I press my face against the monster's chest, keeping my hand between us to absorb his body heat, taking comfort from him.

Three chilling realizations hit me at once.

He's not taking me to the Gallaghers.

He isn't working for the pirates.

He wants me for himself.

And that might just be worse.

9

*V*ASZ

I glare at Ordus' human as they swim ahead to the island, too fast for me to keep up.

I don't like the female.

She's noisy and didn't offer me the respect I deserve by leaving me a pile of—oh, is that another coconut?

I dive away from Ordus and the loud female to the beautiful, perfect, most stunning fruit half buried in the sand.

Thank you, octo-shark-dog Goddess, for blessing me this night.

I have been spoiled for choice today. I saw many, many, many coconuts—and crabs. They must have spread word that I am fearsome and to keep clear. Oh, I can only imagine how glorious my den will be with all my new coconuts. I can throw away the chipped and bad broken ones to Ordus' lair to free up room in mine.

My tail swishes side to side, ears bouncing against the current, saliva mixing with the water and coating the coconut in my maw. Excitement blossoms all the way to my toes. Sand plumes around me as I bounce from paw to paw along the ocean floor, not stopping until the divine fruit is within reach.

I butt my nose into the sand to dislodge the coconut, jumping back to get a good look at her.

Oh, she's beautiful. Truly majestic. More stunning than anything on sea or land.

And she's all mine. She's coming home with me.

I lunge for it, jaws wide, soul open to welcome my true love home. But I...I knock right into it?

Huh? That doesn't make sense.

My ears flatten. I try grabbing it again, and it floats further away. I narrow my eyes, calculating my next move.

Ohh, yes. I see what I did wrong.

I drop the coconut out of my mouth and pick up the new one.

Ha. Success.

I turn back to catch up with Ordus, a bounce in my step, only to freeze. I turn back slowly. There's still a gorgeous, round, green fruit rolling in the sand.

Wait. That's... I tip my head to the side. That's the coconut I brought with me from the mainland.

I drop the one in my mouth and pick up the old one, then frown at the new one steadily floating away from me. Why is this not working?

I repeat the process, letting go of one to get the other.

Old coconut. New coconut. Old one. New one. Old. New. Over and over.

A frustrated growl rumbles in my throat. I keep trying, letting loose a whine. I can't fit them in my mouth.

Now, I understand. A tortured, pained whimper tears from the deepest part of my chest.

I cannot keep both.

One must be sacrificed.

I screw my eyes shut, fighting the wave of tears. The grief is eating me alive. How am I meant to choose? The Goddess is cruel. She has gifted me with beautiful, perfect coconuts, and she's forcing me to abandon one of them, to leave it behind so another may throw it aside, abuse it, not cherish it the way it deserves.

A broken sob shatters my throat. She's a cruel, cruel woman.

I drop to my haunches and dip my head, trying not to wail. Why does the Goddess wish to punish me? What have I done to deserve this?

I will remember this day until I perish; the night where I said goodbye to my love, the one that got away.

"I will do everything in my power to return for you, my sweetness," I whisper to the mate I must leave behind when I only just met her.

I sink my teeth into the coconut I found by the human's house. I must be loyal to my first love. It is the honorable choice.

10

ORDUS

My mate won't stop shivering, and I don't know how to stop it.

I've tried summoning my magic to raise my external temperature, but it's using up my energy and making me swim slower. I've cradled her close, right up against my chest. I've stroked her back, purred louder, whispered my undying devotion, and still, the deep crease between her brow remains.

I am at a loss. There is nothing more I can do until we get to our den. It isn't safe out here. Some krakens prefer hunting at this time of night. If they see me carrying a human, they will tell the Council and rally other krakens to have my mate killed.

My muscles pump harder, slicing through the stormy ocean, my human lungs itching for air. My ears and suckers focus on sensing any danger. There are several sharks in the area, but they wouldn't dare come near. I dislike swimming back into my territory from the mainland. The further I get, the worse the water quality becomes. It feels like dirt burrowed into my pores that needs to be scrubbed.

Cindi whimpers, and it's like I'm being flayed. I finally have my mate in my arms, and I am failing her. Nothing has gone right, and the look she gave me when I shifted sits at the forefront of my mind.

Cindi is my fate-ordained mate. Yet, I could hear her calling me an abomination without uttering a single sound. I disgust her. My mate is disgusted by me.

I thought it would be different because the Goddess deemed it so. She was meant to look at me with nothing but awe like she did the first time we interacted—before her scent went sour. Before she feared me.

I'm just as cursed as my kingdom. One was cast upon me by the Goddess to forever be nothing more than a disgrace to krakens, humans, and my own mate.

I'm meant to protect her, keep her safe, healthy, and happy, and what have I done since meeting her? Five men have harmed her. She's cold to the touch, clutching her arm with a single, jagged scar running down the middle.

Fury simmers beneath my skin. I grind my teeth, regretting everything about tonight. I should have been gentler with her, talked her through what was going to happen, and explain that I, as her mate, would rather perish than cause her harm.

But my incompetence has also hurt her. It's unforgivable.

Yannig would have never allowed this to happen. His mate would never have screamed or looked at him like he was the most hideous creature to have ever lived. His mate wouldn't have hated him.

I hold Cindi tighter, tearing my sights away from the darkness to look at her, wishing I could taste her sweet skin against my suckers again. I will fix this. I'll make her see being my mate isn't her curse. She will never have a reason to abhor me. I'll need to... I don't want to spend the rest of my life in human form just so my mate finds my appearance tolerable.

But if it's the only way my mate will feel something

toward me other than loathing, it is a sacrifice I am willing to make. For her. *My* Cindi. I can't lose her and continue living this life alone anymore. The solitude has developed its own pulse that will continue to beat when the rest of me has withered away.

I want to be someone's priority, just once, even if it's not because they want me to be.

The entrance to my den looms ahead. I'm tempted to slow my pace to hold her for a little longer, but I do not want her to suffer. I am a bad, selfish mate.

There is no thrill in having her in my space because I have done little to nothing to prepare. Yet again, I have failed. Always failing.

I glance down at Cindi, considering whether to seek out a healer to look at her hand. We may not even have one of those anymore; it's been years since I've checked. They may have fled our territory to seek better conditions.

Diving closer to the sea floor, I scan the rocks littered beneath the cliff, spotting the large, oval stone. The entire island is mine. Other than Krokant, it's the only other area with any biodiversity —except it's not the kind me or my people could survive off. The island has a different relationship with the Curse no one has bothered to figure out.

No other kraken nor creature but Vasz is permitted to enter it, though that doesn't mean I trust my people or bandits not to try to access my den.

I hesitate before approaching the door. Cindi will find our home lacking. I had wanted to take out my finest treasures and line our bed with the softest moss. I planned on stocking up on food so there would be no reason for me to leave after we consummate our bond.

Yet, I have none of those things. All trivial matters.

My human is delicate and small. Why do I not keep healing supplies? Or bring fabrics from the mainland to keep her warm when I hunt? My siblings would never have made such foolish mistakes.

Cindi deserves better than me.

My mate's soft whimpers spear my soul. This is all *my fault*. I shouldn't have been so reckless and impulsive.

The symbols engraved into the stone glow when I whisper the opening command. It groans as it slowly rolls to the side. The door slides shut behind me, encasing the tunnel in total darkness, silencing the roar of the raging storm.

I can navigate the channels with my eyes closed. It has been many years since I've cut myself on the jagged edges sticking out from the rocks, but I still slow, careful to keep Cindi close so she doesn't get hurt.

The first patch of glowing algae stirs my mate. Some give off streaks of purple or green, even the occasional pink.

She peels her eyelids back to reveal her deep brown irises. The soft blue light illuminates the hard curves of her face as we pass another patch, and I slow down before reaching the next group so I can soak in every detail of my precious mate.

Her lips part, and she sits up straighter. Cindi's gasp brings me more joy than she'll ever know. I spent years harvesting and planting the glowing algae, keeping it alive through the Curse. My mother taught me how when I was very young, and it took a long time for me to get it right. That my mate would appreciate it makes the years of work and frustration worth it.

Cindi's eyes widen in awe as we approach my den, where the algae is abundant and brighter than anywhere else in my cavern system. My mate is impressed by our home. Maybe…maybe there is hope.

The magic air bubble around her head dissipates when we break past the surface of the water into the cave hidden beneath the island's cliff. Oxygen fills my own lungs, and my chest instantly feels less tight.

I carefully and reluctantly set her on the edge of the pool, missing the feel of her the second she's out of my arms. She wobbles unsteadily for a moment, wincing when she places pressure on the hand she was clutching.

Silence floods the space between us, and I watch with bated breath as her eyes roam over our den.

It is...plain. There is nothing special about it. No king would ever live in such barren quarters. I never saw the need to improve it or have anything beyond the bare necessities. Mutants have no need for nice spaces. I moved from the palace the moment I could. My human lungs could not stand spending so much time in the water.

In an alcove on the other side of the cavern is a shrine to Edea, the Sea Goddess, with a woven basket of jewelry dropped by humans, shells, and a jar of sand from a distant island where she was last sighted two hundred years ago.

A pile of coconut shells lies in the corner, leftover from the many times Vasz has come up here and forgotten to bring them back down to his little grotto off one of the shoots from the tunnel.

There are some human gadgets around the place I thought might be useful: chains, knives, some type of metal tool, a bowl, cups, a bag I can carry across my body, fabric I'm weaving into ropes and mats, and other random bits I've managed to find uses for.

I didn't dare have keepsakes of my family on display. I have enough reminders of my shortcomings, I refuse to add to them. The treasures I've been gathering over the years are kept in another cave.

During the day, some light trickles in through the hole on the side of the den that leads up to the land. At night, the only source of light comes from the algae threading through the crevices of the rock wall and around the pool.

Emboldened by her blatant approval of our den, I slowly move closer so she doesn't notice.

Cindi blinks blearily at the algae residue glowing on her fingers. Her gaze swings to me. I puff my chest out and rise out of the water so she might look at me with the same astonishment. I am big, larger than every other kraken I have met.

I am an adequate hunter. I'm fast, strong. I have won every battle I've fought. I have access to my people's riches, and I am protected by virtue of being the king.

I flex my muscles and expand my chest, making myself larger so she can see I am a worthy mate. Her gaze drops down to my partially curled fingers. I may have been cursed with claws, but I have honed them into a weapon. Cindi is smart. She will understand that.

But there is no astonishment, no awe or gratefulness. Everything stills, silent for a heartbeat. Then, pure horror flashes across her face.

I deflate, staggering back. She isn't meant to look at me like that.

My mate isn't meant to find me revolting.

What is it that she finds wrong with me? Do I lack the charm my brother had? Or the lethal tact of my sister, so Cindi thinks I cannot protect her? Is it my appearance? My size? Is she disappointed I failed to protect her? Our den?

It makes me sick to know if we weren't destined to be together, she'd pick either of my siblings over me. Or any other human *but* me. Everything in my life has been by chance: the throne falling into my lap, my mother's accidental pregnancy, even finding Vasz's unconscious form on an island far from my lands after being attacked for the way he looks.

I am never a choice. I am an unwelcome consequence.

Given the option, my people and every person on the Council would choose another to lead them. My own mate would rather be bonded to someone who isn't me.

The Curse requires my bride be willing, and my Cindi does

not find me worthy. She will not be willing. More than anything, I know this to be true.

My hearts hollow as I watch my precious, beautiful mate scramble away from me, leaving the scent of her fear behind. Her eyes dart around the cavern, landing on the human objects placed around.

"Cindi," I start, but nothing else comes out. The words are lost on me. What could I say in this situation? Apologize for my birth? For the decision of the Goddess to bind our souls together?

What's done is done. There is nothing I can do to change our destiny.

One of my tentacles reaches for her.

"Get the fuck away from me," she hisses, clambering back toward the rock wall with the human objects.

I feel sick. My own mate is frightened of me. Oh, the Council would be laughing if they saw this.

Cindi grabs what I believe the humans call a wrench.

Her eyes jump to the tunnel beside me up to land. I hold my hands up like I've seen the people on land do when they're in trouble and slowly exit the pool to block her path. She's safer from the storm inside the cavern than outside. Cindi is so small, I worry she may be swept away in the wind. "I will not hurt you, mate."

"Stay back," she threatens, holding her makeshift weapon with one hand while the other remains tucked to her side. My human is so precious. She's adorable to think she is the least bit frightening.

It's hard to focus when the fabric of her dress is sticking to her, hugging every curve. One of the ties has come undone, hanging her dress lower with the added weight. The tops of her pert breasts peak above the teal, rising and falling with her heavy breaths. My mating arm twitches when my eyes fall on the slit ridden up to the juncture of her thighs.

My eyes widen when she uses her good arm to throw the wrench at me. It hits one of my appendages, then clatters onto the ground.

"Touch me, and I will tear you limb from limb, asshole." Cindi bares her blunt little teeth at me and grabs the knife off the ground.

I don't mind having a violent mate if it's the only form of touch she offers.

"Asshole?" I echo. I've heard the word before but never understood why humans enjoy mentioning their anus in conversation. Perhaps it is a form of offense? Or endearment?

"Yes. You are an *ass-hole* for fucking kidnapping me, you fucking monster!" She swings the knife, pointing it at me.

Monster.

One of my tentacles develops a mind of its own, slithering along the ground to touch her, desperate to prove that I might be, but not to her.

"Don't you dare!" Cindi cries, hopping away on one leg to avoid me.

Her bad arm swings back to hold her up against the wall. It buckles the moment she applies pressure to it. More of my limbs shoot outward to catch her before she can fall.

She screams, batting me away. "Let go of me! Put me down!"

I scrunch my nose. Cindi's acrid fear stench reaches new heights when I pull her against my chest where it's safe and she cannot hurt herself. My chest rumbles with a purr, and I release the venom from my suckers into her skin to relax her. The effects are almost immediate. Her muscles incrementally unwind as she stares up at me in astonishment.

A tentacle dips beneath the top of her partially fallen dress and wraps around her upper body to keep her steady. The sudden shift in Cindi's scent slows my movement. It's warmer, spiced, morning mildew mixed with the sweet tang of fresh kelp.

My suckers contract, latching onto her skin, puckering

around the small nub on her breast to taste her more clearly. Her nipples stiffen into perfect peaks, and my breeding organ hardens.

She shivers, breathing hard—the good kind. The type that brings hope to our damned situation. Her lust permeates the air, and my nostrils flare, filling the smell into my lungs. Blotches of red blossom along her golden skin as her rounded eyes stare up at me, lips parted wide.

My mate finds me attractive.

"Cindi," I groan, sucking her nipple harder.

Her desire seeps from her pores. I wind between her legs to smear the aphrodisiac over my limbs, the scent marking me as hers. I feel drunk on her and the dream that she may say yes to me. Maybe tonight, we'll bond, and my life will change.

Her breathing hiccups as she squirms. "What are you— don't—"

A slight prick makes me pause. I frown, looking down at a tentacle. We both stare in silence at the knife sticking out of my limb.

My mate has... She's marked me.

A mating mark.

Sparks skate across my skin as my sex arm begins to raise, seeking her out. She's accepting me—albeit, it's not in the usual place, but I didn't think this would really happen. Liquid drips from my mating organ as I fight the need to bury myself in her delicious core.

Cindi's forehead pinches in confusion when I cup her cheek and tuck her hair behind her curved, human ears.

She needs only say the words, and I will mark her in return.

"Thank you," I rasp, blood soaring with elation. "I would have preferred my chest or throat, so it is more obvious, but I suppose this will suffice. I will still wear it with pride. All will know I belong to you."

I pull the knife out with my free tentacle and offer it to her.

The blade digs into my limb so she does not accidentally hurt herself, but the pain isn't noticeable beyond the excitement of having her mark me as hers for the rest of eternity.

Her jaw drops. I like this Cindi much better—when she's not fighting me and her scent is only tainted by her underlying anger. And...she looks rather intrigued by me.

But my mate's bewildered expression? I can't place the reason for it.

"You want me to stab you *again*?"

"Only if you're offering." I try to hide my hope. Cindi could engrave her name on my chest if she wanted.

"What the fuck?" She gasps.

"I will not force you to do it, but it would be my greatest honor if you did." I dip my head.

I try not to notice my blood pouring onto her skin—I'm unsure whether she is the type who dislikes such things. Still, it drives me wild knowing I am marking her in my own way, covering her with my scent so every creature knows this treasure is mine.

My sex travels over her body, leaking and spilling my seed all over her supple flesh.

Cautiously, her soft fingers curl around the handle as she timidly takes the knife from me. She seems to be more settled when she has the weapon. I will find her more if that's what brings her comfort.

I release her face, lowering my hands to her back and waist. Then, I tip my head to the side to expose my neck and chest. Even if she wishes to mark my cheek, I will be the happiest kraken in existence. My Cindi can do no wrong to me.

Instead, the joy of having my mate in my arms is severed when she slowly says, "Put me down and take me back home."

Her steady confidence makes my chest swell with pride. Then, her words settle in.

My forehead wrinkles, and my tentacles clutch her tighter,

refusing to let go. My sucker puckers hard around her nipple, and she jolts, perfuming the air with her sweet arousal, but her expression is tense and unhappy. Why did she mark me if she wanted me to take her home? Humans make no sense.

"I cannot do both. To return you, I must hold you."

Cindi makes this thrilling squeaking sound when my tentacle latches onto her other nub. I can still taste her lust on my tongue, but her skin is dampening with fear. It lessons as I release more of my venom, making her body relax further like I wanted to in the water, to treat her injured arm.

"Fine. Then do it." Her voice is just above a rough whisper through her gritted teeth. "We'll go back tonight."

I dip my head once. "No, thank you."

Manners are a human value, are they not?

See, I do not need Yannig to tell me how to speak to my mate.

Like a gentle kraken, I keep my suckers exactly where they are, even though it is the greatest torture. My suffering means nothing as long as it brings her pleasure.

Cindi tries to wriggle away, but my suckers refuse to let go, inadvertently pulling at her breasts. I relish in the way her lips part on a silent gasp. My sex winds around her leg, rubbing my seed over her skin. It takes all my strength not to inch closer toward her heat.

My tentacles move with her as she lunges forward and presses the blade against my throat. Her fearsomeness almost makes me smile.

I say a silent prayer to the Goddess that she breaks skin and leaves a scar. My mate would never kill me.

I hope.

"I won't let you take me to your fucking spaceship," she hisses, her injured hand resting limp yet stiff on one of my limbs.

My brows knit together. I did not see any fresh cuts on it. Is my venom not helping? Is it a bone issue? Maybe healing it will be one of my first acts as her mate.

"My…" What is a spaceship? Oh, I believe I understand. "My boat is small and would leave you exposed to the elements. I mostly leave it by the hut."

She blinks. "You mean to tell me aliens have no fancy technology?"

I am…confused. An alien? How does finding me unfamiliar impact technology?

"I have magic." Is that what she's referring to?

Cindi's eyes dart around the den. "Like crystals and sage and stuff?"

I point to the wall. "I believe it is pronounced *rock* and *algae*." Maybe I'm getting my English wrong.

"No, that's not what I—" Cindi tightens her grip on the knife as she returns her glare on me. She wavers, slumping forward lightly, like the energy has suddenly been sucked out of her. Is she sick? What's wrong? Do I need to find the healer tonight?

"Tell me what is wrong with your arm," I demand.

In a matter of seconds, she rights herself, crackling with the same fire like she didn't have a moment of weakness.

"What are you then?" she presses, disregarding my question.

I study her carefully for signs of the Waste. Her eyes are slightly sunken, but her skin doesn't have the green tinge, and the whites of her eyes are clear. It would be far too soon for the water to make her sick. It would take months to years for it to affect her.

Is it a human sickness, then? Her skin isn't hot to the touch. What else should I look out for?

"Kraken," I answer.

"Like an octopus-squid thing?" She scrunches her nose, seemingly fine.

I frown, attempting not to take offense at her insinuation I'm dimwitted. "No, like a kraken."

"You know what? Never mind." She shakes her head, pushing

the serrated edge of the knife harder against my throat. "I don't care. Just take me back." My mate's tone sharpens.

"No."

"Yes."

"I cannot let you leave." Ever.

Her eyes search mine, scent turning bitter with fear, chasing away any evidence of her lust. My lips tic, and I suppress the urge to growl. We were making headway. She was beginning to understand. Why is she upset again?

Cindi lowers her voice. "Are you…" Her voice holds vulnerability I don't like. "Giving me to them?"

I snarl. I wouldn't give her to anyone.

She flinches and turns her head to stare at the ground in a sign of submission. It makes me angrier.

She is my mate. I am hers.

I may be the king, but I bow to her, and she bows to no one. Between us, the only one who will submit is me.

"I would never give you to anyone, Cindi. Any man who touches you will die. I have killed for you before, and I will kill for you again."

"I don't want you to do that." She shakes her head, voice barely above a whisper. I would take her violence and her fury over her fear and sorrow.

I grasp Cindi's face between my hands, and something shutters behind her eyes. I've seen it happen twice before when I touched her with my fingers. She shoves me away like I burned her.

"It is my duty, a privilege, to spill blood for you, mate."

Does she think I am incapable of it? That I'm unworthy of protecting her? Well, she is now my sole purpose, whether she wants it or not.

"Why won't you stay?"

"I—I don't belong here. I don't care about what you think

you're entitled to." She hiccups like she's fighting back tears. "I don't know you. You don't know me. We don't owe each other anything."

I hold her face again so she might truly see me. "You are my mate. There is nowhere you can go where I won't follow. This is our den, so this is where you will stay. You will be happy and want for nothing. I will take care of you. I am all that you need. You are mine, and I am yours. Fate deemed it so."

And one day, if I am lucky, Cindi will grow to love me too.

Something in my chest splinters when she flinches, averting her gaze. "I want to go back. Please."

Why must she fight our bond?

"I forbid it."

The lines of her face harden. "You can't forbid me from doing anything. I—I'm not something that can be owned. I won't let that shit happen to me." *Finally*, the blade breaks the skin of my neck. "*Take. Me. Back.*" Another prick pinches my tentacle, and I glance down to see the knife protruding from another appendage.

Oh.

It wasn't a mating mark. My mate was trying to hurt me.

"I don't want you," she spits, glaring at me with the same seething hatred as every other kraken I've met.

Those four words hurt far more than a blade.

I lower her to the ground and move back. I can't look at her. I thought I might be able to withstand such scrutiny from my own mate, but it's too much. I'm underwater and can't breathe.

Turning away, I slip into the pool without looking back at her.

I was wrong to think my own mate might want me. No one ever has, and it was a fool's hope to think Cindi would. She doesn't think I'll ever be enough for her. I shouldn't be surprised, because my family thought so too. They loved me, but they never thought I could hold any kind of leadership position. I've always questioned if it was a result of my appearance or because of what my appearance did to me.

It's clear it never mattered. The Goddess's curse upon me is mine to bear. Not even my fated mate can break it.

11

CINDI

Did he just… "Where the fuck did you go?" I yell at the pool, mouth dry.

Nothing.

Nada.

Silence.

Fucking *prick*.

I grab the knife off the ground and chuck it at the wall. It clatters off the rock with a high-pitched ring. I want to hit something. Scream. Throw things. Cry until my voice is completely hoarse. Rage. Burn this world to the fucking ground.

So, I do it.

I scream like shards of glass are tearing through my veins. I turn the cave upside down, smashing rocks, splintering wood, ripping moss away from stone. It's not nearly satisfying enough.

I'm dimly aware of the pain in my hand and the tears rushing down my cheeks as I run around the cavern to search for an exit.

I barely wince when my foot slices open on the harsh rock floor, hardly swallow when my mouth feels like sandpaper.

Oxygen rushes from my lungs, and I stumble, head swimming. A fresh wave of tears pours down my cheeks.

I'm so *sick* of being sick.

I have to get out of here. Staying isn't an option. I was *free*. I escaped Tommy. I was *this close* to getting the hell out of here.

How did I end up right back where I started, but with a… Jesus Christ, I can't believe I'm even thinking this. But with a goddamn, living, breathing, eight-armed fucking *kraken*.

A kraken who does things to my body I can't explain—relaxes it, lulls it into a faux sense of comfort.

A kraken whose suckers I can still feel around my nipples.

A kraken who wants to own me. Keep me as a pretty pet. Lock me in a cage, throw away the key, try placating me with pretty words or flowers to get me back in line.

Tommy told me I would want for nothing, that he'd *take care of me* because he loved me more than the moon and the stars. There would be *nothing* that would keep us apart. Little did I know, it was because he chained me up, then threw away the key.

Maybe I should be scared shitless about the mythical sea monster aspect of my captor. Sure, his size and the knowledge he could kill me with a single swipe is frightening, but it's nothing I'm not used to. Size and shape and looks mean fucking nothing.

Tommy was beautiful. He had the most dazzling smile I'd ever seen, like he just walked off the cover of *Vogue*.

Look where that got me.

On the other hand, Dad had friends who towered over me, could pick up a tire with a single finger, push trucks without breaking a sweat; one guy could even lift his Harley as a party trick. Despite their intimidating size, the leather jackets, and *fuck you* attitude, they were gentle giants, patched up teddy bears.

I don't need to go out to sea to find a monster; they exist on land. They hide under human skin and call themselves men.

I don't want to be around to discover whether the textbook monster is just as evil.

The cavern alone is as big as the small, two-bedroom cabin I was stolen from, lit by the glowing matter slimy to the touch, the last vestiges of moonlight pouring in through the hole above the pool.

I skitter to a stop at a deep alcove to the side of the cave, saying a silent prayer I'll find an exit. Instead, beds of moss stare back at me, rich greens illuminated by the threads of blue and purple bioluminescent matter climbing up the walls.

Everywhere smells like him but better, and it's sending me into more of a tailspin. It makes no sense as to why I'm having this kind of reaction to someone—some*thing's*—smell.

My eyes dart to the crooked archway on the opposite side of the cavern. I half limp to the opening, spreading my blood over stone from the cuts on my feet. If he doesn't decide to eat me, maybe I'll die from infection instead.

Or dehydration.

The entrance could be a gateway into hell, a black hole where things go to perish. The light from the main cave doesn't reach more than a few steps into the tunnel. I swing my blurry stare to the undisturbed pool, swaying from the exhaustion that sank its teeth into me and is gnawing on me like a dog with a fresh kill.

The monster could return at any second. If I want to get out of here, I need to do it now.

I take a step forward, muttering a string of profanities.

He left.

That creature actually *left*.

Without me. Without any response or weak attempt at assurance that he won't leave me here and check up on me once a day to drop off food and take his pound of flesh. I can't fathom why else he'd want me here—*me*, of all people.

Maybe he's got other women trapped around here.

I don't believe his promise of protection for one second.

Maybe he doesn't plan on sharing his things, but I've been a fool once, and it's not happening again. Being Tommy's fiancée afforded me certain protections too—from everyone *but* him.

Tommy was *exceptional* at keeping other men away because he instilled the fear of God into me that it would somehow be *my* fault if someone's gaze lingered too long. The one time someone played with his toy, I heard the echo of a gunshot, followed by total silence.

My mind races as I squint against the darkness. There's no telling where the tunnel leads. I could get lost in there or come across something *other*.

I rub the muscles in my sore arm and glance back at the hole above the pool. There has to be another exit besides that.

Getting to it is a feat I'm not sure even a seasoned rock climber can achieve. The rock wall is curved with hardly any prominent grooves that I can make out. Jagged stones await at the bottom of the hole, promising injury if there's one slip—and there *will* be a slipup with the state of my arm and shitty vestibular system.

Then, there's the way we came in.

I'm a decent swimmer, but there's no way I'll be able to get out through the underwater channel without drowning.

I'm out of options. The tunnel is my only choice. It leads either to an unknown place or something far worse than the devil I know.

I swipe the tears from my face and grit my teeth against the agony throughout my body as I put one tentative foot in front of the other, using the damp cave walls as a guide. Minutes tick by, or maybe they're a matter of seconds, possibly hours.

I can't tell.

"Shit," I hiss, losing my footing and crashing my knee into something hard and jagged. Pain slices up my leg. I rear back and almost lose my balance.

My hands fly out in front of me to land on a solid surface.

Harsh breaths echo through the tunnel. Every sound I make is like an alarm that will alert the monster to my attempted escape. I squeeze my eyes shut. Rotting away isn't how I wanted to go.

Pull yourself fucking together, I scold myself, drawing whatever is left of my sanity to gain some semblance of control over my emotions.

I quickly feel the walls around me to gain a sense of direction.

No.

It can't be.

My heart hammers in my chest as I keep turning in my spot, hands out to orient myself. It's the perfect 360 spin.

It's a dead end.

"*Fuck, fuck, fuck.*" Tears of frustration burn down my cheeks. Hopelessness, raw and guttural, pounds down on me.

Why is this happening to me? Why me? What could I have possibly done in my past life to deserve all this?

My knees buckle, and I narrowly stop myself from falling. I'm so tired, exhausted from constantly running, fearing for my life. There's never going to be an expiration date to this feeling—it makes me question the point of fighting.

Dad said he'll always be happy as long as I'm doing what makes me happy. He's not even here, and I can feel his disappointment. Happiness isn't on the table for me. The only thing I can offer him is my survival, however fleeting that might be.

I have to go back to the cavern. Climbing out of the hole is my only option.

I swallow, attempting to bring moisture to my dry mouth. When was the last time I drank something? Ate? The lack of food and water wouldn't be helping my condition either.

My head swims as I trudge forward, the vestiges of my adrenaline chipping away until I'm struggling to stay upright. Today has consisted of trauma after trauma. Exhaustion has me by my throat.

I'm panting by the time I stumble into the cave, coated in a layer of cold sweat, grime, and blue liquid I can only assume is the evidence of my attempted attack on the kraken. I pause, narrowing my eyes against the sudden light and waning energy. At the edges of my blurry vision, I spot something circular and brown.

My brows furrow as I close the distance, half crawling, half walking. *A coconut.* It sits atop a pile of shells, all husks of different maturity that have been broken, or…gnawed on?

My stomach grumbles. I snatch the fruit at the top, and my heart sinks. It's empty. *Dammit.*

Movement sounds behind me. I whip around, holding the object up in defense. *That's not the krak-*

My eyes widen. I clamor back from the *thing* that just stepped out of the pool. What the ever-loving *fuck* is that? I saw it briefly back at my cabin, but up close…

The shark-dog tips its head to the side, watching me with keen curiosity. Beneath the low light, I can make out more than his silhouette this time. It's shaped like a dog, but with fins and a wider, rounder, more stretched out snout like a shark—although with a black nose at the very end like a canine.

It has the same coloring as one of the common octopus breeds in the area: cherry brown, with yellow along his snout, around his eyes, and like socks on his feet.

I find myself leaning closer, noticing the white dots on his stomach and below the fins on the backs of his legs. Are those…suckers?

A shiver rolls down my spine when I catch sight of its razor-sharp teeth. Between its maw is a greenish thing shaped like a ball.

My muscles lock when it steps forward. What are the chances I can outrun that thing?

Nil. Absolutely zero.

Looking it in the eye is a bad idea, but I can't stop staring, brows stitching together. The creature is really quite fascinating. What did the kraken call him? Chad?

It isn't quite staring back at me. I follow its line of sight to the coconut in my hand, and I glance at the teeth marks on the pile of husks beside me.

Oh shit. I'm playing with its toys.

My hand trembles, raising the coconut as an offering—no, bad idea. Don't invite it closer.

Throat bobbing, I slowly—*so* very slowly—lower it to the ground and roll the fruit its way, inching from the creature's pile.

The green ball—another coconut—thuds onto the floor from his mouth. He looks up at me, and I hold my breath. Then, his piercing stare drops to the coconut I rolled his way. Up at me. Back to the fruit. Me. Coconut. Me. Back to the coconut. Me again.

It steps toward me, and I suppress every one of my instincts to jump back with a scream. It presses its snout to the coconut, making the cute aggressive sniffing sound like dogs do. Then, in a move that has me questioning everything I know about biology and animal behavior, its shark tail starts swishing side to side.

The good kind of tail-wagging.

I blow out a breath, feeling like I've passed a test I didn't know I was taking. Before I can question my next move, it spins around and trots back toward the pool, leaping into the water in an unceremonious cannonball.

I blink.

What just happened? I'm hallucinating, surely. My attention drops to the coconut it left behind, the only proof I have that my interaction with a shark-dog took place.

I glance up at the hole above the pool and check the alcove with the bed of moss to make sure I'm the only one around. Whatever. It's gone.

I blow out a breath.

It's now or never.

12

My bag flails against the current, the fish inside it no doubt trying to make their escape. I only caught four for Cindi, which is not enough variety to be worthy of someone as special as my mate.

The muscle in my jaw feathers. I should have searched for crab as well. Many humans enjoy eating it, and I could have fed her myself to avoid her getting hurt by its hard shell. It will take too long for me to swim far enough from my territory to hunt.

Every second away from her feels like my soul is ripping apart —even if it hurts just as much to be around her.

I was a coward for departing without a word. I can only imagine what she thinks of me for leaving her in our barren den. I couldn't... It was too painful to listen to her rejection. I needed to clear my mind, to think about how to earn her forgiveness and accept me as her mate.

When she sees I have returned from my hunt with plenty of food, maybe she'll realize I am a capable provider. I do not mean her any harm. I have already shown her my strength by killing five males for her. I... How does one woo their mate?

How do I get her to look beyond my appearance?

I wish Yannig were here so I could ask him what to do. He was my sole source of guidance when I was young. He helped me navigate the other kraken to make myself less...*less*. My sister may not have concerned herself with such trivial matters, busy studying and ruling our people, but she would know what to do as well. Her mate wouldn't fear her, even though she's the deadliest kraken to ever exist.

The thoughts and questions keep piling up, stealing my focus. The water shifts, and I sense another creature's presence too late.

"Your Majesty."

Anger surges through me. Someone dares to keep me from my mate, *dares* to be so close to my island. My lips peel back with a snarl. A low growl builds in my chest, though not loud enough to be heard above the storm.

A dead weight sinks in my stomach when I spot the kraken emerging from the shadows of a stone structure.

"Counselor Lazell." Lightning thunders in my veins. He is a snake amongst kraken.

His eyes dart to my dark hair floating around me. His lips twist in distaste.

My mother killed his brother when he campaigned for my execution a few months after I was born, then later attempted to carry it out himself. Since then, Lazell has been a thorned pest, leading the Council in his vision, keeping hatred toward me alive.

It's a pity my mother didn't end his entire family line.

I would have long ago if it wouldn't have resulted in my certain death.

Our interactions are few and far between. The Council has been operating on its own for several years, running the kingdom without my interference. I wanted nothing to do with it, and my subjects were all too happy to take the proverbial crown from me. Their contempt toward me worsened after Yannig died and I refused to marry the first kraken female they sacrificed to me.

Now, for the most part, they leave me alone, acting like I don't exist, only bothering me every so often to check if I'm any closer to shackling a female to me.

"I see you are still alive," Lazell observes in relief and disgust. The lines on his face deepen when they land on the two fresh wounds left by my mate.

He tears his stare away at my growl. I don't like him looking at Cindi's gifts to me.

The kraken has aged centuries since I last saw him eight moons ago. His cheeks are sunken, and there's the barest green tinge to his skin—a telltale sign the Waste has reached his body. I have yet to see a kraken without the coloring in recent years.

Lazell's long, thin tentacles slither over rock and sand before jettisoning close to the surface to mimic the movement of my limbs. It's the same habit Yannig had.

He uses the webbing between his arm and ribs to keep stationary against the strong currents. The tapered edges of his four fingers ripple. It's the greatest offense that his coloring is similar to my brother's—brown and white stripes like a lionfish.

Grief hits me every time I have the misfortune of seeing Lazell, only to be quickly staunched by seething hatred.

Every word out of his mouth is a concealed threat.

I may be the king, but he is the one who holds the power over our people. If he chooses to follow in his brother's footsteps by rallying krakens to kill me, it will happen. If he knew I was hiding a human in my den, the Council would be demanding Cindi's execution. Our kind's continued anonymity is one of the most sacred values we hold.

The only reason I'm not dead is because I am their only hope. Lazell and every other kraken who loathes me are losing sleep over having no choice but to place their faith in an abomination.

"It has been many months since you've joined our meetings."

"It has." Why would I want to be in the presence of those who would sooner poison me than willingly speak to me? My attendance only serves as an opportunity for the Council to berate and pressure me into marrying a kraken.

He raises a brow. "I assume your search for a bride has not been successful, and the people will continue to starve." My inner beast rears its head at his condescending tone.

I clamp my mouth shut to stop from bragging about finding my mate, from proving to them that I was right. The Goddess deemed me worthy of having a fated mate.

He would insist on seeing her, and then he'd try to have her killed.

Once our bonding settles the blight over my territory, I will parade my beautiful female for all the vile krakens to see so they know *I* saved us with the help of my *human* bride. My people will seethe, recoil from disgust, but it will bring me no greater joy than to know every time they hunt, it is because a human and their monster king permitted it.

Until then, Krokant is all that remains, an hourglass showing how much time remains before all is lost. It has been two years since I last visited. I can only assume it has halved in size. It's anyone's guess as to how much time we have left before the Curse wins.

And they come for me.

"My search for my mate remains," I lie, balling my hands into fists to stop from tearing him apart.

He forgets my human attributes have turned me into a far better hunter and killer than any of them. Their webbing is a weakness—one cut, and they could bleed out. My claws are a weapon in themselves. Thumbs are an advantage in every form. I have yet to find a purpose for my hair. I assume there is one, but thus far, I have not been able to find a reason.

"Perhaps it is time to look at marrying—"

"No," I snarl.

I would sooner sacrifice my soul to the Goddess than even *think* of bonding with anyone other than Cindi. Whatever kraken bride the Council sends will either be one who is rejected and hated by society, or a strong female who will kill me the moment she has my cub in her stomach.

His eyes darken. He's probably wishing his brother never failed at killing me. "Time is running—"

My tentacle shoots out and clamps around Lazell's throat. Bubbles explode around us, and a streak of lightning flashes above the surface to illuminate his panicked face. "I do not appreciate repeating myself, Counselor." My voice is low.

His own pathetically weak limbs fly out to push back against my tightening grip. My limb spans wider than his neck, forcing him to stare up at me. I chuckle as his eyes bulge as he uselessly grabs at my arm with his tapered fingers.

"If I say no, that means no. If I have to question your ability to listen again, I will remove your ears because, clearly, you have no use for them. Do you understand?"

His mouth gapes. Air bubbles replace words.

"Nod if you understand."

Lazell frantically bobs his head, a barely noticeable movement against my tentacle.

I release him, throwing him aside. "The Council will be informed once I have taken a bride," is all I say before going back toward my den.

Rage simmers under my skin. I swim harder to dispel the energy and the need to tear another kraken apart—"limb from limb," as Cindi said.

Letting my vapid Council look at—or even *speak to*—my mate wasn't a thought I delved into with much detail. It filled me with too much rage.

It has been at least a moon since I came across another kraken. I once went half a year without interacting with anyone other than Vasz. Most barely spare me anything more than a sideways glance.

I'm obviously a fool. My wishful thinking had me believing my mate would want me back and I could have Cindi to myself, away from every other kraken.

The runes at the cave entrance glow silver beneath my touch. The stone groans as it slides against rock, a low, grating sound that can only be heard if nearby.

A confusing mixture of excitement, dread, hope, and fear winds my hearts into a tight knot. She cannot hate me forever, right? At some point, she will soften to my efforts because… because fate deemed it so.

Fate. Fate. Fate.

It's never because of me.

The gills along my neck bristle, and I steel myself to weather the disgust Cindi doles my way.

I'm torn between racing through the tunnels or leaning into my trepidation by prolonging the inevitable pain. I want to see my mate, make sure she's okay, but I…I don't want her to see me. I never thought I could feel such joy from simply touching another, yet such pain at the same time.

The glowing algae illuminates the path into the den before I can decide what I want to do. My senses tip closer to the edge. My nose twitches, suckers pulsing as I taste the saltwater.

Blood.

I speed up, splitting the surface, claws out, chest puffed, muscles coiled, ready to defend my mate to the very end.

The stench of her fear, anxiety, and the metallic scent of her blood permeates the air. My stare swings around the den to locate the intruder, but there are no new scents. A gasp pulls my attention toward the large stone near the side of the cavern.

Cindi's frightened eyes burn into mine, and my muscles tense to strike…Vasz.

"What…" I frown, lowering my limbs to the floor. The creature, blissfully ignorant to my and Cindi's panic, continues gnawing on a coconut as my mate presses herself flush against the rock, tucking her limbs close to her body beneath her dress to create more distance from Vasz as he wags his tail, happily playing with a husk.

"Tell me if he bit you," I demand.

She shakes her head at the same time Vasz huffs, "I wish."

Try as I might, I can't figure out why she's sitting beside his coconut pile or how a piece of driftwood made it from Vasz's quarters to my mate's lap.

My nostrils flare. I cannot see where the blood is coming from. She doesn't look like she's badly wounded, but even the slightest scratch is unacceptable.

"Come here, mate," I say. A tentacle sneaks along the ground toward her.

"Fuck off," she hisses, batting me away with the driftwood.

Vasz rises to his haunches to snap at my limb in warning. "*Vasz,*" I growl.

"Fuck off."

My brows hike up to my hairline when he places himself between me and Cindi—or his pile of coconuts.

Disregarding him, I meet Cindi's wide stare. There are deep bags beneath her eyes, and her hair stands up at odd ends, tangled and nest-like. "You're hurt." *And you need rest.*

"You're right. I am," Vasz responds instead. He holds his paw out, dipping his head in earnest. "Yes, you may treat my wound."

"Fuck off, Vasz." I test the words.

They have a nice ring to them.

He whips a wounded glare my way, snapping at me when I push him aside to get to Cindi.

She smacks my arm with the wood. "Don't touch me."

"Don't touch her," Vasz echoes.

"I will throw out all of your coconuts," I threaten.

He gasps. "You wouldn't dare betray our friendship like this."

I lower myself to look him in the eye. "Try me."

"You can talk to it?" Cindi's bewildered attention flicks between me and the walking, talking irritant. "Can it...understand me?"

Vasz snorts in answer, and her jaw drops. "That's incredible."

I swear on Yannig's grave that Vasz preens, batting his eyes and rumbling what I could only describe as a giggle before he straightens. "I am," he agrees, a cocky tilt to his voice. "Isn't that right, Ordus?"

Goddess, give me strength.

"Leave. Now." He snarls when I pick him up by his stomach and deposit him next to the pool. I almost lose part of a limb to his teeth. *"Go."*

His harrumph is loud enough for even Cindi's human ears to hear. His own points to the ground as he skulks toward the water. "If you asked, you'd know the human tried to climb out of the tunnel as I was returning with my gift, so I bit her. Just a little nip—"

"You—" He jumps into the water and swims away before I can catch him. "Did Vaszeline hurt you?" I ask, getting as close to Cindi as I can before she hits me with her little stick.

My stomach sinks as my mate gawks at me like I sprouted suckers on my face. A stone lodges in my throat as I await her rejection.

"Did you just call that thing Vaseline?"

Jealousy spears through me. Why is my Cindi asking about the creature and not me? "Vaszeline, yes." I force the words out even though I don't want to be discussing any males with my mate—even if that male is part dog. "But it's too difficult to say when angry, so I call him Vasz," I continue in the hopes civility will encourage her to speak more.

I like the way she sounds when her words aren't barbed and made to cut.

"Like..." She blinks at me, then the water Vasz escaped through. "The petroleum jelly?"

It's my turn to gape at her. "No," I say carefully, so as not to offend her by sounding like I am questioning her intelligence. "Like Vaszeline."

It isn't the name I would have chosen for him; rather, it's one he chose for himself. When I found him starved, battered, and injured, attempting to hide beneath a coconut, he was curled up around a plastic jar with the name *Vaszeline* on it, a name the Witch must have given him.

I believe he has the bottle in his cave somewhere, probably beneath a mountain of husks and random objects he's chosen to bring back.

My tentacle moves against the floor, tasting my mate's blood on the stone. If I discover he's harmed Cindi, I will revoke his access to the underground system of the island.

I reach my hand out for her.

"What are you—get away from me." She stumbles back, that familiar shuttered expression crossing her eyes, souring her scent the same way it does each time she looks like this.

Her dress falls away from her legs to reveal the small cut on her shin and the blood coating her feet.

Guilt burns up my throat. I should have brought her shoes so she can move without worry. My siblings would never have made such a foolish mistake.

"You're bleeding because I wasn't here to keep you safe." *I let you down.*

Her brows stitch together in a flicker of confusion she quickly wipes away. "You give yourself too much credit. Rocks aren't the danger here." Cindi gives me a pointed look, as if *I* might be the one to hurt her. I'll prove her wrong. "I'm fine." It's a sentiment she poorly confirms by wincing, stumbling when she attempts to stand.

I point two clawed fingers at my face. "Do you know what these are?"

She blinks in shock, glancing around the cave like she's uncertain I spoke. "Uh…are you talking about your eyes?" Cindi's words are partially slurred.

"Yes. *Eyes*. And they are seeing you are not fine." I motion toward her injuries. Sighing, I raise back up to my full height, watching the way she stiffens as I do. It infuriates me that she thinks I would hurt her.

"It's a little cut. I'll live—where are you going? You can't leave me here," she calls when I turn, moving toward the water.

First, she wants me to get away from her. Now, she doesn't want to leave. Humans are very confusing.

I try not to let the false hope get to me that she might actually want me to stay. I have done nothing to garner her change in feelings toward me since coming back, and I doubt she has seen sense in the past couple of minutes since my return.

The muscles in my tentacles stretch, pushing me higher off the ground to reach the nook in the rock wall where I keep my meager supplies. Cindi's wild stare never leaves mine, but there's something else there too. It lightens her scent and brings some familiarity back to her face, like when I was watching her from afar.

I bite back my irritation at the spike in her fear. I am just putting the chest on the ground? Why does she perceive that as a threat?

I force myself to release it, fighting my inner beast's need to hold her in my arms and reassure her she will never know a moment of pain.

But even if I think it, I know it will not be true.

Cindi will suffer as long as I live because the Goddess has cursed her to be my mate. She will spend the rest of her days resenting my mere existence, lips curled into a perpetual sneer from being in my company.

Like she is now.

Violent, hateful, afraid. The scent from her emotions is scattered through the air, thick enough to choke on.

My jaw aches from clenching hard. Emotions do not matter. I must tend to my mate's injuries. *That* is the priority. Humans do not have the magical healing powers krakens do, and I intend to keep my mate alive at all costs.

The hinges of the chest creak as it opens to reveal the few pieces of kelp, clean cloth, and a half-empty tub of healing paste I made. Regret churns in my stomach over putting off its restock for months. I only ever use it when Vasz picks a fight with something a quarter of his size then cries at the smallest bit of pain. The only thing that would make him stop talking about it is if I treat his nonexistent injury.

Now I have a mate with real wounds, and she's acting like it's barely more than a scratch.

They will both age me. I'll be a fifty-year-old kraken looking a hundred in no time.

I move to grab Cindi with my tentacle, and the ensuing whimper chills me to my very soul, a sound that echoes and vibrates like the strings of a guitar. Every instinct tells me to attack whatever it is causing her distress, even though I know it's all my fault.

I'm the problem.

Always the problem.

"Stop being stubborn." My words come out sharper than I intended them. How is one meant to react at the realization that the hope I've been clinging to since I was a cub is a lie?

"You're the one who insists on touching me—" I disregard her protests and hold her in my limbs. My other tentacles wet the cloth in the pool. "No!"

As blissful as it is to have my Goddess-sent mate, it's hard to find true joy in it when Cindi is acting like I'm going to suffocate her. I am just trying to help.

I take care not to sneak my arm beneath her dress. I need to be completely focused to tend to Cindi. It's what she deserves. I can't mess it up. Yet, my cock is hardening from having her in my arms, recalling the smell of her lust, the red blossoming on her skin.

I force myself to think of anything else: stargazer fish, rotting shark, the rubbish near the mainland.

"I am trying to clean your wounds, human." It doesn't come out as delicately as I would like, more of a rasp than anything else.

"I don't need your help," she huffs, poking me with the driftwood. Her hair stands up at odd ends as she wriggles in my grip, foolishly thinking she stands a chance. Not wanting her to hurt her arm further from the tiny punches she's throwing at me, I gently wrap my tentacles around her arms, trapping them to her side.

"Ugh," she complains. "Take me home. I can deal with it myself."

Must she keep repeating the same thing? "The Goddess decided you are my mate. You are home—" Time stills as I watch her sink her teeth into my tentacle.

Not only has my mate marked me twice, but she's...*claiming* me?

The breath rushes from me, mind reeling at what might be her true intention, making me lightheaded. I don't think humans are aware of the significance behind such an act. The marks a female leaves on her male is used to complete a marriage under kraken customs. For a female to bite her male is a marriage in the eyes of the Goddess, a promise that not even his death will separate her from him. It's one of the rituals to fulfill a bond.

My cock thickens, and there's nothing I can do to stop it from moving toward her.

Oh, that will anger her.

I clear my throat. I'm struggling to think clearly. I'm certain it wasn't her intention, but my body does not understand that. "My beloved, you can try biting me later. You're hardening my breeding arm when you do that, and I am trying to be a good mate to you."

"Your what—" Her eyes round at my sex sliding up her leg. It's much the same as my tentacle, except it has a bulbous end that swells with my seed when I'm aroused—which has never happened before this day. "Holy fuck. What is that?" she breathes out.

"My breeding arm," I grunt, moisture leaking under her attention. It spills onto her leg when the smell of her lust hits the air.

I want to roar from the possessive instincts surging to life. I'm marking her with my scent. Every creature will know she belongs to me. And she isn't screaming.

Her breath comes out in a rush. Cindi's eyes have an awed bewilderment to them that matches the sweet notes of desire and curiosity from her. The heat of her gaze has a low groan rumbling through my chest.

The sound snaps her out of her trance, making her go back to fighting me. "Get that thing away from me," she says, voice heavy with something other than disgust.

I grit my teeth. Her words are at odds with the way she clearly desires me too. My mate looks at me like I'm a monstrosity, and yet, this is the second time her body has reacted in such a way.

It's likely fate forcing Cindi's hand, her physical form responding to our connection.

She doesn't actually want me.

My anger rises at the realization—a muted thought somewhere beneath the cloud of lust.

She suddenly stiffens and lowers her gaze in an act of submission. I force myself to relax, wanting to shower her with my devotion to prove that though my fury runs deep, she will *always* be safe with me.

My breeding arm bobs against her, seed dripping onto her

smooth skin. I open my mouth without thinking. "Yes, that's what I was trying to say. Do you have problems with your hearing—" I clear my throat. This is my *mate*, not another kraken.

My tentacles have locked up around her, refusing to release Cindi or put space between us so I can deal with the agonizing distraction. No matter how hard I try, my repeated attempts at softening my sex or lowering it back down isn't working. I'm going to keep saying the wrong thing.

"Show me your feet," I try softly. Focusing my attention back on her injury might make my limbs compliant again.

Her jaw drops, and her earlier show of placation vanishes. "While your cock is staring at me? I think the fuck not. You've got the wrong girl for that, buddy. Why are you—"

Cock.

A shudder works down my spine from hearing that word on Cindi's lips. It's a new word I've been hearing humans use more and more. I never found it very appealing until my mate said it.

My bulb hardens until it's excruciating. I clamp my mouth shut to suppress my pained groans, stars flashing behind my eyes.

My hand wraps around the knot, imagining it's Cindi's instead, and I stroke, trying to lessen the tension enough for my limbs to settle so I can think clearly. The pressure sends stars shooting behind my eyes as more of my seed drips onto my tentacle before pooling on her smooth skin.

"You're getting your cum on me!" I grunt when her nails sink into my arms. It thickens my cock, undoing any progress I've made. "Stop it. Stop it right now, kraken."

"Ordus," I rumble, breathing in her desire fogging the air. "My name is Ordus."

This was not how I wanted to spill my seed for the first time, with ashen notes of my mate's fear tainting her lust. It feels like a waste not to coat my mate's sex in it. I doubt any such suggestion would be forthcoming.

"Fine," she pants, darkened eyes still firmly on my breeding arm as the pretty red blush colors her chest. "Stop jerking off like a fucking barbarian, Ordus."

I chuckle, cock leaking all on its own at hearing her say my name. "Mate, you are not helping the situation."

She gives the angry, swollen tentacle a pointed look since her arms are still trapped. "I'm telling you to let go of your dick! How is that not helping?"

"Your voice, little mate." I blow out a breath, shivering when I move my fist up and down, picturing it's her wet sex wrapped around me. "If you want me to stop, I suggest you stay quiet, or else the sound of your voice will make me harden more. I cannot make it—I did not—I'm trying—" I clear my throat and drop my head in shame. "I apologize."

I feel Cindi's eyes searching me. I'm not sure what she's looking for or what she finds. All she offers is a resounding, whispered, "Okay," before falling silent. Eyes locked on me as I massage the bulb, squeezing and shifting, grunting and swallowing groans, spraying my seed onto my tentacles and her skin, wishing to the Goddess that my mate will offer to relieve the tightness so I can do right by her.

My own body hates me, an uncontrollable monster deserving of all the scorn I've received my entire life.

I wish I could tell what she's thinking. Her scent isn't as sour as it was the other times I've touched her, but she's as rigid as a board.

When I've softened enough for the organ to deflate, I revert my attention back to what matters: caring for my mate's injuries. The unease hangs heavy between us. I keep my head down, letting my wet hair fall to hide my embarrassment.

Ribbons of cloying tension tangle around my throat, suffocating me with her silence. Cindi hardly moves as I carefully dab at the wounds on her feet and shin. She allows me to dress them and wrap them with the seaweed without interference.

No words are shared. No glances. Nothing is needed for me to know I've multiplied her hatred toward me.

The feeling is mutual.

"You can't keep me here." Her whispered words slice through the silence.

I know I shouldn't subject her to endure my Curse, but I am a selfish, awful mate. I do not want to keep living in solitude.

"I need food, water," she continues.

Pointing at the pool, I say, "Water." I pull the bag from around my body to show her the fish flopping around. "Food." I puff my chest out, just a little, but I know it will mean nothing. "I hunted the fish myself." It's foolish to think such an admission will change anything.

She shakes her head. "I can't consume either of those things. I need *human* food."

Her response flays me open. My mate would lie to me?

Humans have been hunting in our seas for centuries, depriving us of our sole source of food. They catch more than they can eat when they have game on land.

"I understand," is all I say. Because I do.

It is not the first time someone has refused to eat what I have caught. One of Yannig's friends spit it back out, claiming I poisoned it when everyone knew its only flaw was that I had touched it.

I throw the fish into the water so it can remain fresh for a while longer in case she changes her mind.

"Come," I say, lifting her up and cradling her to my chest, even though I'm carrying the knowledge she will forever refuse to be here. "You must be tired."

"Ordus, please." The rawness in those two words tears me in half. She struggles weakly in my hold. "Take me back."

I squeeze my eyes shut, relying on my limbs to safely get us to the alcove where I sleep. "No," I grit out. "We will rest now."

Perhaps the Goddess will pity me and open my mate's eyes. Our union could be good. She might see me as a friend. But I know it won't happen. It probably never will.

13

CINDI

Ordus' dick looks like one of my dildos.

There.

I said what I said.

I'm not ashamed—yes, I am—to admit that for one embarrassingly long second, I was imagining how it would feel to have the real deal inside me.

Don't get me wrong, the tentacle dildo in my bedside drawer doesn't have a bulb on it, but I did potentially make an impulse purchase last week after reading one too many shifter romances. One thing led to another, and I have a knot waiting for me if I ever make it back to the house.

I keep throwing glances at all the limbs wrapped around me, but I can't for the life of me figure out which one is his dick.

Or why kraken dick isn't as scary as human dick.

I yawn against his chest, fighting wave after wave of exhaustion as I tighten my grip around the knife he gave me. His weird purring sound is going to make me lose the war against sleep.

A particularly loud snore has my eyes snapping up to his face, and I scowl at the memory of how his stupidly pretty face looked as he got himself off. How the muscle in his jaw feathered. The tendons in his arms rippled. His heaving chest paired with rasping breaths. The way the opalescent liquid beaded at the tapered tip before spilling onto my chilled skin. I can still feel the thick residue coating my thighs.

He was my only semblance of warmth, both inside and out.

It was a mortifying, exhilarating, partially heartbreaking experience I still haven't got a clue how to process.

On the one hand, fuck him, the piece of shit, for forcing that situation on me.

On the other, holy fuck, I know he's a sea creature, but how dare he get me wet like that?

And lastly, most disconcertingly, the guilt riddled on his face made me almost… I don't know. Pity him? Sympathize with him? I truly believe he didn't want to do it, didn't have a choice.

I don't give a shit if he couldn't help himself. After the shit I've gone through, everything is a choice, and he made the wrong fucking one—as sexually enlightening as it was.

I want to absolutely despise him, hate every fiber of his being and gut him a thousand times to fix every wrong, but he's making it hard for me to place him on the shelf Tommy is on.

They're in the same building, but not the same room. I'm not sure how to make sense of it.

Everything this monster has done was with a gentleness I haven't been afforded in a long time. Ordus' hands might be larger than my face, but there was never a moment of hurt as he dabbed at my wounds with a delicateness I didn't think would be possible by a man—*monster*—of his stature.

He wrapped my feet with so much care—care I wouldn't have given myself. I was certain he was going to say something horrific to balance it out, make him a true monster, inside and out, but it never came.

He never told me I was pathetic, stupid for hurting myself, useless for not staying put. There was no inkling of disappointment or disgust, no displeasure over having to deal with my injury.

He never raised his hand against me. Put his tentacles around my throat. Yanked me around.

No snide remarks have come over my injured hand either. I expected... I don't know what I expected him to say when he noticed it. Maybe talk about how weak I am? Laugh at it? Goad me. Tease me. Tell me I deserved what happened, and I wouldn't be sore if I hadn't *pushed* him to do what he did.

None of that has come.

He's a monster, but he's not acting like one.

When he was raging so hard, he left to calm himself down. Then later, he forced himself to breathe through his anger. His touch was soft, and even though I could tell he wanted more, he didn't even try to take his pleasure out on me, didn't ask or suggest. He could've pulled my dress down or spread me wide and taken what he wanted, but he didn't.

And I don't know how to deal with that.

I don't know how to deal with any of this.

Not how gentle he's been. Not the weird, romantic, creepy shit he's been saying. Not the fact that he's taken me "to bed," which apparently involves zero funny business. The man—*kraken*—slithered us over to the side-cave, lowered us to the moss, wrapped both versions of his arms around me, closed his eyes, and started snoring ten seconds later.

I was gobsmacked.

I've been fighting sleep for the past two hours; this façade of his is bound to break soon. He's luring me into a false sense of comfort before he does whatever it is he plans on doing with me.

Tommy's needs never waited for daylight or full consciousness. Even if I was fast asleep, anything went. If there is a way to stay awake forever, to avoid opening myself up to that vulnerability, I would do it.

I don't want to be around to find out what Ordus' true intentions are. I don't want to find out when it's being forced upon me.

No one kidnaps people from their home if they're a good person. Maybe this is a common occurrence amongst his kind— if there are more of him—but as far as I'm concerned, it's not an excuse. Every creature is capable of good and evil. He's choosing the latter.

With nothing to do and every intention of watching him like a hawk in case his plan was to fake sleep then pounce, he's been my sole focus.

Light trickles in through from the ribbons of bioluminescent algae. It's hard to pinpoint Ordus' exact shade, other than the fact that it's very distinctly not quite human. Sometimes his skin holds a blue coloring, while other times, it's a medium tan over the center of his body that radiates into a reddish brown along his shoulders, arms, forehead, and the bottom half of his body. The light, spotted markings are more prominent along his tentacles like the local reef octopuses, dotted around his brow bones, beneath his eyes, along his shoulders and arms.

I've noticed his tentacles sometimes change colors as they move over the ground, darkening over the grey stone before shifting to a lighter brown over the driftwood and coconuts, then glimmering blue close to the algae. Even now, there's a greenish tinge to the tentacles resting on the moss or over my damp teal dress.

It's fascinating.

In Ordus' sleep, he carefully wrapped his tentacle around my injured arm, keeping it slightly bent at the elbow, the wrist cushioned over the thick limb. Maybe I'm losing my mind, but the appendage seems warmer than all the others. The suckers might also be puckering slightly—I can't really tell from the pins and needles. Either way, the combination is weirdly soothing.

I would rather be knocked out by painkillers, though.

Movement sounds from the main cavern, jolting me out of my half-asleep state. I whip my attention toward the noise, unsure whether I should wake Ordus up or hope to whatever god listening that nothing bad is about to happen.

There's a steady *clack, clack, clack* of claws against stone, and before I know it, the shark-dog is flopping himself against my back, shoving closer so he's flat against me, sandwiched between me and Ordus.

I hesitate. "Can you really understand me?"

His tail thumps the ground.

I'll take that as a yes.

"Can you get me out of here?"

He snorts.

"I need to get out of here. My friends will be—"

He slaps me with his tail, as if to say, "Shut up. I'm trying to sleep."

"Are you going to eat me?"

I contort my neck to watch him turn to look between me and Ordus. He shakes his head no but shows me his teeth in a confident yes.

That's not very assuring.

Vasz—or fucking *Vaszeline*—lies back down, effectively dismissing me.

If someone really did lace my drink, I must be absolutely tripping balls to be able to come up with any of this.

I swallow, attempting to lubricate my mouth and throat. I'm half tempted to wake Ordus up to demand he fetch me water, but I'm pretty sure he's just going to direct me to the pool.

I can't imagine explaining humans only drink out of clean, bottled water will go down well.

Or that I can't eat the fish unless he's going to start a fire.

I fight sleep tooth and nail, forcing myself to keep my eyes open and mind alert to any change in breathing, atmosphere, or twitching. But at some point I lose the battle, because everything goes black.

The sound of movement comes from all around me, and my brows stitch together at the odd sensations. The taste of salt spreading over my tongue registers in my senses as something glides over my gums. Something is wrapped around my waist and legs. I can't move.

No.

No.

Not again.

Panic sinks its claws into me like a vice. My eyes snap open, and I clamp my teeth down without caring if something gets bitten off. The *thing* leaves my mouth in an instant. Screams rip from my throat. I throw every ounce of my weight against the ropes holding me down.

I can't fucking breathe.

How is this happening again?

He's dead

Tommy's dead.

I killed him.

He can't be here.

My legs hit the soft floor, and I scramble back, choking on terror as the tears start to burn my eyes. I can just make out the shape of a giant through my blurry vision, and reality comes crashing in.

Ordus. The kraken.

Not Tommy. Not the Gallaghers.

But a ten-foot-tall monster who has me imprisoned, starved, dehydrated, and injured. He's strong enough to kill me with a single swipe. And he was—he was doing something to me while I slept.

There's nowhere for me to go. I can't outrun him. I'm trapped with a raging bull, and I'm guaranteed to lose.

I can still taste seawater on my tongue and Tommy's battery acid at the back of my throat.

I whimper, curling up against the wall, hugging my legs to make myself smaller. God, I wish I were anyone else but me. I wish I could rage and have the strength to tear his throat out instead of huddling up to the wall, hoping and praying it doesn't hurt that much.

Ordus isn't going to be happy by my reaction. I hit him, just tried to bite him. Not for the first time, but I would've worn his patience thin already. Bile lurches up my throat, and I swallow it back down to keep from angering him further. If I throw up, my punishment would be brutal enough to leave me twitching on the floor, unable to move.

Nothing good ever comes from sleep. I was right.

God, I want to fucking scream.

People don't wake up and feel better, open their eyes then forgive and forget. The memory of all my indiscretions would still be fresh in his mind. I was given a pass yesterday. It never extends to the next. Tommy taught me that, and I've been too stupid to remember.

"Cindi." His voice is quiet, cautious. Ordus lowers himself closer to the ground, slowly approaching me with his hands out, palms facing upward.

It's a lie. He's not surrendering. He's lulling me into a false sense of security.

I swallow an angry, fearful sob, keeping my head down, gaze averted, not daring to make a sound, even though I want to scream for being the way I am, for not being strong enough to look him in the eye and tell him to go fuck himself.

I wish I buried that blade into his neck yesterday so I didn't have to discover every fear I had was true.

Ordus is a monster, one as bad as the rest of them.

I was beginning to think maybe he isn't a monster. Maybe he's just misunderstood. Maybe he's nothing like the faces I passed day after day, fooling me into believing the true monsters are the ones hiding beneath the bed while they smile with their straight teeth.

I'm a fool for thinking he held any goodness in him last night when all he wanted was to wait until I was asleep before taking advantage of me. I don't know what he's done to me. My underwear feels like it's in place. My dress is right. It doesn't feel like anything has been *in there*.

Still, I have no way of escaping. Scaling the wall to get to the hole proved impossible. With Vasz playing guard dog, I won't make it far. And what? Do I think it'd be even remotely possible to outswim Ordus if I fail at killing him?

This is all my fault.

I should have stayed awake, ran at the first sign of trouble *days* ago. I should never have stopped moving.

My tongue flicks over my dry, chapped lips. I covertly feel the ground around me for the weapon I fell asleep with, but I come up empty. I start to shuffle back, only to stop when an indiscernible rumble starts in his chest.

"Don't," I whisper, staring at the two tentacles coming toward me.

I flinch when one gently wraps around my ankle with hardly any pressure; I could yank myself out of his hold with ease. Ordus speaks before I get the chance to run.

"I was looking at your teeth."

My stare flicks up to his. "*What?*" I run my tongue over my gums to make sure nothing is missing.

"You were obviously badly injured, yet you told me you were fine. I was...checking for anything else that might be bringing you pain. Sometimes—sometimes, my tooth aches, and I do not want to eat. I thought perhaps..." Ordus' brows flatten as every guilt-laden word drips out from him. He sinks onto the moss across from me, shoulders slumped, filling the cave with his tentacles.

I study his face for signs of malice or manipulation in the crinkle around his eyes or the downward tilt of his lips. Except it's like looking at a reflection. His self-loathing is written in the pain behind his eyes and the slightest tremble in his hands. That's not something anyone can fake. My chest squeezes, and I'm struck with the urge to tell him it's alright, to apologize for accusing him of something so heinous—but I can't have that type of weakness.

"I—" He stops, clears his throat, and drops his gaze to the tentacle wrapped around my ankle. "I am unsure how to help with your arm, but it is possible for me to forage for supplies to treat other issues."

I notice belatedly that the sound he started making is his purr, not a growl.

My attention falls on the fresh wrapping around my feet and shin. He's...he's telling the truth.

Ordus might have been taking advantage of me while I was asleep, but it was just… It was for my benefit.

At least, I think it was just for my benefit.

"Why do you care?" My words crack and scratch from the lack of water.

The tentacle curls up around my calf. He raises his hand like he wants to touch me. Thinking better of it, he drops it to his side, holding my gaze with a weight that's suffocating in its reverent intensity. "You are my mate."

My stomach drops. He's said it a few times already, called me his *mate*. Whether out of pure delusion or genuine fear, I disregarded it, shoved it to the back of my mind. Too many crazy things have happened.

"Are you Australian?" I blurt.

Please say yes.

I've read enough romance books to know the alternative is something I'm not willing to accept as fact.

Even though, apparently, krakens are fucking real.

If a *mate* or soulmate means the same thing to him, as it does in every single fated mates book on the market and the general world renown meaning of a soulmate, then there is absolutely no way I'm getting out of here.

"Your soul called to me from across the sea." Ocean-blue eyes hold mine with the ferocity of a chemical fire. It's an oath, adoration packaged in possession. "The moment I saw you, the course of my life was altered to become wholly devoted to you, your every whim, your every thought, need. The Goddess deemed I belong to you, and you belong to me. The rest of my days are yours. If you are not with me, I will cease to exist."

Oh.

Oh no.

Oh fuck.

I'm screwed.

Completely and utterly screwed.

I think I'm going to have another panic attack.

My pulse races. "The Goddess was wrong."

Ordus' look of honeyed admiration fractures. The brittle edges of his cracked mask splits open. His guilt and sorrow seeps through, casting his skin in a sullen shade. "She is never wrong. You feel it too." He adds the last part hesitantly.

"I feel nothing but contempt."

What I feel is, I'm about to relive years of abuse in a less-gilded cage. My experiences have made me soft and touch-deprived enough that I would seek any semblance of pleasure from someone who's keeping me hostage. I've been without warmth for so long, I'm willingly touching fire.

What I am *feeling* isn't the effects of fate or a divine being. No, it's the side effects of a broken psyche drowning beneath a decade of failures.

We aren't *mates.*

I'm not here to question the existence of the concept or the will of who decides pairings. I know deep in my heart that my reaction to him isn't the result of fate, but of desperation. Ordus is attractive, strong, and has been gentle with me in a way I forgot was possible.

Whether he's lying to me or he genuinely believes it to be true, whatever it is, it's not because we're mates. He's got it wrong.

Ordus winces like I've struck him. I almost feel guilty for it. The reaction is more extreme than the times I really did stab him, and those cracks widen. His guilt and self-loathing aren't oozing out anymore—it's pouring, spilling down my paling skin to pool at my torn feet.

"I'm sorry." His shoulders fall, dejection thick in his voice. "There is nothing I can do."

"Let me go," I whisper, frowning at the building pain in my elbow and fingers. I massage my shoulder and tricep muscles. "Return me to the house."

He tips his head to the side to study me. "You're like that bird that repeats the same words."

"A parrot?"

"Yes, yes." He sighs, eyes brightening at my amusement. *"Let go of me. Take me home. Don't touch me."*

Is he...teasing me? What the fuck? "Probably because that's what I want," I snap.

I gasp when a tentacle wraps around my bad arm and does a weird, warming, puckering thing that distracts me from the pain,

"Then I suggest you find new desires, mate." The creases around his eyes soften.

"No, Ordus." I shake my head slowly. If there's one thing he's said I believe to be true, it's that he'll never let me go—the jury's still out about my safety. He needs to understand staying here will kill me. "You care about me, right?"

"Of course." He nods, brow wrinkling in annoyance that I'm even suggesting he doesn't. "More than anything."

His answer tips my axis. I believe him at the same time I reel at the blatant manipulation.

I'd rather be a cynic than be made a fool of again.

"Then you can't keep me down here. I'll grow crazy. I need food and water," I insist.

A piercing pain shoots through my stomach at the reminder. The last time I was deprived of food and water, it was because Tommy thought I embarrassed him at dinner because I reached over someone to get something. It was so mundane, I can't remember who or what was involved.

Ordus tenses like he's about to get up.

"*Human* food," I correct before he can catch fish again.

He falters, lips pursed, hesitating as he glances between me and the cavern. Slowly, like he's scared I might bolt if he moves too quickly, he offers me his hand. "Come."

The tentacle caresses my leg. I swallow. "Where are you taking me?"

"Land."

14

"We're not gonna fit."

"We'll fit," I assure her.

It'll be a tight squeeze—it already is without my mate clinging to me, a fact that has my purr doubling in volume.

Cindi, my mate, the human who despises every part of me, is holding me like her life depends on it.

Likely because it *does* depend on it.

I won't let her fall, of course. The thought of the cuts and bruises that would mar her body from the fall is enough to momentarily replace my purr with a growl.

"Let go of my neck." It kills me to say it.

"Are you crazy?"

"It is not a term—"

"I'm not letting go."

Oh, she did not expect an answer.

How am I meant to know when her questions require a response? Are all human females this confusing?

Cindi's stomach vibrates against me, and I frown. I'm worried she still has not eaten. How often must humans feed per day? Once? Twice? Five times?

The food shops on the mainland are always busier during midday and at night. So...only twice? She has to feed more often than that. Cindi is so small, I can feel her ribs through her dress. More concerning is that she feels more weightless than she did yesterday, yet she continues to refuse the fish I caught for her.

If my mate will not accept the fish I hunt for her, she may be more willing to feed if it was brought by Vasz. A sound of displeasure startles in my throat. I don't like any male giving anything to my Cindi.

Cindi glances at the rocks below and defeats all forms of impossibility by tensing even more. I flatten my palm against her upper back, silently urging her to comply with my request. I prefer her arms not be exposed to avoid injury.

A moment passes, both of us staying completely still in the narrow passageway above the pool. There are two different accesses from the cave to get to land. This is the fastest way. The alternative is through the tunnel to the side of the cavern I blocked to keep bats from flying into the den.

I would have taken the longer route if Cindi hadn't insisted on walking. Her feet are wounded because of my lack of attentiveness. I will not make that mistake twice.

The tunnel is very narrow. Some rocks jut out with sharpened edges. I had intended on cocooning around her, sacrificing my own skin to the stone, but she continues to insist on being difficult.

Humans.

"I will not let you hurt your hands." Her legs are already wrapped around my waist after minutes of arguing. Despite the many times I've assured her I will not let her fall, that my arm and tentacle will hold on to her, she refuses to comply and let me take the brunt of any scrapes.

In truth, I don't want her to let go. I never do. The feeling of being held—willingly touched—is foreign. I could get addicted to it. I'm already mourning the moment where she'll inevitably let go.

"No."

"You're being unreasonable."

She shoots me a scathing glare.

I sigh, readjusting my limb beneath her backside and around her waist to take more of her weight.

I continue through the tunnel, using my free arm and tentacles to suction us to the path and keep moving us upward. Her thighs tighten around me, and my breeding arm hardens. It remains that way as we crawl closer to the sunlight.

Alone, I can get to land in a matter of seconds. Today, I take my time, tightening my hold on Cindi so she's flush against my chest, making her small breasts push up. I can't help stealing glances when she isn't looking.

Her sex is taunting me. I can taste her warmth on my suckers through the layers of fabric. My cock twitches against the rock. I want to dip my tentacle beneath her dress and suck on her nipple again to see if I can get her to make the good type of sounds.

But every inhale is sobering. Her scent is tainted by fear, and not the kind that leads to her screaming and fighting, only cranky. Maybe it's because of her hunger as well.

Vasz gets that way when he hasn't eaten.

With her silent—and only partially trusting—in my hold, I can almost imagine what it would be like if she didn't hate me. We would lie in our den, and she would wrap her arms and legs around me just for the mere fact that she wants to. Because she *wants* to feel me. We'd stay like that for hours while my hands and limbs roam over her.

Then she'd look up at me, and she'd smile. A real smile. A genuine one. Only for me. And my hearts would swell because the Goddess blessed me with a mate capable of loving me back.

147

But that is a fool's dream, wishful thinking that holds no merit.

At least like this, her head tucked beneath my chin, warm against me, I don't need to see the evidence of her disdain written all over her face. My suckers pulse, releasing a whisper of toxin into her to relax her muscles.

I carefully maneuver her body to avoid any scrapes as we reach a bend in the tunnel. The edges of dull green leaves sway up ahead, and light descends on us. Cindi's arms and legs tense around me. She looks up, unnervingly quiet. A sinking feeling settles in my stomach. I spare a glance at her calculating face, and her eyes brighten, like there's a plan forming behind them I won't like.

Buka, I think as I approach the mouth of the tunnel.

The invisible door pulses an iridescent blue only noticeable with great focus.

Hot air assaults my skin the moment I pass the magical barrier that stops the elements, creatures, and critters from coming in. I scowl up at the blinding sun, feeling the sensitive skin of my tentacles wither against the scalding heat. They rapidly change to a lighter brown to match the dirt and keep cool.

"Wait," I tell Cindi, wrapping another tentacle around her. "Do not make a sound."

She stills, breath no more than a whisper against the gills of my neck. The sensation makes me shudder, and I have to remind myself I'm meant to be surveying my surroundings for predators.

At most, there will only be the bats that survive without the fruit that no longer hangs on the many trees on the island. Krakens are forbidden from accessing the island—not that they would even if they were permitted.

Malediction Island, as my people have named it.

When I first inhabited it forty years ago, many were tempted to steal leaves or wood for their homes. The only reason it stopped was because krakens spread rumors the island is contaminated with my disease, and I've somehow poisoned all life here from the blood running through my veins. Some even began believing they may look like me if they so much as swam near my den.

The island sits in the middle of the ocean. The nearest body of land is nothing more than a giant rock formation that barely scratches the surface of the water. The palace. It's where I should be residing as king.

I moved out decades ago when Chlaena still lived. It was hard to sleep knowing krakens were beyond the rock walls, whispering about me, wishing for my demise, finding a way to sabotage me. Plus, my body hated being underwater for long periods of time.

Taking post out here, away from the main eastern city, at the edge of the territory, was packaged to our subjects in a way that made it sound more like military strategy, rather than cowardice or weakness.

I held post here, watching for intruders, bandits, enemies from neighboring territories. I have killed many in protection of my kingdom. I was foolish to think if I tried hard enough, my people would accept me, but not once have I ever received thanks or commendations for what I've done.

Now, without threat of invasion, there's nothing for me to occupy my days with, except hunting or experimenting with the human tools I've found.

"What are you searching for?" Cindi whispers when the silence stretches on for too long.

"Threats."

"What—" She swallows, fingers digging into my shoulder. "People?"

My tentacle presses to the dirt to sense for any kind of magical interference or new presence. It's possible humans have come to investigate the island. It wouldn't be the first time. The runes hidden around the island and the palace *deter* them from venturing this way, not *prohibit*.

As for krakens, we may not have passed any on the way here, but there would have been a trail of her scent the seasoned hunters could follow. I can only hope the storm diluted her scent enough to make her impossible to track, and no one is foolish enough to investigate.

"Krakens," I answer, closing the distance to the beach to scan the shoreline. "Witches. Sirens. Ghouls wouldn't swim this far out. But you needn't worry. You are safe with me."

Her jaw drops. "Did you just say ghouls?"

I nod.

"They're *real*?"

I dislike how much interest she's showing them. "Have you interacted with them?"

"What? No." Cindi's brows flatten. "Are vampires and demons real, then? What about the grim reaper? Dragons? Faeries or fae or whatever you're meant to call them."

Uh. "I am not familiar with the creatures on land, although demons come in many forms." I can't say I've had the misfortune of encountering any.

I brace myself for her disappointment. It never comes.

She huffs out a breath. "It's better I don't know."

I like this. I like when Cindi is talking. Her eyes get brighter, and the lines around them soften. The sunlight kisses her tanned skin as I step out of the shade onto what my people call *Mutant Shores*. She's not glistening beneath the light as she did the other times I saw her. Her shade isn't as rich and warm, doesn't appear as feather-soft to the touch.

Is she sick?

Is it because she hasn't been eating?

Exhaustion?

Was it because she was attacked?

"Is it safe?" she asks.

I blink, forgetting what I was meant to be doing.

I nod. *For now.*

"Can you put me down?"

"Yes, but I do not want to."

"Put me down," Cindi orders.

"You're—"

"Don't you start with me being injured. Put me down right this second." Cindi's voice is infused with the confidence of a queen and the rage of a provoked shark. Her scent is the only thing giving away her fear.

I almost smile. I never want to see her show neck again.

Slowly, I lower her. I fight my instinct to pick her back up when she flinches when her feet touch the ground. The poultice has worked quickly to heal the worst of the wounds, but even slight discomfort is unacceptable.

Cindi stumbles away from me and carefully turns on the heel of her foot to survey her surroundings. I hold no pride over this island. It is both a source of shame and a place for a coward to seek comfort, a prison of riches and freedom.

Cliffs taller than the human buildings on the mainland surround the beach. It's a mix of rock and forestry that homes insects and bats that are of no concern to kraken-kind. Much of the island is too steep for humans to climb, and more effort than it's worth for me to attempt it a second time.

Ten minutes from where we are is an elevated, flat patch of land untouched by seawater. Other than our den, it's the only part of the island I've made to be my own.

The breeze flows between the thinning leaves of the forest, dancing to the tune of the Goddess' song and the tumbling waves against the shore. Mingled within the smell of saltwater and damp earth is my mate's sweet scent.

Confident Cindi will be safe from any and all threats, I divert my attention to her, always keeping my suckers pulsing, alert to any changes in the atmosphere.

My hands fist at my sides as I watch her limp along the shore, searching for something between the thick trees at my back.

She wants to run, I realize belatedly.

It's obvious from her fluttering pulse and jumpiness and the way she keeps flicking her gaze to me, as if calculating how quickly I'll be able to catch her.

My throat tightens. Cindi is a female who has gone through many things I do not know about. The one thing I am certain of is that she is woefully unimpressed by me and anything I have to offer.

I follow her line of sight to the sprawling expanse of deep blue. "My people call this beach *Pantu Aknora.*"

I've closed any opening or tunnel hidden beneath the water. This beach is the only part of the island directly accessible from the sea. If a threat comes, it'll be on this shore.

She raises her good hand to her brow line to block out the sun. Her tongue flicks out to wet her lips before she speaks. "What does it mean?"

"In your language, it translates to Mutant Shores."

When she blinks up at me, I'm struck with the desire to learn how to stop time so I can stare at her forever. She doesn't look like she hates me.

A little divot forms beneath her brows that I want to trace with the tip of my claws. "Why is it called that?" she asks.

I purse my lips. It's best she doesn't know what my people say about me. "Because there's a monster living here."

She blanches, taking in the surroundings with widened eyes.

"You will always be safe, I promise. You...you can trust me, Cindi." Repeating the same words won't change her mind. It never does. But it isn't a waste of breath.

I will remind her every day until she believes it.

Movement from the water catches my eyes. I grab Cindi to hide her behind me, a warning growl rumbling in my chest. Two yellow dots pop out from above the waves, then a brown fin.

I narrow my eyes at Vasz as he comes trotting out of the water, ears flopping, the fish I caught for Cindi dangling from his mouth. I move aside to let my mate resume her perusal of my island and pretend not to notice her stand close beside me.

But I notice.

I very much notice.

And because I'm a coward, I also pretend not to notice her gasp when my tentacle wraps around her ankle, and the taste of her floods into my system.

"That was Cindi's lunch," I scold Vasz.

He throws a fish in the air and eats it in one go. "What was?" Water sprays across the sand as he shakes out his skin.

"Vaseline," she mutters under her breath. I almost miss it. "Unbelievable." Her mood suddenly falls.

I spear Vasz with my wrath for upsetting my female. He stops trotting, looks at me, then falls into the sand to show me his belly.

My fury rapidly multiplies into a venomous mixture of grief and rage when Cindi's croaky voice breaks the silence. "I have to go back, Ordus."

Ordus.

Ordus.

I like when she says my name, just not the way she lets it fall from her tongue.

"Why?"

She has not been here for a full day cycle, and she's been desperate to leave from the very beginning. Am I so dreadful to be around? Does she hate me that much?

How can she not care we are mates? Was I so delusional to believe she might feel it too?

Cindi meets my anger head-on. She rounds on me, raising her voice and throwing out her hands. It's amusing a creature half my size could be so explosive. "Because I have a life! People counting on me. A job. Friends."

Jealousy burns a path from the base of my spine to the tips of my tentacles.

Friends? She has me.

I haven't had any friends in decades, and I've been fine. She doesn't need them. I will be enough for her.

We glare at each other, neither of us backing down. Cindi breaks the contact first to dart her gaze to the shore where Vasz is running up and down the beach, attempting to eat the foam gathered atop each wave, barking and leaping into the water before going back to sprinting. The barest trickle of sweetness in Cindi's scent has me grateful for Vasz's distraction.

My jaw tightens.

Fine. I will try to do as my mate asks.

"Okay." The words taste bitter. "We can compromise."

Her attention snaps up to me, lips parting, like she's unsure whether to wait or say more.

"I'll let you be friends with Vasz. And you'll be happy."

There.

It is a good compromise.

Although Vasz may not agree, I will bribe him with coconuts.

Cindi blinks.

Once. Twice.

If I thought the little human was angry before, it is nothing in comparison to the static that zaps from her, electricity thundering through burning water seconds before an explosion.

Oh no. I think I broke my mate.

"That is not a compromise," she screams. Her eyes are so round and wide, I worry they might fall out. "A compromise is you saying yes because you care about me in exchange for a souvenir. A compromise is returning me to my home and getting far the hell away from me."

I consider for a moment, as a good mate should, but her proposals are only setting fire to my veins. As much as I try to convince myself she'll be happy here, wanting for nothing, I know I'm only making my mate suffer in this cage with me.

Letting her go would be the right thing to do.

But am I not a monster?

"I don't like those compromises. They're too unrealistic." And because Yannig once told me females like when you ask them questions, I say, "Do you have any more proposals?"

"*Unrealistic*? You're a real-life *kraken*, and there's a shark-octopus-dog"—she points at Vasz—"named after Vaseline—*Vaseline*," she enunciates, incredulous. "And you're telling me what's *unrealistic*?" Her fingers rake through her knotted hair. "You kidnapped me just as I was about to save myself. I don't belong here. I belong out there—that's where humans live."

I stop myself from reminding her many humans live on boats.

Those weren't the type of compromises I wanted. Nonetheless, I understand this is an important conversation for her, and I am trying. I truly am.

There isn't much more I can tell her that I haven't already said. My soul is hers, and hers mine. The Goddess decided it. Fighting fate will not get her anywhere. I'm not sure what I could say or do that would give us what we both want.

I recognize that much of this would be a shock to Cindi, and I never thought of much beyond what destiny might entail—that she would see me, instantly know what we are to each other, and every piece would fall into place without issue.

I…I haven't considered many things, but how am I meant to know what it is I should be aware of? There's no one I could speak to about this, no one I could learn from. My grandmother was the only one who engaged with humans, and she died long before my birth. And Yannig… He's not here either.

I grind my teeth. The Goddess was wrong to give me a mate. I do not deserve one. She should have ignored all my prayers and refused my offerings.

But still, she gave me a mate, and now I need to try and keep her happy.

Compromise. I can do that.

"I will bring your friends to the island." I can lock them in a hut on the flat patch of land on the island. That way, Cindi can visit them whenever she wants.

"No! You're crazy." She stomps on my tentacle, and I recoil. "Fuck you," she screams. "I hate this island and your stupid cave. I don't want a mate. I never asked to be your mate. I don't *want* to be your mate. Just get me out of here. Let me go. I don't want to fucking die like this."

Pain ricochets through me with each word. I want to fix this without giving her what she wants. A good mate should put the female first, but I am not good. I spent my early years doing whatever others wanted, but it never changed anything.

"You will stay here, Cindi," I say sternly, throat tightening. I know what's coming next. "That is final."

Tears well in her eyes, and I freeze, unmoving when she shoves me. "I hate you!" she cries, hitting me again. "I hate you. I hate you. I hate you." She claws at me every time she says it. I take each attack, wishing it'd hurt more to make up for her pain. I deserve it. "You piece of fucking *shit*. I was getting out of here! Fuck—ugh—Tommy—I—" A sob wracks through her body.

I want to touch her, kiss away her sorrows, hold her until her tears stop flowing, tell her everything will be alright. I want to demand she tells me about this *Tommy* so I can kill him for making her so upset, but she doesn't want me to. She's getting paler, cheeks red as she heaves, stumbling to the shore.

Vasz gives her one dismissive look, rolls his eyes, then dives into the water. She doesn't notice, whipping her head side to side to find an escape along the shoreline.

My mate doesn't want me.

There was no mistaking her words. She meant them with every fiber of her soul. Cindi hates me.

I feel sick. My chest constricts and my arms tremble at my sides, skin pulsing as I melt into the shadows, blending in with my surroundings to give Cindi the illusion of space.

Any other kraken would know the right things to say to stop her crying, to bring her comfort as a mate should. But this is the fate the Goddess bestowed upon her, the curse she was given. I will not free her from it. I cannot.

She has no choice but to go along with it. The sooner she realizes it, the easier it will be for her.

15

CINDI

Everything I endured was for nothing.

Those are the words repeating in my head as I watch the sun descend beneath the shoreline.

I was beaten, abused, starved all so my father could die alone, waiting for me to call him to restart our Sunday routine like we did before I fell into Tommy's trap.

I stabbed my husband. I ran to the other side of the world.

And all of it was for nothing.

I'm going to die out here, at the hands of my so-called *mate*. Whether by plain ignorance or pure naivety, he's going to be the death of me.

Hunger pains stab at my stomach. My throat is raw from crying, the heat, dehydration, and many mouthfuls of saltwater. My skin feels like it's peeling off my body from the hours I've spent in the sun, staring into the distance, willing someone to see me. I think the tattoo on my back has blistered.

I've circled what I could of the island, coming face-to-face with a steep rock wall or the edge of a cliff every time I think I've finally found a way back to civilization.

But no one is coming.

The only form of escape I could find was a dinghy with a rusted, busted engine. There wasn't a single salvageable part.

I searched the trees as I ran around the island, hoping to find any fruit or vegetable I could eat or drink, but nothing. No freshwater stream. No coconuts I could attempt to pick. No way to make a fire because I'm far from being a Girl Scout.

A person can last three days without water. I'd venture I'd die in less, based on how the past twenty-four hours have played out, not to mention the whole *chronic fatigue* thing I've been sporting for the last six months.

The last thing I ate was a single lumpia yesterday afternoon, followed by two cocktails later that night. By my calculation, I have until tomorrow evening to get out of here before I waste away.

At one point, I considered jumping into the sea and swimming until I reach land, drown, or get eaten by whatever fucked-up thing is out there, but I figured Ordus would catch me before I could make it far.

I haven't seen him, but I know he's out there somewhere, sulking, watching, doing mental gymnastics to come to some justification that keeping me—his supposed *mate*—out here is fine.

He'd rather let me die on this island than take me back.

Just because a monster has a gentle touch doesn't mean he isn't a monster.

I'll do well to remember that.

The water splashes against my feet, sand sticking to my grimy, sweat-stained skin. The fabric of my dress feels like matted cardboard. I've turned into a slab of meat for the nearby mosquitoes to feast on. I'd kill for many things right now. A shower is near the top of that list.

I need to find the silver lining in this, right? That's what Dad always did. Oh, I got seven out of ten on my spelling test? At least I passed and learned from my mistakes. Burned dinner? Once you shave off the char, the inside is edible.

He was an optimist, a yes-man through and through. He wouldn't hurt a fly. He'd say I was enough of a pessimist for the both of us. Well, he only said that once I started seeing Tommy.

So, silver lining? The Gallaghers can't reach this island.

I squeeze my eyes shut against my plummeting blood pressure and sugar levels that send my body on a toxic tailspin where I want to discard the nonexistent contents of my stomach.

My body sways with the gentle breeze, eyelids drifting open and closed.

The sea isn't giving me any peace like it usually would, but still, if there were ever a place for me to die, it would be here, overlooking the ocean as the water cools me down. Because when all is said and done, my corpse will be mine alone. I'm trapped on this island where no one will ever find me here. The Gallaghers can't turn me into a warning if they never find my body.

With that thought, I weakly dart my eyes to the trees in case one of the Gallaghers magically teleported here. For a second, I see a glimmer of Tommy's ghost, but I know he isn't there. It's been...nice not looking over my shoulder every minute I've been outdoors, waiting for the Gallaghers to be around the corner.

My fear of them isn't at the forefront of my mind. Paranoia isn't choking me. Natural survival is the only thing I'm thinking of. That, and Ordus, who's left me to my own devices, watching me slowly wither away.

Movement sounds behind me. I don't bother turning. I know who it'll be. I have no desire to give him more attention than he deserves.

I hate that I flinch when he raises his arm, that I instinctively tuck my chin up against my collarbone to brace for a strike that never comes. I never used to be like this. I was a stranger to hurt until pain became all I knew.

What I hate even more is watching Ordus' fingers curl into fists, how my heart hammers in my chest at the memory of what knuckles feel like against soft tissue.

Maybe somewhere deep down, there's a part of me that believes he'd never raise a hand against me, but that's what I believed about Tommy. I gave him the benefit of the doubt, and I paid for it with my life and a screwed-up arm.

Ordus lowers himself to the ground and very intentionally hunches to seem less imposing. The silence stretches for long minutes as I watch the water draw his tentacles in and out of the shore.

It's on the tip of my tongue to open my mouth and demand the same thing I've been demanding since I got here, but he beats me to it. The monster clears his throat, offering me his hand. "Come, female."

Of all the things to be mad about, that sets me off. Maybe it's the exhaustion. Maybe I just want to argue to feel something other than hopelessness.

"Don't fucking call me that," I snap, my voice a garbled rasp of shards of glass that tear through the fibers of my throat.

"Female?" Ordus questions, bewildered.

"*Woman,*" I correct.

It's a stupid argument, a waste of my precious energy when I should be conserving whatever moisture is left in my mouth and throat. But I don't want him to have a moment of peace. I want him to hate me as much as I hate him for putting me through this.

My eyes heat once more. Exhaustion. Frustration. Despair. It hits me, spilling down my salt-burnt cheeks into my lips.

"Or Cindi." I almost say Kristy, because I might as well let someone else know my real name, since I'm going to die anyway.

But Kristy is already dead—even if her ghost is insistent on haunting my every waking moment.

I ignore his outstretched hand and jump to my feet, hating that he towers over me either way.

"Do not lessen my person to the organ between my legs," I yell. That's what Tommy did. His family. Every other person I came across during the three years I was with him. I was nothing more than a thing to hang off his arm, a toy for him to throw around when no one was looking.

If I'm going to die, I want to do it without feeling less than human, even if the kraken sees me as nothing more than an object of fate.

"I'm a person. A human being with feelings. Emotions. Needs." I don't know why I bother. He's not going to change his tune. I doubt he's capable of it. He's a monster through and through. Being humanoid doesn't give him humanity. "And you're a monster," I seethe.

He says nothing, staring at me with eyes I can't read. Muscles bunched. Lips twitching. Arms stiff.

I'm torn between cowering away and doubling down. Tommy would have hit me before a sound could come out.

I hate Ordus, but not in the same way I hated Tommy. I hated my husband with a force that moved mountains and raised hell to my feet.

I hate Ordus because he looks like Tommy in certain lights. He's giving me the same clouded look Tommy used to give me before he twists his words until they're sharp enough to puncture an artery.

Except Ordus doesn't speak. He's looking at me like he wants me to say more, to lay everything out at our feet in the hopes he can pick at the words to see them from a different angle and figure out how it works out of plain curiosity.

"You're killing me," I croak, tears stinging my burnt cheeks, vocal cords like sandpaper.

A look of pure torture crosses his eyes. Then, a flash of guilt, followed by unbridled desperation. Every hair on my body stands on end, though not out of fear. I just... I don't know how to react to him.

He doesn't want me to die, but he won't do what needs to be done to keep me alive. He doesn't want to hurt me, but he's letting me starve.

"I need water, Ordus," I whisper.

He motions to the sea. "The—"

"*Water*," I repeat. "Drinking water. Human water. Fucking mineral water. Aqua. *Air*," I say in Indonesian, in case that registers in his thick skull. "And I need to wash and cook the fish."

No one ever fucking listens to me. It's like I'm mute to everyone, and I'm screaming at a brick wall.

I can feel his distress oozing off him. Well, if he's upset about this, how the fuck does he think I feel?

"I...I do not understand." His eyes dart toward the sea once more.

"Take me back! Take me back. Take me back. Take me back," I chant. Scream. Heave. Hit. Cry. Drop to the ground and sob some more.

I feel like a petulant child throwing a tantrum. I keep waiting for the other shoe to drop where he starts yelling back, berating me, or exerts some level of force to make me stop seeing any semblance of good in him.

He says nothing, staring into the distance as I try to get my breathing under control. Over and over, one of his tentacles comes toward me, and another snatches it away, as if each of his limbs has a mind of its own.

It's...nice having someone there. I'm too tired to think of a better word to describe how it feels to have another person beside me as I let go of the restraints on my emotions. To not be touched. To simply sit in the silence.

Even if he is the cause of my meltdown.

This is the most fucked-up situation any person could imagine. It's nice when it shouldn't be.

It could be worse. It's not the metric I should use to judge my situation, but there's no escaping the truth.

I could be the Gallaghers' new punching bag. Lord knows what the pirates would do to me, who they might sell me off to.

The kraken could be intentionally harming me. He could have forced himself on me.

Or worse: I could still be with Tommy.

I hug my knees, wishing for a different life, staring out into the vast unknown and wallowing in my misery beside a monster who isn't acting how I thought a monster would.

"Krakens would…" I watch Ordus out of the corner of my eye. His gaze drops to the hands in his lap. The striking familiarity of that single, pained look winds me. I can recognize grief anywhere. "I would die if you left." His voice is just above a whisper.

"I'll die if I stay here." I sound like a broken record. "Look, I've read the books. My kind has a vague belief in soulmates. I know… I think I understand the magnitude of your…" I search for an appropriate word. "Position."

I can't possibly know what *mates* mean to him. I'm unconvinced he's right about what I am to him. I spent a solid six months certain Tommy was my other half. We'd laugh at the same jokes, have the same interests, listen to the same music.

Yeah, I've met people who I've gelled with immediately or felt something low in my stomach from a single look. It doesn't mean anything. He's putting too much stock into a concept with no real basis.

"Word of advice," I rasp, tasting ash, sand, and salt in the back of my throat. If I'm dying anyway, I might as well give the monster a piece of my mind. "Fate's a bitch."

Ordus' eyes damn well nearly pop out of his head.

Fate got my dad killed before I could say goodbye. Fate took my mother before I could meet her. Fate made my rabbit die a week after I got it. Fate gave me appendicitis the day of my exam. It made me spill Ribena all over my cream prom dress. It caused a motorcyclist to ram into the back of my car and break his shoulder when he was a single parent of three. Fate gave my friend in eighth grade cancer, then let her live and took her mom instead.

Fate put me on Tommy's path, and now, Ordus'.

Fate is a downright wretched bitch, and I'm sick of being her victim.

I continue before he can respond. *"Vibes* don't equal compatibility. And you and me? We will never be compatible."

My subconscious seems to be taking the "gently break up with the kraken" approach, since nothing else seems to be working. It's not like it's a lie. How could we possibly work?

Size is one thing. I'm not made to live underwater is another. Oh, and let's not forget one tiny, itsy-bitsy matter. *He fucking kidnapped me.*

"In time," is all he says.

As if time is going to change any of the reasons I listed.

"You can't love a corpse." Either now, or in two days. I'm already dead.

"Love would surpass death." The atmosphere grows somber. "Our bodies would decay, but our souls will forever be one."

I'm not about to argue metaphysics with a mythical creature, so I don't reply. Clearly, I don't know a thing about how the world works. Sea Goddesses? Sirens? Actual, written in stone soulmates?

"What happens after death is none of my concern," I mumble. It will finally be over. I wouldn't have to run anymore or look over my shoulder.

My entire life feels like a lie, and I don't know if I can keep myself up above the water.

I'll probably meet Tommy in hell to kill him all over again.

There's a pregnant pause before Ordus says, "My kind buries our dead beneath stone so reef may grow from their physical body to allow for new life. Existence is a cycle. A fish feeds from coral so it may one day be food for a shark that will end up in the hands of a kraken that'll end up back feeding the coral so the fish can eat once more."

The golden light of the setting sun kisses his bronze and deep russet skin, illuminating the iridescent threads that glimmer in golds and blues more prominent along his tentacles. The white dots along his shoulders and brow area look like a smattering of pearls. Streams of silver and sea glass glitter in his cerulean irises as he stares at the horizon.

He might be a monster, but right now, he looks like a broken shell of a man. A pretty disaster.

"The soul sets each individual kraken, human, siren, bird apart," he continues. "It's what gives the body drive beyond food and shelter. Personality beyond natural instinct. Different patterns of a million threads no mortal being could deign to understand."

Ordus' voice is rough, yet smooth all the same. It's thick but glides over my bone-dry skin in a gentle caress. The deep, warm tenor threatens to put me to sleep. I rest my chin atop my knees, facing him, too tired to hold my weight.

As awful as my circumstance is, I like hearing him speak. It feels like a messed-up safety blanket.

"A mate is the soul's drive, two pieces of a puzzle designed to fit perfectly with the other. Once it meets, they become inseparable, braided and wound together. To tear them apart is to come undone." The weight of Ordus' attention falls onto me. "I cannot let you leave, Cindi. We will both surely die."

I avert my gaze. I don't believe him, but I don't think it's an outright lie either. For all I know, those could be rules that apply only to krakens. I doubt he knows much about the inner workings of humans if he thinks he can feed me raw fish and ask me to drink seawater.

My mind conjures memories of Dad.

For the first decade and a half of my life, we would have fish for dinner every eighth day in memory of the woman who gave birth to me. Apparently, Mom was horrendous at fishing. After years of trying, she finally caught one, then eight days later, she caught another. By a stroke of luck, another eight days rolls around, and a fish ends up caught on her line. She never managed to catch another fish after that, so it became their thing to eat fish every eight days. A little inside joke.

My father never cried. He didn't when he broke his arm, or when he fractured three bones in his hand. He didn't when my grandparents died, or when my uncle was diagnosed with cancer. But on those nights, every eight days, I'd see him shed a tear when he thought I wasn't looking.

He didn't believe in soulmates, but she was the sun, the moon, the stars, and every wave he'd ride. She was everything to him before I came along, and she was still, long after I took my first steps or rode a bike alone. Not once did I see him look at another woman or go on a single date after she died.

Dad loved me with every fiber of his being, gave me the world and then some, but there was always something missing. Mom.

A dry cough rattles through my lungs. I choke into my shoulder before rasping, "What makes you so certain I am your mate?"

A deep divot forms in Ordus' forehead. A tentacle curves around my lower half, staying on the ground, and I don't bother pushing it away. It feels nice. A cushioned chain. Bedazzled shackles.

His stare lands on the spot where our skin touches. He softens, eyes brightening like I've just given him the world. "As cubs, we are taught about souls and the Goddess' influence on them. I spent an entire lifetime thinking she forgot to grant me one, or that she may have started with mine but left too many fractures she did not want to bother fixing. When I saw you, that was the first time I felt my soul sing. I felt complete."

I shift my gaze, unable to look him in the eye. "I feel nothing."

Is that a lie? I'm not experiencing the full scale of hatred and loathing someone in my position, with my background, should feel.

I'm sympathizing with him, thinking he's attractive. I even felt tingles between my legs last night when he took advantage of my vulnerabilities. Is that because of fate, or because I'm fucked in the head?

"You are human," Ordus answers, confirming my earlier assumptions. "Damaged." My eyes fly to him. *Excuse me?* "By the hands of another," he explains before I can lash out, even though he's correct. "Lost. Running. Alone." I'm not sure if he's talking about himself or me. "Do you feel your soul, Cindi?"

I... My throat bobs.

If I had one, there's nothing left of it. I got rid of it for the sake of keeping my heart beating. Is that why I don't feel the pull toward him, or am I entertaining the ramblings of a species different to my own?

The waves brush my feet, sending cool splatter up my thighs. I focus on it to keep myself from spiraling, reliving everything that happened over the past five years.

This would be a good surf spot. I'd have the whole beach to myself, decent waves, silence, an aquatic lifeguard.

My brows knit together as I watch Vasz bustle out of the sea, drop something on the beach, then hack up liquid like he's a typical dog who thought drinking saltwater was a good idea.

Fucking Vaseline.

We both watch as he picks up the round thing he dropped and coats it with his slobber before trotting over to us, tail wagging, ears flopping, paws pitter-pattering on the ground. He disregards Ordus, coming to a stop in front of me. The coconut thuds as it hits the sand, and he noses it toward me, growling when the waves move it back to him.

I blink at the green-yellow item. A *coconut*.

Wait.

I hesitate when I reach for it. "Is it for me?" I swing my gaze between the two creatures.

Vasz chuffs a noise that sounds eerily like "Duh."

I snatch the coconut off the ground before he can change his mind. I use more of my energy reserves to turn the fruit around to search for major cracks. There are holes from his teeth, but they haven't punctured very deep.

"The knife." For the first time today, a flutter of hope starts in my chest. "Get me the knife," I repeat to Ordus.

He leaves without question, saying something to Vasz in a language I don't understand. The shark-dog rolls his eyes then fixes his focus on me, tipping his head side to side. I study the fruit, praying to every god and goddess it's not filled with seawater.

I look around the beach for a solid surface and pull myself onto my feet to stumble for it. I'm panting from the minute walk it takes to reach the stone.

Ordus returns soon after, handing me the weapon with no care that I might use it to kill him. I stare at the blade for a moment. It's different to the one I stabbed him with.

Grabbing a fistful of my dress, I clean it as best as I can. I'll just need to accept that food poisoning is my other greatest threat.

Taking a deep breath, I balance the coconut on the stone and raise the knife above my head. *Here goes nothing.* I use the force of gravity to plunge the blade into the upper half of the fruit before taking it out.

Liquid sputters and spurts from the gap, foaming around where the thin hole is. I repeat the process three more times, careful not to crack the husk. Each stab takes more energy than the last until I'm buckling over, my injured hand splayed out to hold my weight as a wave of lethargy hits me.

I can feel the two creatures watching me—a quick glance at Vasz tells me he thinks I'm committing sacrilege.

There are better ways to be doing this, but I don't trust myself not to fuck it up and waste any juice that might be inside.

I rock back on my heels, inspecting the banged-up square I've made, wedging the pointed edge to dislodge the lid so I can peek inside. It smells like coconut and the sea, and I can't for the life of me figure out if the liquid inside will kill me or not. I don't know jack shit about what the inside is meant to look like. I only know what it looks like in a can, plastic bottle, or a glass mixed with rum and pineapple.

Giving up, I bring it to my mouth without hesitation, ignoring the fact that I swear I can taste Vasz's slobber. The first drop of liquid hits my tongue, and my eyes drift shut. Sweetness explodes over my taste buds. It trickles down the back of my throat. A moan builds deep in my chest, and I'm out of fucks to stop it.

I might as well be drinking the elixir of the gods.

It's the best thing I've ever had.

I can't think about pacing myself. I drink every last drop, tipping my head back and shaking the coconut until nothing else comes out.

I grab the knife and chop the top off with renewed energy, scraping the flesh before I put that baby right into my mouth, nibbling at the meat I've never dared to eat before. I try stripping the skin off instead to savor all I can.

By the time I'm done, the sun has fallen beneath the horizon, and I learn what a shark-dog looks like when he's mortified.

"Good boy," I say without thinking, patting his head.

My stomach is full, my throat doesn't feel like sandpaper, and I think I could cry from such a simple joy.

I scratch the back of his ear, muttering, "Good job, Coco. You're so good. You're such a good boy."

His eyes light up, and his tongue lolls to the side like he's in heaven.

"Coco? Yeah? That's a better name for you, huh?" I coo. "Can you get me more coconuts?" Hope is alight in my tone.

He yips and runs back into the water, faster than I've seen him move.

Maybe I won't die after all, and it might all be because of a shark-dog named after petroleum jelly.

16

Vasz

I am brave. I am strong. I am fearless.

I have traveled across the sea in search of the most special coconut for my queen. A coconut worthy for my mate—whatever that is. Ordus keeps using the word. I assume that's what human females are called.

She tasked me, and only me, because I am the best soldier in her arsenal. A *good* shark-doggopus.

I have not rested for eight days. I feel the exhaustion in my bones. My queen needs me.

I am a good boy. The *best* boy. She said so.

The stone door rolls to the side, and I swim with all my might, keeping the...twelve coconuts in my mouth, careful not to bite too hard so my queen can—I don't know what the human did to it. It looked wrong, dangerous, to defile such a beautiful thing in a horrifically gruesome matter. The love of my life was being tortured right before my eyes, and I could do nothing but sit and watch. It was agonizing.

Still, I live to serve. Cindi bestowed upon me a coconut the night she arrived. I gave one to her in return. It was a fair trade. But her words... They spoke to me.

Yes, I am a good boy.

A *very* good boy.

It's about time someone acknowledged it.

Bubbles curl around me as I breathe hard, pushing myself through the tunnel. I break past the surface of the water to find Cindi leaning against the wall with Ordus—a very, very *bad* kraken—nearby.

"Mine," I pant around the coconut, dragging my feet over to her.

"No, *not* yours," the stupid, loud, ungrateful beast growls. *"Mine."*

"Be nice," she snaps at Ordus, and I give him a smug grin. "What have you got there, buddy?" Cindi rocks forward onto her knees.

Buddy. Me. *Her buddy.*

A sick thrill ripples down my spine. I am her bestest, most loyal buddy.

I drop the coconut at her feet. "My Queen Mate is fierce," I heave, collapsing onto my side in front of her, tongue lolling out of my mouth.

"You don't even call me king," Ordus complains. "And she *isn't* your mate."

"Silence, peasant. The Queen is—" Stars explode behind my eyes when her small human hand rubs my belly. My back leg kicks out and starts sprinting without me meaning to.

"Good boy," she praises.

I did good. I did *very* good.

Cindi asked for coconut. I brought her coconut.

Now, she is rewarding me.

This is how I should've always been treated. The stupid pest of a creature needs to learn from my human.

"Vasz, come here," Ordus growls.

"No, not Vasz." I stretch my shoulders out, rolling onto my back to give her more belly surface to rub. "I am Coco now."

Ordus huffs. "You wanted to eat her two days ago."

Cindi snatches her hand away. *"What?"*

Oh yeah. I flop onto my stomach. What part should I take a little nibble of? Foot? Arm? Maybe fingers as a little snack so I can save the rest for later?

Mmmm. No. Maybe the hand.

I open my mouth and jolt back when she hits me on the head. "No. Stop it. Bad dog."

Bad...?

I whimper. "But...but I'm a good boy."

She *told* me I am.

"Yes, Cindi." Ordus glares at me all smug and dumb. "Vasz is a bad dog."

The betrayal strikes me through the heart.

New plan: must eat Ordus.

17

My skin is only getting paler. Dryer. My body weaker. The pounding in my head is worse. I can barely keep my eyes open. The only thing I'm capable of is sleeping.

I shouldn't have spent so long in the sun yesterday. Sweating and burning has made it worse.

Ordus keeps trying to bait a reaction out of me, probably thinking it'll keep me alive. All I can muster is a faint mumble before turning over, clutching my stomach, and letting my eyes drift shut.

There's only one thing I've asked for: to be taken back to the mainland.

The two coconuts I've had since being here have only worked to prolong the inevitable.

Ordus' selfishness will kill me, and I think he's starting to realize that. In the short moments of consciousness, I can feel his frantic energy as he moves around the cave, trying to get me to eat or drink things that will only make me worse. I'm cradled in his limbs more often than not and have woken up to gentle poking and prodding more times than I can count.

I jar awake when cool water engulfs my body. I whimper from the shock, curling up against Ordus' warm, hard torso. Peeling my heavy lids open, all I can make out is the glowing algae and Vasz watching me from his corner.

"Shh, Cindi. I have you," he whispers, lowering us into the pool.

My head is plunged beneath the water's surface. Oxygen slams back into my lungs before I can panic. The giant air bubble is the last thing I see before I succumb to sleep again, drifting in and out of consciousness, waking only when a gust of wind slams into my face. I sputter a cough, shivering against a warm body as I force my eyes to open against the weight of exhaustion. I can't feel my fingers and toes.

How long was I out for?

Water crashes against my face. I gasp, swallowing saltwater and whimpering, squeezing my eyes shut against the harsh moonlight.

A roaring sounds in my ear.

Is that my pulse?

I force my eyes open again.

Not my pulse. A beach. It looks familiar, but I can't pinpoint from where. I can barely think beyond the stabbing pain in my head.

I blink, and the sea shifts to sand.

Blink, and it's dirt.

Another, and palm leaves hang overhead.

Once more, and suddenly, there's a beeping sound.

I groan, twisting my head to the side. Someone says something, but I can't make out their words. The world turns, and a ringing noise starts in my ears from trying to make sense of my surroundings in the darkness.

Tile floors. A dismantled battery generator on the coffee

table. Laundry on the couch. Dishes on the kitchen bench. A screwdriver and a bottle of glue beside an upside-down chair. Pliers above the microwave, next to a container full of different pills. A rug with one corner burned. The unplugged speakers around the TV.

Ordus brought me back.

I'm so happy, I could cry.

Adrenaline surges through my veins, filling me with energy I haven't had in however long. I point to the fridge, mouth refusing to work.

The world spins and sways as he rushes over to it. I wriggle in his grip, wordlessly ordering him to set me down. He keeps saying things I can't make sense of, but eventually, he relents, keeping me upright with tentacles wrapped around my body. I fumble for the fridge door. It takes three tries to get it open, and I don't think it was me who did it.

The blast of cold air pushes me closer to consciousness. The only reason I don't surge for the big bottle of *Pocari Sweat* is because Ordus changes my movements to a gentle reach by manipulating my body.

I grip the cap with my trembling hands, struggling to get it open. When Ordus takes it from me, I whimper, desperate to do anything for even a drop.

As soon as he hands it to me, I bring it to my lips and greedily gulp the sweet beverage without regard to the cramps piercing my stomach. Liquid streams from the corners of my lips down to my collarbones, mixing in with the saltwater trickling from my matted hair.

I don't stop until I'm sputtering on the floor, coughing up a storm that rattles my bones. The bottle clatters across the kitchen as I heave for breath. Dark spots swim in my vision, fatigue sinking into my marrow.

More.

That can't possibly be enough to replenish me.

I scramble through the fridge for another bottle of anything with electrolytes. I only manage two more gulps before I'm hacking it up on the tile like Vasz does when he chases the waves.

I'm distantly aware of the hand caressing my back. For a second, it belongs to Tommy, not the ten-foot monster who had me trapped on an island in the middle of nowhere. But the instant the thought takes hold, that purr starts up, deep in Ordus' chest, that has my body relaxing for reasons I can't begin to explain.

This time, when I move, I'm not buzzing with frantic energy. I grab the leftover *nasi goreng* and *sate ayam* and spoon the rice and chicken combo into my mouth with my pruning fingers. My stomach growls at the fifth mouthful, and I lurch to the side, feeling everything I've consumed rush up my chest.

Fuck, maybe I should have gone easy.

I pant as I keel onto my side to lean against the kitchen cupboard. My eyes drift shut in my concentration to keep the contents of my stomach on the inside of my body. Carbs, protein, and electrolytes. Surely, that's what doctors recommend. It's the best I've got, since I doubt Ordus will be escorting me to a hospital to get IV'd anytime soon.

When I finally have the energy to reopen my eyes, morning light streams through the slits of boards on the other side of my bedroom window.

My brows furrow. How did I get in here?

How long was I asleep?

I groan as I push myself up on the mattress. The pounding in my head isn't as bad, but it's still there, a constant irritant that makes the light stab into my eyes like I'm being lobotomized.

The room is the same haphazard mess I left it in; a suitcase ready to go next to my emergency "fuck-off" bag. The newest addition to my place is the sprawling tentacles between me and my escape, plus a shark-dog rolling around my rug with a coconut husk in his mouth.

I won't delude myself into thinking I'll be able to outrun him. I couldn't at full capacity, and I sure as shit can't when the grim reaper is picking his nails, waiting for me to kick the bucket.

Now, I somehow need to convince a literal monster staying here is a good idea.

The soft cotton sheets feel wrong against my dry, grimy skin. Every inhale is sandpaper against my dry throat. I need water. Hell, a coffee would make me worse, but I would kill for one.

The bed creaks when I move, and both creatures whip their heads my way. Ordus is up and on his feet—*tentacles* the moment his eyes land on me.

His eyes are crinkled at the edges, looking at me with enough concern to hit me in my windpipe. All over again, I'm wishing I could hate him for all this, wish I could forget the way he touched me so gently, how he sometimes softens from the mere sound of my voice. He brought me more fish and a couple different crabs, spouting something about how one of them might be right for me, and then he holds my bad arm and massages the tense muscles.

He's lonely. He didn't need to say it for me to see it when his sheer desperation for me to show him even an ounce of positive attention oozes from his pores. His eyes brighten with a flicker of *something* every time I look at him. I don't miss the barest curve of his lips every time I let his tentacle wrap around me.

Also, it's not an excuse, but I don't think he knows any better.

I can't entirely fault him for not being familiar with how another species feeds, but I'd expect some level of research first before taking one prisoner.

I won't thank him for bringing me here when he's the reason I'm like this to begin with. If you thank people for the bare minimum, you'll teach them mediocrity is the standard.

I suppose this means he will do whatever it takes to keep me alive, but being alive and comfortable are two separate things.

"Cindi, are you well?" Ordus' voice is smooth yet pinched, like he's holding himself back from doing his own check.

"A million bucks," I murmur.

He tips his head to the side.

Yeah. You don't understand the reference. Got it.

I shift to the edge of the bed and take a deep breath before pushing myself up to my feet. Fatigue hits me like a bad case of vertigo, combined with a mushroom cloud exploding somewhere behind my eyes, and I drop back down.

I've felt like shit before, but this well and truly takes the cake. It's as bad as when me and a couple of friends decided to finish a bottle of absinthe between the three of us back in college. I thought I was going to see God.

Ordus could've brought me back to the island while I was unconscious. Why didn't he? I'm weak. I wouldn't have been able to fight him.

Curling onto my side on the bed, I watch Ordus from beneath my heavy lids. One of his tentacles—it's always the same one—snakes around my leg, always so gently, pulsing and warming like it's trying to comfort me. He inhales deeply, tension unwinding from his shoulders as he closes the distance.

I guess at some point during the past however many days, my subconscious realized tentacles don't need to hurt, and despite the dehydration and hunger, his intention isn't to hurt me. He truly believes I'm his soulmate.

I hate that my broken shards have splintered too many times until there is no longer any part of me I recognize.

I hate that his hands don't hurt, because then it would make it easier to hate him.

I won't lie and say being looked at like I'm a being of the divine isn't a...nice experience. Maybe under different circumstances, in another life, *maybe*.

But what if...what if we really are soulmates? Would it be so bad to be with a kraken like Ordus? I mean, the physical attraction is there. He's somewhat amusing, I guess, if not bewildering or maddening. And—

No, I can't think that. I didn't get out of one cage to end up in another.

"I need more water," I croak, standing back up and shuffling past him, his tentacle still awkwardly hanging on to me. It feels more like intimacy than shackles.

The fridge door squeals, and the motor rumbles to life when I slump onto the floor and pull it open. I stall with my fingers on a plastic bottle. Where's the high-pitched whirring gone?

The contents of the little *Yakult* bottle are in my mouth before I form another thought, followed by the satisfying *crick* of the *You•C1000* bottle cap before the carbonated vitamin drink is bubbling down my throat.

If I can't get an IV drip in me, grocery store probiotics and vitamins are going to have to do. This time, I pace myself by drinking a few sips of milk, *Teh Botol* for the sugar, and plain ol' water. I manage little spoonfuls of fried rice and chicken in between, careful not to get to the point where I throw up.

Ordus studies the contents of the fridge like memorizing every bottle I pick up and bring to my lips and the cans I steered clear of. A dip forms between his brows when I use a pump on the Aqua water gallon sitting on a plastic stool.

I manage to find my last little jar of chicken essence and brace for the worst. I crack it open, pinch my nose, and swig it back. The putrid taste makes me gag; I have to wash it down with more tea. Most of my childhood trauma comes down to Dad pressuring me into drinking the alternative medicine whenever I got sick. He swore by it—always preached something about how it's all the vitamins and nutrients from a chicken or whatever.

But Christ, he really was onto something. It's always given me an energy boost.

I feel Ordus watching me, always a couple of feet away, still as a statue, like it might make him appear less imposing, or he's scared I might freak.

Leaning my head back against the cupboard, I try to even out my breaths. My sights land on the power generator on the coffee table, the one I've been meaning to fix for weeks. It's been put back together, the red light flashing. It wouldn't turn on a week ago.

And the fridge… It stopped making that weird sound.

I crane my neck toward the broken chair that was upside down on the floor last night. It's fixed, now upright, leg in the correct place, perfectly angled with no uneven lift off the floor. The glue, wrench, and screwdriver sit on the table.

My eyes swing to Ordus, lips parted. He fixed them?

Why would he even bother? The gentle giant confuses me.

I reach above my head for the edge of the kitchen counter to haul myself up. A tentacle wraps around my waist and carefully raises me to my feet before I can attempt to do it on my own. He lingers there, coiled around me, brushing against the underside of my boobs, and I stop breathing.

My skin pebbles, and my cheeks heat for reasons unbeknownst to me.

That's a lie. I very much know.

The memory of the suckers around my nipple flashes like damn high beams, and I suck in a breath to forget about it, but it's too late. It's there. It's so vivid. So is the way his cock hardened, how his cum dripped on me.

That near-death lethargy creeps back up on me for entirely different reasons. I can barely get my body to comply with my demands to extract myself from the memory and the feel of his solid warmth around me.

Next comes the exhaustion, the crushing weight of months of running without pause, years of pain under pretty hands. His tentacles don't hurt. *He* doesn't hurt. I miss knowing what it feels like to endure the touch of another person without fear of leaving with bruises on my skin.

Ordus eases the rest of him over to me, curling his tentacles tighter as he crouches to avoid hitting the roof. Tentatively, he slowly holds a hand out to cup my jaw.

And I let him.

I don't know why I let him.

I can't even begin to explain why I lean into his touch, why my eyes drift shut to focus on the feel of his warm skin against mine. The tips of his claws scrape the edge of my jaw. A shiver goes down my spine, and not an unpleasant one.

Maybe it's the effects of dehydration. Maybe it's the weight of history.

He's a beast of a man. I've watched him kill three people in under a minute. He crushed their skulls, ripped apart their limbs, made them bleed for what they did to me.

I still remember the cold panic on his face when he noticed the few cuts on my feet. The manic rage when someone hurt me. The unbridled jealousy when a guy approached me at the bar.

I'm not afraid of him. He won't intentionally harm me.

His expression is bewildering. I can't pinpoint it. It borders on awe and betrayal and something else entirely. Unease churns in me. My breath catches, waiting for him to make the first move. What if he decides to drag me back to the island? What if he thinks I've consumed enough, and he'll be giving me the bare minimum for survival from here on out?

Ordus never indicated he would do it, but it's not like I haven't missed signs before.

He breathes hard through his nose. "Are you mated already?"

A tremor works down my spine. "What?" How does he know about Tommy? Apart from the pictures of me and Dad, there shouldn't be anything in this house pointing to that demon.

His nostrils flare and his eyes darken. "A male was here."

A ma—? Fear sinks from my stomach down to my feet, twisting and churning. The food and drinks turn into bile.

"H-how do you know?" Dread seeps into my bloodstream like poison.

"I smell him."

No, no, no.

"Let go of me," I rasp.

Ordus hesitates. He must sense my panic, because he quickly releases me.

I scramble for my workroom in search of my laptop. It isn't here. Fuck. Where did I put it? I tip the laundry off the couch, then try my bedside tables before moving to my go bags.

It's not there. Neither are my passports.

He's found me. Tommy's found me.

Fuck.

I rip open the curtains. Where the hell is the car?

My feet thud against the tile as I scramble outside. Why are the wheels missing from my bike?

My phone. I need to check my phone.

I tear the house apart, emptying out my bags, turning over furniture, checking pockets. *Where the fuck is my phone?*

My eyes dart up to the cameras hidden around the room. Undisturbed. Without my phone or laptop, I have no way of knowing who broke in—but they would've been scrubbed the second the timer went off, and I didn't type in the disarm code.

Shit. Shit. Shit. What should I do?

Was the door's alarm beeping before we got here, or did it only start when Ordus tried it?

What if it was Tommy's brother, John? He's the worst of the two. I've never seen a genuine smile on his wife. She always wore long sleeves to hide the bruises that would peek through if she raised her arms.

I don't know any of the pirates by name, but I've seen faces. What if it's one of them? I mean, if it were, they wouldn't be fucking with my head by only taking two items. My house would be empty or destroyed.

It wouldn't have been some random person either—who came for my tires and personal electronics, but left the TV and wallet sitting on my bedside table?

I tip over the mattress. Nothing. It's a small place. There's nowhere else it could be. I scrub a hand down my face, ignoring Ordus' calls, the wedge driving deeper into my soul as I feel the phantom pains from the horrors the Gallaghers would rain down on me.

But right now, there's only one thing standing between me, the Gallaghers, and freedom.

I zero in on the gun lying on the floor. I could shoot Ordus and get out of here, finally be free of him and this whole *mate* bullshit.

But I hesitate.

I stare at the weapon, imagining its weight in my hands as I aim for his head. I feel my finger press against the trigger, the recoil rippling up my arms.

I can't do it. *Why can't I do it?*

I can't bring myself to grab the gun and put a bullet through the monster's skull. The thought alone makes my chest constrict.

A cry tears when I'm swept off my feet and spun to face a hard, bare chest. And it's like a dam burst. I couldn't stop myself even if I tried. I kick and shriek, sink my nails into anything I can reach. He keeps saying my name. The wrong one. Or is it the right one? *Cindi.*

Every time I blink, there's a different person holding me.

Tommy.

Ordus.

Tommy.

John.

My arms become plastered to my sides. I throw every ounce

of my power into throwing them off, but each failed attempt sends my panic rocketing to new heights.

"You can't take me!" I'd rather die than go back.

"Cindi," Ordus repeats. Puckering tentacles tighten around me.

Tentacles.

Ordus. Not Tommy. *Ordus.*

Even though my body is stiff, battling with all my might, he easily contorts me to his whim, cradling me against his chest so I have no choice but to feel the vibrations of his purr against my cheek. My lungs expand with my sharp inhales. His sea breeze scent washes over me. The sounds coming from him hit like a bucket of warm water, drenching my coiled muscles, dampening my twisted sobs.

His large hands are firm around my back, keeping me steady in place. Suckers pulse where our skin touches. The same misbehaving tentacle travels up and down my body in a soothing caress. A storm cloud drifts into my mind that turns my thoughts into fuzzy static.

Adrenaline ebbs out of me, dwindling my fight with each minute until I'm nothing more than a pile of sweat, bone, and tears in the arms of a monster.

A monster who has done nothing but try to take care of me in his own twisted way. Trying to feed me. Fussing over the wounds on my feet that have healed over. Putting a paste on my sunburned skin when I was sleeping. Using his limbs as cushioning against the hard rock.

"Cindi, tell me what is wrong."

I blink my bleary eyes up at him, expecting to be seared by his rage. I never dared have any kind of meltdown in front of Tommy. The only time I did was when Dad died, and I vaguely remembered the flash of white teeth as he curled his lips before leaving me on the floor to "sort out my own mess."

Tears trickle freely down my cheek. The signs were there.

Why did I ignore them? How did I completely miss all the red flags when I was raised surrounded by green? I'll never understand.

"What..." I start, scrambling to disperse the wool from my brain to get my shit together and come up with some kind of plan. "What do you smell?"

Ordus' nostrils flare. The tips of his canines catch the glint of the afternoon sun. "A male. The scent is old." He works his jaw. He appears so human when he does this, even with the gills and the webbed ears. "Who is it?"

Tommy's name catches in my throat, but saying it makes it true. "I can't stay here. I need to leave the country." I don't want to, but what choice do I have? They'll follow me to the ends of the Earth. I just have to keep running. "They've found me."

"Who is after you?" he repeats, ocean-blue eyes intent, bordering on obsessive. The rumble in his voice betrays him—a tidal wave stews beneath the surface, intent on destroying everything in its path.

A foreign warmth unfurls low in my core. It's strange, having someone's rage directed at something other than me. *For me.* With me.

But it's not enough, and I'm not selfish enough to drag him into my mess.

"It doesn't matter who. You need to let me go," I plead, imagining what people would do to him. He isn't human. I'm sure the Gallaghers would sell him to someone to be tested and experimented on. They would break him until he's barely even a shell.

I can't let that happen. I won't. I may not know Ordus very well, and he may be my jailer, but he doesn't deserve that kind of fate. He isn't...he isn't evil.

"They have guns. The best-case scenario is, they kill you and do far worse to me."

"I can keep you safe. Trust me, mate."

"You can't." I shake my head, struggling in his grip. He can't possibly know that. "You can't help me. You can't save me." He carefully lowers me to my feet, keeping one tentacle firm around my waist. "I made the decision to marry him. I'm the one who decided to kill him instead of leaving without a trace. I made my bed; I need to lie in it. There's nothing you can do to help. I need to leave."

He doesn't respond, doesn't bother singing the same ol' tune he's been saying since the moment he captured me. He reaches behind him and passes me a waterproof bag I bought when I was delusional enough to think I could go kayaking. "Take everything you need. We will return to the island."

I jerk my head side to side. "That's not what I meant." He's not understanding me. This is serious.

Ordus holds the bag to the side. For the second time today, when he reaches for my face, I let him. I should be screaming, fighting, throwing everything I have into making him realize the magnitude of the threat. I shouldn't be seeking comfort from the creature who decided I'm his prisoner. I shouldn't let him touch me when I watched him kill three men in cold blood. I hate that weak, pathetic part of me that still doesn't have the strength to draw away from him.

I hate that my broken shards have splintered too many times so there is no longer any part of me that I recognize.

I hate that his hands don't hurt, because then it would make it easier to hate him.

"Plagues, humans, and krakens alike have tried killing me since the day I was born. You are my only purpose. I give you my word. No harm will reach you." He nudges the bag against my hand. "Take it and bring what you want, or I will choose for you."

I swipe the tears from my cheeks. "Stop telling me what to—"

He cuts me off, gripping my chin between his thumb and forefinger. "Cindi, listen to me. No one can reach you on the island. There is only you, me, and Vasz. Whoever it is you are running from will not reach you there. So take the bag and let me take care of you."

My gaze lands on the black sack.

I mean, he's right, isn't he? How will anyone know to look on an island in the middle of nowhere? No one would find me in the caves.

My plan was always to lay low in the middle of nowhere or hide out on one of the islands in Thailand. This isn't any different, is it?

No civilization. No cameras. Nothing to give away my location. Stowed away with a powerful creature intent on protecting me because he thinks I'm his divinely chosen soulmate.

There's nowhere on Earth safer for me than Ordus' island. It's the one place the Gallaghers will never touch.

I hesitate before placing my hand on the bag. "Okay."

18

CINDI

It took a total of seventeen hours to get from San Diego to Shanghai. I spent the thousand-and-twenty minutes shaking, thinking Tommy or his family would appear out of thin air and drag me back to the mansion.

I never saw a single Gallagher. Not when I found a place to stay, two cities over, or further north, when I was too scared to stay stagnant for another day. It wasn't until I saw Matthew—one of Tommy's friends—in the crowd while I was at the market.

Every day since the night I killed Tommy has felt much the same, paralyzed by fear and paranoia.

Except now.

For the first time in a year and half, I let myself simply *be*. I feel...safe, like I can finally take a breather from running and looking over my shoulder. Like there's someone else in my corner looking out for me.

I could get addicted to this.

Three bags rustle against the currents, oscillating and pulling against Ordus' powerful propulsions as air bubbles climb over the oxygen dome over my head. The nonperishables and food in wrappers are in the nylon bags strapped to his back. The waterproof one has the basic necessities.

My legs tremble around his waist from the hour we've already spent in the sea on the way back to the island. Pain lances my arm, from my shoulder all the way down to my fingers. My elbow throbs from the use, and the cold is making it even worse. The wetsuit isn't helping nearly as much as I want, and I don't want to admit how much I want Ordus' suckers to do that thing it does that makes my arm hurt less. Being carried bridal style isn't an option when he's holding a gallon of mineral water in each hand.

To add insult to injury, it feels like someone lit a fire on my tattoo, then took a grater to it. At least I feel the best I have in days—it was probably the chicken essence. I can hear Dad's "I told you so" from the grave.

Still, I feel sick to my stomach. What might have happened if Ordus never intervened? What would those guys have done to me the night of Nat's birthday? What if I decided not to run that day, and some man showed up at my house? I could have found out firsthand what is worse than death.

Silver lining? I have a *semblance* of a plan when it comes to preventing death by lack of food and water.

I packed some plastic containers to collect rainwater. I managed to find my old, barely functioning tablet to access the internet. Reddit suggested filtering seawater with a T-shirt, and in my nonprofessional opinion, it sounded like bullshit. If I'm desperate, I'll give a solar a go.

If all else fails, Ordus can swim to the mainland to get me another couple gallons of distilled water.

The crappy, lagging, jailbroken iPad also helped teach me how to start a fire so I can cook water and fish—shit, I forgot seasoning. Whatever. It doesn't matter. This is one long episode of

Survivor. I'm not about to fuss over the fact that I can't have sambal with crab.

But chances of me successfully starting said fire? Closer to zero percent than a hundred. I'm crossing my fingers the matches and lighter I packed stay dry.

A cramp goes through my whole body, and I bite back a whimper. I untuck myself from his neck to glance at the surroundings. Sunlight streams through the waves. Silver beams of light illuminate the surrounding blue.

Minutes pass. I stare over his shoulder, waiting for pops of color or evidence of sea life, but...nothing? Just trash floating around like water bottles, cigarette buds, straws, plastic, the occasional wreckage of what I can only assume came from a boat.

No fish. No reef. No evidence to suggest we're swimming though something other than a graveyard.

It continues for miles. It's like a wasteland—rocks, sand, the corpses of animals long dead.

Are these the side effects of global warming scientists warned us about? Where are we on the map? Are we going north through the Java Sea, where we'd eventually hit Borneo or Sulawesi—or the Philippines, if we're going through the Strait? Singapore if we're heading northwest.

Or south toward the Indian Ocean. Or southeast to Australia.

All I know is, the scenery doesn't change as we head further away from Bali, other than there being less and less trash the further away we get.

"What happened here?" I ask, more to myself than to Ordus. I can't hear much of the other side of the bubble, so consider me unnerved when the dome expands, and suddenly, another person's breathing fills the small space. I lurch back to put distance between our faces—as if I hadn't spent the past few hours leaning my head on his shoulder.

"My kingdom is now known as the Dead Lands," he says quietly, as if he doesn't want anyone to hear.

I'm sorry. Did he say *his* kingdom? The proper noun or whatever would be *our* pronoun—as in *us krakens'* kingdom, right? It's a slip of the tongue.

"Now? Has it always been so..." *Don't say dead.* "Barren?"

He shakes his head once, watching me closely from the corner of his eye. He's on edge, stiffening every so often, darting his gaze all around. It's putting *me* on edge.

What if Ordus isn't the biggest creature out there? I tighten my grip on him.

"My territory was booming with life fifty years ago. Game was ripe. There was coral of every color each way you looked."

My.

I swallow. "Global warming?"

His brows pinch in confusion. "A Curse," he says, like he isn't sure if they're the same thing.

The air in the dome grows frigid, but the water's temperature increases with the shifting landscape. It rises by at least ten degrees, rapidly ticking upward until it feels like I'm swimming through a hot pool in my wetsuit.

Worse is the scene below. The sand changes from grey to pitch-black, broken only by the protruding white bones.

The energy feels all sorts of wrong. The atmosphere is staticky, cloying, like stepping into an abandoned hospital, or standing alone in a forest when all the insects have got silent.

Ordus stops us before it reaches jacuzzi level. I slowly pry myself away from him. The reprieve of moving my aching limbs is instantaneous. One of his tentacles helps me turn to survey the area, still close enough to him that the air dome remains around us.

In the distance, a single boat lies on a pile of animal corpses. It looks like one of those traditional Balinese fishing boats, the old-timey ones that often find their way to the bottom of the ocean, except this one has more color and parts.

Dad's buddy Marcus would take us out on his boat every

summer to go fishing or tubing with his two kids. When I was nineteen, Dad, Marcus, and a couple of their other friends took us snorkeling at Wreck Alley.

Majority of us were way too beginner to check out the Ruby E, but Dad's biker friend Saul had been snorkeling since birth and showed us the pictures he took after he went down.

The Ruby E looks nothing like the fishing boat in front of us. The photos showed the deck and hull covered in pinks, yellows, and greens from algae, every inch of surface left exposed to the unforgiving elements.

This boat isn't blanketed in moss. Streams of green aren't floating off it or winding around the lines. The lines of blues and reds painted on the bow and hull look like they could've been done in the past year. It isn't rusted either.

If I didn't know any better, I'd say the boat just went down in the past day.

"What is this place?" I whisper. It doesn't feel right to talk here.

Sensing my unease, Ordus draws me closer to him. I shouldn't be breathing a little easier with him near, but nothing about this place is natural.

"Fifty years ago, a kraken killed the daughter of a sailor." His voice is low. I watch him over my shoulder, listening intently. "He stole her from the ship and killed her before swimming away."

My lips part as I shift my attention back to the boat. Are there dead people in there? I instinctually move closer to Ordus.

"My mother, the queen—" His mother, the *queen*? Excuse me? "—wasn't aware of what he had done until that very vessel returned a month later, bringing with it the woman's mother. A witch. An incredibly powerful one."

Witches. Queens. Krakens. I clench my jaw and silently urge him to continue.

"And so started the Witch's tirade for revenge. She didn't care who the offending kraken was. In her eyes, all kraken-kind was complicit, all suffering for the crimes of one. She sacrificed her crew, used the energy from their souls to kill my mother and cast a Curse over our territory for all plants to wither and die so krakens will starve to death or succumb to the Waste," he says, like he's repeating a story out of a kid's book, not something he's lived through.

I stare at the boat. His story makes sense. In a way.

It justifies the miles upon miles of desert land we passed. It explains this eerie place, the lack of vegetation on Ordus' island.

I believe him.

"My sister was agile." There's the first inflection in his tone, a dip that says this isn't just a story for him. "She snapped the Witch's neck, but it was too late. The damage was done. My mother was dead, and our territory cursed. It is why..." He clears his throat. "Why my kingdom is known as the Dead Lands."

I'm not sure whether I'm more shocked by the fact that one witch could cause this much destruction, or that Ordus is a fucking *king*.

"Forever?" I whisper, turning back to face him. The Earth is already screwed because of human greed. I'm no scientist, but I'm fairly certain the last thing our world needs is for part of the sea to be uninhabitable for all forms of life.

The full weight of his attention falls on me. "No. The Curse can be lifted."

Ordus' tentacle squeezes my waist. The blues of his irises have darkened into thunderclouds, the glint of sunlight in them a thunderbolt. The intensity makes me suck in a sharp breath, wanting to turn back around to avoid seeing his gaze.

I wet my dry lips. "How?" Something tells me I don't want to know.

"By the ruler marrying their destined bride."

His words slam into me, heavy and suffocating. *Me.*

I'm his so-called mate. How much more *destined* can it get?

"My brother and sister both married krakens their souls didn't call to. The Curse remained."

The dome is running out of oxygen. I don't think I can breathe.

Me? Save kraken-kind?

No. *No.* That's not me. He's got the wrong person.

Being his mate is hard enough to wrap my head around. Having the fate of his species rest on my shoulders? The same shoulder that was dislocated the one time I tried protecting myself from Tommy? The same person who jumps at her own goddamn shadow? I don't think so.

Wait. So this is the real reason why he wants me? Not because I'm his mate, but out of moral obligation to protect his people? That stings more than I care to admit.

Does that mean he will force me to… Panic roars in my veins.

His eyes round in alarm. "The bride must be willing," Ordus quickly adds.

"I'm not willing," I seethe. Like fuck am I getting married again. Been there, done that. Got the T-shirt and bruises to prove it.

I expect Ordus to argue or go on about how he'll protect me and blah, blah, blah. His reaction surprises me instead. "I know." Nodding solemnly, he says, "I want anything you are willing to give. Even if it's nothing, I will spend the rest of my life eternally grateful for the chance to be in your presence."

Heat blossoms in my chest. Why couldn't he say something that would piss me off? When he's all nice and somber, it's hard for me to villainize him.

I break eye contact and wrap my arms around his neck to resume the position we were in before we stopped. "I want to leave."

He says nothing. Neither do I. I can tell he doesn't miss I never said I wanted to return to my cabin, because there's something easy about the way he moves.

The grating silence stretches well beyond the site of the casting. The tension is palpable. He shrunk the dome back down so it's large enough for me to stew alone in my turmoil.

The right thing to do would be to give him my hand and let him pop a ring on it. But one, who says he's telling the truth about this whole thing? And two, I'm not going to do something just because a man wants it. I need to put myself first.

A few more hours roll by before the landscape shifts, more rock than sand. A dark wall looms ahead, spreading as far as the eye can see, reaching toward the heavens. A field of promised death borders the island. Rugged chunks of spear-shaped stone with sharpened tips protrude from the ground. A single wave would send a human crashing into it. I can't imagine how horrifying it would look at night or during a storm.

Suppressing a shudder, I tighten my weak grasp around Ordus. At some point, he shifted one of the gallons to his tentacles to keep me upright with his free hand after noticing my slipping grip.

He rubs slow circles over my back, and I glare over his shoulder. It feels nice. I hate that it feels nice. Nothing Ordus does should *feel nice*, but it does. Too much does.

The stray tentacle that always seems to seek me out feels nice.

The suckers feel nice—especially when they start plucking.

The way his claws brush against my cheek as he tucks a loose strand of hair behind my ear feels nice.

The approaching wall of rock snags all my attention. The gargantuan, round stone stands out against the expanse of sharp edges. It looks like the "he rose on the third day" type of tomb, minus the sentries. Some type of inscription has been engraved into the eroded surface of the wall and door. I gape when the sigils glow piercing blue before the stone painstakingly rolls to the side with an earth-rumbling groan.

Ordus tucks me closer to him, and I let him. He dives into the tunnel, slowly navigating the pitch-black darkness with what feels like ease. I use whatever energy I have left to force my muscles to comply and keep my limbs as close to his body as possible—which is nice too.

When was the last time I had my legs wrapped around someone, and they happily held me back? Nathan Chen when I first started university? He was an on-again, off-again biology major whose interest in me was purely physical, which was fine by me because I wanted the touch of another person.

Thomas Gallagher was never the cuddly type. I had foolishly assumed his way of showing me he cared about me was through gifts and quality time. In hindsight, he was only buying my freedom.

Blue light filters through the darkness, and I blink against the first pass of the glowing algae. We're plunged into darkness again before the light grows until it's near blinding.

The dome pops. Saltwater rushes into my mouth before I break past the surface, gasping for air. I swing my attention toward the sound of movement. Vasz perks up into a sitting position and patiently watches as Ordus lowers me to my feet.

My legs wobble from fatigue and overuse, and he catches me before my knees can slam against the hard ground. He sets me closer to Vasz, deposits my things against another wall, gives me a swift, "I will return soon. Stay," and he's off, leaving me in my jail cell for the indeterminate future.

I blink at the space he once occupied. Before I can begin to question where he's going in such a rush, Vasz nudges my shoulder then stares down at the coconut skin he's dropped beside me. His eyes flick between me and the fruit.

"Thank you," I say, cautiously patting his head. "Keep it." I sigh, pushing the coconut back to him. "You deserve it."

Silver lining? I've always wanted a dog.

19

ORDUS

"Please," the human begs, throat bobbing against my hand.

I believe it might be his third time saying that word. Or the fifth. I'm unsure. I was distracted again.

Leaving her behind on the island makes me nauseous, but I'm comforted by the fact that she isn't alone. Vasz is protective of what he deems as his. I'll allow him to view Cindi as his Queen Mate if it means he will play guard while I'm away.

I don't like it, but I will allow it—for now.

He's cheap labor. That mutt will do anything for a coconut husk.

"Is it money? Do you want money? I have money?" the tourist rambles.

No. I have money, should I need it. If I do not have any, I can just take it anyway.

I squeeze his throat and use a quarter of my power to slam him against the wall. His yellow hair falls over his face as he grips my arm in panic.

As I left the island, I didn't have a set plan as to *whom* my prey would be, only that they be in the right place at the right time for me to drag them behind a building enshrouded in darkness.

The tourist was the first convenient male.

He opens his mouth too much. And should bathe. And look into his oral health—teeth shouldn't be that yellow.

"I have questions," I say carefully. I'm in my human form, but anything I ask cannot give away that I am…not as I appear. Granted, I do not look like the average human either.

The male shakes his head frantically. "I don't know anything, man."

He's a human. So, yes, he does know.

"How do you make fish edible for your ki—*you*?" I correct myself, loosening my hold to allow him to speak.

"I… Is this a joke?" His brow line flattens. "Did Mitch put you up to this? Because if he did, you can tell him I'm kicking his ass and telling Chelsea he was chattin' up a hooker last night." He forces a chuckle.

"*Answer.*" My patience is waning.

"Seriously?" He chokes when I retighten my grip. Humans are so annoying. Not my Cindi, though. Well—no. She's perfect. "What the fuck is this? It ain't funny, man."

I want to kill him. It would take me less than two seconds. He wouldn't have time to see it coming.

Alas, I cannot kill the human yet. His brain still holds use.

For now.

"I will ask you one more time. *How do you make it?*" I'd like to learn for my mate, prove to her I can provide for her and any future cubs we may have.

"Okay, okay." He holds up his hand in surrender. "I cook it? I don't know. What do you want me to say?"

"How?" I growl. Does he take me for a fool?

"Are you—" I shake him. Have humans always been this difficult? "Okay, fuck, okay." He raises his hands, palms up again. "On —on a pan, or a skillet, or—or a grill."

What are they? "From the start. Step-by-step—"

His forehead wrinkles. Whatever useless thoughts filter through his head must be put aside, because he does as I command. "I—I mean like—" He swallows. "My pops would skin it, gut it, and give it to me sealed. I'd wash it, pat it down, drop some butter in a pan, throw some seasoning in, then add the fish. Fuck, I think that's it. I don't know, man. I can't cook for shit. Is that what you want to hear? Can I go now?"

This *pan* again?

"No. Show me." There are human establishments that serve food. I've tried looking, but there's no way for me to see how they do it without arousing suspicion or killing more people than necessary.

"Like—like a video?"

I nod. I've heard humans talk about *videos* before. It's not a word I have been able to translate into my language.

"Okay, okay. Yeah. A video. Yea—" He reaches into his pocket and holds his hands up to stop me from slamming him into the wall again. "Woah, woah, woah. I'm just taking my phone out. Chill."

Phone. A sound? Voice? What is that?

The tourist reaches into his pocket, and I frown. I do not understand how the small rectangular box helps. I've seen many, many humans hold something like that—more so recently. They sometimes hold it up to their ear or stick wires into it. I've never cared to look closer. Maybe Cindi has one of these *phone* things? Will she be happy if I give her one?

The male's hands shake as he taps the black box. Light suddenly flashes, and a still dog appears on it. A photo, I believe the humans call it. I've seen many on paper around the mainland. It is far superior to the paintings and art we have at the palace. It's like magic in the way it glows.

My eyes widen as the images on the box change with every flick of his fingers.

Maybe I will also get myself a...*phone*. It may be useful.

"YouTube good?"

I nod. I don't know what that is either.

I release his neck to stand beside him to better see this...*phone*. He taps on a square, then symbols appear on the screen.

I never learned how to read English, but Mother insisted we learn the native language of the humans on the mainland. Admittedly, it's been many years since I've attempted to read anything, and I'm finding it difficult to recall the phonetics for the tourist's language.

Several images of human food pop onto the box. He clicks on the one with a snapper, and the picture begins to move. A male's voice filters through the device.

Fascinating.

I will gift a phone to Cindi. My mate can watch the moving photos too, if she wishes.

My full concentration is on the device as the male talks through scraping off the scales of a fish, gutting it, then what they call *filleting* it.

"You do not like the bones?" I confirm with my prey.

"Uh...yeah?"

I nod. I understand. The scales are sharp, and the bones sometimes get stuck between my teeth. Cindi should never experience that.

I continue watching the human on the device clean the fish, then tap it dry. The male sprinkles salt and pepper—I will search for this—on both sides before pouring oil—I will add this to the list as well—on a flat silver item with curved sides.

Is that what that is called? A pan? Cindi packed something similar, except it had rounded edges that looked more like a bowl.

Now that I really think about it, I think I saw one in that shape but much smaller, in black. She was running around the house throwing things into bags, taking it out again, putting it back in, swapping it out for another item. I did my best to catalogue every item she was interested in bringing, but my efforts were mainly spent moving around to cushion her as she inevitably stumbled. I lost count of how many times she would've hit the edge of a table if my tentacle hadn't been there.

I'm curious to see how the fish tastes when it's prepared in such a way.

"That." I point at the metal thing the pan is on. The box goes weird when I touch it.

Wait. Yes.

The humans burn their food first. On fire. How did I forget?

I paid attention to where the humans were and where their attention was locked onto, but never much more than that.

I never cared to know how the humans lived beyond the trivial matters of where they congregate or the words coming out of their mouths. Had I known my mate would be human, I would've begun learning their customs years ago.

"A stove?" I do not appreciate the tourist's condescending tone. "Seriously, dude. Is this a prank? Are you high? Because I'm—"

"Get me one," I snarl. My incisors threaten to make an appearance.

"I don't live here. I don't know where—"

"*Now.*" No more excuses.

"Holy fuck. My Airbnb has one, okay? Is that fine? Just—just don't hurt me."

He speaks too much. "Take me there, and say nothing more."

I snatch the *phone*—interesting choice of word—from him and shove him back toward the main street. I follow closely behind as he lumbers along, casting frightened glances back at me. "Will there be other hu—males there?"

He shakes his head. "Will you—"

"No speaking."

I only like when Cindi speaks.

It isn't long until we're entering an older villa in a quieter neighborhood not far from Cindi's house. The male hands me the *stove* he mentioned. It's much smaller than the one in the video. There's only one of the places the fire comes from instead of six, but it's little and can be easily carried back to the island. It'll do.

The male shifts and slowly backs away. "Look, I don't want any trouble—"

I throw him across the room. He must hit his head in the process, because he doesn't move again. I revert my attention back to the stove.

Yes. Tomorrow, I will cook a fish for my mate.

Cindi is a hoarder, I have learned.

She has many of the same items—which I do not understand. She has over six pairs of shoes, just as many pants, over ten dresses, and at least twenty tops. One or two, I understand, but ten seems a lot.

I suppose this means humans change clothes many times. How often are they meant to do it? Will they get sick if they don't? Weren't the sailors I saw always wearing the same thing?

Krakens do not require such things, but the noble ones flaunt their wealth with jewels they've acquired. Some wear belts with pouches to carry more supplies, or necklaces made from the finest shells they've found.

Cindi has very little jewelry. No matter. I am a king. She has plenty to choose from.

My nostrils flare as I sort through the clothes on the floor. The male's lingering scent is faint. Vasz was unable to pinpoint his smell to track him. My mate says someone is after her. I need to change that. My stomach ached seeing her upset like that. I wanted to hold her and reassure her nothing will happen, but words mean nothing to Cindi. I have to prove it.

I stalk toward the open closet door once more. Did Cindi bring enough clothes for her to be comfortable on the island? She only had three bags. It couldn't have been sufficient.

I place the clothing in the hard-shelled rectangular item on the floor that opens like a grey clam with four little wheels at the bottom. Like a chest...except not. There were some items in it already, but I want my mate to have as many of her things as possible.

Content that Cindi will be sufficiently warm, I move to the cupboards beside her bed. One side has been emptied already; the other remains standing, drawers still intact. I cautiously pull the drawer out lest I break the contents inside it and upset my mate.

I stare at the bright blue object at the very top. I tip my head and frown, then tip my head to the other side. What is...

I pick up the rubber object. It's nearly as long as my hand, yet my finger doesn't reach my thumb at the base. Why does Cindi have a tentacle?

Cindi's scent is all over the house, lingering on every fabric. It's different now. Stronger, mustier, more... I inhale deeply.

My cock hardens, moisture immediately leaking from the tip. The tentacle smells of my mate's sweet sex.

Did she...she... Blood rushes from my head, and I sit on the edge of the bed, staring at the rubber tentacle that's similar in shape to my own. I breathe her in again, imagining her taking my appendage instead of a toy. The sounds she'd make. How her eyelids would flutter. How her full lips would pout.

My human mate is attracted to krakens.

The thought both thrills me and makes my hearts ache all the same. Clenching my jaw, I place the item in the clam-chest.

Attempting to dispel the thought from my mind, I move to the bathroom, where she has jars of potions along the shelves. Some are in plastic, some in glass. I've seen them in the human stores before, and I am unsure what purpose they serve. But if Cindi bought it, she must have use for them, no?

They go in the clam-chest as well.

As do the packets in the kitchen cupboards. The bottles of thick liquid. A large grey box she was tinkering with. The blankets on her bed. A cushion.

Once the chest is full, I heft one side of the clam over the other, and the zipper glides around the rectangular shell, shutting it tight so none of the items fall out. I lift it by the handle, pleasantly amused to find the wheels rolling along the floor.

Yes, I will keep the clam-chest. Cindi is a good procurer.

I jog down the steps to the dinghy I carried from the shore. I have to move the carved stone about arm injuries I took from the palace library aside to fit the clam-chest, placing it over the tools and other hardware I found in Cindi's workroom and kitchen. The pans and the bowl-like instruments go in next, as well as the big board and a tire—just in case. Then I cover it all with a bright blue plastic I found in the building beside the house that acts as a messier, dirtier workroom for my mate's land vessel. I strap it down with the rope I found there too.

With one last survey of Cindi's house for things she might want, I close the door behind me, waiting for the beep to indicate it's locked.

There's not a cloud in sight. The water was calm on the way here, and the only time I can use the boat is under the cover of night to not alert the humans of an unmanned vessel traveling across the sea.

With the slightest grunt, I haul the boat above my head to make for the beach, then set it out to undress from my mainland clothing once I hit the shore. I thread thick ropes through the hoops I fastened beneath the vessel and tie it across my chest so the two cords intersect over my sternum.

I wade into the water, tugging the boat behind me. Once the waves hit my stomach, I check no one is around to witness my shift and then grab hold of the magic to release my true form. I dive into the water, swimming as hard as I can, careful to stay close to the surface so the dinghy doesn't capsize.

I want the den to feel like home to Cindi, or else she'll spend the rest of her life seeing it as a prison, and me, her jailer. But it is the truth. There's no other way to put it. She didn't come back to the island with me because she wanted me.

She didn't choose me for me. She came because she had to. Because whoever it is she's scared of is worse than me.

I've had days to come to terms with the fact that I will always be the problem, but it isn't any easier to accept.

She wants to be on the mainland. She wants her cabin and her workshop and the loud music along the busy streets. I can't give her everything, but I can bring her house to her. I'll give her space, keep my mouth sealed shut, and watch her from afar, because my presence will only make matters worse.

My distance will be my gift to Cindi. She'll be happier if she forgets I'm there. I'll keep my silence—even if it eats me alive.

It's one of the only things I can do for her.

20

CINDI

Breathe. It's not Tommy.

My house is inside a cave. One minute, I'm asleep on a bed of moss—which isn't as comfortable as being all cocooned by Ordus —and the next, I awake to clattering in the main cavern.

I thought I'd find a brigade of Gallagher men with weapons trained on me while Tommy does his bloodcurdling, sadistic laugh. I imagine the gleeful pity in his eyes as he berates me for being caught. He'd hold up the knife I stabbed him with and promise to use it on me.

But none of those things happened. Apparently, I'm well and truly moving in.

My luggage is here, bedside table, bookshelf, more food, the car tire that has a slow leak, a couple plastic bags with stuff inside, tools, nuts and bolts, a stud finder near the pool, the cushion that was on my sofa, the sofa pillows themself.

The gun trembles in my hand as I drag my eyes over Ordus and the items.

Not Tommy.

I blow out a ragged breath and tuck the gun in the waistband of my shorts. "You brought me my things." It's obvious. There's no point saying it. But he's barely acknowledged my presence, and it feels—wrong, like I made a mistake somehow and I need to fix it.

Ordus gives me a sideways glance and grunts, using a single tentacle to suction onto a bookshelf and move it to a solid surface.

What I should be asking is how in the fuck he brought it all here without getting a single drop of water on it? And, follow-up question: why didn't I get the dry mode of transport option? I'm ashing up like a motherfucker from living life like a drenched sea rat.

Oh, right, and lastly, *why* are my things here?

But he still doesn't say anything, doesn't look at me. His shoulders are stiff, muscles bunched, vibrating with an emotion I can't pinpoint.

My anxiety spikes.

That's fine. It's fine. Ordus hasn't hit me or yelled at me. Just because he's giving me the cold shoulder doesn't mean anything. Sometimes, no attention is good attention. It means I'll be left to my own devices.

Or it means that whatever is wrong will fester.

"How did you get all of this here?" I settle on. Baby steps. We'll get to the bigger issues eventually.

My muscles scream with each incremental movement from yesterday's events.

"Boat."

And we couldn't have boated me around? I take a deep breath. Fine. Next question. "Why?"

He doesn't grace me with attention when he throws over his shoulder, "For our den." No further detail. No follow-up explanation. Just, *it is what it is.*

My hackles rise. What's gotten him in a mood? He stills and casts a careful glance my way as he very obviously lowers himself to the ground to make himself smaller. He can do that all he wants; the scowl betrays him.

The stone floors shift to eggshells, and the grey walls turn into the alabaster white of the mansion.

I dip my head on instinct to avoid furthering his...irritation? Anger? Disgust?

Averting my gaze to my water shoes, I shuffle to the opposite side of the cavern where my luggage is, always keeping my front facing him.

As if a couple yards is going to mean anything.

But this is Ordus. My supposed mate. A monster who is apparently the king of the Dead Lands.

He won't hurt me.

No matter how many times I tell myself that, I don't find myself relaxing as my stiff muscles tug at the zipper. The glowing algae casts a bluish light on the hardcase luggage I bought for ten bucks at the market. I grab the water bottle from inside and gulp the whole thing before reverting my attention back to the contents of the bag.

It takes me a second to process everything, but once I do, I almost burst out laughing, forgetting I'm meant to be frightened.

All my skincare is there. A paintbrush. Whiteboard marker. Sunglasses. My Bluetooth speakers. A fake Chanel handbag. The generator I was fixing. Multivitamins I opted not to bring. A raggedy hoodie that's three sizes too big. Tablecloth. The Bulbasaur squishy Nat gave me for some reason. Books. Measuring tape. A spare PopSocket. The tennis ball I use to help undo knots in my back. A scrunchie. My dil—

My cheeks burn bright red, and I quickly cover the dildo with one of my clothes.

"What is that?"

I yelp, clambering away. When did Ordus move so close? His

brows pull into a frown, and he moves into the kraken version of sitting on the other side of the luggage. The stray tentacle instantly reaches for me, and one of the other ones snatches it back before it makes it beyond the makeshift barrier between us.

"Nothing," I say quickly, cheeks heating. *No follow-up questions, please.*

"It is a tentacle." A hint of uncertainty trickles into his nonquestion.

I blanch white. "Yup."

He keeps glancing between me and the sleep shirt the blue dildo hides under. "What is it for?" His voice echoes against the cave walls.

Is he kidding me? "None of your business."

It's hard to be frightened of him when he seems so genuinely perplexed about the silicone, *uh*, appendage in my luggage.

The luggage he filled himself. Which means his large, thick hands have touched it.

I chastise my perverted brain, because the first thing that comes to mind is wondering which is bigger: the ten-foot monster's hand, or the *thing* that's been my only source of action in over a year.

Ugh. I've only used it like four times max. I just bought it about a month or two ago. I've been too unnerved about putting anything in me, and I figured if it didn't look remotely human, maybe that would trick my brain into being more receptive to—I don't know—reclaiming my sexuality, I guess.

And now, he knows about it—the creature those dildos are vaguely fashioned after.

I want to crawl into a hole and die.

"Are humans aware krakens exist?"

Wait. He seriously has no idea. Fuck, his mind is going to blow once he hears about hentai and the romance books I've been reading.

"No." I don't think so, at least. If America knew, I'm pretty sure they would have figured out how to drain the ocean and twist it to say they were protecting democracy by now.

Ordus nods at the luggage. "It smells like your sex." He says it so innocently.

Jesus H Christ.

"Too far. Boundaries," I snap. I'm burning up. I feel red from my hairline to my toes. "We are not talking about my—what's between my legs."

His gaze drops to the area in question, and I squirm. Wearing shorts wasn't a good idea.

That perplexes him even more. "I like what's between your legs. The human music on the beach always mentions the female—"

"Boundaries," I repeat.

This conversation is physically paining me. And because my mind is a traitorous bitch, she's decided to remind me how it felt to stretch around the base of the dildo, and she's taking it a step further by replacing blue silicone with Ordus' brown, spotted tentacle, the same stray tentacle fighting tooth and nail to break free from his hold to get to me.

By a stroke of pure weakness, I fall for the compulsion to look at his ocean blues, and I wish upon everything I never did. Stormy black has eaten every drop of clear seas, ready to devour me whole. They're heated and starved, a beast pulling on his last thread, ready to pounce.

His nostrils very obviously flare, and his eyes flicker to my thighs and back.

He—fuck, can he smell when I'm aroused?

My gaze darts to the tentacle leaking an iridescent liquid onto the stone floor. Try as I might, I can't help but squeeze my legs together. I'm telling myself it's to conserve the modesty I left dead alongside Tommy, but I'm well aware at a certain angle, the pressure from the seams of my shorts pushes *just right* and feels a little too good to be acceptable.

"Are you a witch?"

My jaw drops. *"What?"*

"You have potions like our healer," he says cautiously, nodding at the skincare products in my luggage.

I say a silent thank you to whoever is listening for getting Ordus to change the subject. I pick up the white dropper bottle. "This?" He tips his head in confirmation. "It's…"

Am I really about to explain my skincare routine to him? I suppose someone would've accused me of witchcraft for it two hundred years ago if they saw it.

"Niacinamide," I read out the label. "It's for, uh—" I don't remember. Someone recommended I use it, and I did. "Pigmentation. I think."

He looks at the other bottle at the top of the bag, a silent question.

This one, I know. "That's hyaluronic acid to hydrate your skin."

Tommy practically forced me to get beauty treatments— Botox, dermablading, LED therapy, IPL, facials, the works. Early on, if I ever refused or pushed back, he'd subtly compare me to the other Gallagher women. *They do it,* so I should. Lily's thirty-five with two kids, but she looks like she's in her early twenties. Olivia's on baby number three, and she's making sure she's on top of her figure.

Well, why would I be selfish and inconsiderate regarding my body when Tommy's the one who had to have me by his side at events?

Aren't I embarrassed? Don't I care? He's doing this for me, not him. It's because he loves me. He cares about me.

I grind my molars. *Fuck you, Tommy.*

"So the potion is like water on your skin?"

"I, uh, guess so?" I'm not about to explain the science about it. I couldn't if I tried. I could spend hours explaining to him what robots and aliens are, but I highly doubt he knows what they'd mean.

"What is this for?"

It takes me a second to get my bearings over Ordus changing the subject again. His attention is cast toward the bag, almost —regretful?

I don't let myself read into it. I follow the line of his pointer finger to the red satin scrunchie. Is he oblivious, or does he not visit land often? He must spend enough time around my kind if he knows our music, but somehow, he doesn't know we eat and drink different things? It's hard to wrap my head around.

He doesn't strike me as the people-watcher type. The Gallagher head of security was broody as hell and wouldn't talk much, but Nolan knew every detail about his surroundings. No one could drop a crumb without him noticing. You could tell he was the type from his eyes. They were always alert, cataloging everything.

Ordus is like that all the times we're in the water, except it's a different type of observation. Ordus is on the lookout for threats for survival, but Nolan watched for weaknesses to strike.

Tommy was kind of like that, except cockier. Most of the time, his arrogance outshone his conniving intelligence. Nolan's was always there. You knew the moment you looked at him that he'd taken a mental snapshot of you and done an entire analysis already.

But Ordus' eyes hold a heart-wrenching familiarity too. It's the same type of eyes my dad wore for most of my childhood, and later, whenever we had fish for dinner.

He lost someone he loved. If yesterday's conversation was any indication, he lost three. I've seen this island, searched this cave. Everything is bare, empty. I don't think he has anyone else, and something about that has all my defenses dropping.

My throat bobs as I pick the scrunchie up and pull my matted strands up into a messy bun. "A hair tie."

Gnawing on the inside of my cheek, I rock forward to fish out the other scrunchie I saw in here. It came in a pack of three: red, green, and blue. I pause before holding it out to him.

A peace offering. Maybe also an apology for stabbing him —*twice*—even though he seemed grateful for it.

Ordus' eyes bore into mine. He tentatively raises his hand like he's unsure whether he should. My gut sours. He's looking at me the same way I do when Tommy asks me to come closer, and I don't know if I'll walk away with a new bruise.

I don't like that Ordus is looking at me like that. It doesn't sit right with me.

I lean forward and pull the scrunchie onto his wrist. "For your hair."

His throat bobs as he stares at it like I've just given him the moon. The corners of his eyes crinkle, body utterly motionless, as he stares at the little green scrunchie around his thick wrist. Slowly, almost like he's afraid it'll disappear if he moves too quickly, he brushes his fingers over the fabric. In his distraction, the stray tentacle breaks free and joyrides straight to me, curling around my leg. Ordus shudders at the contact, and something innate settles in my soul.

He isn't going to hurt me.

"You can..." I start, wanting to break the pregnant silence. I feel like I'm going to choke from how heavily he's looking at the scrunchie. "You can braid your hair back if it, um, gets in the way."

What a stupid thing to say. What the fuck else would he use the hair tie for? I don't need to mansplain it when I did a demonstration not sixty seconds ago. He probably uses seaweed or something to keep his hair out of his face.

I'm pretty sure krakens have figured out their hair business, and I'm being a dick for running my mouth.

I twist my hands in my lap, waiting for him to say something.

Anything. Maybe resume whatever it was he was doing. This whole exchange has gotten weird.

With nothing better to do, I reach for a dress to begin folding my clothes.

"How?"

Huh? I flick my attention up to him and raise a questioning brow.

"I braid flax and seaweed into rope or a basket. Krakens do not..." He trails off like he's embarrassed, eyes lowering in dejection. "Krakens do not have hair."

My chest pinches at his tone. He's tense, as rigid as the stone walls around us. I'd get like that whenever I said something I knew might upset Tommy. It's not obvious. Someone like Nolan might notice the flicker of fear, but no one else would, not unless you've been in that position—like you're waiting for hurt.

"You have nice hair." I'm not sure why I say it. It just feels like I should. But it's true all the same. Ordus' hair looks like the smoothest silk, even though he's spent all his life in saltwater. Mine feels like a nest birds wouldn't dare go near.

His eyes dart up to me, disbelieving. He's braced for an attack. Hell, something in my chest shatters at that.

"May I?" I point to the scrunchie around his wrist.

His brows lower, and his lip twitches, like I'm trying to steal his toy. It's animalistic. Eventually, he relents, albeit extremely reluctantly. His muscles are bunched, movement sharp, acting like it physically pains him to give it back.

My legs protest and groan as I rise back onto my feet. It takes me a second to stop wobbling and straighten my legs completely, but I get there eventually. It's like I've ran a marathon twice over.

Ordus stalks my movements, tensing the nearer I get, so much so that even the tentacle around my ankle tightens. I swear he stops breathing when I settle behind him.

Why am I doing this? What if that was a manipulation tactic? He's pretending to be afraid so I lower my guard and—I don't know. Be an easier prisoner? Fight him less? I find that hard to believe.

I take a deep breath. Even sitting, the top of his head reaches the bottom of my chin. Steeling my spine, I use both hands to pull his hair behind his ears, onto his broad back.

He visibly shudders. I pause to study him. There's a slight bulb on his breeding arm, but it's not as thick or leaking as much as it was when we were talking about my dildo.

It's heady knowing such a simple act has goosebumps pebbling over his flesh. His skin itself seems to shiver—I'm not sure if that's the right word for it. The pores kind of flutter, changing his coloring to make the iridescent blues in his skin glow.

I pull his hair over his shoulders once more, and his skin ripples, rapidly changing between brown and blue. It continues as I comb my fingers through his hair. It's softer than anything I've ever felt—even smoother than silk.

What...what would it feel like against my cheek? His skin is already so soft and velvety. Everything about his appearance does things to me. Even the scar on his ribs has my heart pitter-pattering because it accentuates his rugged appeal and ups the fear factor at the same time it calms my senses that such a frightening, domineering being has become my protector—of sorts.

Unable to stop myself, I brush my fingers over the gills on his neck. He makes a sound close to a hiccupped groan that sends a line of fire down my spine. His responsiveness has me on a power trip.

Ordus' breaths are coming out strained, the tentacle around my ankle frozen. He's so tense, I'm afraid he might snap in half. I'm no kraken, and I swear I can smell his unease.

I'm not sure what compels me to take my time doing the best French braid I've ever done instead of parting his hair into three and getting it over and done with to release him of his misery, but I do. His breathing never evens out, though, slowly—so painfully slowly—his tentacle relaxes and pulses, warming my body from the inside out.

My hand and elbow are cramping like a bitch by the time I finally get down to his mid-rib. I finish off the braid with the scrunchie, then lower it over his shoulder so he can see my work. Retaking my position back on the floor in front of the luggage to busy myself with folding, I tell myself it's no big deal. I just braided his hair. It's stupid. It's whatever. His silence doesn't mean anything. I don't need to look at him.

But I do. I keep stealing glances at him holding the long braid in both of his hands. He's staring at it like I gave him not just the moon this time, but the sea and the stars, plus the clouds that bring reprieve on the hottest of days.

It has to be more than a minute before he finally looks at me. My cowardice takes hold, and I keep my gaze fixed on my work, folding and refolding just to keep from looking up at him.

The shelving is probably for my things, but I don't want to assume or get comfortable by unpacking my suitcase. This is temporary. It's just until I can come up with a plan on how to escape.

My nerves stutter when he rises to his normal height, but I don't dare look up until he says my name.

"I would like to show you something, Cindi."

Oxygen leaves me in a rush. He's stunning. His jaw is sharper with the hair off his face, the shadows of his cheeks more lethal. The gills on the side of his neck are more obvious now too, and it's weird how well they suit him.

The tentacle does an excited little tap on my knee when I stand on shaky legs. One of Ordus' limbs dips into the pool to scrape algae off the walls. Then he smears it over his shoulders and onto the piece of driftwood I was wielding the other night, handing it to me. I take the makeshift torch from him and follow the kraken into the pitch-black tunnel I tried escaping through on my first night.

"I will grow algae in here too," he says, more to himself than to me as he moves into the darkness.

The torch and his glowing shoulders offer a surprising amount of light that reflects off the mildew on the walls. My steps are still slow going, because the last thing I want is to trip again—which seems to be a possibility, even if the stray tentacle has moved its residence around my waist. My wounds have miraculously healed so only a scar remains, but I'd rather not go through the pain again.

Between focusing on not breaking my leg and moving forward, there aren't many openings to ogle Ordus' muscled back. I half wish the braid would stop swinging so I can study every inch of his exposed skin and engrain it into memory for me to enjoy later with the tentacle dil—

Bad. Very, very bad.

Ordus' body is none of my concern. Absolutely none. I'm his temporary housemate who can't leave without his escort.

I'm sweating by the time we get to the dead end that turned me around. Only this time, I can see the symbols etched into the walls like the boulder in the underwater tunnel.

"*Buka*," Ordus whispers.

The sigils glow the same shade of blue before the stone groans, rolling to the side. Natural light seeps into the damp space, opening to a clearing with a...a cottage? Shed? How did I miss this when I was running around the island the other day?

I check over my shoulder and between the trees for evidence of the Gallaghers, and I blink back surprise when my brain is put at ease with only a single survey.

It's a small structure about twenty square feet, elevated off the ground, with unvarnished wooden walls and a straw roof held up by logs. There are windows and a tiny door that looks ridiculous against the twelve-foot-tall wall.

It appears structurally sound, I guess, but it's a far cry from the level of acceptability by any architectural measure. It's not exactly the most visually appealing thing either, with its lack of symmetry. I don't need a leveler to know everything is off by at least a couple of degrees.

"How did this get here?" My forehead pinches when I inhale, and a familiar smell makes my nostrils twitch.

"I built it."

"By yourself?" Surprised is an understatement. But also, yeah, I guess that checks out with how it looks. "How? Where did you get all the supplies?"

"Mainland."

He's really not chatty today. Is it because I refused to marry him? Can he really be shocked by that? I shake my head. His silence is a good thing. It means…I get my space? I can't think of any other benefit.

I circle the property and come face-to-face with the answer to my earlier question of how he brought the supplies over. A boat. Well, more of a dinghy with two lengths of rope hooked onto the keel. A log is hanging on either side of the vessel like a double rigger to help stabilize it.

When he said he brought my things by boat earlier, I stupidly imagined him messing around with an engine, hunched down behind a steering wheel, or using his tentacles like propellers to push it across the sea. Pulling it makes a lot more sense. I can't imagine it'd be easy, but it's far more logical.

I eye Ordus curiously. He built a shed by himself, modified a dinghy, fixed my generator, chair, and fridge, yet he had no idea how to keep me alive?

I'm having a hard time wrapping my head around that.

Ordus glides easily up the wonky steps onto the fenceless porch, then into the shed. He holds the anti-insect netting aside for me to enter first. The inside is much the same as the outside— plain, functional, no aesthetic, the same mismatched wooden walls.

The smell of cooked fish assaults my nostrils, but I'm too distracted trying to figure this place out to follow my nose.

I was wrong to call it a shed. It's a shed—or, more accurately, a workshop. There's a running ceiling fan tied to various rigs, tubes and plastic bottles powered by a watermill to circulate airflow. A DIY'd bench in the corner is tall enough for him to comfortably use. There are random bits and bobs he collected from humans, what looks like half-made creations lying around. A wheelbarrow made from flax. A spade fashioned from steel sheets. There's a transmission part from some kind of car, hooked up to a series of wires, ropes, and pieces of wood—no idea what for.

And no sign of the Gallaghers, my brain helpfully supplies.

I turn to survey the area behind me, lighting up at the surfboard leaning against the wall with a green-and-pink hammerhead shark Deedee painted for "Cindi's" first birthday. As for the organized mess on the homemade shelving beside my board? Ordus didn't just move my bedroom—he brought my whole damn kitchen to the island.

There's salt, pepper, bay leaves, tamarind concentrate, *Sambal Jempol*, a whisk, tongs, cupcake tins—the list goes on.

The kraken managed to fit almost my entire life onto a dinghy. If I ruminate on that, it'll make me sad.

My eyes narrow on the other workbench that comes up to my chest. A portable camping stove and one of my pans sits atop it. It's the source of the smell.

Fish.

Cooked fish. Fucking warm, *pan-seared* fish.

Wait. "Did you kidnap a chef?"

Ordus' eyes flare in alarm. "No?" He looks around the hut like he's double-checking.

Well, I haven't seen anyone else around. Based on the purple spatula handle hanging over the edge of the pan, I'm going to guess no professional was involved.

"You made it?" It's somehow a more ridiculous statement-question. *Hold up*— "You had this the whole time?" I point accusatorially at the stove, my anger rising. What the fuck was the point of almost killing me? "Because it most definitely didn't come from my house."

The stray tentacle that dropped down to my ankle frantically rubs what's meant to be comforting circles over my leg. "I brought the—stove, I think it's called—this morning so you may eat fish." He picks up a pot from the shelf. "The pan is from your home. See? I was not hiding it from you. What's mine is yours."

I gape at him. This ten-foot giant really learned how to cook for me? Traveled hours to get me my things and everything I might need to eat and…entertain myself?

"Why?" I demand.

His ocean-blue eyes cast to the pan before fixing back on me with a questioning look. "So you can eat," he says, like it's the most obvious thing.

A dangerous warmth slithers into my stomach. I feel my eyes burning with pathetic, unshed tears. The only person who ever put in any effort for me was my dad. It's been years since anyone has done something solely for my benefit without wanting anything in return.

But that's not true, is it? He does want something. An exchange, of sorts. He wants me alive and to accept being his mate, to end the Curse. It's as much for him as it is for me.

Even so, he didn't need to bring me my surfboard to keep me alive—in fact, it's putting my life more at risk. He brought spices, books, more clothes, skincare, a fucking dildo, all so I don't have to survive off bare necessities.

My throat bobs. At no point while I was packing did I point the gun at him. I had countless opportunities to put a bullet in his head while we were still on the mainland, and I didn't. I let him live. I let him bring me here.

Giving him the side-eye, I amble over to the bench to peer at the source of the smell. Right there, in black and off-white, is the fish my nose picked up, skinned, filleted, and deboned.

"It's for me?"

What? Like he's about to eat it? Think before you talk, Kris —*Cindi*.

He nods, giving me the universal "try it" look. My stomach rumbles at the thought of food. My lips press into a thin line as I grab the handle. I mean, it looks legit? Seared on both sides. A little burnt, if anything. If the waft of pepper is any indication, it's seasoned as well. Maybe overly.

"Did you wash it?" I grill him.

Ordus hesitates. Nods.

Fuck it. I don't care. We'll find out later if I'm poisoning myself.

I cautiously scoop a bite into my mouth. My body's rejection of it is instantaneous. Out of pure stupidity, or a misguided affront to make him feel good about his cooking, I swallow the salt-and-pepper-drenched fish and start hacking up air like I'm Vasz after he drinks half the ocean. I sputter and cough, eyes watering from the pepper in my eustachian tubes.

Ordus is on me in a second, clutching me to him, rubbing my back, voice panic-stricken. "Tell me what is wrong, Cindi."

"I'm fine," I rasp. He passes me two of the *Aqua* cups I point to, and I down a whole one in a single go.

Oh, motherfucker, I already feel my indigestion coming on.

I lean back to catch my breath. I can't help but laugh at the ridiculousness of what just happened. It's the sweetest thing anyone has ever done for me that has failed so horrifically.

"Next time, less seasoning, 'kay?" I chuckle hoarsely, glancing up at him. The corners of my lips twitch up, because his head is lowered, all bashful.

"Seasoning?" Ordus' hand goes firm on my hip, claws grazing me over my tank top. He sheepishly scratches the back of his neck and stills, as if suddenly remembering his hair's been braided. He drops his hand to his side, a slightly panicked look in his eyes, like he's worried he's ruining it.

I point at the jars and bottles on the shelf he no doubt used. Ordus takes the pan and spatula from me with his spare hand and a tentacle. He breaks off a piece only slightly bigger than I did and slowly brings it to his mouth.

Has he ever tried human food before? Maybe I should warn him what he made is lethal.

But I don't, because I'm a sadistic bastard who wants to see how a monster reacts to over-seasoned food.

My lips curl into an excited little grin, and dare I say it, he becomes both alarmed and downright gleeful at the same time. Blue orbs glint like a misty-teal sea against a cloudless sky.

This is the most at ease I've felt in…in a long time. It's foreign, not feeling compelled to check out of each window every few seconds, not feeling like there's a gun trained on my head, or that I'm perpetually running. God, I can't remember the last time I felt comfortable with my guard this low.

Whatever Ordus sees in me gives him a boost of confidence to take a bite. Barely two seconds pass before he's choking and sticking his pointed tongue out.

"Vile," he spits.

Laughter tumbles out of me. It's absurd to watch this monstrous giant gagging over his home-cooked meal. He repeatedly swipes the back of his hand over his tongue to get rid of the taste, gagging and making pained sounds.

"It burns," he hisses. I rip open the plastic seal of the water cup and shove it into his hand. He gurgles and gulps it down before agreeing, "No seasoning next time."

"*Less*," I correct, grinning up at him.

His eyes drop to my lips, and his own curl to match mine. "Less. Next time."

21

CINDI

I bat a fly away from the *properly* cooked fish before dipping it into sambal, letting my bad arm rest at my side. I showed Ordus how to make it properly this morning, then supervised his dinner attempt. Then he grabbed a deck chair, and we made a ten-minute trek through the forest to the beach to watch the sun set beneath the shore.

I've bathed, moisturized, cleaned, and de-matted my hair. My organs still feel a bit rough from the whole dehydration thing, but I'm feeling exponentially better. Refreshed—at ease.

The breeze is cooling my face, the sand soft beneath my feet, I have good food, and no human could be hiding behind any tree— I cast a brief look around to be sure.

The fear is still there, but I haven't felt this truly at peace in so long, I forgot this feeling existed.

Ordus' stray tentacle has been wrapped around my bad arm every chance it gets. I should probably hate it, but whatever magic it is that Ordus has, his little ministrations make the pain in my arm subside enough for me to have a coherent string of thought.

We spent the day setting up containers around the island to collect rainwater. Ordus never asked why, or what the purpose of the containers was. He just did it happily without question. But when I explained to him what it's for and how it'd work, I half regretted it.

The only time Ordus left my side was for about half an hour, when he came back with three big drums. I felt like throwing my bachelor's degree out the window when *he* was the one who suggested a filtration system with mesh from the mainland.

I am equally impressed and mortified that a kraken out-engineered me.

I'm pretty sure he picked up on it, so he took the back seat and let me order him around as we put it together—not that I was much help, since my elbow decided to become completely useless after I made lunch. At least the rain saucer was my idea.

I peek at Ordus out of the corner of my eye. His braid falls over his shoulder, and he carefully touches the green scrunchie as if it might break. Every time I see him looking down at the hair tie like it's the most precious thing he's ever seen, my stomach does a flip.

He looks at me the same way, I realize. That same awe, like I'm more than just a body he needs to marry to end a curse. Like he might want me for me, not because I'm something a divine being threw his way—or out of a sense of duty.

It doesn't matter whether I like it or not. My feelings mean nothing.

I won't stay here permanently. I need to figure out a way to leave so I can keep running until my eventual death. But... would it be so bad if I hung around here for a while to catch a break? Whoever was at my place will probably think I did a runner again and be looking for my trail in the wrong direction.

It'd be a chance for me to regroup and recover, make a plan, then go for it.

Just the thought of needing to start again makes me sick.

But when I think about the Curse...it doesn't make sense. How could the fate of all krakens possibly be on my back? I'm a random human plucked off the street. There's no way a *Goddess* picked me to be the supposed savior.

"There's no...back door?" I think out loud.

Ordus casts his attention to me.

"For the Curse," I clarify. "You can't use reverse psychology on the Curse and make it take someone else's land—okay, not like that. But, I don't know? Maybe bounce the Curse to a parcel of land not being habited. Like...like the space cemetery in the South Pacific Ocean by..." I click my fingers. *Where was it?* "Point Nemo!"

"Uh..." He glances to the side, like he's finding a way to nicely tell me I'm insane. "I...do not know where that point is...or a space cemetery."

"It's where countries dispose of their spacecrafts like satellites and space debris." I read an article back when Dad was alive, when I still had interests outside of pleasing Tommy. "There are no oceanic currents in the area or something like that, so there's no marine life. If there is, there would be even less life caused by the chemical spillage, radioactive material, general waste, and collision shock. If you deflect the Curse to the cemetery, it would be *perfect.*"

Ordus scratches the back of his head then snatches his hand away like he doesn't want to ruin the braid. I bite back a smile—another foreign feeling. Did I smile or laugh with Deedee and Nat?

He frowns. "Even if that was possible, I wouldn't have the slightest inkling on how to do it. Any kraken who may have ideas are either dead or have gone to seek sanctuary elsewhere."

"Fuck."

"I do not have the magical capabilities to wield that type of power," he adds.

I tip my head back and squeeze my eyes shut. I can't have the fate of all krakens in my hands. I just can't. How many krakens are out there? A hundred? Three hundred? Thousands?

"May I ask you a question?"

"No," I say immediately. Ordus' face falls, and my gut constricts with guilt. "Maybe," I amend.

"Who is after you?"

I take a deep breath. It's the question I've been dreading. I figured he'd ask sooner rather than later.

My hand wraps over the scar on my wrist like it might hide the evidence of my past. As I rub it, pins and needles pierce my flesh from my elbow down to my fingers at the thought of Tommy.

There's not a single person who knows who and what I'm running from, or even my real name. A name carries weight. The moment I say his name, Thomas Gallagher, people will start connecting the dots.

But who would a kraken know? Yes, he's a king, but he had no idea what a scrunchie was. He thought my skincare products were potions, that humans drink seawater.

I could scream my ex-husband's name, list every single person in his family, mention every company they own, and Ordus still wouldn't know who the hell they are, because this is another universe. I'm on Earth, but in another realm entirely.

"Tommy Gallagher." I haven't spoken his name out loud in over a year. It tastes bitter and liberating. I stop myself from mentioning pirates, because that probably has a different meaning to him.

Ocean blues turn stormy as a vein in his temple ticks. "Did he harm you?"

I flinch at the memory of my marriage. Ordus knows the

answer. I think he figured it out long before I uttered my demon's name.

"I will kill him," he snarls, teeth bared, incisors on show.

It's...touching. I forgot what it's like to have someone in my corner. The only person to slay my demons has been me.

"Too late. I beat you to it." I don't mean to sound sad, but it's the first time I've confessed my sins out loud, and it's like this great big weight has been lifted off my shoulders. I can finally breathe again, release a hand off the reins and let someone else grip them for dear life with me.

It's a premature feeling, but it's there all the same.

"My mate is deadly." Ordus dips his head in appreciation. Our gazes clash, and the glint of pride in his eyes makes me want to crawl into a ball and cry. "You will not need to kill again—not unless you enjoy it, in which case I will bring you many bodies."

I blanch. Right, I forgot we both have a different set of morals and ethics. "You aren't meant to condone murder, let alone enable it."

No, the giddy feeling in my chest isn't because his declaration of bloodshed is kind of romantic. If I'm swooning, it's from the heat and the many near-death experiences I've had as of late.

"I would kill every male alive for you—monster and human. It makes no difference to me whether you take their last breath or I do." I inhale sharply and still when he trails a finger down my jaw. "Ask, and I will make it so."

"You—" I shift in my seat and clear my throat. He lowers his hand back to his side, disappointed. "You don't need to kill anyone for me."

Kill all the Gallaghers for me, and make it hurt, is what I want to say.

"I have done it many times before. There is no version of existence where I wouldn't do it all again for you." His voice is a deep rumble that sends a dark thrill through me.

Tommy killed in my name before, but it was never *for me*. The wounds he left behind have scraped and reopened a hundred times. They've been infected, inflamed, bloodied, and bruised, but they never healed. The best is a moderate itch begging to be scratched.

Because I lied when I said I'd sleep peacefully after killing Tommy. I haven't known a moment of peace since I shoved that knife into his neck. I'm afraid it'll never get better.

"How do you sleep with all the blood on your hands?" I whisper, staring at my plate. I've lost my appetite.

"Alone." Ordus' face betrays nothing. It's only the tightening of his tentacle that tells me our words have any impact. I watch him soften when he looks back down at the braid, and my tummy does a low whoop despite the somber shift in atmosphere. "Sometimes, I rest still feeling their blood on my skin."

My fingers twitch, remembering how it felt to pierce skin and sinew, how the warmth of his blood felt splattered on my face.

"Sometimes," I start, thinking of the nights I've spent staring at my hand and the two-and-a-half-inch scar on my wrist. "Sometimes, it's a blanket that warms you to the core."

"Other times, it leaves you cold," he finishes for me. My injured arm prickles under the heat of his attention. His hand covers mine, engulfing the scar and each of my sore fingers in his protective embrace. "But you are not alone anymore. You have no need to fear."

Inhaling deeply, I explain. "His family will not rest until they've captured me."

"No one will find you here."

I know that. More than anything, I know that in my very soul. John and the rest of the Gallaghers won't, but Tommy's ghost will follow me wherever I go.

The second I think it, a knife twists in my stomach. It's like a premonition. I'm setting myself up for failure. I want so badly to not see Tommy in every man I encounter, to stop running and hiding.

Just being able to mention his name without fear of repercussions is like having a stream of light break through the cracks so there's one corner of the world where his ghost can't touch me.

Ordus is nothing like the Gallaghers, who all hide their faces. Ordus sometimes wears his heart on his sleeve, and maybe I might have thought it was manipulative before, or a mask, but it's clear this is just who he is. There's nothing hiding in the closet. He's just...sad.

"He was my husband," I whisper, unsure whether I want Ordus to hear. I wince when I move my elbow to get more comfortable. Ordus freezes and snatches his hand away, like he's worried he's the issue. "It's a...an old injury," I assure him. "I've had it for years."

The muscles in his jaw pulse. He touches the scar on his ribs, and a flicker of rage crosses his face. My heart sinks. It really is like holding up a mirror. When you survive certain things, you develop a knack for recognizing other survivors.

"Does it still hurt?" I ask, nodding at his rib.

He drops his hand, lips set in a grim line. "Only when I remember." His throat bobs as he fixes attention back on my scar. "One day, I hope I can help you forget."

My chest swells with that dangerous feeling. *I hope you can forget too.*

"One day," I agree.

It's a dream. Hope is as deadly as a gun, but one will hurt far more.

Soft snoring filters through the cave as Ordus' chest rises and falls beneath my hand. Suckers pulse against the skin of my arms like a heated massage. Fingers are threaded in my hair, at the nape of my neck. Tentacles are wrapped around my legs and my waist. The moisture from his breath kisses my forehead as he dreams of—do krakens dream? They probably do.

Lord knows where Vasz is. Probably harassing a poor, innocent fruit.

Ordus has been asleep for an hour already, I think. He's been falling asleep well before I do since I've voluntarily returned to the island. Ever since we had our talk a few days ago, things have been...tense. Not *tense* tense, but more like there's a strange rift between us that almost feels forced. It feels like I've done something wrong, except all he's done is give me space to explore and do things at my own pace—except sleep.

Hell would freeze over before Ordus imposes a cuddle-free sleep routine.

Slowly, with the precision and finesse of someone defusing a bomb, I try to extract myself from the gentle giant. Like every other night I've tried to escape, it doesn't matter whether it's the blue wire or red—it blows up on me.

His soft purrs pour into the small cave, and it's like a switch that instantly changes the chemicals in my brain to turn me into mush. Suckers glide over my skin, warm and nice. Very nice. Too nice. Sliding up my leg, close to my core—too close.

Molten heat spreads from my stomach, out to the tips of my fingers and my toes. My lungs constrict as his thick appendage parts my legs in its pursuit to climb higher, closing in on the apex of—

I gasp, snapping my eyes to his sleepy face to check if he's aware of what he's doing. His solid limb grinds against my pussy over the thin cotton fabric of my sleep shorts, sneaking higher to wrap around my hips, holding me firmly in place as his suckers pucker over my clit.

Pure, raw desire shoots up my spine, and I clamp my lips together to stop my moans from breaking loose. My hand stiffens over his hard abs, and it's like his scent has seeped into my bloodstream to make me see double.

The sudden pressure and sensations have my nipples hardening, and I've lost the ability to breathe, too scared I might make noises that will wake Ordus.

Goosebumps rain over my flesh. Something momentarily turns off in my brain, and my body develops a mind of its own; back arching, hips bucking up to meet the length of hard muscle. It's like I'm seeing God.

The forbidden, delicious heat curls through me, and I bite the inside of my cheek to stop myself from doing it again as the thick appendage continues to glide over my center. Each sucker is like another nail in the coffin of my undoing, because I woefully fail. My hips shift to grind against him—one more time. The need to be filled is all-consuming. By him. My dildo. I don't care which.

His tentacle halts its travel up my aching body, but my panties are already saturated. My core is aching with need, and every fiber of my being is begging me to ride the tentacle nestled between my thighs. I breathe hard through the fog in my brain and nuzzle my face against his chest like I can hide from the world.

How does one level up from a tentacle dildo? By graduating to the real deal, of course.

Because completely and undeniably, I have the hots for a kraken. I have no idea how to unpack that with a therapist.

22

V_{ASZ}

Day and night, I guard the parameter.

Ninety-eight have passed since I have been tasked with the most important role in existence. I do not rest. I do not squander. My Queen Mate's life depends on me.

I am her guard shark-doggopus.

My eyes narrow at the wooden plank, daring it to drift closer and disturb my human. It is not easy protecting Cindi. Everything is a threat.

Ordus has granted me permission to bite any foe who dares come near my island. Even once the kraken has returned from hunting, I do not rest.

My trust in him is...fickle. She was sick, and it was I who brought her the coconut. *I* brought her back from the brink of death. If she needs another coconut, I will be ready. I cannot rely on Ordus to do right by her.

Also, she likes me more. Cindi has never called Ordus a good kraken. She calls me a good boy whenever I see her, and I make her laugh.

Ordus doesn't make Cindi laugh.

Whenever I haven't seen her in a long, long time, I sprint up to her, maybe pee a little—a moment of weakness, on my part— tail wagging as I jump all over her. She smiles at me and tells me she missed me too.

Does she tell Ordus she missed him? No.

Does she sneak Ordus her food when no one is looking? No.

Does she rub his head and call him a good boy? No. *I'm* the only good boy around here.

She once called me the bestest of all boys, and my Queen Mate is not a liar.

The waves are strong today. Cindi always comes out into the water to sit and stand on her board whenever it is like this. It makes my job harder, because there are always more threats and greater risks with her out in the open.

The plank floats closer. My warning growl renders it still. I stretch my paws out so it sees my claws. I take my duty very seriously.

It drifts closer once more. I lower to my haunches.

"Leave now. This is your last warning."

It sways *closer.*

The audacity.

"Do not test me," I growl, peeling my lips back.

This time, when it moves, I pounce, tearing Cindi's potential attacker to shreds until it's littered over the sea floor. It was not a worthy opponent.

Satisfied the threat has been eliminated, I straighten to stare down my nose at the plank. "If you want blood, you will see blood."

23

CINDI

Surfing would be a lot more relaxing if I didn't have to keep an eye out for Vasz the entire time. The fucker likes to graze his teeth over my foot.

Whenever I've been sitting on my board for too long, he likes to take a nip. It scares the shit out of me. He hasn't done it in a week, but I don't trust the little prick one bit.

When I get mad at him, he acts like I've cussed out his entire bloodline. He has a pair of killer puppy dog eyes he shoots me with every time I tell him off. It makes me feel like a complete ass after.

It's unnerving how almost humanlike he can be.

I check the surrounding water again before letting my eyes drift shut, bobbing along to each wave.

Aside from the constant fear I may lose a limb because of Petroleum Jelly's boredom, I've been stuck on this island for five weeks, and I wish I could say I've hated every moment of it.

My arm hasn't felt so goddamn good in years. With the relaxed island lifestyle combined with whatever it is Ordus' suckers do to me every night while we sleep, I'm reminded the baseline for the amount of pain a person should be in is zero, not five.

Assuming I'm not calling in a sick day—which has been happening far too often lately—I've got a routine down pat: wake up in Ordus' many arms, eat, surf, read, eat, surf again, eat again, maybe workout, maybe tinker away in the workshop to try to rebuild the boat's engine.

If I'm not doing any of that, I'm making the island my own.

I've tried planting some fruits and veggies to see if I can get something to grow, but I'm not an agricultural specialist, and I've never had much of a green thumb. I'm trying to build an irrigation system to see if that does anything as well. My efforts are probably pointless because of the whole Curse thing. Still, I like the challenge.

I also have plans to explore some type of renewable energy source. Somehow, Ordus managed to find me a book on it. So far, without a lab to make half the stuff I need, I'll need to go really old school and summon my inner Faraday.

Even though my arm is better, I haven't been pushing it too much. I've been coming up with ideas of things to make, like a swing, hammock, shelving, and other random stuff, and then Ordus puts it together.

Ordus has been giving me my space—Vasz most definitely has not. He's the definition of a Velcro dog. Whenever I lounge around the beach, he drops a coconut on me to throw. For hours. He literally doesn't stop. Ever. If he's panting to the point that he's foaming at the mouth, all he needs is a ten-minute nap, and he's rested and ready to go.

The Coconut Princess has developed this new thing where he refuses to chase fish through the underwater tunnels for his meals. He now requires all fish be prekilled and served to him by me on one of my plates, and he refuses to start unless I praise him first.

Some days, he requires I pretend the raw fish is actually my dinner, so I have to take a fake bite then give it to him.

He might be a little shit, but he's starting feel like *my* little shit.

A fin pokes out of the water and starts swimming toward me. I lift my legs out and cross them on my board, watching him closely.

Vasz sticks his head out, a long stick between his teeth. He growls when I reach for it, and I roll my eyes. "Wow, Vasz." I pat his head, entertaining his need for constant praise. "Look at what you've got there. Good job."

He chuffs, all cocky, as if confirming that it is, in fact, a good stick, then dives beneath the waves, swimming off to God knows where.

It's on my to-do list to ask Ordus why they're currently giving each other the cold shoulder, or they'll argue with each other to the point that Vasz barks, and Ordus says something that sounds a lot like "*She's not yours.*"

But he's not really talking to me much.

Sometimes he huffs and gives me shit for encouraging Vasz's spoiled ass, but hell, sometimes I just want to dress the shark-dog up like a hula girl or something.

I drop onto my stomach and paddle toward the oncoming wave. A smile pulls at my lips at the flash of red and yellow gliding through the water alongside me. He's always around somewhere.

The stage-five clinger sleeps with me every night, so I have approximately half an inch of breathing space at any given moment, with Ordus on one side and Vasz on the other. Sleeping while touching someone took some getting used to—I'm not even sure I *am* used to it yet.

Vasz races me back toward the shore, doing loops around me

when I slow to a stop, patiently waiting for the next wave that tickles my fancy.

I crane my neck toward the beach, hoping to see Ordus somewhere, but, as usual, he's nowhere to be seen.

Other than the forced sleeping arrangement, Ordus gives me more breathing room than I expected. He's normally lurking around somewhere, but without fail, he's always there for lunch and dinner, only really speaking to ask whether I've eaten enough—which I most definitely have.

Otherwise, our communication consists of me talking at him, ordering him to get this or that, hammer a nail here, set the wood at that angle there—a little higher on the left, nope, too high.

The few times I've covertly tried looking for him, I found him at the workshop, either making improvements to the shed or creating something. Every two or three days, he's gone for long stretches of time, returning with food, water, and random knick-knacks from the mainland and sea life he's hunted for us.

Space from Ordus was good at the start.

I don't find it so good anymore.

I miss the mainland. I miss interacting with people. I miss feeling like I'm not the only person in existence.

Vasz is great, but not quite enough.

Tipping my head up, I spot the angry storm clouds in the distance and internally grumble.

Red sky at night, sailor's delight. Red sky in morning, sailor's warning. That old sailor's adage was utter bullshit. It was nice and blue when I woke up today.

If I had known the weather was going to turn, I would have spent the entire day reinforcing and adding more rainwater traps so I don't have to take really pathetic baths in the blow-up kiddy pool Ordus brought me.

Ordus promised to get me a proper bathtub one day, but my current digs suit me just fine. At the start, it was a little demeaning to use it, but then Ordus brought me a bottle of vodka, and one day, I got loose and limber and started feeling like a mermaid in that thing. Ever since, I've been kind of fond of it.

Plus, it's not like I'm staying here forever.

It's just temporary, until I feel ready to venture back out into the real world and go back to jumping at my own shadow. Or until Ordus gets bored or tired of "running around" for me and takes me back.

Some unpleasant feeling churns in my gut at the thought.

I shake my head and paddle back to shore. We need some kind of tank to store all the water to limit further contamination. The drums are okay for now, but I'd feel better if I had a backlog in case of a rainy day.

Well, in case it stops raining.

I jog back toward the shed with my board. Vasz runs alongside me, tongue hanging out the side of his mouth, yipping, thinking we're on some kind of mission.

One of our newly acquired chickens screeches when it sees us and dashes back to the coop Ordus made.

"Don't," I warn Vasz.

He doesn't listen, snapping at the poor animal. I swear it loses a feather.

Prickles skate over my skin, and I come to a halt, leaning against a nearby tree to catch my breath. Bile lurches up my stomach, and I slap my hand over my mouth, willing my body to solve itself.

I thought rest would make whatever is wrong with me go away, but it's shown no sign of disappearing. Vertigo—or whatever the fuck I have—is a bitch. Pushing off the tree, I herd the chickens back into their cage. Then I check the containers along the way to the shed to store my board, seeing if the rain catchers need taping down or if the funnels and filters for the drums need fixing.

Ordus usually checks them—and the swing, hammock, and chair—every couple of days to make sure they're all in perfect shape. I still like to do a once-over as well. Not that I don't trust him, but sometimes, he's modified it or improved it in a way I never thought of.

My footsteps slow as I approach Ordus. The threads of blue in his skin are more prominent next to the plastic, cyan drum.

I chew the inside of my cheek, watching the tendons in his back strain and feather as he tightens a bolt. Every inch of him is pure, hard muscle, each one prominent and bulging from years of honing them to lethal perfection.

Ordus glances back at me, eyes dropping to my bare legs for half a heated second before averting his attention back to the funnel.

Clearing my throat, I say, "Storm's rolling in."

He grunts.

Ordus never really talks anymore. At most, I'll get a handful of short, clipped sentences.

Last week, I snapped at him because I spiraled over the fact that he only wants me at a shallow, physical level, so I told him he's welcome to drop my ass back off on the mainland whenever he wants, and his mature response was to bare his canines at me and stalk off.

"How are your teeth?"

"Fine." I bite back a smile. It's one of three questions he only ever asks me—I think it might be his attempt at an inside joke.

He nods, and the would-be smile wipes off my face. Ordus may hate me, but his tentacle seeks me out the moment it notices me.

"What are you doing?" I probe, saying a mental hello to the appendage curling happily around my leg.

Something that feels unnervingly akin to butterflies erupts in my stomach when I spot my scrunchie still around his wrist. I haven't seen him without it. Ordus kept his braid for four days after and only reluctantly took it out when there was more hair out of the braid than in it.

The same thing happened the other three times I offered to braid his hair.

"Checking on it."

My shoulders slump. At the start, the silence was nice. I could seethe from afar, loathe him for putting me in a position where I had two options: go with him or pull the trigger, and I couldn't do the latter. It was easier for me to pretend he's the villain and I'm the victim, perfectly innocent to fault.

But the silence has grown claws that pierce soft tissue. Every drop of blood beading onto the surface is a reminder I'm complicit in all this.

My husband was a bad man. That alone made his hatred toward me *understandable*. To an extent. Ordus' disinterest in me...it's grating on my nerves. The little voice in my head screams it's my own fault. My own supposed Goddess-sent soulmate doesn't like me because all my splintered pieces have turned me ugly. I know that's not the real reason why, though.

At the end of the day, Ordus has been the perfect jailer. He gives me more space than I'm finding I want. He's doing everything he can to keep me fed and happy. He's kept me safe like he promised, turned his barren island into my own slice of paradise.

And my perfect jailer is wishing he ended up with someone other than me.

I shift my weight. "I've checked the containers between here and the beach."

Ordus grunts.

"Should I check the one near the eastern cliffs?"

He shakes his head.

"Okay, what about the northwest drum?"

Another shake.

I fist my hands. "Do you need help?"

"No."

I take a deep breath, looking around for ideas on what to say.

"Is there anything you need me to bring inside?" Sometimes he has pastes or seaweeds drying out.

"I've done it." I wouldn't say his tone is dismissive, but it's definitely not suggesting he wants to keep talking.

I wipe my clammy hands on my soaked shirt. "I'll, uh, make dinner so I don't need to leave the cave once the storm hits."

"It is already made."

"Oh." We take turns cooking. He likes to watch and learn, but he also likes surprising me. Or, at least, I think he likes it. Ordus usually hands the plate to me, face devoid of emotion, and grunts when I say thanks.

Once we've cleaned up after dinner, he leaves me to my own devices and only seeks me out when it's time for bed, when he wordlessly pulls me into his arms, and it becomes a race to see who falls asleep first—usually Vasz. He might be a little thing, but he can shake the walls with his snoring.

I clear my throat. "I'll just...have a bath, then."

"No."

I frown. "Why not?" He's usually very probathing, because I'm a lot happier when I can't feel grime and saltwater sticking to my skin.

He finally—*finally*—looks at me. "Eat first. I want to show you something."

I do as he says, mind whirling with possibilities. Maybe he hauled a water tank from the mainland, or a box of *Kacang Disco*. Or he could've stolen the solar panels I previously mentioned wanting—he does stuff like that very often. He might not talk or look like he's interested, but he listens to every word I say.

I once asked if it were easy to catch crab or squid, if he's ever tried human meat like chicken. The next day, he came back from hunting with both. A week later, I saw a chicken roaming around the island.

Now I am the mother of eight chickens, craned to me by boat

in the dead of night, and much to Ordus' confusion, I can't bring myself to do more than cook their eggs.

Ordus says nothing when he shows up midway through my meal. I'm camped out in the chair he made, staring out the window. It's too windy to sit outside only in my swimsuit and rash shirt.

Once I finish, I follow him silently through the tunnel into the main cavern, the stray tentacle wrapped around my waist in case I trip—a common occurrence. Ordus and I have begun planting the glowing algae along the channel walls so I'm no longer going in blind. The light is still faint, but it's miles better than it used to be.

He leads me to the pool, where he holds his hand out for me to take, the one with the green scrunchie on it. If I didn't know better, it looks like a seaweed bracelet.

Pensive excitement soars through my veins. He acknowledges me so little that in the dead of night, when it's time to creep into our bed of moss, a needy bud comes to bloom at the knowledge I'll be in his arms. That when he touches me, it won't hurt. When he trails a finger down my arm, the goosebumps aren't out of trepidation, but the ecstasy of being recognized as a being beyond skin and bone.

Ordus thinks I don't know he stares at me before he falls asleep, that he presses his nose close to my hair and takes four deep breaths as his eyes drift shut.

But I do.

Every night, I let myself fall for the delusion that fate and magic don't have anything to do with his interest in me. That whatever this is between us is more than physical. I...I want him to open up to me.

"Where are we going?" I hesitate, glancing between him and his outstretched hand.

"We will stay on the island." His face is impassive; it always is nowadays. I hate it.

It doesn't make me uncomfortable, not the way Tommy's blank face did. This just kind of—hurts?

I brush my fingers over his calluses, watching as his hand dwarfs my own. His skin pulses different colors with his shudder. Tugging, I inch toward him, gnawing on the inside of my cheek while he reaches for me, curling his arm around my waist to hold me to him. I wrap my legs around him and try not to think about how his abs contract against my core.

Ordus' fingers weave into my matted, postsurf hair to tuck my head against the crook of his neck, and I let him. I melt into him, breathe him in, soak up every inch of his warmth to fill the empty space in my heart where my loneliness grows.

His thumb snakes beneath the sliver of skin between my rash shirt and the top of my bikini bottoms. It stays there, a threat and a temptation all in one.

The silky strands of his raven hair twine and thread between my fingers as I cradle the base of his skull. A strained purr rumbles to life in his chest. The buzzing in my veins heats at the way his muscles ripple beneath my touch. Feminine satisfaction sends a bolt of desire right to my core that I can have such a profound impact on him from such a mundane motion.

Sometimes, at night, when I dare let myself dream of something good, I replay all the times I've watched him stare at his scrunchie. I want to do it again. I want to braid his hair so he's moving through space with my touch evident on him—as a reminder to the both of us that my touch doesn't need to hurt either.

Maybe I also want to do it because it gives me a possessive thrill. Or maybe it's the self-satisfaction of knowing Ordus might feel less alone when he looks at it.

His next breath comes out ragged. A forbidden touch in a dark cave. We don't speak. We don't dare move, like we're both afraid of scaring the other off.

My eyes flutter closed when his thumb glides along the few

inches of skin. Back and forth, a pendulum that keeps me on edge, waiting to see if it'll ever stop.

I fist his hair against my wishes. My hand has a mind of its own. I don't want him to know how badly I need the connection. I don't *want* to need the connection. I wish I weren't so hungry for it that I could let the desire fizzle into nothing. I wish I could go back to trying to stay alive. But still, my hand stays in his hair. His thumb continues to caress my skin until it feels like I'm raw.

Ordus breaks the spell first by snatching his hand away like he's caught fire, and then he jerkily lowers us into the water. The warmth around me shatters, and I try to keep myself contained so he doesn't see my disappointment.

The air bubble forms around my head not two seconds after I'm fully submerged beneath the cool water. I tighten my legs around him and flatten my torso against his to absorb his warmth. A shudder rolls through his body, and it just…confuses me.

Whenever I start to convince myself he's disgusted by me or wants to get rid of me, his body reacts so viscerally. Like the way his cock hardens when I walk around in my bikini. Or how his abs clench when I rest my hand on his stomach at night. His breaths come out ragged when I stand close to him.

It's just physical. I hate it.

I squeeze my eyes shut, letting him hold my weight. He only likes me like *that*, not for me. It's probably that stupid *mate* thing. He wouldn't tolerate me if it weren't for it.

But on the other side of things… Deep down, maybe he does want more, but the walls he's built around himself won't let him have that, whether out of self-preservation or self-loathing. The things I've said wouldn't have helped matters. I can't get anywhere if he doesn't talk to me.

Do I really want to get anywhere, though? Aren't I leaving soon?

A blue glow stirs me up, and I open my eyes just as the bubble pops. I sputter against the crash of saltwater.

"Give me warning next time," I sputter as I cough and rub my stinging eyes. Ordus eases horizontally onto his padded tentacles.

He grunts.

I glare at him. Fucking hell. Enough of the grunt—

Oh, shit. Molten heat shoots straight to my core, and I suck in a sharp breath. He can grunt some more if he's like this: towering over me, arms on either side of my head, caging me beneath him. Under the glowing light of the algae, water sluices down his bulging biceps and each dip of his abs before traveling down the sharp V that spreads out into thick tentacles.

My vision goes blurry as the muscles in my core contract, and my nipples push painfully against the fabric of my top. His harsh breaths fan my aching skin, nostrils flaring with every deep inhale. In the span of a heartbeat, ocean-blue eyes blow out into a stormy black void of hunger.

My nails dig into his shoulders of their own accord. What is happening?

One of the tentacles cushioning my back from the harsh, rocky surface of the cave floor shifts. A thick appendage slides around my upper thigh, suckers puckering against my skin. It grazes the throbbing flesh between my legs and sends stars shooting straight behind my eyes.

This shouldn't be happening.

It's wrong. He kidnapped me. He doesn't even like me. He prefers the idea of me.

But one more second won't hurt. Just one. A single second doesn't change anything. I can afford *one*. A moment to be looked at like nothing in this world exists except me, as if the seas could drain and the skies could fall, and he won't feel the burn as long as I'm there.

It's a suffocating addiction. I could choke on it and still come back day after day for another hit to feel like I'm more than a pile of skin and broken bones.

A strangled moan splinters out of me when pure, hard muscle grinds against my sensitive core.

"Cindi," he purrs.

I clamp down on the inside of my cheek.

Just one more second.

A second won't hurt.

Slowly, my back starts to arch. I jolt when something clatters beside my head. I snap my attention toward the sound, hackles rising, memories of another life clawing up to the surface.

It all stops short.

"Holy shit." I gasp.

Bioluminescent algae crawls along the stone walls, casting a blue and purple glow over the riches hidden in the cavern, the heat from our interaction forgotten as he helps me to my feet.

There has to be almost thirty square feet of treasure in here. I can only imagine how crazy archeologists and history buffs would get looking around. There are various gold coins that could've been from the Ottoman Empire, golden statues, porcelain vases, silver trays, jade carvings, curved swords with tasseled ends, a crown of diamonds, and chests upon chests of jewelry.

The British Museum would have a fucking field day.

"What is this place?" I whisper.

"My treasures." His voice is gruff.

Ordus won't look at me.

Why won't he look at me? I want to scream. He was all over me when he first kidnapped me, and now he's acting like I'm his roommate he doesn't particularly like talking to.

"I…" Ordus clears his throat, leaving two tentacles around me before giving me a wide berth. I lean against him as ripples of fatigue chip away at my energy. "The collection is bare. My family's hoard remains at the palace, guarded by krakens and magic."

"Bare?" I echo, marveling at the chest holding a ruby the size of my fist.

Bare is most definitely not the word I would've chosen.

The items in this room would set me up for life. If not my whole life, then for sure the few years I have before someone decides I need to be taken out.

"This is amazing." I've never wished I took ancient history at school before, but there's a first for everything.

One of his tentacles drops away when I move deeper into the cave, stepping on coins to get close enough to make things out. There's so much treasure everywhere. I don't know where to start. I feel like I need to use gloves to touch anything.

I practically have to wade through piles upon piles of gold coins and gem-studded jewelry: belts, necklaces, brooches, earrings, bracelets, rings.

My heart is hammering against my chest with the panic levels of someone carrying out a heist. Alarm bells go off in my head, blaring that I shouldn't be here. I'll get arrested for theft, or breaking and entering, because none of this is real. There's no way krakens are real, and there sure as shit isn't any way this room exists beneath an island in the middle of nowhere.

And there's more at the *palace*? I thought nothing else could surprise me, but *this*?

Forgoing any kind of proper ancient-artifact-handling etiquette, I pick up the giant ruby—I think it's a ruby, at least—as big as my fist. I gawk at the light catching on it—and it was just *thrown* on top of the gold coins and pearl necklaces.

"The elders claimed this belonged to a princess whose ship sank."

My jaw drops. Fuck off. Really? "Which one?" Diana?

"I don't remember."

I wouldn't have known who even if he did. I carefully set down the ruby and pick up an emerald—I think—the size of my palm. "Is this from the same ship?"

His lips tighten. "Unsure."

I pry for information regarding everything I pick up: an oval sapphire necklace as big as my thumb, another necklace covered in teardrop, bluish diamonds. I don't know jack about any of this, but Tommy's mom was in love with this type of thing.

Ordus' response eventually condenses down to a stiff shrug paired with a clenched jaw, like he committed the gravest crime by not having the answer.

I grab one of the many necklaces in the cave, but this one is different from the rest. It's in its own special, handwoven basket, a mix of diamonds, pearls, sapphires, opals, and seashells.

"It was my sister's." I snap my attention up to Ordus, and he nods at the necklace. "Mother gifted it to Chlaena on her name day before I was born, and it became her favorite necklace." The gold glints as I turn it over in my hand. There's a damaged mechanism bent at a bad angle, at odds with the perfection of the rest of the chain, but it still works. "The clasp snapped when I was a child. I remember seeing Chlaena cry for the first time in my life."

"And you fixed it," I guess.

He dips his chin. A small smile pulls at my lips, imagining a mini Ordus fussing with a human item the same way I've seen him do many times over the past five weeks.

"The last time she wore it was on her wedding day, two months before she was killed."

My mouth dries. *Oh.* "I'm sorry," I whisper.

"It was a long time ago." He's impassive again, or at least, he's trying to be. The strain around his eyes is a dead giveaway.

"I never had any siblings, but I—I can imagine the hole they left behind." I still have a gaping wound in my chest from Dad's death. I never met my mother, and there's an empty spot where she's meant to be.

Ordus grunts and turns away.

I guess we're back to silent time. I try to tamp down my hurt and disappointment.

Sighing, I pick up a dagger with precious gemstones on the hilt. I'm not sure what exactly is on it, but my jaw is somewhere on the floor.

"We took this off a ship sailing near our territory."

My eyes flash up to Ordus, and a stone drops in my chest from the sorrow etched over his face.

"My brother and I were both very young at the time, long before the Curse." His voice is low, like he doesn't want to speak but he's forcing himself to. "Yannig loved challenging us to do foolish things—I'm sure it was to see how far the line was for him to cross." He adds the last part more to himself. "One night, we dared each other to get things from a passing vessel without being caught. It's not something we'd ever done before, and I usually wouldn't have agreed, but it was his name day. It was night, so the odds were in our favor. I must have been around thirteen at the time, Yannig twenty-two. I knew it was too far. Our laws were and are clear: krakens cannot reveal themselves to humans."

The stone in my chest grows into a boulder, and it becomes harder to breathe. I don't think I'll like what's coming next.

"I knew I could get on and off the vessel without issue. Blending in is my specialty, even as a cub. Yannig's, his words. He could convince anyone to do almost anything. It made him arrogant. Words wouldn't keep him from detection. A human spotted him a moment before he jumped back into the water." Ordus fidgets with a belt, not meeting my eye. "Our mother was furious. She forbade us from leaving the palace for a month and sent us to clean with the servants for a year. But the Council, they blamed me for it, said I corrupted Yannig's mind and made him do it." I suck in a sharp breath. "So, I was punished."

His fingers hover above the scar on his ribs. *Oh, God.*

Flashes of Tommy's *discipline* assault me. Other than my wrist, he never left scars on my skin. My broken bones are another story altogether. "Punished?" I croak.

What did they do to Ordus that left a jagged, six-inch scar? On a fucking *kid*.

Ordus' jaw is tight, body primed for a fight. Even the tentacle usually always touching me has recoiled away from me.

"A Council member—Lantoli—always disliked me. They all did, but he was the most vocal. He was biding his time, waiting for an excuse to—" He stops himself, skin pulsing and paling until he's the same shade as the sand. "Lantoli convinced krakens I almost single-handedly caused the eradication of my species, that I was feeding humans information about our kind."

He clenches his hands into fists. "Lantoli led a group of krakens to grab me as I was coming back from a hunt. They chained me to a large fishhook with the intention of dragging me to this island. Yannig found me before they could make it. My mother killed Lantoli and his conspirators, but the damage was done. They almost—" His voice breaks. "They almost succeeded."

Ordus stares at the dagger in my grasp. It falls out of my hands like it's poison. Why would they do that? What the fuck was wrong with them? "You were a child."

He gives his head a single, stiff shake. "It does not matter. I was impure."

What? *Impure?* That's a load of bullshit. There's nothing okay about harming a kid, monster or otherwise. "I don't understand why they could hate a *child* so much." Why is Ordus excusing their behavior? He sounds like Kristy, taking Tommy's abuse by some misguided allusion it's out of love or I might have somehow deserved it. "You did nothing wrong."

"*I did.*" A growl breaks his voice, and my fear receptors stand on end. "I did many things wrong."

"Like what? What could a thirteen-year-old have done?" *I was twenty-three when I met Tommy. What did I do to deserve it?* "Did you give humans information? Were you trying to get your brother killed? How could you possibly be—"

"Because I am a monster!" he snarls. Piles of treasure fly

across the cave and crash around us. The vein in his temple pulses, his anger developing its own heartbeat. I stagger back to get away from him. The spike of fear ebbs away as soon as my sights land on the heavy rise and fall of his chest. His sharp teeth are on display, muscles rippling like he's a hair away from striking. This is the first time he's looked *truly* monstrous.

I'm not sure what shocks me more: the sudden outburst, or that the one constant feeling I've had for the past four years isn't there. I'm not afraid. Not of him, at least.

That mustn't be what he sees on my face, because he recoils, horrified of himself.

I step forward, close enough that his stray tentacle can wrap around me again. He moves back like he's frightened he'll hurt me.

"Ordus," I say quietly. "I've met monsters. You are not one."

"Look at me," Ordus roars, pointing at his chest. "I am an abomination!"

I've lived under the same roof as one, shared meals with him and his even more abhorrent family. I know better than most what a monster looks like. After all, I fell into its trap.

"As it is in nature, the prettiest ones are the most poisonous. You are one of the most attractive men I have ever met, but you are far from poisonous."

I hated that he wasn't, confused at myself that I've stopped fighting him, that I look forward to nightfall so he can hold me, that he had me under him moments ago, and my blood heated with need.

"I want you to talk to me, Ordus."

Ordus' face contorts into a venomous scowl as he glares at me like I'm the reason for the reopened wound. "I took you from your home, almost killed you, cursed you to suffer on this island with me. Do not lie to me, Cindi," he hisses. "I know what I am."

Broken.

I don't know why, but his words get to me. And the look of

utter self-disgust? It lands on the wrong side of my brain, and it's like everything explodes at the same time it comes into crystal clarity.

"Get over yourself," I bite. I regret it the moment I say it, but I don't back down. He can't keep shutting me out if he expects me to stay.

Ordus rears back. "Excuse me?"

"Don't get me wrong, you're a fucking asshole for what you've done and how you've gone about it—how you're keeping me. Isolated. Alone. I need something other than a spoiled dog for company—one I can't even speak to, by the way." My voice keeps raising in volume until it suddenly drops, and it's like trying to pry screwdrivers out of my flesh. "Despite all of that, everything you've done, I don't hate you. I'm not lying awake at night wishing you were dead. I've spent every fucking day wanting you to just *talk to me.*"

I thought my husband was the most handsome man to ever walk this Earth, and I found out the hard way that he was the ugliest.

I swallow the lump in my throat. "Any flaws you have are over what you've done, not because of your appearance. So get over yourself, Ordus."

He shakes his head. I know he's not listening to me, not hearing what I say. "My hands, Cindi. I have claws. My hair, my fingers, my arms, my head. It's all wrong."

"Why? If your nails were nicer, maybe people would like you more? If your arms were a little smaller, maybe people would take you more seriously?"

Ordus paces the small path, curling and uncurling his fists. "You do not understand."

"No, I don't. I'm fully aware I have no idea what it was like growing up in the sea, what type of cultural and social aspects are involved, but our minds are still the same. They've convinced you to hate your own reflection, and you have. What are you doing to change that?"

What am *I* doing to fix all the things Tommy fucked up?

It wasn't all Tommy's fault. Something had to be misaligned in my brain that I let myself walk into that and did nothing to get myself out.

Maybe I was desperate for the love Dad had with Mom.

Maybe I was so used to Dad picking up after me, I didn't know responsibility unless it slapped me in the face, and I figured someone else would clean whatever mess I got into. Maybe it took me four years to figure out how to do things for myself.

Because that's exactly what happened. Tommy swooped in with the job, the money, the house, the nice cars. He took me to the fancy restaurants and dressed me in the expensive clothes. I didn't have to lift a goddamn finger, because Tommy did all the thinking for me. When to eat, when to sleep, who to talk to, when to fucking breathe.

It wasn't even a slow progression. It practically happened overnight.

I stayed with Tommy because I…I thought I didn't have a choice. Dad died, I lost all my friends, and I thought I was stuck. Grief turned me stagnant.

Or, fuck, maybe it was nothing at all. I had on a pair of cherry-tinted glasses, and my first serious boyfriend could do no wrong in my eyes. Narcissists are manipulative. I got played, and I fell for it, simple as that.

I never learned how to survive until I lost my safety net. I had to gouge it out to find my backbone. Now, I'm surviving again, but it…it's different. It's not like with Tommy.

Ordus and I are working together, like the rainwater drums. I thought up the saucer; he came up with the filter. The chickens were his idea, but the coop was mine. He wanted to keep fish closer so he doesn't need to go hunting as often, so I drew up a cage with what we had on the island.

And the crops I'm trying to grow. He made a garden box; I designed the system. I come up with the natural electricity plans; he'll execute them. I wash laundry; he built a clothesline.

When was the last time I demanded Ordus return me to the mainland? A week? Two?

Ordus stops pacing, his back to me as he motions to the treasure, ignoring what I said. "It is yours to do with as you please." There's finality in his voice. It echoes against the cave walls and weighs a hundred tons.

I shake my head. "What? No, I can't accept it."

"All I have is yours." He looks at me over his shoulders, and it almost knocks me off my feet. It's not just adoration. It's...hopelessness. He's a man at the edge of his rope, and he doesn't know what to do anymore.

But it's not mine. It's too much. I don't deserve it. They're his memories. His treasures. I've done nothing to earn them.

Yet, all that comes out is, "I can't accept it, Ordus."

He grunts, and just like that, we're one step forward and two steps back.

24

VASZ

Sand sprays across the beach with each wag of my tail. I sigh, staring up at the big, white, forbidden coconut in the sky.

She's so beautiful.

"Goddess?" I whisper, pausing my movements to wait for a response.

Sometimes, she talks back. By talk, I mean scream. The trees usually bend when she does, and I almost fly away. When the bright coconut in the sky is hidden behind—I don't know what she's behind—and it's all wet, loud, gross, and cold, the world goes bright and the Goddess roars.

Tonight, the Sacred Coconut bathes my surroundings in black, grey, more grey, and light grey. It's the only time I get to see her, when Cindi is getting ready to sleep and Ordus is watching her, and my stomach tells me I won't be fed for a long, long, long time—until I wake Cindi up, usually, so I like to do that nice and early.

Chuffing, I try again. "Shark-doggopus Goddess." My tail slaps the ground once. "I'm talking to you."

Nothing.

"Please? I've been a good boy." My ears drop, and I lower my head to my paws, swishing my tail behind me as I stare at the Sacred Coconut longingly. "Goddess, I... You may know me as a warrior, a valiant protector. I have faced many fearsome battles— as you are aware—and I return the stick to my queen every time she throws it."

Why must everyone ignore me? I am *perfect*. I have never done anything wrong in my entire life.

"I ask—and I don't ever ask of you—but I want this one thing. It's small. Not a big ask. Easy for you to do because you're a Goddess." Flattery will get me far. "If you could fill this entire island with coconuts... I know, *I know*. Ordus would be angry, but he doesn't worship you like I do. What matters is that I, your humble servant, am repaid for my service."

The bushy *thing* drifts over the Sacred Coconut. A silent answer.

The Goddess does not think I am a good boy.

25

ORDUS

It's worse than I thought.

The last parcel of land left untouched by the Curse is nearly as small as my island. Though rich in game, it is rapidly shrinking with each passing week.

Once it's gone, there's no telling if the Curse can still be broken.

At this rate, we may never know. She will never agree to marry me, and I have no intention of coercing her into it.

I can either be a bad king or a bad mate. Already, I am monumentally failing at both. If it is a decision between killing the people who wish me dead or doing what's right for the female the Goddess chose for me, I pick the latter.

I've been unsettled since I left Cindi alone in our den this morning. The feeling worsens when a kraken female swims out from behind a stone archway. Like the others I've passed on the way here, her skin is stretched over bone in a sickly hue. If she came closer, I'd be able to count every one of her ribs.

The kraken female freezes when her rounded gaze lands on me, and then she dashes away. The four other krakens I came across did much of the same, running away the moment they saw me. One dared glare at me over their shoulder as they jetted off in the opposite direction.

It enrages me every time it happens. I must suffer the cost of existence, pay the price for the blood thrumming through my veins. I have defied nature, and the consequences must be reaped.

Cindi claims I am attractive, but it cannot be true. How can she say I am not an abomination when my own kind is repulsed by the sight of me?

Her question has been replaying in my mind for the past two days. She has barely spoken since. At night, she doesn't relax in my hold. I'm frightened this will continue as a result of my outburst.

It's my fault. My decision to distance myself has upset her. I have to make it right. I must say something, do something, to make her look at me. Words have never been my strong suit. If I open my mouth, I will make it worse.

You are one of the most attractive men I have ever met, but you are far from poisonous.

I want so badly for Cindi's words to be true, that she might not hate me. I might not be the monster everyone makes me out to be.

Only her opinion matters, but she doesn't get it. They've made me hate my own reflection, but what is there to like?

The hairband around my wrist grows heavy. Cindi likes my hair, does she not?

The last time she braided it, she tied it off then came to stand in front of me. There was a soft smile on her lips and a gleam in her eyes that stopped my breath. She tucked a loose strand behind my ear, then said, "There. Now I can see your face clearly."

I spent the entire day worried I'd burst from happiness. I could hardly contain it. She doesn't want me hidden.

The currents shift.

A new scent taints the water. Another kraken.

My claws dig into my palms. There are too many around. I've seen more in a day than I have in months. It has been years since non-Council members have dared speak to me. Still, my nerves refuse to settle.

I am larger than other krakens, stronger. I hold value. They would not dare attack me, but words can still hold venom.

A growl erupts in my chest when Lazell comes into view. He's like an urchin, vermin that needs to be killed—exactly as he thinks of me. I swim harder, hoping he doesn't try to engage in conversation that never ends well for one of us.

"Ordus," he calls.

I'd rather be attacked by a swarm of jellyfish than endure a minute with him, but alas, I must.

"*King* Ordus," I correct, slowing to a stop. It sounds like a joke, even to my ears.

Lazell adapts to the movement of my tentacles the closer he gets until it is like looking at my own reflection. Strong and sure. It doesn't suit him. Or me.

His eyes are sunken, cheeks more prominent. His skin has taken a pale, sickly hue. He looks nothing like the kraken who smiled as I was hooked and dragged away.

A warning sound vibrates in my chest when he looks me straight in the eye and sizes me up like he wants to finish what his brother couldn't do. As if he senses my thoughts, his lip twitches when he looks at the scar on my ribs before averting his gaze in faux respect.

"Out with it," I snap. The sooner I visit the healer, the sooner I can return to Cindi. I want to make her dinner again.

I want her to acknowledge my existence again.

Lazell's lips peel back for a split second before he rights

himself, but not soon enough. I puff my chest out in a show of intimidation. He bows his head, palms out as a sign of submission.

"Speak."

The column of his throat bobs. His mantle enlarges in irritation before he boldly looks me in the eyes again. "One of our sentries on the border reported seeing you haul a boat to your island twice in the past month."

I dislike the insinuation he has eyes on me. My inner beast slams against the walls, begging to rip the male to shreds for posing as a threat to my mate. It's an ugly, bloody feeling that raises my internal temperature to the point of boiling.

I know which two occasions he speaks of. I sensed the kraken female nearby but chose to forge ahead on my path. I saw no point in diverting my route to avoid her detection when bringing loot from the mainland is an activity I've been doing since my mother lived.

Lazell tilts his chin up to look down his nose at me. His brazen disregard for authority has always enraged me, but he's becoming far too emboldened for my liking. He mustn't think he has anything to lose—he likely doesn't anymore. "I believe you understand the risks posed by such—"

My claws dig into my palm. Blue blood twines in the murky water. "I did not ask for your recount of a report."

His nostrils flare before his attention drops down to my fist. I scowl when he flexes his four fingers. "Your Majesty, I only raise it as a concern for our people. Adding rubbish to decorate your island is not worth jeopardizing kraken-kind. If a human were to—"

My inner beast tears at the walls. I lurch forward. "The only one who saw is a kraken who should not be spying on their king. Should it happen again, I may find it is a punishable offense."

The wrinkles around his eyes deepen as he brazenly glares at me. "We are losing more viable land every passing day. As our king, it is your duty to ensure the survival of your people. Your continued gallivanting amongst humans is killing your people. Females. Cubs. They either leave or perish. The sooner you take a bride—"

I've heard enough.

"I will not be lectured about *duty* by a pest who shares blood with that demon who tried to kill a child. If I ever wish to seek your counsel, I will." My lips peel back, my sharpened teeth on display. "Now *leave* before I decide to act upon your insolence."

He holds my stare for far longer than he should. I have to remind myself killing him would harm Cindi. The masses would flock to my island and demand my head for ending their precious leader. If they don't take me out, my mate's death would be the only thing that would appease them.

Just as the thread on my control is about to snap, Lazell dips his head and swims away, muttering something I can't catch.

I'll have to do more parameter checks around the island from now on. Lazell's waning patience for me to take a bride is making him desperate, and desperation leads to recklessness.

Growling in frustration, I swim closer to the water's surface, swinging left toward the mountain range. Concentrating on the cool water or thinking about something other than the threat to my mate doesn't unwind the maddening tension in my chest. Nothing will calm me until my eyes are on her.

It isn't long until I descend toward the trenches where the healer made her home and spend the better part of an hour searching for the doorway I know all too well. It all looks so different without color.

Elder Adina was one of the few who cared little about my differences. I've spent more time with her than I have any other kraken I have no blood relation to. She's had to treat one too many of my ailments—especially when I was younger. I was born with modified human lungs, an organ no other kraken possessed in their natural form.

Mother gave her a residence at the palace to see to me daily. For a time, there were concerns whether I could continue living in the sea, or if I had to live on land if they wanted me to survive. It's another reason why I was moved to the island, why I spent so much time there growing up. I can only hold my breath for two or so days, but being on land will always be more comfortable.

My stomach sinks when I finally spot the healer's residence. Rubble covers the entrance, an offering basket woven around one of the stones—a sign the den has been vacated and its occupier is seeking the Goddess' blessing for luck and safe travels to find their new home.

I clench my jaw. Adina was our last living healer. Who will treat Cindi's injury now? Or her *vertigo*, as Cindi calls it. The information stones I've taken from the palace library have offered me no assistance.

She is clutching her arm less and less, but that is unacceptable. She should not be experiencing any kind of pain. I've asked her about it before. She claimed she is *semicertain* about what's wrong, and that time and rest is the cure.

Not good enough.

Huffing in frustration, I swim toward the edges of my territory in the direction of the island. I catch the breed of crab Cindi likes and spend the passing hours thinking of ways to make the island better suited for my human mate.

I want her to feel the same way I feel whenever I look at the *scrunchie* thing she gifted me. I feel...cherished. Deserving. *Accepted.*

Every time I look at my wrist, I can almost believe I am enough for her.

The sun is high in the sky by the time I make it back to the island. After depositing the crabs in the cage we made, I seek her out.

I already know where I'll find Cindi. She never stays in the den, even when her "vestibular system is being a bitch," preferring to keep busy with making the island her own or burning her skin on the beach.

Her scent dances in the water leading up to the shore, growing stronger with every wave the closer I get. Vasz is swimming somewhere nearby. He no doubt sensed me long before I sensed him.

Cindi's legs dangle in the water on either side of her surfboard. Most nights, she returns to the den bright red along her forehead, nose, and cheeks. She'll hiss and groan as I apply the healing paste. The next morning, she'll *hmm* and *ohh* when she looks in the mirror I installed in the hut, then repeat the whole burning process again.

Oxygen trickles into my lungs once I break the water's surface, slowly swimming toward my mate. Her eyes are closed, head tipped back with an easy expression. Watching her out here is the highlight of my day. It settles my inner beast, eases the gnawing ache of inadequacy.

I force myself to keep my sights on her face, not her soft breasts pressed against the tiny blue triangles of fabric with white trims and strings. My breeding arm hardens painfully whenever she forgoes the long-sleeve top that covers her arms and stomach and "protects her from the sun," as Cindi says.

I'm not sure why she needs protection from the sun. It's an odd human superstition.

From this angle, I can't see the fabric covering her sweet sex. Still, the sight of it is seared into my memory. My appendage twitches, instincts telling me to prowl forward, sink into her, and fill her with my seed.

A shudder works down my spine when I wrap my fist around my bulb. Moisture drips into the water, alleviating the pressure enough for me to approach Cindi without frightening her.

Cindi bobs with every wave, stretching her neck side to side. She doesn't have the thick, white, sticky residue along her nose and cheeks that she likes to wear whenever she plans on spending a long time out in the water. I don't like when she uses the paste. It tastes bad. Vasz always gags and shakes out his tongue as well.

Her eyes open, immediately finding mine. A soft smile spreads over her lips, plumping her sharp cheeks.

She's looking at me again.

A trail of fire rushes through my body, ravaging every doubt I have about her feelings toward me. If she hated me, would she smile at me the way she is now? Light up like she's *happy* to see me?

"You weren't in bed when I woke up," she says.

My lungs rattle like they did when I was a child and couldn't get enough air.

I grunt.

"The filter on one of the drums broke from last night's wind, but I managed to fix it—used almost an entire roll of tape to keep the fucker together."

I nod.

I want her to keep talking. Her voice is like finding shelter as rain patters against the grounds. It's bird song in the morning after a storm. The crash of waves against the shore after deafening silence. Cindi is my favorite sound.

She's my favorite everything. Mate or not, I would choose her every time. There is nothing about her that doesn't make my hearts skip beats.

The way she sits beside me and draws shapes in the sand before we work on building something together. The delicate touch of her hand as she helps correct my work and teaches me a better way to do it.

How she once offered a bat her food then screamed when it flew toward her. The string of conversations she has with Vasz, even though he isn't following what she's saying.

When she offers me her food, and the laugh she suppresses when I swallow the foulest thing I've ever tasted. Then, the brush of her skin against mine as she passes me one of her drinks to wash down the horrid taste.

Her soft snores, and the way she rubs her nose against my chest before thrashing around in her sleep to get comfortable. Then the drool that follows, the bright red on her cheeks when she notices the next morning.

How she continues to speak to me when I offer her nothing but my presence. She seeks my company out, and every day, I make her suffer the price.

I watch in silence as she stares up at the cliffs lining the tops of the island.

Every day, I question whether my silence is the right choice. It's what Cindi would truly prefer. It's not *me* she wants to talk to. It's anyone willing to listen.

If I don't speak, there's no chance for me to say the wrong thing—like I did in the treasure room.

Cindi looks back down at me. "What does the island look like?" There's a hopeful lilt to her voice.

That hope has dimmed with each passing day.

"Hold on," I tell her.

She yelps when I pull her board forward with my tentacles. Her small hands grip the front of the board. I do my best to find an opening with the least amount of surface motion, but the waves on this beach can be violent.

I swim hard against a wave to keep her from crashing against it, but it's no use. One of my tentacles grabs her arm when she sways dangerously. She bats me away, drops down flat onto the board, then says, "Now you can."

A smile threatens to break across my face at her confidence and overt trust in me.

That's who I am. A male Cindi trusts.

I use one tentacle to wrap around her and the board, keeping my senses open for any foreign scents in our surroundings. I spot

Vasz's fin in the distance, popping in and out of the surface before disappearing back under.

That mutt better not try anything stupid. He can hunt for his own food tonight if he nips at me.

Once we're further out from the island in calmer water, Cindi wriggles against my hold until I release her so she can sit back up. Water drips between her breast, and I force myself to look away, willing my breeding arm to go down on its own.

Goddess, I can still imagine the glint of sunlight as it trickles toward her sex.

The sex in my direct line of sight.

I must think of something else.

Urchins. Sea lice. The sound of Vasz's cleaning routine when I'm trying to sleep. Cindi's cooking. No, I can't think of anything to do with her.

"It's like a banana boat." Cindi chuckles. I snap my attention back to her when she starts splashing her feet, gazing out at the scenery, a beaming smile on her face. "I haven't been on one in years."

I know what a banana is, and I know what a boat is. What I don't know is how those two words work together.

She must see my questioning look. "It's an inflatable boat shaped like a banana."

I am no closer to understanding.

"I didn't realize how pretty it is," she whispers.

I grunt, and a divot forms between her brows. I wish I could take it back. "I suppose," I grumble.

I've never paid much attention before. The island simply...*is*. I hold no opinion on its appearance. There are jagged cliffs and small openings along the rock surface for bats to nest. Greenery and moss, sharp edges against rounded trees. The golden beach glitters from this distance.

So, yes, I suppose it is pretty. But if my mate is sitting beside it, there is no question as to which takes my breath away.

"By the way," Cindi begins, glancing back at me, "I think we need to redo the chicken coop. Cheeto ate a hole through the wood—or pecked, more like."

Of course the—as Cindi says—little shit has.

I brought Cindi chickens from the mainland after I tracked down the human male tourist and made him show me more videos on his phone that doesn't want to work without him. He said his favorite is the big animal that sometimes has horns. A cow? It would have been too difficult to bring it to the island.

After he showed me the chickens, I managed to find a few and a couple bags of feed, boated them to the island, and let them loose.

Cindi was shocked more than she was impressed. Then she paled and refused to eat them, instead naming the pests and allowing her favorite—*Cheeto*—to hang around with her on the beach.

He's the most annoying chicken. Made my tentacle bleed twice.

Five times, actually. Not only does Vasz want to bite me and my mate want to stab me, but I have to be on constant lookout for a chicken that wants to fight me for dominance. It is exhausting.

Cindi shifts, pulling her legs out of the water to lean back on the board.

"I was also thinking a fridge would be nice to preserve food." This is the third time Cindi has mentioned a *fridge*. I will ask the tourist human what it is. "Ice would be great too." I nod when Cindi casts me a glance. "I want to look into drying fish." I can't imagine anything worse. "I know you can with the really, really little ones, so I want to test it out one day." They taste terrible. "Not sure how you'll catch them, but it's just an idea." I'm sure I'll find a way.

We continue moving in silence. I want to say something, maybe ask her about her day. I hope she may eventually come to enjoy my company. I want to tell her she said my name in her sleep for the first time last night while I've been dreaming of her every day since I met her.

But I can't bring myself to speak for fear I will say the wrong thing and upset her. I opened my mouth two days ago, and look what happened. I made Cindi scream at me then ask to return to the mainland—something she hasn't done in a while.

So the silence builds and builds until it's suffocating. Cindi puts me out of my misery when we're halfway around the island.

"Oh, and we need batteries too. I would kill for a fan." I've learned this is what Cindi calls *sarcasm*, and she wouldn't actually kill someone for it. It has been a learning curve. "Another generator would support a lot of things if my whole renewable energy idea doesn't work. I could hook a fridge, fan—*oooh*, and a radio or something so I can play music."

I'm about to grunt, but Cindi's lips twist in preempted disappointment before I can utter a response. It spears me the same way it does whenever she stares blankly at the horizon or plucks at the grass, expressionless.

I've never been one to think things through; it's no different now.

"What—" Cindi cuts off in a scream when her board capsizes and she falls straight into my awaiting arms. I tug her against my chest, her arms and legs immediately wrapping around me like it's second nature, and there's nothing I can do to stop the contented purr from rumbling to life.

She doesn't hate me.

"You did that on purpose," my pretty mate accuses, hitting me playfully.

I try to hide my smile by looking down at the water. "Vasz must be around." It's not a lie. He is nearby, just not quite within biting distance.

"I could've drowned."

My tentacle that can never seem to keep to itself taps Cindi's leg as if offended she'd imply such a thing would happen.

"You're not slick," she huffs, a smile playing at her lips.

That... Okay. No. This must be sarcasm again, because I do believe I am quite smooth.

I lean back in the water with an arm around her waist so she can fully relax and let me do all the work. She props herself up, straddling me like she does on the board, her hands flat on my chest, staring out at the island as we continue our slow swim around it.

I may not trust myself to speak, but this? Holding her in place, touching her in reverent worship? I can do this for every waking moment until I die.

Minutes pass before she readjusts her position. She lies against me, head tucked beneath my chin like we do at night. Bumps erupt over my flesh when she traces the scar along my ribs before wading her hand through the water.

My purr increases in volume, drowning the sound of the surf-board bobbing against the waves. Her little sigh goes straight to my breeding arm, and this time, I do nothing to settle it. My mate is in my arms, fed and well, placing her full trust in me to keep her safe. I want to absorb every moment of it.

"Do you have any stories about this place?" Cindi timidly asks.

I wish I could take back my weeks of silence. Cindi should never be timid, and I made her that way. It's getting hard to remember why I'm so insistent on keeping up with it.

Still, the only answer I can give won't be what she wants to hear. "None you will enjoy."

She tenses, and I place my hand over her back to stop her from running. "Ordus..." She peers up at me through her lashes, brows pinched in worry.

I quickly scan our surroundings for any new scents. Other than Vasz, there's not another living soul around us.

"You said your people call this place the Malediction Island, the beach Mutant Shores."

"Yes." I nod.

"I think you should rename it. It's your home. You should treat it that way." Her frown deepens for reasons I can't decipher.

She may not see it this way, but it's Cindi's home too. She's made the island hers. Our den is made up entirely of her belongings. The land is covered in things she's made or needs for survival.

At this point, the island is more Cindi's than mine.

"You should have...positive thoughts about this place." My mate says it like she's uncertain that's the correct word.

The only good thing to happen on that island is the woman in my arms. Nothing else compares. She's the only light left.

I run a finger down her spine, and her scent sours, but only for a moment. "What would you suggest?" I ask.

"Not Vaszeline and sure as shit not petroleum jelly." She chuckles, shifting back up to look at me.

I hope Vasz didn't hear that. He already thinks it's *his* island. Cindi's rejection would make him spend a whole day sulking.

"Your name, then? Cindi's Island?"

She sighs, releasing my gaze. "My... That's not my name."

What? Have I been calling her the wrong name this entire time? I'm a bad mate. An awful one. Why didn't she correct me?

"I changed my name to Cindi after I ran from my husband because as far as I'm concerned, Kristy is dead. So, I mean, yeah. I guess Cindi is my name."

I'm both relieved and enraged. How could anyone want to harm her? Why would she have to kill a part of herself to survive?

I inhale deeply, pulling her scent into my lungs to calm the need to act upon the anger.

Swallowing, I force my voice to hide my emotions. "Humans have two names, do they not? Yannig said the female sometimes takes one of the male's names when they marry."

She nods, lips curled like she's tasting something bitter. "Yes, I took my husband's last name. Before then, I had my dad's." My mate softens at the mention of her father.

Cindi has spoken of him once during dinner. She pointed at one of the items I took from the mainland and told me how her father taught her about the automobiles. Based on the way she hung her head and the water gathering on her tear line, I assumed her father passed.

She offers me a sad smile. "He would've loved seeing this island. If he had his way, he'd live by the sea, spending every day fishing or surfing. In my first year of college, he and his buddies built a raft I helped design and were betting on how long it would last out on the water."

"Did he win?"

She snorts. "Dad put money on it staying afloat for two hours. It lasted four minutes and twenty-three seconds."

I smile up at her, and her own widens. I run my hand up the length of her back, reveling in the feel of her soft skin. "What was his name?"

"He went by his last name: Saelim."

My hand travels back up her spine to cup her jaw. "Then it shall be called Saelim Island, in memory of your father."

Her lips part with a wobble. I hold myself back from grabbing one between my teeth and taking her worries away. She searches my face for a lie she won't find. "Really?"

This time, when I grunt, she lights up.

"I like that."

Her attention drops to my lips when my lips stretch into a smile. "Yes?"

She smiles back at me. "Yes."

26

CINDI

Would Dad be absolutely chuffed about having an island named after him?

Shit yes.

He'd make it his opening line to every new person he met. He'd print out a map, circle the island, then make it his phone screen background and have it framed.

Would Dad be absolutely pissed about me being a willing captive on said island?

Eh.

My gut says no. My logic also says no.

Am I still thinking of plans on how to get the fuck out of here? Also, no. In the early days, the best thing I could come up with was holding a gun to Ordus' head to force him to take me back—which I was doubtful would work.

Yes, I want to go back to the mainland. I miss it. I want a change of scenery for a bit.

But no, I don't want to spend every waking moment scared

the Gallaghers will find me.

And *marry* Ordus to save all krakens and probably slow down global warming in the process? I—I don't know.

Where does that leave me?

Well, I at least know that leaves me cradled in the arms of a monster who's killed for me, goes the extra mile for me every day, and has abs hard as rock that contract whenever I wriggle.

So I keep wriggling, keep squeezing my legs around his waist to feel his breath hitch, his hand tightening around my thigh.

And because I'm an awful human being, I play with his hair to watch his eyelids flutter and grow heavy.

I ignore the weight of the future to focus on the sound of his shuddering breaths in the small dome around our heads. I gnaw on my lip, barely paying attention to how the island looks underwater. We returned my surfboard to the shack and ate dinner before Ordus asked whether I wanted the full outdoor tour.

I jumped at the opportunity. I'm telling myself it's out of pure curiosity, not because I want to spend more time with him, but I know the truth.

It's addicting to see someone be so responsive to me in a way that doesn't bring pain. Tommy had a hair-trigger reaction, but it's nothing like Ordus. This man is like a puppet on my string, and there's nowhere else he'd rather be.

I'm enraptured by all of it.

If I really think about it, sure, there's likely an element influenced by the alleged soulmate thing. But it's still more than that, right? He doesn't need to bring me chickens, build me a hammock and swing set, or learn how to cook human food.

I just can't make sense of his distance, though. He went from singing his undying love for me every two seconds to grunting and the occasional sentence here and there. If he really, truly wanted me to marry him and end the Curse, why hasn't he mentioned it? Not even once?

Why he isn't trying harder for me to marry him so his people don't starve to death? My gut tells me he genuinely is giving me the choice, simply happy to have someone else on the island... which doesn't sit right with me. His people are suffering because of something I could supposedly prevent.

I don't know what to make of it.

We dip suddenly, swerving to the left. I yelp and accidentally grab a fistful of his hair. His eyes widen in surprise, and a low chuckle sends a questionable thrill down my spine. He does it again, and I gasp, clutching him harder. We can't be steady for more than eight seconds before he takes us for another dip, then twirls us through the water like a torpedo.

My stomach flips. It isn't wholly unpleasant. For a moment, it's like I'm fourteen again, with my friends, screaming with our arms up in the air, going this way and that on the roller coaster.

That same giddy feeling has me shrieking when Ordus dives straight down toward the sea floor before straightening out at the very last second. A smile splits across my face as he keeps doing it until unexpected laughter peels right out of me.

I only just catch his own smile for a second before he's swirling us again. My fist is still in his hair, and I should feel bad and worry about my supplies—scold him for changing the subject.

It's the same freeing sensation of being carried through a wave, never knowing if you're going to crash or make it to the other side in one piece. It's exhilarating and invigorating and saddening because I remember a time when laughing like this was a daily occurrence.

My stomach lurches unhappily, and I tap his back in silent command to cut it out before I throw up the crab I had for dinner. He straightens immediately without question, swimming along like nothing happened.

The temperature of the water drops as we descend closer to the ocean floor. The familiar cave entrance looms ahead.

I survey the water. It feels so wrong for there to be no other life around—not even any moss on the stone, only the plants higher up the cliffside that are untouched by water. Will the island be destroyed if the Curse isn't ended?

I blurt out my question before I chicken out and keep fretting over it. "What happens if you don't..." Mate? Bond? Shackle me to you? "Marry?"

Ordus' face tightens. "My territory will be completely uninhabitable, and krakens will be forced to leave or die."

That's what he said last time, but it still doesn't add up. "Why don't they just—I know I sound like a dick—but why don't they just leave, then? If there's no food here, then why stay?" *Why aren't you pressuring me to marry you?*

My stomach swoops when we loop around a protruding rock. Ordus mutters the word to open the entrance to the cave, and the sigils glow blue, groaning as the rock rolls aside.

His voice rumbles in the small space as we become engulfed by darkness. The lack of echo and reverberation plays tricks on my mind. "Because this land belongs to our kind. To leave it is to risk death from trespassing into another creature's region, or from natural causes from incompatible climate. Many have already left."

A shiver slides down my back from the plummeting temperature. "Shit, it's cold." I curl around Ordus to steal his body heat, hoping and praying he doesn't feel my nipples poking through my bikini.

One arm curves beneath my shoulder and engulfs my waist and half my back to cradle my head against his chest, covering as much of my exposed skin as he can.

The other hand travels up my thigh, catching on my bottoms. My breath labors. Liquid heat curls through my core. He settles at the base of my spine, right above my ass, fingers dangerously close to dipping beneath the fabric.

Ordus presses the lower half of my body to his hard stomach. Sparks detonate behind my eyes from the sudden pressure against my sensitive flesh. The complete lack of orgasms I've had since coming to this island is catching up with me and rewiring my brain chemistry.

I don't think he's aware of what he's doing. There's nothing that suggests any ulterior motive other than to warm me up. He's doing what he set out to achieve, because my internal temperature has soared to an uncomfortable boil filling my veins with fire.

I clear my throat. "Did they survive?" I rasp.

"I do not know. The odds are not in their favor." His voice is far too hoarse for this topic of conversation. I wish I could see his expression in the dark.

"So unless you marry, krakens will be extinct?" I confirm.

Ordus' hand slips lower, practically cupping my backside. Only this time, I choke. His fingers brush the hem that leads down to my heat that's rubbing against Ordus every time he moves, scrambling my brain.

He needs to move his hand. Right now. I need to move it for him. It's not appropriate. Wrong.

It's too hot in this tunnel. Cuddling is fine.

This? This is not fine. But I can't bring myself to move.

What are we talking about?

Right. The Curse. Marriage. Our collective existential crisis.

He grunts. It's strained. I hear him take a deep breath. "They will be endangered, forever skating the line of extinction, yes."

Is he wound up because of the topic, or because of—his finger dips beneath my bikini as he drags me up his chest, adding friction to the neediest part of me. I clamp my mouth shut to stop any sounds from coming out.

His hand returns to the base of my spine. It was an innocent gesture to readjust his hold on me. Gentlemanly. I'm the pervert here for getting all hot and bothered by it.

Get it together. Focus. Ignore it. Ignore him. This is a serious, important conversation. And—I take a deep breath. *Okay. Concentrate.*

"Will you leave, then?"

"Where you go, I follow." His deep tenor wraps around my aching body. I shudder against him. He means it. To the deepest recesses of my soul, I know he means it.

He says it with intent, like he's trying to tell me something I'm not getting.

"The area surrounding the mainland belongs to the humans and is the safest place for us to hunt to avoid encountering scavengers or creatures far deadlier," he explains. Ordus shakes his head just as the first batch of glowing algae illuminates his face before plunging us back into darkness. "But hunting near the mainland comes at the risk of discovery, which is a sure death as well. We are quickly running out of krakens strong enough to make the journey, and they are needing to swim further and further out."

That sobers me enough to push my libido to the background.

"Damned if you do, damned if you don't." I sigh, frowning from the painful tingles going down my arm.

Fuck, not again.

I hang my arm limp at my side, letting Ordus take the brunt of the effort to keep me against him. I maneuver my sore arm beneath his to rest my hand under the scar along his ribs.

Ordus makes a sound of agreement. "All soldiers have been assigned to bring game back from the mainland to feed the people, but even then, the water alone has become unsafe. Only the strongest kraken will survive."

"Is there no other way to end the Curse?" I ask hopefully.

I feel his head shake. "The Witch is dead. The elders suspect there may be an anchor of some kind that enables the Curse to continue without its caster, likely two because of the severity of the Curse."

I rake my teeth against my bottom lip as another wave of light hits us. My only knowledge about magic comes from TV and fiction books. I have no authority or experience to be throwing out ideas, but I might as well try. "You have sigils on your doors. That's a witchy thing, isn't it? Don't you use magic to shift as well? Shouldn't your people have more of an idea?"

To his credit, he pauses to think about it. "My mother was once friends with a witch. Her strength was incomparable to the one who cursed us. Beyond basic healing pastes and protection spells, we knew very little. The krakens of the royal line's ability to shift is inherent because we are the only ones with any power. Our magic is different. It is not an outward manifestation."

If an entire population of krakens can't come up with a loophole around the Curse, where do I get off thinking I, a human woman who didn't know mythical creatures existed until about a month ago, will think of something?

Which means there really is only one solution.

"And…" I swallow, pulse hammering. The algae is becoming more frequent, so I can't hide in the dark. "You mentioned marrying to end the Curse. You've also spoken about bonding. Is there…a difference?"

"The term is used interchangeably." His eyes drop down to me, rendering me frozen in his arms as another flash of light catches the longing etched into every crease in his face. "I will not force you to marry me, Cindi. We move at your pace, even if there is no pace at all."

I frown up at him. "Aren't you tired of me?" I say, breath catching when his hand glides back down to my ass to keep me stable as we take a sharp bend. Like everything else, it's an innocent gesture that skyrockets my heart rate. His fingers are mere inches from my core, and I'm frightened to think how wet he'd find me if we weren't in the water.

One bump, one turn, a single swoop, and he'd be sliding over my slit like his thick appendages have done before. Images flash in my mind of all the times his tentacles have come dangerously close to sliding over my heat.

I shiver. Ordus squeezes my flesh to push me up his vibrating chest, rubbing my sensitive nipples and sex over his hard abs. It's pure sin. My nails dig into his shoulders. I want to arch my back so fucking bad to add more pressure somewhere. Anywhere. I just...

I want him to make me feel good.

Which is wrong, bad, and shouldn't happen for so many reasons, but fuck, can't I have something nice for once in my life?

Whether it's an accident or his gentlemanly façade drops, he gropes my ass, grabbing at the flesh so it pulls at my folds. My lips fall into an O.

My eyes round when his hand threaded into my hair uses the strands as leverage to force me to hold his suffocating gaze. "You fascinate me." His breath skates across my tingling skin. "Everything about you fascinates me." He carefully kneads my backside, getting closer and closer to the forbidden area each time. "The mark behind your ear. Your voice. How you tap your right thumb against your thigh when you're thinking. Scrunching your nose before eating crab. The stretch you do when you first wake up. Sometimes, when you're working, you make these small humming sounds. It's rare, but it always brings a smile to my face."

I flush red against the chilled water. He noticed all that? "This is the most you've spoken to me in weeks." *Outside of the treasure room.*

He stops massaging me and looks away, pretending to focus on navigating the tunnel, even though the pool is right above us. "It's for the best."

I take a deep breath just before the bubble bursts and saltwater floods around us. It's not a full second before we're breaking the surface into the cave that's quickly becoming my own safe space—like the swinging chair hanging from the ceiling, handmade by Ordus using the trees around the island. He set it up next to the shelf filled with books he smuggled for me from the mainland so I can stay inside and read if the weather is bad, I'm too tired, or to wind down before bed.

Then there's the thick mats made from layers of woven bamboo to protect my feet from the unforgiving stone, and the little bed of dirt, moss, and coconut husks I made for Vasz.

I've made this entire island my own faster than I made the cabin my home back in Bali. It took six months before I even dared buy new clothes or used a dining chair that wasn't a couple bucks and made from plastic.

Yet here I am, changing this place into my vision, away from pirates and the Gallaghers, from the claws of crippling paranoia and the brink of hysteria.

My greatest threats on this island are the sharp rocks, bats that leave me alone as long as I return the favor, Vasz's teeth, and the organ between my ribs that wants too much of Ordus' attention. Companionship. To beat without feeling the twinge of the shards encasing it.

My attention fixes on the monster before me, carrying me like I'm his greatest treasure. Lips thin and wary. Jaw tight and clenched. Voice brittle. "I can't say the wrong things if I never speak."

The water quietly laps against us as I draw my hand over his hair and shoulders, down to the center of his chest where the purrs have stopped. It's a sound I've come to long for, soft rumblings I hear as sleep lulls me into its clutches every night.

"You should talk more anyway," I whisper. "You have a nice voice."

A small smile tugs at my lips when the soft vibrations stir beneath my fingertips, unraveling every knot in my muscles.

Ordus' eyes slowly travel down to my hand. He stills beneath me, so stiff, he could shatter. My eyes round, and every cell in my body screams in panic. Something's wrong.

I frantically follow his line of sight to my breast, and the internal screaming turns deafening. My bikini shifted during the swim; now Ordus has a first-row seat to my exposed nipple.

Mortification stains my body in bright splotches of red. Before I can scramble to cover myself and collect the last vestiges of my dignity, a tentacle loops around my thigh, and the pointed tip brushes over my center.

I suck in a sharp breath, looking up at Ordus. Whatever pain painted him earlier has morphed into pure, unbridled desire.

He pinches my chin between his thumb and forefinger, the tip of his claw curving over my lip. "The Goddess made you perfect, little mate."

My eyelids flutter at the heat in his voice. It's deeper than I've ever heard it before, a fraying thread about to snap.

Oxygen whooshes from my lungs at the press of a pointed edge along the inner seams of my bikini bottoms before moving across my ass to hold me up. A growl thunders beneath his purr.

There's an unfamiliar comfort in knowing I could say a single word, and this will all end. He'll let me go, maybe even fix my top for me, turn his head to give me privacy. The tension would evaporate.

He hasn't pushed me to marry him because it's my decision. He hasn't touched me in inappropriate ways or said anything that makes my skin crawl because he won't do anything unless I ask for it.

I shift my hips against his tentacle, grinding along the hard limb. Ordus' nostrils flare, and his lips peel back to reveal his sharp teeth, his expression twisted with rage and desperation. I'm not scared. On the contrary—I want to wrap my arms around him, trace his harsh jaw, and hang on every word he's willing to give me.

"Cindi," he warns.

A bulb drags along my inner thigh. It pauses over my sex.

Oh. He's just as affected as I am.

"You should talk more often," I whisper, lips moving against his clawed thumb that could rip me to shreds.

I poke my tongue out, swiping across the harsh pad to taste the saltwater clinging to his skin.

"Tell me what you want," he rasps. His fingers twitch against my ass, eyes never once straying back to my exposed chest.

Control. He's giving me every ounce of it in this moment.

This is for me, not him. Everything he does is for me.

Goosebumps erupt over my flesh as he draws us out of the water, settling me against his thick limbs on the side of the pool. He towers over me, his hand still inches away from finding out it's not the water making me wet.

His tentacle tightens around my leg, and warm liquid spills onto the delicate skin of my inner thigh. The muscles in my lower stomach spasm, and he takes a deep breath. The blacks of his eyes devour the blue, more beast than man.

And the monster is still giving me the reins.

I want to take them.

"It...aches." I almost don't recognize myself.

Ordus' purr jumps in volume. "Tell me where it hurts." He trails his finger along my cheek, bending down to brush his lips up my jaw to the shell of my ear. "Let me fix it, *mate*."

My breaths come out in short bursts. My free leg falls to the side, knee resting on his waiting tentacle. I arch my back, pushing my ass into his hand before grinding myself against the V of his abs.

He snarls, a sound so animalistic, my heart rate leaps.

Without warning, my bikini bottom is reduced to shreds, a pile of ribbons on the ground, swollen flesh exposed to him.

I'm distantly aware of the sirens blaring in my head, warning bells urging me to step on the brakes, to stop us from crossing a line I can't uncross. I know what this would mean for me. What would it translate to for the monster who thinks I'm his soulmate?

Whatever the answer is, the question evaporates from my mind as soon as a tentacle sinks into me. A moan tears from my throat at the same time as he releases a growl that vibrates through my bones.

It's a gentle move, cautious, like he's holding himself back and doesn't want to hurt me.

I clamp around him. Somewhere in me, there's a long rope with dents and tangles. In a single second, it's obliterated. His sucker pulses around my clit, and there's nothing in this universe that exists except his tentacle in my pussy.

Ordus draws back before pushing back inside me, over and over, deeper each time. I look down as warm liquid drips from his bulbed appendage onto my core and trickles around his thrusting tentacle.

He's fucking his cum into me.

"You stretch so pretty for me, little mate." He's all monster. There's no hint of the man behind that voice. "Is this where you're hurting?"

I grunt. Choke. Whimper. I couldn't speak even if there was a gun to my head. He might have given me power over him, but in this moment, I'm completely and utterly powerless to my own whims.

"Perfect." Ordus sucks my clit harder, and I thrash against him, clawing at his arms, bucking against his limbs. It's pure ecstasy.

I'm not sure what happens, but my breasts fall victim to the cool cavern air and my top is on the ground right before a long, pointed tongue laves at the hard bud. "My sweet mate," he purrs. I scream when his sharp teeth prick my nipple, and he does it again and again, alternating between licking and threatening me with his teeth.

Nothing about what he's doing is rough. There isn't an ounce of hurt or an inkling of incoming pain. Still, he isn't treating me like I'm breakable. He's looking at me like I'm the Goddess he spends his life praying to, and he's on his knees appeasing me, worshipping my flesh and tasting me like I'm his first and last meal.

I lose all sense of composure when a sucker wraps around me and—dear fucking *God*.

Ordus' pleased chuckle splashes my desire with fury that fizzles away when his tentacle eases into me, stretching me out until it stings.

"Is this what you wanted to hear? My voice?" He pulls out, keeping his tentacle an inch away from my entrance. My muscles spasm angrily at the loss. "It's only fair I hear yours too."

"Ordus." It's my turn to sound animalistic.

"That's it, little human. Louder."

He smiles a full, sadistic smile, plunging back into me in a single swoop. I scream, fisting his hair, then snarling in frustration when he deprives me of his appendage.

"Again," he demands. He thrusts back into me, tentacles curling around my limbs to keep me in place, like he might die if I left.

I cry out, arching my back to take more of him. I'm not quite sure what goes through my head at that moment, but I slam my lips against his, and everything stops. He doesn't move, doesn't dare breathe.

Shame washes over me. I misread this.

Kissing is too much. I shouldn't have. This probably means something else to him, and I—

Ordus grabs the base of my neck and kisses me back as if his life depends on it. It's unpracticed and unsure, but he follows my lead, moving with me. He tests out each nibble the way I do, sliding against my lips, tasting each other as he resumes thrusting into me and sucking my clit.

"Do you want to leave?" he breathes, expression tight. "Do you want to go back to the mainland, Cindi?"

His question hits me with a wave of clarity. It disperses the lusty haze and brings me back to reality. Do I want to leave this safe haven and never return?

Is he really asking me that? Is it a real offer?

My answer should be a confident, immediate yes, but I hesitate. The few-second delay it takes me to nod my head speaks volumes. That I never use my voice is even louder.

I *need* to go back. Have to. There's no other option. I'm meant to agree. I don't belong here, and I don't *want* to stay here for the rest of my life. I'm feeling the oncoming of stir-craziness after a month. What will I be like in a couple more weeks?

The lines of Ordus' face soften at my hesitance. He exhales like a boulder has just been lifted from his shoulder, and in its place, an emotion cripples me: hope.

For the first time in weeks, he looks truly *hopeful*.

Guilt and dread suffocate me, but I can't do a damn thing about it when he eases out of me, notching another tentacle at my entrance.

My pulse roars. "What—"

"Every tentacle I fit in your sex is another hour I will allow you to spend on the mainland."

Wait. Does he really—

"One." He slides a single tentacle in.

Frustration claws at me, question forgotten. I need more. Deeper. God—*fuck*. It's not enough. He needs to move.

My mouth falls open on a moan when another appendage slides into me. The stretch is almost too much. He slips in slowly to allow me to adjust to the mind-altering fullness. My pussy stretches around him, taking sucker after sucker. I swear, I can feel him in the back of my throat.

"Two," he rasps, eyes heavy and glazed over.

Ordus is breathing harder than I am. His breeding arm is off to the side somewhere, but I can still feel his cum dripping down the inside of my thighs.

Two. Two hours on the mainland.

I could accomplish so much with two hours. I can't think of what right now, but I'm certain I can do something.

A string of curses flies past my lips when he pumps into me, slowly, so agonizingly slowly. His suckers catch on my clit with each pass, pulsing and warming, making me relaxed and wilder at the same time. My vision darkens as bright spurts of white flash behind my eyes.

I don't know what's up or down, left or right. I can barely breathe with how—I can't even describe it. Out of this world. Extraordinary. I'm at the gates of both heaven and hell, and I have no idea whether I'm going to ascend or perish.

My climax hits me, and I don't know how I react. I think I scream Ordus' name. I think I slap him. His arms might be bleeding from my nails.

But he doesn't let up.

He keeps going, and I think he might kill me from it.

Nothing coming out of my mouth is coherent, not a single thought comprehensible. The only thing I manage to register beyond the pure pleasure in my core is his guttural, *"Three."*

I'm screaming, sobbing, moaning until I can't make a sound because I've become blackout delirious. When did he put a third one in?

Tears spring from my eyes. I'm trembling. Bucking. Crying for him to stop and keep going. Another orgasm is coming, I can feel it. It's going to take me out.

Ordus leans down, his long, blue tongue sliding over my cheek to capture my tears. His purrs grow impossibly loud. "Is that all you can take, mate? Three?" His eyes shine with curiosity. "How badly do you want to go to the mainland?" He tips his head to the side, studying me as another tentacle wraps around my leg, up to my core. "A fourth?"

I shake my head. "I can't—I—It won't fit."

The pointed tip prods at my back entrance. "Hmm," he muses, pushing in slowly. "Here?"

No.

No, no.

Fuck.

I don't think I can hold it back. My climax is chasing me, coming stronger than ever before. I'm falling, and I know eight limbs will catch me. I'm so far from being in control right now, but at the same time, I have it in my grasp.

I want this. I want to orgasm around this monster's tentacle, and I want to scream because I fucking deserve it.

I walked through hell. I have the burns to prove it. I want to feel free from everything for one fucking minute. I want to let go.

Just this once.

Because one more second won't hurt.

There's a silver lining in all of this, and I want to cover myself in it.

When my climax hits me, I let it knock me off my feet and descend into the dark depths. Fireworks explode around me, erupting blues and browns and golds. And when I finally settle onto the ground, it's in Ordus' arms, wrapped up in his safe embrace, my head against his chest, engulfed by his sea salt scent and rhythmic purr that grows louder at my whimper.

The emptiness that follows is so profound, I almost ask him to put his tentacle back inside me. "It aches," I mewl.

He presses his lips to the top of my head before carrying me to our bed. "I will take care of you."

27

ORDUS

I can still taste her.

On my tongue, on my suckers, in the pores of my skin. I can taste her, and I feel complete. I was hopeful, but I never thought I'd ever be welcomed into her sex, or press her lips to mine, or hear her say my name with such demanding need.

I throw glances at Cindi as she surfs while I continue building the shelter to install by the beach so she can watch the waves even when the skies open.

I like a lot of things.

I like the meat in a crab's legs. The smell of the air after a storm. When I put together the final piece of a project and it works exactly how I planned.

I like Cindi's smile the most.

I like my mate. A lot. Even if she pretends not to like me back, I'd still like her. She's a fighter. Strong. Smart. Observant. Snappy. When I get angry, she holds her ground—sometimes. Chaotic but organized.

Cindi prefers to sit and watch. That's what I like to do too. And she's a tinkerer as well. She has a workroom that's messier than mine, with just as many unfinished projects.

Most of all, she trusts me.

I've spent all morning and afternoon distracted, replaying every moment I spent with my Cindi.

She laughed. I made my mate laugh.

And I made her moan. She was—*is* so beautiful.

I want to do it over and over again, because it was the most breathtaking thing I've ever seen. It is all that has played on my mind, an endless loop that fills me with more joy than I can contain. It was the sweetest melody, more potent than a siren's song.

She used to always be so dour that her delight is the greatest blessing the Goddess could bestow.

My breeding arm hardens even more when I look at her again —my bulb has been leaking since last night.

Last night was perfect in every way except for the words that left my mouth. Asking her whether she wanted to return to the mainland was foolish. Of course, her answer would be yes. I was an idiot to think what we were doing would somehow change her desire to leave me.

Offering to take her back was even more foolish. She may smile at me and close her eyes when I purr for her, but nothing has changed. The moment we depart this island, she will be plotting her escape. She will run at the first opportunity she gets, and I will drag her back here so she can spend the rest of her days despising me while my territory becomes uninhabitable.

I'm failing my siblings, their deaths meaningless in the name of my mate's freedom to choose whether to marry me or not. I could've spent the past few weeks convincing her to bond to me to save my kingdom, but I couldn't bring myself to mention it even once. I don't want to manipulate Cindi into doing anything she doesn't want to do. She'd only resent me more.

And kraken-kind might die for it.

I understand now why I'm considered a monster, because only a monster would be willing to allow the hundreds who remain to die.

I want my mate more than I want my people to survive. I can only imagine the look of disgust on my family's face over my self-ishness. I have failed at every kingly duty I've been given. What's one more? The gravest one.

If I'm unveiling the full truth to myself, I'm not even certain marrying Cindi would end the Curse. The territory might be too far gone for anything to be done, and Cindi may not be the *destined* bride—even if she is my soulmate.

Destiny is too subjective, especially when it is placed in the hands of an all-powerful being. It's too vague and nonspecific. But if I had to wager, a soulmate is the closest answer.

I tie the log off then grab another to continue building the roof. A commotion draws my attention back to the sea.

Vasz comes sprinting out of the water, barking, "Krakens! Krakens coming! Many, many krakens! "

The blood drains from my face. I launch toward the beach to grab my mate. "Cindi!" I roar. "Get out of the water."

Brown eyes swing to mine with panic. She drops onto the board and quickly paddles back to shore, casting frightened glances behind her.

Vasz rushes besides me, panting, *"Must protect."*

It isn't until the first wave hits me that I sense them. There are at least twenty different scents contaminating the water. They're close—*too close*. They'll arrive in a matter of seconds.

They know Cindi is here. There's no way they wouldn't. Her own scent is strong from all the time she spends surfing.

None have ever dared venture this close to my island before, for fear of what I might do to them. Something must have changed. Someone could have seen Cindi, or her scent might have traveled further than it would have from the storm the other day.

I swim faster than I ever have before, lashing my tentacle out to suction onto her board before tearing her toward the beach. Vasz swoops beneath the water to help push her forward.

"Ordus, what's happening?" Her voice shakes.

"Go to the den. *Now.*" Red tints my vision. They dare approach? They *dare* put my mate in danger?

She stumbles onto her feet, narrowing her eyes out at the water. "What is that—? Holy fuck."

Panic, raw and all-consuming, grips me by the neck. Our den is the only place they won't be able to get to her. The enchantment only allows for me, Vasz, and my mate to enter. But how long would she survive down there if I died?

"Cindi, *leave*," I snarl, putting every ounce of my desperation into the word.

But it's too late. The first kraken appears above the waves. A hunter. Our strongest one. She carries out the most trips to the mainland to bring back game. Marussa is smaller than the last time I saw her, less flesh and more bone, with sunken eyes and pale skin.

One by one, krakens breach the surface, each looking as tired and starved as the last, all sporting the same faint, greenish hue. Females, males, they all appear, crowding my shore.

In the center of it all is Lazell, surrounded by the twelve other members of the Council and our few remaining sentries.

Vasz growls beside me, barking in warning. Cindi makes no move to run like I demanded. I force her behind me, my fury flaring. My chest and limbs expand, making myself bigger, primed for battle.

All eyes are directed on the human behind me.

I want to kill them. I want their deaths to be long and torturous, their organs littering my shores.

Lazell gnashes his teeth at me. "What is the meaning of this?" he hisses, nodding at my mate, speaking the kraken tongue.

"I should be asking you this." My rage lashes at the kraken who's been pining for my death since the moment I was born. "You are trespassing on my island. Leave before I kill you all."

"Some king you are, threatening your people," he spits. A chorus of agreement echoes through the crowd. "You brought a *human* into our territory. You let her see our kind. *You* broke your family's own rules."

"Lazell was right," Mailien, another Council member, starts. "You're consorting with humans. Have you learned nothing from the Witch?"

"They should have killed you," another jeers.

"Vermin!"

"The humans will come for us!"

"Seize him!"

Each cry is another knife in my chest. It's like I'm thirteen years old, swimming back home with my latest catch. I can feel their phantom hands clawing at me, the pierce of the hook into my ribs that narrowly missed my lungs. Their words echo in my head, clanging against my skull before striking again, over and over.

Hands grabbing me. Hitting me. Snarls. Jeers. Taunts. Sharp pain in my side as a chain is wrapped around me.

Make it stop.

I heave for air. They're screaming, louder and louder. I'm going to die. And my mate—I need to protect my mate.

Make it stop.

"*Silence,*" I roar, breathing hard. Think. *Think.* I bare my teeth and slash my tentacles across the water. Krakens jump out of the way. I want to hit skin—*need* to see blood.

"You told me to pick a bride, so I pick this one." I motion to my mate, whose burnt scent permeates the air. My fury multiples tenfold.

When Mailien barks "It's hideous," I lose it.

No rational thought takes hold. The ugly beast inside me rears its head. The hatred and pain curdles, boiling until it breaks out of my skin. Years of hate, a lifetime of cowering, the grating silence—it all comes out.

The cage is broken. Only blood will settle the beast.

I'm bigger. Faster. Stronger. Mailien's head is ripped clean from his shoulders before he can blink.

A sentry lunges for me, staff raised, and I dodge it easily, cracking his body beneath my tentacles.

The world is tinged red. Blue bleeds from the krakens onto the shore. I can't hear their screams, can't see the disdain written across their faces.

More.

They all need to die for what they've done.

I prowl forward, claws poised to tear into skin. Only the softest voice coming from behind me stops me in my tracks.

"Ordus."

Cindi.

The beast halts long enough for a single thought to break through: if I kill my people, more will come.

They'll circle the island so we're trapped until we've finished our food reserves. Once I'm weak from starvation, they'll attack. I won't risk Cindi's safety by attempting to swim for the mainland. I can't kill them.

"You want me to be a monster? Then I am your monster," I snarl, chest rising and falling, looking every kraken in the eyes. Some bow their heads in fear while others raise them in challenge. "Does anyone else dare insult my mate?"

Lazell glares at me in mortification, blue splatter on his striped skin. "Your mate? Have you gone mad? The Waste has gotten to you."

The rest of the Council are stiff in their spots, glancing between me and Lazell. They'll flee the first chance they get. The krakens before me are no true warriors. Some may have fought alongside my brother and sister, but they've weakened since then. I may not be afflicted by Waste, but I have had no issue with hunger or sickness.

Still, they'll be hard to take as a group. Too many for me to ensure Cindi remains protected, even with Vasz's assistance.

I wrap a tentacle around her, needing to know she's safe. "I marry her, or I marry no one."

"Even if mates exist, the Goddess would not curse a land creature to be your mate." Lazell scoffs, and my limbs flex. One day, his hearts will stop beating beneath my hands.

"I recognize my own mate," I defend. Her scent may not call to me as the tomes described a mate would, but I feel her in my chest. A pull. A thread connects me to her, even though our scriptures only describe matings between krakens, never a human.

"Please," Lazell sneers. Krakens cast nervous glances between us. I'm sure they're wondering if they're burying another friend today. "You are an abomination who calls himself a kraken. You don't recognize your own reflection, yet you think you'd recognize your *mate*?" A snarl rips from my throat. He ignores it. "Since you are incapable of logic, let me put it in simple terms for you. The Witch would have never forced a human to suffer the fate of marrying the very kind that killed her offspring. You have one chance. Do not *waste* it on pests."

My nostrils flare. I have no rebuttal. Other than my grandmother, a mating of any kind between a kraken and human is unheard of. There is nothing for me to go off.

"Watch how you speak of your future queen. It is an affront to the Goddess to question her will. Is that what you intend to do? Offend Edea?"

"The Goddess has no domain over humans, *Your Majesty*." He says my title in mockery.

"Had you not cowered in the palace and continued your schooling, you would know this."

Again, nothing.

I have no basis to deny his claim beyond personal belief. The Goddess has taken the life of many humans, both in the water and on land. Our teachings only ever concern krakens and our worship of Edea. It makes little sense that she reigns over every being in the sea, yet her powers end with the souls of humans.

Lazell continues. "There are krakens for you to choose—"

I've heard enough.

"I have decided!" Cindi is my mate. This is not a point of debate. "Or have you forgotten the Curse requires the bride to be willing? That *I* be willing. We have one final chance, and I pick my *mate*."

"Mate?" He arches a brow, dragging his blatant perusal over my torso and the notable lack of marriage mark. "Yet you have not bonded with her."

My teeth grind. "I will not be rushed."

"We are *starving*, and you want to take your time with the *human* female?" He hisses. "You will never deserve to be king."

"We'll kill her," a kraken barks. I snap my attention in their direction, unable to pinpoint the culprit.

Counselor Ronet nods her agreement. "We will not bow to a human."

My blood burns. I shift forward to gut every kraken on this shore for threatening my mate. I forget I'm holding Cindi, her small hands falling onto the width of my tentacle, halting me in place. It's a silent reminder she's alive and my stupidity would be the death of her.

My response to their claim is simple. Certain. The weight of my venomous glare falls on Counselor Ronet. "Then I kill myself, and all hope will be lost." She shifts her weight, referring to Lazell for his support. "Then there will be no saving these lands." I hold up two fingers, a reminder to everyone that even though my hands are different to theirs, their existence is in the palm of mine. "You have two options, and I suggest you think carefully about your response. Leave and never return, or learn why I am just as deadly as Chlaena."

A collection of sharp gasps echo through the crowd. Their last hope is the two things they despise most.

That would be the Witch's last laugh.

"Kraken-kind will be eradicated because of your selfish delusions," Lazell states, cutting Ronet off before she can speak.

My lips peel back, and I bring Cindi right up to my side for all to see me stake my claim. "*Decide*. Die by my hands or the Witch's. One is more certain than the other."

I tuck my mate tighter against me when everyone's attention falls on my woman. There's a pregnant moment of silence. Cindi sinks her nails into me. No amount of pumping my venom into her makes her relax. Finally, Lazell speaks.

"You have until the full moon in eleven nights. If the Curse has not ended by then, we will come for the human, and our kind will finally be rid of you." He turns and begins his descent into the water.

The blood drains from my face. Eleven nights? Cindi will not be any closer to loving me by then.

Or I could leave, reside on the mainland with Cindi where we'll be safe. But then, all of kraken-kind will be damned, making my family's death meaningless. They would have died for a kingdom I'm too selfish to try to save.

One female at the cost of an entire race, and the memory of the only ones who ever cared for me.

I snarl in frustration. I want to save my territory. I want any cub I may have to see the beauty of our land—the land every person I've shared blood with has sacrificed to save. I want to look my mate and my offspring in the eyes and tell them a whole kingdom is at their fingertips. A kingdom I, my brother, and my sister all brought back to life.

I address Lazell, making all krakens pause to look back at me. "Then a blood oath, here and now. If the Curse is broken, no harm will befall my female or me."

I can't lose her. It can't all be for nothing.

He stops but doesn't grant me the respect of turning his body to speak to me, angling his head to the side.

"I will not spill my blood for you, most definitely not for a human." Before he dives into the water, he repeats, "Eleven days, *King Ordus.*"

28

CINDI

I dig my trembling fingers into Ordus' meaty limbs. They're looking at me. The fucking krakens are *looking* at me.

They say there are only two responses: fight or flight. But *freeze* needs to be added to that list.

Shock made me stupid.

I should have run for the cave the moment Ordus told me to. Instead, I'm out here being stared down by *actual* creature-of-the-night monsters.

Monsters stare me down like they want to eat me alive and gnaw on my bones like a drumstick. I've seen that look on the Gallagher men a hundred times. But now, I have no doubt I may very well be turned into octopus chow.

They could be talking about how to season me right now, and I wouldn't have a clue. Nothing in their language sounds remotely similar to anything I understand—not Indonesian, Thai, or English. There's a lot of weird clicking and gulping being thrown around.

I wouldn't stand a chance against them. With every fiber of my being, I trust Ordus to protect me, but one against thirty isn't exactly a fair fight.

They're frightening. Hideous-looking. The stuff of real nightmares. Not a single one of them has Ordus' beauty—shit, if I didn't have context, I could be convinced they're an entirely different species.

They have elongated oval skulls that protrude well over the top of their spines. Their heads look squishy. If I were to poke one, it'd cave under my fingers as I imagine would happen to a real octopus. I think it's called a mantle—something Ordus most definitely doesn't have hiding beneath his hair.

The similarity with Ordus starts with eight tentacles and ends with two arms and a humanoid torso—minus the webbing between their ribs and biceps.

It's a good thing. A very, *very* good thing. If any of them showed up at my house and kidnapped me, I would have put a blade through their chest, and I wouldn't have missed.

No two kraken look the same, other than the general attributes of their bodies. Some have spiked ears like Ordus, others are tube-shaped like Shrek. Hell, some don't look like they have ears, just a hole in the side of their head.

That's not the worst part.

A couple don't have lips that close, so their sharp, toothpick-shaped, yellowed teeth are on display. My skin prickles imagining what those incisors would feel like turning my skin into ribbon.

There's no two coloring that's the same either, but they all remind me of the octopuses I've seen in the area; the blue-ringed octopus, coconut octopus, reef, mimic, and a bunch I can't name. Deedee is obsessed with them and always took me out to snorkel.

But none are nearly as big as Ordus. A few are my size—one male who's at least a foot shorter than me, with a face weathered with age.

The females are differentiated from the males by the small lumps on their chests and the—dare I use this word—*softer*, more feminine faces. Although, their build isn't impacted by sex. They can be as big and burly or as small as the males.

One woman at the very back of the congregation has a protective hand over her rounded stomach, pressing herself to a male's side every time Ordus speaks. She flicks her sunken eyes between me, Ordus, and the lanky kraken who keeps talking. It doesn't land on Ordus and I with hatred. The same goes with the male beside her.

It's fear.

Not of Ordus, but for themselves. For the life growing in her.

Even from this distance, I can count her ribs poking out against her baby belly. The edges of her bones stick out against her taut, pale skin. My heart aches as I study each bony finger and deep ridge of her collarbones. I may not be familiar with kraken biology and anatomy, but there's no way she has enough meat on her to be carrying a baby. It can't be healthy. It must be a miracle she was able to conceive, let alone carry the child this far along.

None of the krakens here look like they're well-fed. All of them have the same exhaustion written over their gaunt faces, with bodies that consist of more skin than flesh. The evidence of their starvation is clear in their emaciation.

Yet Ordus looks like he spends three hours at the gym each day, hits his protein goals, and meets the necessary sleeping requirements. He couldn't be more different from his subjects even if he tried.

Is this...is this my fault? These people—*monsters*—will die because of me? My selfishness.

I glance at the pregnant kraken. Oh, God. There would be children as well. *Kids, little babies*, would be dying because I can't say yes to Ordus. I'm so in my own head over what I want to do with my life when there are people who want me dead and people who *will* die.

An entire species has been turning to flesh and bone while I've been playing fucking *house*, caring for chickens and tending to a garden on an island in the middle of nowhere. And what else have I been doing? Complaining I haven't been getting enough attention, that I want to go back to the mainland when I don't at the same time. Worrying about a marriage proposal that isn't being forced upon me.

This is too much.

There's no way I'm supposed to save them when I can't save myself.

I make eye contact with one of the women off to the side. My cheeks burn. It's hard to look at any of the women when their nipples are pointed right at me with not an ounce of shame. It's even harder to stare at any of the men when they're looking a lot like the Gallaghers.

I drop my gaze, which was a big fucking mistake. Bile lurches up my throat at the empty eyes staring back at me. A lone head bobbing in and out of the beach floats along with the waves. Dark blue ink seeps from the hole into the water, washing out into the sea—the same ink splattered over Ordus and smeared across my skin from his tentacles.

My breathing comes out in shudders. *Oh, God.*

I think I'm going to puke.

Movement from the crowd stops me from losing it to hysteria. The talkative kraken turns, and the others follow suit. A few grab their fallen friends and the severed head. The talkative one throws one last barbed comment before diving beneath the waves.

I can't move a muscle, frozen even when the only creatures in sight are Ordus and a growling Vasz. Dread seeps into my bloodstream, poisoning me until the fear leaks from my pores.

He's going to force me to marry him.

He's going to force himself on—

No. *No.*

I can't live like that again. I won't do it. I refuse.

A hand clamps over my mouth. I scream, kick out, thrash my entire body against the tentacle tightening around me. We're flying through the island, between the thickets of palm trees and shrubs, heading west toward the tunnel into the den.

He's really going to do it. He said I had to be willing. He lied to me. Ordus lied, and he's going to prove my fears true. He's just like Tommy, manipulative and violent. They take, take, take, even if I don't want to give.

I let my guard down. It crumbled to the fucking floor, and I spread my legs and let it happen. I let him in without remorse, and now, he wants to sink in his teeth.

I'm so stupid.

It's happening again.

I didn't learn the first time.

"Calm yourself, Cindi," Ordus growls against my ear.

Angry, frightened, hot tears spring from my eyes and trickle onto fingers muffling my cries for help. My reality turns bleaker with every tree we pass, descending deeper into the island.

No one's coming to save me. No one ever does. Not anymore.

Vasz is barking and nipping at Ordus, but what can a shark-dog do? He can't get me out of here or keep me fed. He won't be able to fend off a kraken at least quadruple his size.

Kristy died a long time ago. I should've begun digging Cindi's grave the moment I stepped foot in Indonesia.

Ordus is going to kill me the same way Tommy did, and there's nothing I can do about it.

The cave entrance glimmers under Ordus' command. He lunges for it. Vasz sprints back toward the shack to get to the tunnels. His hand leaves my mouth, and I suck in a breath. A chorus of "no, please," and "don't" fall from me. My cries and pleas echo through the dark tunnel. I angle my head toward the light, reaching for it. It'll be last time I see the sun.

I'm being taken into the basement again. This time, I won't be let out.

No one will check on me. There will be no escape, no solace, nothing but a monster who will take his pound of flesh.

"Please, Cindi," Ordus rasps, rubbing his hand all over my back and arms in a move that's too reassuring for the fate I'm about to endure. *"Please."*

I whip my head side to side. "You can't. I won't let you. Please, don't do it."

We make it out the bottom of the tunnel faster than we ever have. Panic shreds me to pieces, frozen and scorching. My vision is blurry from the tears, voice raw from screaming.

I got *out*. I was free. I was surviving.

Ordus turns me to face him, cupping my cheeks in his big hands. "Listen to me."

Black hair morphs to blond, brown skin to white. It's Tommy, back from the dead to haunt me, lips twisted into a crooked smile —the type that promises a world of pain.

Logic and reason escapes me. I can't summon the image of Tommy lying dead on the floor, because he's here right in front of me, touching me.

"Please. I will not hurt you."

Tommy can't purr. He doesn't have tentacles. He doesn't live in a cave with bioluminescent algae. He doesn't give reassurances or promises not to cause me harm. But it doesn't matter how loud I scream it in my head—I can't escape.

I choke on the memories. The feel of the silk sheets against my cheeks as Tommy pushes me down and yanks my skirt up around my waist. Tommy's rough, calloused palms that grate against my cheek followed by the *smack*.

The man before me grabs my hand and places it over his

heart. I struggle against him. I don't want to touch him, but there's no getting away.

The rumbling in his chest grows louder than the blood roaring in my ears. His pulse is erratic beneath my hand, and I'm only vaguely aware of the suckers pulsing hard against my flesh. I screw my eyes shut, trying to push everything out of my mind and focus on the feeling, on the vibrations coming from him, because tentacles don't hurt. They never hurt.

"Kristy," he begs, tentacles holding my thrashing arms still. "You are safe."

"That's not my name." I gasp for breath. It's not. She's dead. She doesn't exist anymore.

Tommy—*Ordus* tips my face up, coaxing me to open my eyes. I shake my head. If I look at him, I'll see Tommy.

"Listen to me, Cindi."

Cindi, not Kristy.

Cindi, Cindi, Cindi. Tommy doesn't know that name. This *isn't* Tommy.

His eyes waver between green and blue, hair flickering between long and short.

Yes, that's right. My name is Cindi. Kristy is dead.

Tommy is dead.

I try to stabilize my breathing, focus on pulling oxygen into my lungs. When I was younger, there was a cove Dad would take me to after school if I got a really good grade on a test. He'd take the afternoon off and get us a snow cone and a hot dog, and we'd sit and watch the seagulls swoop and squawk. Sometimes, a seal would bark at us, and I'd squeal, insisting Dad let me pet it. If the weather was good, he'd let me swim there.

When I breathe in Ordus' ocean breeze scent, filling my lungs until I'm completely consumed, I can almost feel the love and safety I felt hanging out with Dad. It's that irreplaceable, childlike trust in someone. I know I can throw myself over the edge and there will be someone there to catch me.

I inhale deeply. There's no hint of cheap cologne or the lemony cleaning products I used to clean the mansion's marble kitchen, only Ordus and the musty cavern air.

When only the occasional shudder racks my body, I brave peeling my eyes open, and I shiver once I do. Before me stands a man with worry lines all over his face, concern in every divot and fold of his spotted tan-and-brown skin. The intensity would've knocked me off my feet if he weren't holding me upright.

"Please, Cindi," Ordus says like it's a question. He's asking if I'll give him a chance to explain. "Listen to me. I promise you, I will not harm you. I swear it on the Goddess and my family's honor."

My fingers shake against his chest. If he wanted to force himself on me or make me marry him, he wouldn't have waited for me to get a hold of myself.

If those krakens planned on killing me today, there would be more dead bodies on the beach.

"Why were they here?" My voice is hoarse, like it was whenever Tommy choked me.

Ordus' gaze drops to my hand on his chest, working his jaw. "The Curse."

"They want to kill me." It was clear in the way they watched me. My anxiety spikes, flashing back to dinners with the Gallaghers, men with guns who'd leered at any woman who walked into a room or spoke without being spoken to.

His purr shifts into a displeased rumble. "I will not let them."

"You can't stop them."

A haunted expression casts over his face. "I can. I am their king," he says with conviction not even he believes.

"It didn't look like that mattered to them, Ordus."

Ordus nostrils flare, one hand falling to my shoulder. "They need me. They will not..." He can't even look at me.

"What did they say?" I prompt when his eyes grow tortured.

Ordus suddenly sets me on top of a smoothed-out stone that

acts as a makeshift table. The loss of warmth and stability rocks me to the core, and the panic rises up my spine.

His pacing only makes it worse. He's rubbing a hand down his face and batting away hair that refuses to stay put. His anger and fear leaves a pungent note in the air I can taste in the back of my throat.

"Ordus, you're worrying me."

There are a million things they could have discussed. Every idea I have is worse than the last.

My heart lurches when something emerges from the tunnel, calming when Vasz's panting echoes faster than my racing pulse. He and Ordus gnash their teeth at one another before Vasz takes his spot beside me, lying alert on his stomach.

Ordus keeps opening his mouth and closing it, like every time he thinks he knows what to say, he changes his mind. "That..." He snarls, tentacle lashing out to hit the pool, and I flinch, swallowing a whimper. *He's not Tommy. He won't hurt you.*

Ordus halts his pacing and turns to me, guilt riddled across his face. He pulls his tentacles close to his body and forces himself to lower to my eye level. Still, he's coiled tighter than a spring.

His throat bobs, like he's trying to choke his emotions back for my benefit. "The only way to end the Curse is through me. They will not do us harm."

Ordus' delusions are irritating me. I don't want to accept sugarcoating of a situation that's going to hurt me. I burned my rose-tinted sunglasses for a reason.

"You can't know that. They're starving! Desperate. I saw them. They looked like they were dying right in front of my eyes. You said it yourself. The only way to break the Curse is to marry me. And they *hate* me. They hate me more than they hate you."

I'm itching to jump off the rock and pace like he did. I want to scream, because maybe then he'll hear me. This will be just like before, when I told him to take me to the mainland or else I'll die, and he still didn't listen. History has to stop repeating itself.

He stares at me with big blue eyes filled with too much for me to pick apart.

"What happens if I say yes and the Curse ends?" I continue, barely blinking so he'll *see* how fucked this is from every angle. "They'll have no need for me, and I'll never agree to a life where I'm subjected to a cave, only seeing the sun through a hole in the wall."

I feel like I'm about to explode.

Ordus might not even listen to me. He might shove our problems under the rug again because his priorities and relationship with himself and his own kind are all twisted.

"What do you suggest we do?" he asks.

I blink. "I…"

He doesn't confirm it. He doesn't deny it. He's just as unsure as I am. That should scare me more, but instead, it's taken a weight off my shoulders. There's a problem. He recognizes it, and he wants to fix it.

Together.

Like we're a team.

I'm stunned speechless.

There's a tremble in his hand before he places it on my knee, rubbing circles around the cap like he's trying to comfort himself from the toxic mixture of desperate hopelessness.

His throat bobs, voice strained. "I will not force you to marry, but I meant what I said. I will follow you wherever you go. I don't want to exist if I cannot exist with you."

I suck in a sharp breath. Is he implying what I think? That he'd live on the mainland with me? Even if that *was* the path I chose, I need to move countries. I can't stay in Indonesia anymore, but I can't take him from his own kingdom. How will he react if we moved away from the equator to colder temperatures? What would he be like amongst humans? I can't imagine either reaction will go well. He kills easily and without hesitation.

What about Vasz?

But why would I want to lock myself to a life surrounded by people who tried to kill a child just for looking different?

My mind conjures images of the pregnant kraken, only this time, she's dead, all sinew and bone with a baby who never got a chance at survival—to be different from everyone else.

The woman and the male were scared. They didn't look on with hate. There was a moment where something...light flashed behind their hollow eyes. A flicker of hope.

Not all monsters are monsters.

If I've learned anything, it's that sharp claws don't always cut. A monster can be gentle, sweet, the light amongst darkness. Monsters hold no fake veneer or twist words to hide their venom.

I don't know if I could sleep at night imagining their dead bodies, knowing I could've prevented it.

What if I snuck away from Ordus after marrying him?

My stomach sours as soon as I think it. He's not Tommy. I can't leave him out here for dead. It's not... I wasn't raised like that. Despite everything, Ordus is a good man—to me, at least. The universe was just pitted against him, and he had no one in his corner to help him out.

His mom died. His sister. His best friend and brother. I'd be adding *mate* to the list, and that thought makes me sick.

But I'd be doing the same thing to myself. I lost all my friends and the one man who truly cared about me. Maybe I don't truly believe soulmates exist, that Ordus is mine, but fate has given me another chance. I have someone who will always have my back, protect me, never leave my side, bend over backward to please me.

I'd be losing a man who lights up whenever he looks down at a hair tie on his wrist, who purrs for me every night until I fall asleep. A monster who learned how to cook and brought an entire kitchen and a farm to a secluded island so I don't have to eat the same thing day in and day out. He's building me a shelter so I can watch the sunset, handwove a hammock for me to snooze on.

He looks at me like I'm the only reason he's still breathing when I've done nothing but fight him or talk his ears off.

I'd be losing my mate too.

The words *I'll do it* are caught in my throat. I can't make myself say it. "I don't know," is all I manage.

I need to process everything and *think*. I just clawed my way out of one marriage; I can't jump straight into another.

"I promised I'd take you to the mainland."

My brows knit together. I can't believe I forgot about that. At the time, I thought it was said in the heat of the moment, not a promise.

Ordus dips his head. "Forgive me, I had planned on taking you after lunch, but it is too dangerous. My kind will likely be waiting for me in the waters."

Something *is* happening again.

The familiar coil of paranoia wraps around my lungs. The need to look over my shoulder hits me with full force.

But it's not as potent as usual. Before, there was the doubt, the never-ending question of whether someone hid around the corner.

Now, I know nothing's there. I want to check for peace of mind, because three sets of eyes are better than one, but no one would be able to sneak past both Ordus and Vasz, supernatural beings with heightened senses. Still...I feel safe with him.

"Okay," I whisper.

"Maybe tomorrow." He looks guilty, and I can only guess why.

"I trust you."

Ordus snaps back like I've struck him. "You shouldn't. I—they

—" He's back to his normal height, gliding up and down the short path of the cavern, fists clenched and stiff at his sides.

My fear spikes for only a moment before it ebbs. It doesn't stop my body from responding on its own, hunkering down to brace for *something*—anything—even if my head knows better.

The sounds coming from his chest are pure vicious. Vasz matches them with his own warning growl as he searches the cavern for a threat that's not there.

Ordus pauses in front of the pool we've slowly been adding fish to, like a makeshift aquarium with coral and vegetation we're trying to harvest, but it isn't going well. Everything always dies within two days. Three, if we're really lucky.

A tentacle lashes out into the water to catch a fish, killing it with a crack of its head. I wince at the sudden movement, and Vasz jumps up to his feet to check if the kraken needs backup. I press my lips together, attempting to keep my breathing even. I watch him snatch a knife off a nearby shelf and skulk toward a bench against the back wall.

Ordus' hair falls onto his face when he hunches over the bench, beginning the process of skinning and filleting the snapper. He's vibrating, strung so tight, I'm worried if I blink, he'll snap and the threads will turn into barbs.

His life is going up in flames too. He's got everything to lose. That realization is a slap in the face, because I've spent every waking moment thinking the world revolves around me.

The swipe of the blade is jerky, and he slams the innocent creature against the table, flipping it over. Streams of black hair spill in the way, and he releases a full-blown snarl, straightening to hit it away before curling over the short table again.

He repeats the process another three times, growls growing louder. I hesitate for a moment before jumping from the stone and padding over to Ordus. Hesitantly, I place a hand on his forearm. He freezes midway through smacking his hair out of the way. His jaw feathers, and he carefully turns to face me.

Like this, I barely come up to his chest. I roll onto the balls of my feet to curl my fingers around the inside of his elbow and give it a gentle tug. "Let me help."

His forehead wrinkles in confusion. I flick my eyes at his hair draped over his shoulder in answer.

The rage dissolves. One by one, his muscles untense, and the stormy clouds of his irises clear into bright blue. A tentacle latches onto my ankle, and I give him a small, sad smile that says, *yeah, life is shit right now, but we're in the shits together.*

He moves his sprawling limbs out of the way and lets me pull him beside the pool. "Sit."

Ordus studies me head to toe, like any second I'm going to rescind my offer and agree I shouldn't trust him. But I've already made up my mind. I'm doing this.

Like a frightened animal, he lowers himself to the kraken equivalent of sitting, and I stand behind him. A few of his tentacles spill into the pool, some climbing up the surrounding walls while one stays firmly around me, coiling up my leg until there's hardly any exposed skin.

We're closer in height this way. I can sort of see over his head, but not much. He shivers the moment I brush his hair over his shoulders. Otherwise, just like every other time, he stays stock-still.

I thread my fingers through his silken strands to carefully work out a few tangles. I could get the comb on top of my shelf, but I don't want to. There's something heady about seeing a powerful male all but kneeling in front of me, shivering and shuddering whenever our skin touches.

I guess I thought everything would change after what we did last night. Maybe he'd become cocksure or arrogant or *expect* my total compliance, but he's just as uncertain as he was yesterday.

The quiet of the cave—less Vasz's gnawing on a coconut—is peaceful. It's comforting, even if it is the calm before the storm.

Ordus must feel when I'm getting to the bottom of the braid, because he offers me a scrunchie that has most definitely seen better days. I nudge his hand back and show him the little black hair tie on my wrist I was using this morning.

I can only see his profile, but there's no mistaking the way his lips part on a heavy breath. Warmth douses my insides. I could almost forget about this afternoon's fiasco with how much he lights up from such a simple thing.

I tie the plait off and navigate his limbs, plus a tentacle holding me hostage, to stand in front of him under the guise of assessing my handiwork.

The blue-algae light kisses the high points of his cheeks and the curve of his pillowy lips. Shadows dip around his broad shoulders and muscled chest, highlighting the definition in his abs. "You look good," I whisper without really thinking about it.

Our gazes snare like a deer in headlights. Embarrassment flushes my cheeks, and uncertainty colors his.

Does he think I'm lying?

A stone drops in my gut. That doesn't sit right with me. I'm tired of treating him like he's the villain when he's just another victim who didn't get an out.

"I like the way you look," I clarify. "The other krakens were fucking hideous."

His eyes glimmer like the sun reflecting off the water, and the corners of my lips tick up. His do the same, though a little more hesitantly.

"Yeah?"

I nod. "It looked like someone stepped on them as a baby. The one who kept on talking creeped me the hell out. He was a real Eldritch Horror."

Ordus' gives me a small smile that doesn't meet his eyes. It makes my heart ache for him. "Lazell," he tells me. "When I was younger, kraken females would swoon over him, even when Yannig was alive."

I reach around to pull his braid over his shoulder in a covert move to touch him. "I thought your kind had good eyesight."

This time, when I meet his eyes, every sorrow and stress of the past few years washes away. He's looking at me in a way I thought only existed in books, like the purest form of love that could bring rain to a desert. I take his hand and squeeze it, and it's like every little thing is right with the world.

"Clearly not as good as my mate's." His deep voice makes my toes curl.

My fingers graze over the tentacle around my leg. "Clearly."

Because yeah, I guess I am his mate.

29

CINDI

The woman looks at me like I'm about to rob her.

"Uh…" I glance over her shoulder into my cabin—or, at least, it *used* to be my cabin. I'm kind of offended my landlord cleaned out my shit and moved on so quickly.

She shifts, blocking my view, casting a skeptical look over me. I can't imagine I look all too approachable, with my sopping hair and the patches of saturation over my green dress—the same green dress I wore when Ordus stole me.

She says something in Bahasa that sounds a lot like *who the fuck are you, why are you here, and what do you want?*

All great questions I'd be able to answer if language weren't an issue.

I can't see Ordus, but I can sense him itching to come out from his hiding spot amongst the trees. He could probably translate for me, but a strange, six-foot dude with long black hair doesn't exactly inspire comfort in a woman nearing eighty.

I really just want to know if she might have any of my old

316

stuff—not that I'd need it or anything. I have everything that matters, but it'd be nice to know if she had car keys lying around anywhere, or a motorbike in one of her rooms so, if push comes to shove, I'm not relying on a taxi when I don't have a phone to call them or money to pay them. I oh so conveniently forgot my purse in the cavern.

"Never mind. Sorry. Thank you," I mutter, backing away toward the beach. I'm not going to get anywhere with this. The woman slams the door behind her. After a moment, I hear Ordus following along on two feet.

I'm not entirely sure what my plan is. This morning, when Ordus told me we'd be going to the mainland for dinner, I'd figured I'd come up with something concrete by the time we arrived at my old place.

Maybe I would have fully decided how to deal with the Curse and the his-people-want-us-dead situation. Maybe I'd agree to marry him, then find a place on the mainland so he still has access to the beaches he's familiar with. Then the paranoia will start back up, and I'll spend every waking moment feeling like a sitting duck, waiting for the Gallaghers to find me.

Then they'll get to Ordus, which scares me a shitload more.

So, all in all, I've got nothing.

I want to save krakens. I want freedom. I want to stay alive. And I want...

I want Ordus.

But maybe I could try to get in touch with Nat or Deedee to arrange for passports for the both of us, just in case we need to fly out of here. But I'm hoping it never comes to that.

Fuck, can krakens handle that type of altitude? His biology clearly isn't the same.

And what about Vasz? I can't just leave him.

It's just problem after problem.

I huff and whirl to face Ordus once my feet hit the sand. He stands closer than I'd usually be comfortable with. I don't hate it. In fact, I like it a lot. Not that it's surprising at this point.

The golden light of the setting sun catches the faint, silvery-blue threads in his human skin. He's still just as attractive without his spots. His hair came out of the braid at some point during the—*at least*—six-hour swim to the mainland. He hasn't said as much, but I can tell he's disappointed by it.

He reaches for my hand, and I let him. I catch a hint of the barest purr that makes my stomach swoop. After I held his hand yesterday, it has been open season on the hand-holding front.

Ordus studies my face, concerned. "I will make her help us."

"*No*," I quickly say, leveling him with a stern look that would have had Tommy beating me black and blue. For the briefest moment, my bravado falters, and that inkling of fear trickles into my bloodstream, but it's gone just as quickly. "We do not force old ladies to do *anything*."

His forehead wrinkles in confusion. "She has your belongings. She upset you. This must be resolved."

Oh my God. He's serious. "That sweet old—"

His nose scrunches in distaste. "She didn't smell sweet."

What? Never mind. It's not important.

"You smell sweet, though," he says so quietly, almost…bashful.

My cheeks heat—part in embarrassment, part from that fuzzy feeling in my stomach. When was the last time I felt *butterflies*? When I was sixteen?

I'm half tempted to give myself a sniff. I'm not sure how I could possibly smell nice when I sleep in a musty cave and spend my days in the water.

"Would you—" He shifts his weight. I'm not used to seeing him in human form. Ordus on two legs is weird enough for me, but everything else of him is notably smaller. My eyes catch on the bulge beneath his shorts, and my blood heats. I conveniently didn't register he'd be packing human heat in this form.

He clears his throat, and my eyes snap to his, skin blazing. If he knows what I'm thinking, he doesn't let on.

"Would you like to go to the city?"

I blink. He wants to be around humans? "Which one?"

"The busy one." Ordus waves his hand in the general direction of where the main towns and cities are located. "You can eat at a human place."

My jaw drops. When he said he'd take me to the mainland, I didn't think he'd let me go anywhere but my old place and somewhere small where he could easily catch me if I tried to run.

My stomach grumbles at the idea of eating something other than seafood and eggs. "Will you eat as well?"

He blanches. "If you wish."

There's no fighting the tug at my lips as they stretch into a small smile. This man really will do anything for me. "Then lead the way."

Traveling by kraken will never get easier. I'm grumbling curses under my breath, wringing my hair out and squeegeeing the water off my body. I'm just about ready to scream when I shove myself into my stiff dress, flinching at every shadow and sound.

The material sticks to my wet body and scratches the tattoo on my back. It's been fine for the past month, but the six plus hours of underwater travel has pissed it off again.

I huff and quickly stomp out of the shadows toward a waiting Ordus, who looks out of place against the backdrop of racing motorbikes and the flurry of tourists and locals, laughing and checking out the menus of restaurants along the beach.

I take a deep breath and instantly regret it. After over a month of fresh sea air, the smell of cigarette smoke, exhaust fumes, and trash gives me a migraine.

And the noise? *God*, the noise. The cacophony of honks and chatter and engines and clattering. It's overwhelming.

Ordus grits his teeth, jaw feathering, surveying our surroundings. His shoulders are stiff, and he has a white-knuckle grip on the waterproof bag holding our clothes, a hand towel, water bottles, sandals, and cash.

It was too dark for anyone to see us emerge from the water. If they did, well, tough shit. They would've gotten an eyeful of Ordus' human junk I've been trying hard not to look at. It makes my skin prickle with the familiar unease of physical contact.

Consciously, I'm aware it's the same male who has eight limbs and cuddles me to sleep every night, but my body refuses to listen. It recognizes his human body as Tommy's counterpart, and it's setting me on edge.

Everything's setting me on edge.

Each honk. Every male voice. The eyes that glance my way.

I look over my shoulder as I hurry to Ordus' side, pulse thumping in my chest and flip-flops slapping against the pavement. I wipe my clammy hands on my saturated dress. I don't miss this.

I thought I was longing for civilization. Now, I'm seriously questioning whether I do. I hate this paranoia, the constant, sinking feeling I'm about to die.

Ordus grabs my hand and pulls me to his side. "What is wrong?"

"Nothing." I give him the most reassuring smile I can muster.

I throw a longing glance back at the water. I want to be back on the island, lounging on the beach or reading a book in the cave without a care in the world that I might run into a Gallagher.

Or pirates—fuck, I almost forgot about them.

The irony isn't lost on me. I traded the risk of krakens for men who call themselves pirates.

I press closer to Ordus' side, cringing when he lets go of my hand to place his on my back as he leads me down to the more populated street. I can't believe I prefer him in his kraken form.

I watch him out of the corner of my eye. He's hating this as much as I am. I trust him to be miles better at spotting danger, but I can't help darting my eyes to everything that moves—and everything is fucking moving. It's peak dinner hour. The streets are filled.

No one gives two shits about us—I mean, people are ogling Ordus because he's a giant, but no one is looking at me.

My plan solidifies more with every second. We're going to get food and get out. I don't care about the four hours I have. Hell, I'm willing to eat seafood at this point. I want out of here as soon as possible. My stomach will hate the postdinner swim, but I don't want to be this exposed for a second longer.

I can *feel* them. The Gallaghers. They're hiding around the corner and watching me through cameras.

Sweat trickles down my spine. I want to reach for Ordus' other hand and grip it for dear life. He's the only reason I'm not power walking with my head down. At least I have a knife in my bag—fuck. No, I don't.

A familiar tinkling laugh has my feet faltering in front of a food stall. I frown, turning my head toward the sound.

In the outdoor dining area, seated on a wooden stool, is a woman with jet-black hair, glowing tanned skin, and high cheek-bones, arm out to the side, flicking the ash off a cigarette onto the ground.

"Deedee?"

Her perfectly shaped brows slam down into a straight line as she looks amongst the patrons and out onto the street, completely missing me.

The four men surrounding her stop their chatter, collectively tensing. One of them has black ink tattooed on his pale, bald head. Beside him, there's another Caucasian man with an eyebrow piercing. It's hard to tell where they might be from, but the other two men could be Indonesian.

"Deedee!" I step beneath the fluorescent light.

She can get us passports and money, just in case. Maybe she'll know where my shit is so I have the comfort of knowing I have a mode of transport that doesn't involve drowning myself in saltwater.

Deedee's on her feet and running toward me as soon as she spots me. I feel Ordus shift, ready to interfere.

"Holy shit, girl." She yanks me into a hug I'd rather not be the recipient of. I cringe. Ordus moves closer, a low warning growl in his chest that I try to cover by angling Deedee away. "Where the fuck have you been?"

I wrinkle my nose from the ribbons of cigarette smoke wafting toward me, and I bat them away with the back of my hand.

"Someone trashed my place, and I got spooked." I practiced the lie earlier in case I managed to locate a phone to call her or Nat.

Her eyes round, and she steps back like she's examining me for bruises. "What? Are you okay?" She glances between me and Ordus, and her nostrils flare with a deep breath. Something shutters behind her eyes as she cranes her neck to look up at him properly. Her jaw drops to the ground in… *Surprise* isn't a strong enough word.

Astonishment.

Deedee's brows hike up her forehead as she takes him in from head to toe, up to his head again, before turning to me with an emotion I can't quite place. A dash of confusion, a bit of shock, and—I could be wrong—concern? Or is that anger? I can't tell.

Deedee studies me with an intensity I've never seen on her before. I can only imagine what this looks like. I go MIA for a month then show back up with a tall, muscled, attractive guy.

The fact said guy is radiating violence and Deedee is aware I had a piece of shit ex? She's probably thinking the worst.

"Yeah, I'm fine. I found a safe place to hunker down," I say to slice the weird tension. I motion to Ordus, inching toward him to make it clear he's not a threat. "He's been helping me out."

Deedee seems to snap out of whatever spell she's under. She sidles next to me, grinning and batting her eyelashes up at Ordus. "And tell me about your friend?"

Something ugly and green turns my blood to simmering. I want to tell her it's none of her business, to put the focus back on me. "Uh, Ordus."

Her lips widen into a full-blown, satisfied smile. "Single?"

The simmer turns to a boil.

Ordus steps in before I can ruin a friendship. "No," he snaps, like he can't imagine anything more insulting.

I look over my shoulder at the same time Deedee's bald friend stands and snuffs out his cigarette on the tray.

She giggles and playfully bats at Ordus' arm. He jolts away, clutching his elbow like she left a fatal wound. Deedee's attention falls back to me, so she misses him bare his teeth at her.

Her slender hand wraps around my arm as she all but yanks me toward her table. "Come. Sit, sit, sit. Eat. Dinner's on me." She raises two fingers at the woman behind the counter and says something in Indonesian I don't quite understand—other than the words for *babi guling*—roast pig.

The clerk nods, and her flip-flops clap against the tile toward the back of the shop.

Deedee hustles me into a seat beside her and points at a wooden stool at a free table for Ordus. She moves empty plates and cups to the end of the table for the clerk to pick up when she passes, then mutters something in Indonesian to the guy beside her. He nods.

Ordus drops the stool beside me and lowers him onto it more aggressively than necessary. If I move even slightly, my knees will knock into his. I'm struggling to recognize him in a sun-stained, blue *Bintang* T-shirt. I must admit, though, I can focus a little better without his abs on display.

It's comical how much he sticks out amongst everyone else. Sure, he appears human, but if you stare long enough, you'll start to notice there's something *other* about him.

Especially in those murderous blue eyes.

We had a nice, long chat about human behavior, the dos and don'ts when we're on the mainland. One of those things was that there's to be absolutely no attacking or growling at or killing humans under any circumstance.

Based on the sneer he's directing at the four men, he'd be doing the latter right now if I didn't tell him it might put me in danger.

I keep my sights on the street in front of me, making a conscious effort not to look any of the men in the eyes, lest it set off Ordus.

I'm lying to myself.

They remind me of the Gallaghers' men. If I look at them, I might throw up or run out of here like I'm on fire.

Half my butt cheek hangs off the side of the bench. I'm careful to leave a couple inches of space between me and Deedee.

"Where's Nat?" I force myself to ask to keep my mind off things. I may question Deedee's choice in friendship, but I know she would never put me in danger. She's the one who helped set up my surveillance system, and if there's ever a riskier drop, she'll send some muscle to do it for me. We have matching tattoos, for crying out loud. Sisterhood and all that.

"The lab." She huffs, shaking her head. "Works too hard, that one. We got a big order for Canadians. Good timing, though. We just moved the main op to bigger premises. I was about to look for another girl to take your place."

I frown. I was gone six weeks. Before I left, we could barely make a decision on how the lab should be arranged, and suddenly, they're moving to a bigger facility? When we didn't have supplies? "So you managed to fix the machine?"

"Yeah, of course." Deedee gives me the universal "why wouldn't we" look.

"What happened to the stolen stock?"

The guy with the piercing snorts, taking a drag of his cigarette. I drop my hand onto Ordus' lap when he starts growling like a guard dog. He stops the second I touch him. I don't want my dinner flavored with entrails.

Deedee waves her hand dismissively, not missing the mistaken show of PDA. "I told you; it was all a nonissue."

My lips flatten into a straight line, and I try not to glower. "It clearly was an issue. Those supplies cost us—"

I silence myself and mutter a quick thanks to the woman delivering my food. I cast a nervous glance at Ordus, who's looking at the plate like it's a pile of the worst possible thing known to man. His face is warped, like everything about dinner nauseates him.

His hand stops midair above the slice of pork. "Are you sure you want to eat?" I interrupt. It'd be rude not to eat it, but it would be far ruder if Ordus starts retching in the middle of the store. "You had an upset stomach earlier. Maybe we get you something lighter and take this to go?"

Ordus' shoulders sag in relief, and he immediately goes back to staring down the men and watching the street while Deedee studies him with rapt fascination. It's kinda irrationally pissing me off.

It can't be jealousy. I'm not the jealous type. I mean, Ordus can see whomever he wants. It just makes me sick picturing them hanging out—or with anyone else, for that matter. Blind with rage, imagining him fucking her with his tentacles like he did to me...

Ordus drops his hand on top of mine, giving it a reassuring

squeeze before caressing the soft skin there like he's saying he's mine, marriage or not.

I blow out a breath, trying to calm down. Deedee waves down the waitress to pack away his share into a container, and I quickly surveil the streets for anyone who might look like someone I recognize.

"You don't need to worry about any of it. I've got it taken care of." Deedee fiddles with her bracelet, and the smile she gives me doesn't reach her eyes.

I force food into my mouth, chewing without tasting.

"So tell me: where've you been? We were so worried. I tried looking for you everywhere, but you went completely off the radar. I thought it might have been because of the whispers of the American looking for you."

The temperature plummets. I drop my spoon. "What American?"

"Don't know." Deedee brings the cigarette to her lips and inhales deeply. Tendrils of grey twirl from the glowing ember. Plumes of the putrid smoke blow beside my head and stick between the strands of my hair. "One of my contacts said there was a guy going around, offering money in exchange for a woman. He mentioned your—*you know*—your name. Had a photo too."

I stop breathing. My name? *Photo*? It must be the same person Ordus smelled at my cabin over a month ago.

They've found me. I need to get out of here. Now. The very first place that crosses my mind is Saelim Island, and despite the threat of other krakens, there's nowhere else I'd rather be.

"What—what did he look like?" My voice cracks as I press.

Deedee shrugs. "Based on what I heard, like a *bule*."

Like a Westerner. That doesn't narrow down anything.

"And what did your contact tell them?" I want to slap the table so maybe she gets how fucking serious this is.

She shakes her head like this is no big deal. "He's never met you, so he didn't say anything. Just told me about it." Her phone lights up with a notification, and she jumps to her feet. Ordus and I do the same. "Shit. I'm so sorry. I need to go."

Wait. No. I want to insist she stay so I can interrogate her for information. When did they ask? Are they still here? Who's your contact? How many men were with him? Did he leave a number? Did they say anything else?

Deedee taps her phone screen again, and she gives my shoulder a squeeze. "Where are you staying? I'll meet you at yours so we can talk for longer."

My pulse jumps, and I cast a nervous glance at the men going up to pay at the counter. "I'm not giving out my location. Just in case, you know. It's not that I don't trust you, I—"

She stops me with a shake of her head. "I get it."

I lower my voice, trying to inject every ounce of my fear and desperation. "We need passports. As soon as possible."

The men she was eating with wait for her on the sidewalk, splitting their attention between me and Ordus. I subconsciously inch toward him, using the kraken as a barrier.

Deedee walks backward, giving me a noncommittal nod with the same blasé attitude she gives to everything that frustrates me to no end. "Call me, okay? We'll sort it. Everything's going to be fine."

I don't answer. Even if I wanted to, she already turned away, typing furiously at her phone.

Ordus and I watch her walk down the street with her entourage until she's out of view. Cold sweat trickles down my spine. To hell with my four hours, I want to go right the fuck now. But I can't hide out on the island and wait for the heat to die down when there's heat on the goddamn island as well.

"I do not like her," Ordus says, stirring me out of my thoughts. I drop onto the bench, realizing we're still awkwardly standing in the middle of the restaurant. I tug him down. "She touched you and made you unhappy."

He'll need to be specific about which instance he's referring to: the hug, the not-jealousy, that my demons are here, or all of the above.

"I don't trust her or her men," he continues.

I shake my head, staring at the barely touched plate in front of me. I've lost my appetite. Without a word, the waitress boxes up my meal after I point to Ordus' Styrofoam container, then my plate.

"Deedee's my friend," I tell Ordus, tapping the table as I wait for the clerk to return. Is she my friend, though? Would friends wave off every concern the other person has?

"She smells wrong." We sit in silence for a moment. "The American is your dead husband's people?" He frames it like a question when he already knows the answer.

My throat is closed tight. I can't speak. The walls are closing in, and I'm on a sinking ship with a life raft being held together by duct tape.

We stay on the mainland, we die.

We stay on the island, we die.

We leave the mainland and abandon Vasz, and we all die.

We're stuck between a rock and a hard place, and the glass floor we're standing on is cracking.

"Let's go home," I whisper, swallowing down the panic.

Ordus watches me intently with both joy and...shock? I replay what I said.

Home.

I blink, chewing over the word, but it never ends up tasting wrong. Saelim Island is my home. That realization hits me square in the chest. I...I don't want the past month and a bit of my life to be temporary.

Ordus takes the plastic bag with our food from the waitress, then grabs our waterproof pack and pulls me right up against him, leading us toward the beach. It's not making my nerves any better, but knowing we're getting out of here isn't making it any worse either.

I'm surrounded by ticking time bombs from all sides, and the only thing I'm certain of is that I don't want to deal with it alone. If I could choose anyone, I'd choose Ordus.

Still, it doesn't stop my racing pulse or my short breaths. I'm not any closer to being anywhere as delusionally carefree as I was all the times I was surfing on the island, blissfully ignorant to the fact krakens are dying and they want to eat me.

We spill back onto the beach, where people lounge on blow-up seats beneath glowing umbrellas, laughing, eating, drinking.

I follow him left, away from the congregation of people and overstimulating smells. Cigarette smoke, the nutty notes of *sate*, the gag-inducing whiff of nearby trash, spilled gasoline and exhaust fume, cologne, perfume, body odor, alcohol, the hint of the ocean breeze...

The sound of chatter, roaring engines, and the bouncy beat of nearby music aren't any better the closer we get to the portion of the beach encased in darkness.

"I got this for you."

Huh?

I zero in on the black purse in his hands. A *Chanel* bag. What the hell? How did he—I quickly shove it back in the waterproof pack. "Where did you get this?" I hiss, looking around to make sure no one saw.

Ordus frowns. "While we were walking to dinner, I saw it left on a seat." He says it so innocently, I almost feel bad for my tone. "You didn't say I am not allowed to take items from the mainland."

If his plan was to distract me from our impending doom, it's working. The water is in sight. The safety of the cave is only a few long hours away. We can talk about...next steps.

"This is stealing." It's my fault, really. If I have to explain he shouldn't murder someone, obviously I should've mentioned theft is also off the table.

We step straight into the water, since I can't be bothered stripping. My dress is already ruined.

"No, it isn't. No one claimed it." Ordus looks so genuinely confused. "I saw other females wearing a bag, but you do not have one—"

He suddenly goes still. Muscles locked. Unblinking. Frozen like time has stopped. Alarm bells scream in my head. Something's wrong.

"Ordus?"

Nothing.

I gingerly touch his forearm. "Ordus, please."

The hair on the back of my neck stands on end. What's wrong with him? I grab him by the arms and shake him. He tips over, body stiff as stone. Half his head is beneath the waves. I don't have the strength to lift him back up or drag him to the shore.

It's the Curse. It has to be.

Goosebumps cascade over my flesh. "Or—"

His name catches in my throat, a warm, fuzzy ball of cotton that dissolves down my chest and acts as armor around my racing heart. Time slows, and my muscles turn to steel.

Then, everything goes black.

30

ORDUS

Pain lances the bottom half of my body—a sharp, skin-deep, biting pain.

The shrill ringing in my ear makes it hard to make out the muted words vibrating through the current.

My head is filled with the thick clouds not even the sun can penetrate. I groan, waving my limp arm to address the source of the hurt. What could be seconds, or minutes, or hours drag on.

The clouds thicken and disperse, ebbing and flowing like the faint tickle of bubbles skating around my legs.

Legs?

My brows knit together. Why do I have two legs?

I summon every ounce of energy I can to peel my eyelids open. My vision refuses to adjust to the darkness. The only thing I can make out is the outline of a shark with brightly tipped ears.

Vasz? What's he doing here?

I crane my neck behind me. Where's Cindi?

She was beside me on the beach. We were talking about the

bag with the shiny gold emblem on it that she can store her treasures in. I had to breathe through my mouth because the smells were getting too overwhelming, and Cindi's bitter scent of fear was making my instincts narrow to tunnel vision. Then, suddenly, it went cold. I was thrust into a void with no end in sight.

She was *right there*. Panic surges through my blood stream.

Where is my mate?

Power trickles back into my limbs with the rush of adrenaline. I need to get to her. I promised I'd protect her, that nothing would ever do her harm. I cannot fail her.

I cannot lose her.

"Cindi," I croak.

Piercing pain rips through my leg as Vasz dislodges his teeth from my skin. Vasz shoves himself right up to my face, barking and growling, giving me a piece of his mind without saying a single word. He doesn't need to say anything. He has the same question I do. *Where is our human?*

I pull him forward by his arm, fighting the haze of black mist blanketing my vision. "Find her," I whisper as I grab his fin. "Find my mate."

31

CINDI

The rag scrapes against my sweat-stained skin. It burns against the tears and chafes my cheek, and the column of my throat feels like it has been tied off.

I struggle against the ropes around my ankles and wrists, trying to dislodge the makeshift gag, my movements sluggish. Tires rumble against gravel. It crackles and pops, filling the enclosed space.

A trunk.

They put me in a trunk after they drugged me.

Bile lurches up my esophagus. The gag and sack muffle my cry.

This is actually happening.

They've found me.

They got to me.

They're going to torture me until I beg them to kill me.

Ordus, I internally plead. He has to be looking for me, has to come find me, but they already hurt him on the beach. I don't know what the Gallaghers did to him—

Oh, God. What if they've killed him?

My terror flares, and I kick my feet as hard as I can, over and over. It gets me nowhere, other than wasting energy I don't have.

I can already imagine the incoming pain. The feeling of my bones crushing beneath a boot. Blue and black blossoming from a fist. Starving. Dehydrated. Locked away in a basement.

They could traffic me.

Please, please, please.

I pray to a God I don't believe in, a Goddess who's letting her followers be wiped out. *Ordus.*

He's the only one who will come for me, fight for me, risk everything to get me back. There have only ever been two people in my life who've put me first, and fuck, I should've recognized it weeks ago.

I should've acted on *everything* sooner, run away or married Ordus to end the Curse. Now? We have nothing to show for years of suffering and heartache, and everyone is going to fucking die because I've been dragging my feet, too stupid to realize children would be dying because of my choices.

The car comes to a stop. The engine cuts off.

My fight renews. The second the trunk opens, I unleash everything I have. I buck and kick, scream against the rag in my mouth, but it's all hopeless with my hands tied behind my back. Pinpricks of artificial light penetrate through the rag. I can't see anything, not even a vague outline of people or buildings. Foot-steps and tires crunch on gravel, but there are too many sounds for me to work out how many people surround me.

A solid shoulder stabs me in the stomach, leaving me winded. I try kicking my bound feet, wiggling my body to throw the man's hands off me but he's too strong. I keep going, attempting to gather details about my surroundings while throwing my weight around.

The moment we step inside, a door slams behind me, and I know I'm done for.

The smell of bleach, cigarette smoke, piss, and rotten flesh assault my senses. I can hear more people. The slap of sandals. The scrape of a chair against the floor. The crinkle of wrapping. A TV plays what sounds like a game show in the background. Male voices come from another room.

How many people are there? Five? Ten? Thirty?

I'm never getting out of here.

Ordus will die trying to save me.

Fuck. No—he can't. He has to go back to the island and forget about me. There's no point in the both of us getting captured.

I fight harder. I'd rather get a bullet through the head than deal with whatever's coming.

Another set of hands lands on me, shifting my equilibrium by yanking my shoulder and slamming me down onto a seat. It digs into my back, like sandpaper against my inflamed tattoo. They tie me easily to it, like I'm not screaming and thrashing for dear life, and unfasten the sack on my head, though they leave it on.

I beg them to let me go in every language I know, but none of it makes sense through the gag. I strain my eyes, trying to see. Still, nothing but the light's hue makes it through.

The echo of departing footsteps fills the room. The gunshot sound of the slammed door makes things worse. They're calling for their boss. Who is it going to be? Tommy's brother? One of their enforcers? His dad?

The ropes burn my skin as I wriggle, trying to undo the bindings around my wrists or loosen the ties strapping me to the chair.

The bag is ripped from my head, and I scream from the shock and the sudden onslaught of light. Breathing hard, I squint against the brightness.

A single, dreary, white light bulb hangs from the moldy ceiling. Brown and black stains splatter the concrete floors and yellowed walls, a watercolor patchwork foretelling the agony in my future. The peeling wallpaper curls around the rickety table loaded with guns, rusted knives, pliers, and tools I've only ever seen used on cars and construction.

Movement flashes from my side. I jump and cringe away from the person rounding me, body primed for an attack. My brows stitch together, blinking to pinpoint why the blurry face is familiar.

"Deedee?" I croak, inspecting her up and down for bruises or ropes. "What are you—what's happening? Where am I? Why am I here? Untie me."

Her arms are free. She's in the same jeans and T-shirt I saw her in during dinner—how long ago was that? I crane my neck to find a window. Is the sun about to rise?

It doesn't matter. We need to get out of here before those men come back.

Deedee tsks, and the room spins when I snap my attention back to her. "So many questions," she muses.

My frown deepens. "Deedee, this isn't funny—" The realization drops like a stone. I suck in a sharp breath at the smile splitting across her face. "The American," I whisper.

She sold me out.

My *friend* gave me up to the fucking Gallaghers.

That bitch.

Rage slices through me. Anger at her. Anger at *myself.* I was stupid to trust her. We were never friends. Why the fuck did we get matching tattoos if we didn't have some kind of bond?

"Cindi, Cindi, Cindi." Deedee's bottom lip sticks out in mock pity. "I don't even know your real name."

It takes me a second to figure out what she meant. When it finally sinks in, I want to throw up. Deedee said there was an American going around saying my actual name.

Like I'm taking too long to fit the pieces together, she laughs. "There was never any American, stupid."

I think I'm going to throw up.

"But there was a man at my house. He—he took my phone," I say in disbelief.

Deedee purses her lips in mock pity. "Yes. One of mine, babe."

"Why am I here?" I stutter, flicking my attention between her and the door. How long until the Gallaghers walk in? How much is she getting for handing me over?

Her smile twists into an ugly sneer. "Because you found him, and you *really* shouldn't have found him."

"Who?" Tommy? I—I don't understand. If this isn't about the Gallaghers, then what? Wait—*"Ordus?"*

"Yes, *Ordus.*" She spits his name. "Monsters."

I gape at Deedee. How the fuck does she know what he is? Ordus didn't recognize her, and she was acting strange from the moment she saw him.

"They feast on human flesh. *Children.* What type of sick monster are you for spreading your legs for him?" She places her manicured hands on her hips, dragging her scrutinizing eyes over me. "I thought you'd be smarter than to do something as stupid as go near his kind."

"They're not all bad," I defend. Ordus is kind and gentle. Sure, he's a bit crazy and unhinged, but that's only because his culture is different to humans. "I'm his mate," I tack on like it might mean something or explain how I got into this situation. "I won't let you hurt him."

"Cute. Like you'd be able to do anything," she scoffs, looking down her nose at me like I'm the dumbest person she's ever met. And maybe I am. "You're a human, darling. Humans and krakens don't go together. Tell me, why does he think you're his *mate?*" she mocks. "Let me guess: he feels a pull to you? He just *knows* or some stupid childish bullshit like that? Hmm?"

I shift in my chair, throwing nervous glances at the table full of torture equipment. Deedee is who the krakens are afraid of—

337

the humans they've been told to steer clear of because they're hated for their mere existence.

I continue wriggling my hands to undo the ties.

"*Mates?*" A maniacal smirk warps her face. "Hate to break it to you, girl. That's because of me and the pretty little mark I left on your back."

As if noticing the attention, the tattoo on my back prickles and sparks before catching fire. I roll my shoulders to unstick the fabric from it. "What does the tattoo have to do with any of this?"

I bare my teeth like an animal when she reaches over to tap my nose, like this is all some big fucking joke, and any second, she's going to yell "just kidding." "You know, it's a good thing you haven't let him sink his fangs into you, or else the Curse would've lifted, and I'd be very, *very* upset."

I jerk back. Deedee knows about that too? "Why wouldn't you want to end the Curse? They have women, children, fucking newborn babies."

"Ni Luh was just a child, and they killed her!" Her voice takes on a deep rumble. The dark browns of her eyes twist into the darkest shade of endless black. "Everyone in our village loved her, and his kind took her from me. She was *innocent*, and they tore her body to shreds. But you know what they did?" Her expression goes crazed. "They left us her head."

The air crackles with electricity, the type of charged energy of a haunted house, or a cemetery when the moon is at its highest. It's an unnatural shift ten times stronger than the subtle tingle down my spine when the sigils into the cave flow.

Her shoe slides along the bloodstained floor. "There are witches around the world, but none are as powerful as my mother. She was revered across the earth. My sister's powers were manifesting to be just as formidable," she explains, angry creases forming around her eyes.

My eyes drop to the bracelet she always wears. Her *sister's* bracelet. Ni Luh.

"I was the only one in my family who could make sure the krakens suffered for what they did to my sister—long after my mother's death." The rope around my wrist loosens as she speaks. "We knew she wouldn't survive casting the Curse, and the only way for it to continue was for me to act as its anchor and choose the brides so there will always be two bearing its weight. One destined to die, one destined to live. *Balance.* She gave me part of her life force so I could live long enough to watch each and every kraken be expunged for their sins."

Holy shit, she's fucking crazy.

Ordus can't come here.

How the fuck am I meant to fight off *and* run from a witch? A witch who's apparently powerful enough to single-handedly continue the eradication of an entire species.

"I'm sorry your sister died, but an entire species shouldn't pay for the actions of one—"

"They're monsters!"

"You're killing children too. Do you think that makes you better?"

"Yes." Deedee raises her chin. "It makes me stronger, because no other daughter or sister or brother will die by their hands."

"It's genocide."

She smirks. "It's justice."

I shake my head. "You're fucking sick. Go to a therapist and grieve like a normal person."

"You do not understand my pain," Deedee hisses. "I lost my sister and my mother."

"Maybe not, but I'm not going around murdering babies because someone I care about dies after casting a curse to kill krakens and all sea life in the area." She has to realize how fucked up this is. "It's over. They've learned their lesson. They've suffered enough. This ends *now.*"

Scoffing, she paces the soiled room. "Oh, it's not enough. All their deaths will be on your hands too." She points at me. "They might not be as bloody as mine, but you'll be a killer like me. That little tattoo you let me put on your back?" She taps the side of her ribs where she has the same leaf motif. "The one we both have? You're wearing the Curse."

A cold chill races down my spine. "The destined bride," I echo. I was never chosen by the Goddess. I was chosen by *her*.

Deedee nods. "Now you're getting it. If the monster thinks you're his mate, it's only because his magic recognizes the Curse pumping through your veins."

Bile curdles up my throat. It was all a lie.

"Whoever wears the mark is the one the kraken king must marry to end the Curse. They'd have to marry the thing they hate most, the kind they see as weak and lesser." Deedee laughs. "I thought it was an amazing idea."

I breathe hard through my mouth. "Why me?" I croak.

Did she sense the blood already soaking my hands? Did she see me and decide I didn't suffer enough with Tommy?

"I needed a bride, and you were available." She shrugs. "You looked like you were running from an army of demons, and I had the means to make you stay on the mainland. Control you. Monitor you. You hardly left the house, so when would you get the chance to run into him? I figured if the Curse didn't eat your life force after a year, your demons would end you so I could transfer the Curse to the next naive girl. I didn't mind those odds."

Eat my life force?

The corners of my vision go blurry with rage. Deedee's the reason I've been growing increasingly tired. It's not *stress*, it's her. God, I want to fucking kill her. "Why didn't you put it on some random tourist who'll return to their country and never come back?"

Her smile is sadistic. "Because the further they are from the Dead Lands—love that name, by the way, my idea too—the slower the Curse progresses. And you've been right here, pushing the Curse along at breakneck speed. Good job."

"And now you're going to kill me." So children can die. So she can pass the Curse to someone else, wipe out an entire population, and destroy miles upon miles of land so it's forever uninhabitable.

I twist my hands and thrash against the bindings. I need to get out of here.

"It's nothing personal, darling. You were kinda okay to be around, I guess, but I can't let you break the Curse." Deedee huffs. "I must admit, it was cute seeing you worry about the pirates. You were so blind, it was almost endearing."

I still, internal temperature plummeting. "What?" I breathe.

"Darling, I am the pirates. So is Nat."

What? No. "But—but they stole—"

She nods. "For me, yes. I have another factory—a bigger one. I knew you would never have agreed to work alongside the men, but I wanted your brains. Your ignorance was a bonus." I hate the look of pity she's giving me.

That—that can't be right. "The machines had a fifty percent success rate—"

"Don't look so confused. You were always holed up in your house and fell for whatever we told you."

Swallowing, I read between the lines. "You were undercutting me." There I go again, proving I learned nothing. I fell for Tommy's tricks, and I fell for Deedee's.

I try hard to imagine a reality in which Ordus might only be using me for his own personal gain, but I don't see it.

"It's just business." She ambles over to the table and waves at the items on it. "Do you have a preference? Bullet to the head? Knife across your throat? I can arrange to have you drowned, if that's what you prefer, so you can be reunited with the kraken. It'd be romantic—"

Screaming starts before I can answer, followed by a gunshot, then a bark.

Then a familiar, deafening roar rattles the walls.

He's come for me.

The cacophony of ensuing sounds renders me frozen as my eyes slide to Deedee, gun in her hand, sights trained on the door.

Fuck. She's going to kill him.

I struggle against the bindings. Deedee launches over to me before I can break free of the ropes. The wooden chair skitters back against the bloodstained floor, a low screech against the battle cries and snarls rattling the thin walls. My seat teeters on two legs before falling as the back of my head crashes onto the concrete floor. White light bursts behind my eyes as a scream tears from my throat.

Deedee reaches for me.

"No!" The syllable comes out garbled. I blindly kick out, unseeing, gasping for breath against the pain radiating through my skull. My heel makes contact with bone, then a body topples onto me. Something clatters to the side.

"Bitch!" Knuckles collide with my cheek.

My head whips to the side as my arms scrape against the floor. She tries to scramble upright, reaching for the gun several feet from us.

"Fuck you," I hiss, driving my knee up.

She tips forward, straddling me, her legs on either side of my body. "I'm going to fucking kill you," she screeches. Talons wrap around my throat in a bruising grip, cutting off my oxygen.

I sputter and cough, attempting to jerk away. My surroundings blur, deaf to the sounds of death and destruction. Black spots mar my dwindling vision. Fatigue sinks past flesh and bone, burrowing deep into my marrow, spreading its poison to every corner of my body.

Air slams into my lungs at the same time a loud boom shotguns through the room. Then a roar—a thundering crack so loud, I expect a blast of fire to follow. Yet all that's there is him, standing before the broken doorway, crowding the room with his presence until it feels too cramped to move an inch. His shoulders are wide, tentacles suspended in the air, coiled to strike. The heat of his rage bursts from him in violent shockwaves that rip through my flesh.

Deedee drops her full weight onto the hands around my throat, and they're ripped away just as fast.

Everything happens so quickly, my brain and eyes experience a three-second lag. A ball of yellow and cherry brown comes flying out of nowhere and latches onto Deedee's limb. Crimson explodes throughout the room, spraying the walls, the floor, my bruised skin in putrid warmth. The walls bleed with each body part ripped to shreds.

And then I feel it.

The pressing, cloying weight on my chest, like a living entity taking its first breath, a sickly puff of condensation rolling down my spine. It pulses. A thud. A shattered heartbeat right up against my own struggling one.

My limbs are weak, broken without real breaks, muscles atrophied without the passage of time. A presence leeches me of life and warmth.

Somewhere in the back of my mind, a voice whispers. Not my own, but someone else's. Hers. *Them.* The Witch and Deedee.

The Curse made to be carried by two. It's been transferred to one.

I'm going to die.

32

CINDI

Ordus whispers words I can't make out as I slip in and out of consciousness.

I feel it. It's hungry, ravenous. A beast wanting both slaughter and rest.

The moon shines overhead, bright and not quite full. It hides behind the trees we're darting past. I'm not sure how long it's been since I blacked out in the room. Minutes. Maybe an hour. Could be longer.

"Deedee is the Witch's daughter, Ordus." I force out the words between bouts of energy. "She's the reason your lands remain Cursed." My voice is raspy like it hasn't been used in days. "I can feel it, Ordus. The Curse. It—it's in me. It's there."

Ordus slows to a stop, and I have half a mind to survey my surroundings, but I can't bring myself to turn my head.

"We—we need to talk," I pant, held upright by his hands around my back and cupping my cheek. "About the Curse."

"I failed you," Ordus rasps against my lips.

I shake my head, fighting another wave of fatigue. "You didn't." My voice is barely above a whisper as I try to keep myself together. "Take me home."

The request turns his expression tortured. "You can leave, Cindi. Move away from the krakens and those who wish you harm."

Grief hits me at the thought of leaving behind the cave and the beach I know better than the back of my hand. It's like I'm losing someone I care about, and I refuse to go through it again. In the past five years, all I've done is lose: Dad, my college friends, my freedom. Enough is enough.

I'm not going to let myself lose the one place I've felt any semblance of safety. No one is allowed to take that away from me. Deedee herself confirmed I'm the only one who can end the Curse. That gives me massive bargaining power with the krakens.

We can swing it somehow.

Vasz wedges himself in the gap between our torsos, subtly licking my face as he loops around me to circle the area again. There's no universe where I could leave him behind either. I don't care if I have to spend every waking moment in a state of panic; this is Vasz's home as well, and I won't do anything to cause him discomfort. He's *my* dog as well.

"There's nowhere Vasz and you can go other than the mainland."

Ordus shakes his head stiffly. "No, Cindi. *You* must leave. I would rather become one with the sea alone than be the reason you get hurt."

My lips part. He's... Tears spring to my eyes, and I swallow down a sob. "*No.* You—you—" I choke on the words. He *can't.* He's not allowed to die. He's not *allowed* to tell me to leave.

I shove him in the chest. "No!"

"Cindi, *please.*" His forehead wrinkles like he's in agony. "I—I cannot keep you safe. I—"

"I don't give a shit," I scream, shoving him again. Face riddled with guilt, he drops his arms to his sides. "I don't *care* about safety. I don't want to run anymore, don't you get that? I'd much rather die than live a life in which I constantly feel like I'm dying —because that's not living. Life shouldn't be torture. I'd prefer risking death if it means I can be happy."

He reaches for me, and I wrap my hands around the back of his neck. "You wish to stay?"

"Yes." Without a doubt.

"With me?" he says uncertainly.

"Always." As soon as the word is past my lips, worry strikes.

Ordus still thinks I'm his mate.

He thinks his fated mate just accepted him—the one thing he wanted most.

"Take me to your island." If he decides he'd rather search for the one the Goddess chose for him, I'd at least like to say goodbye to my home for the past month and collect my things.

"*Our* island," Ordus corrects. "Yours and mine."

"Yes." I nod, tasting bile as I unthread my fingers from his hair to place my hand over his, pressing a kiss to his inner wrist. "Yours and mine. Take us home, Ordus."

It'll be my home if you let it.

"Cindi," a honeyed voice whispers beside my ear, stirring me awake.

I groan, blinking against the line of harsh blue light before we're plunged into darkness. The cold bite of the water only adds to my exhaustion. My eyelids droop closed again, and a wave of nausea has me whimpering, curling into Ordus' chest.

"I have you, little mate," he croons. A big hand rubs over my back as he tucks me tight up against him, bridal style. "You are safe."

A soft purr vibrates against my arm as I try to orient myself to the present. Memories flash of Deedee, bloodshed, and the stone-cold relief of feeling Ordus' warmth against me.

Muted pain presses against the front of my cranium, like there's a hundred-pound weight sitting on it, and any second, my head is going to go *splat*.

I can feel the Curse like it's a living entity within me, a void of bleak nothingness with fangs and an insatiable hunger for blood. Breathing and hissing, it claws at the inside of my skin, trying to break free. I can feel it gnawing away at my life force. Unless I can rip it out of me, it's going to kill me.

"Are we here?" I grumble, nuzzling into the crook of Ordus' neck, wishing I could sleep for just a few more hours, or days. I'm so tired, I never want to wake up again.

Water sluices down my arm as I bring it into the air dome to rub my eyes. I cringe as the bubble bursts, and I push past the surface of the water into the pool. He sets me down on my side on the padded floor and rushes around the cave in a flurry. My eyes drift shut, and I fall victim to the darkness again.

Loud clattering jars me out of sleep. I blink my bleary eyes up at Ordus as he hunches down beside me, a tray in hand that he sets on the floor. He pulls me upright against him, using his tentacles as cushioning and support. My brows pinch as I try to make out the myriad of objects on it: water, pill bottle, protein bar, a pestle and mortar of something that looks like healing poultices, and a little green jar he cracks open and brings to my lips.

The putrid smell assaults my nostrils, and my gag reflex immediately kicks in. *Chicken Essence*. I could identify that stench anywhere.

I unlock my jaw and swallow it down in a single go, willing my body not to throw it back up. It settles unhappily in my stomach, but Ordus wastes no time offering me a couple of gulps of water before forcing me to eat the entire protein bar and painkillers. I don't have the heart to tell him nothing he's doing is going to fix what's wrong or change the inevitable.

"Ordus," I whisper, feeling energy trickle back into me as his warmth seeps into my body.

Rubbing his hand over my legs and arms like he's making sure I'm in one piece, he cradles the back of my head against his chest. "Rest, mate. We will speak once you are better."

I shake my head, weakly pushing against him. I look up to meet his frown, and I almost burst into tears. What if I lose him? What if I tell him the truth about what we are to each other, and he rejects me? This island will be torn from my grasp, I'll never see Vasz again, and Ordus... I can't do it.

I don't want to think about a future in which I won't have him. I don't want the only thing driving me forward to be a fear of everything.

Panic flares in Ordus' expression as my eyes water, and he starts rubbing the back of my neck. It wouldn't be fair of me to trap Ordus when he has spent his life praying to the Goddess for a mate who isn't me. He—he wants a fucking kraken.

I blink back tears. "I am the destined bride who will end the Curse. But Ordus... I—" I choke, not wanting to say the words. Just a month ago, I was wishing I meant nothing to him. Now, it kills me that I'll get what I asked for. I take a deep breath that does nothing to steel me. "I'm not your mate."

"You are," Ordus responds instantly.

"No, I'm not." He's making this so much harder than it needs to be. "You only thought I was because of the mark Deedee tattooed on my back. You—it's only because I carry the Curse."

He carefully arranges me so I'm facing him, propped up against his tentacles. His warm hand moves to cup my cold cheek while he twines his fingers with mine. "You are my mate, Cindi. Fated mate or not, I choose you. If you do not want to marry me, I will still choose you. If you want to leave this island and move to a faraway land, I will follow, because I still choose you."

"Ordus," I plead, gripping the wrist touching my face. Tears stream freely down my face and over his hands before falling between us. "I wasn't who you prayed to the Goddess for." My voice is barely above a whisper.

He lowers his head to mine until our noses brush each other. "You are better than anything I could have wished for."

"Your real mate might still be out there." I squeeze him, wishing upon everything he won't change his mind. Still, I can't be so selfish as to keep him to myself if he was meant for another.

"You, Cindi. I choose you. Always. If you die, I'll follow. If you run, I'll be there. I will never let you go. I will never *not* choose you." Nudging my face like he's making sure I hear him loud and clear, he says, "I am your mate, even if you do not want me to be."

I search his eyes for any hint of hesitance, and then without any second thought, I crush my lips against his, pouring every ounce of my emotion into the kiss. His mouth moves with mine with the same reverent intensity, like there's nothing in the world that could pull us apart. Even though the Goddess didn't pair our souls together, this is fate, and I'm done fighting it.

Climbing up him, I force my limbs to comply against the weight of exhaustion. I fist his hair at the nape of his neck and curl my arms around him, flattening my body to his so there isn't any space between us.

Fire lights my veins, a single match in the utter blackness of the Curse that then spreads like wildfire. It morphs from a hollow buzz to a rattling roar. With each kiss, another spark turns into flames that burn on water. It extinguishes the frozen chill in my bones until I'm pure molten lava, melting beneath blushing skin.

More, I can feel the Curse demanding, and there's nothing else I agree with.

I pull apart long enough to say, "Marry me."

"Cindi, you cannot take it back. You must be sure."

"Where you go, I go." I steal his words as he grips my hips.

"We're mates regardless of what the Witch or the Goddess or any other asshole thinks. I want to be with you even if marrying you doesn't end the Curse. You make me feel safe, Ordus. Wanted, protected, loved. *Seen*. We had a rocky start, but I was always drawn to you. Even though there were times I wanted to be alone, I wanted to be alone *with you*. I don't want to be alone anymore. I don't want to lose anyone else. I care about you more than I thought I would. So marry me, mate."

Staring at me in dismay, Ordus says nothing, studying me like he's waiting for the punchline, and he's giving me the chance to change my mind or tell him I've decided to go off on my own and never see him again.

I press our foreheads together. "You need me to mark you, right? For the bond? Get me a knife."

Clattering sounds behind me, and I glance at the nearby shelving, watching one of his appendages rummage around for the hunting knife I keep there. I chuckle at his frustrated growl and bite my lip when the stray tentacle smacks things out of the way, opens a drawer, and instantly grabs what Ordus was looking for.

It offers me the handle, and I take it without hesitation, but trepidation makes me pause. This is *'til death do us part*. What if he changes his mind or meets his real mate? What then? Will he—

No, Ordus wouldn't do that. He's a good man—he's *my* monster.

I balance myself with a hand on his shoulder as darkness ripples through me, sapping the little energy I have. I will my body to stay strong, and I raise my chin to meet Ordus' eyes.

"Neck or chest?" I say, recalling the time I stabbed him and the very notable lack of scarring.

His purr is louder and smoother than I've ever heard it. "Anywhere you wish. I'll be grateful regardless."

Carefully, I hold the blade over his left pec. Like hell am I about to bring a knife to his throat after I killed Tommy—

because he's dead, and so is Kristy, and every other ghost who's better left in the past. Cindi is a new woman, a second chance. She is Ordus' mate and future wife. She doesn't cower in shadows or huddle in corners.

Cindi does what she wants with a smile. She laughs. She goes to bed feeling safe, protected, loved.

That's the woman who wants to marry Ordus.

"Do I need to say anything?" I ask.

"Your agreement suffices." His voice is strained as he glances between me and the knife.

Taking a deep breath, I press the blade into his skin, watching deep blue rise to the surface and trickle down his torso as I say, "I accept this bond."

I sway forward. The Curse twists inside me in both pleasure and pain, like it can't decide whether it's going to rip apart or evaporate into thin air. Ordus' hands around my waist keep me steady. Our heavy breaths tangle together as we feel the weight of the union. He takes the blade from me and returns it to its place.

"What next?" I murmur against his cheek.

"Do you remember how well you fit me last time?" His deep voice curls around my body, ratcheting up the heat pumping through my veins.

My core tightens at the memory of being stretched around his tentacles. The pure bliss. The way he looked at me like he felt complete for the first time. I cup his cheek, silently telling him I want him to feel that every day—even if we don't have many left.

I nod, and my throat bobs. Something hard and round presses against my core. I gasp, eyes flying wide open as the muscles in my core spasm.

"You're going to do it again, except this time, I'm going to put my cock in you and spill my seed—" He breaks off on a strangled groan when I reach behind me to grip the bulb.

Oh dear God.

I don't think it's going to fit. The knot is wider than my hand.

I can't wrap my fingers around it or fist it properly, though it looked manageable the other time I saw him relieving himself.

"I don't think—" Warm droplets of cum fall onto my legs.

His clawed hands dip beneath my dress and follow the curve of my thighs until the pointed edge of his nail runs over the seam of my saturated panties. "No? Were you not made for me?"

My brows draw into a frown. Is he teasing me right now?

Then my breath comes out in a rush when his clawed finger slides over my clit. The thin material is the only thing stopping me from feeling its sharpness.

A shiver rolls down my spine. "You are my other half even if the Goddess did not deem it so."

The corners of his lips curl into a smile. "You will fit, Cindi, because the only thing your sweet sex will ever need is my cock and feeling my seed fill your tight little hole. And one day, my sweet mate, you're going to bear my cub."

Ordus tears my panties in a single swipe, and the tip of a tentacle immediately fills me. I squeak in surprise, my inner walls tightening at the intrusion.

He captures my lips at my next gasp, and he sinks deeper into me, stretching me out to prepare me for his cock. My dress is reduced to shreds in the next heartbeat, then my bra, until there's not a single thread on me. He doesn't give me a chance to complain or process the sudden loss, because his suckers latch onto my clit, sending me to see the Goddess he claims exists.

Sparks explode behind my eyes, and I cry out against his lips as he thrusts his tentacles in and out of me. Pleasure reaches every inch of my body. My grip around his bulb must turn to steel, because he snarls, and more cum spurts over me. It's hard to keep kissing him when all I want to do is throw my head back and scream.

The foreign entity poisoning my soul writhes, vibrating inside me angrily and excitedly. It makes my head spin at the same time as pressure rises in my core, growing as he pushes deeper, forcing me to take the thickness.

"You're doing so well, little mate," he croons.

Ordus kisses down my neck, sucking the delicate skin into his mouth to leave behind splotches of blues and reds. I can't help but smile to myself. He's leaving bruises on me, and I like the way they feel.

"Do you want me to stop?" Ordus asks, sensing the shift in my thoughts.

I shake my head, pushing my hips down onto his appendage. I try to lift myself up to ride it, but the Curse leaves me winded after the second grind. He leans back against the rock and uses his tentacles instead to yank me down onto him.

The motion takes me by such surprise, the pressure in my core reaches a detonation point. Pure, unbridled pressure surges through me. My nails dig into his shoulder as my screams echo through the caves. Ordus growls against my throat from the grip I have on his cock, but he doesn't relent, using the opportunity to push another tentacle inside me.

My walls clamp around him. Eyes rolling to the back of my head, I massage his bulb in my fist. It never seems to get smaller.

He slips the appendage back out, thrusting into me with the single limb. Wiggling my hips back, I whimper, trying to seek out the fullness.

"More?" Ordus rasps. His suckers continue their torturous puckering at my clit, and I grunt in response, unable to form any words. "I don't think so, mate. I need to hear you say it."

He slides the second tentacle back in, only to pull it out.

"More," I cry.

Ordus complies immediately, stuffing his limb into me and fucking me until I'm so full, I can barely breathe. He leans back against the rock, and my arms drop forward to balance on his chest.

Moans and cries fall past my lips from the overwhelming sensations. It's too much and not enough at the same time.

He tugs his cock out of my hand, and I feel it skate along my thigh down to my pussy. A violent shudder tears down my spine as he removes his tentacles, notching his cock at my entrance. Warm liquid coats my core and drips down my legs.

"Are you certain, little mate? Once we do this—"

I cut him off with a whimper. *"Please,* Ordus."

The tapered tip slides in, and I gasp at the screech the Curse releases from the depths of my soul. Its panicked cries raise the hairs on the back of my neck, and I crush my lips to his to try and block out the roaring in my ears.

His appendage abruptly stops, and my eyes widen at the hard, flared bulb pushing against me.

Carefully, he contorts my body to the side, easing my legs apart with a tentacle wrapped around each ankle so I'm spread wide for him to see his cock inside me. I turn my head to gape up at him, curling one arm behind his neck to keep stable against the sprawling limbs he has me lying on.

Ordus' purr rumbles against my side as he draws his appendage out before thrusting back into me. I moan when the knot hits me, over and over, suckers plucking at my clit intensely as he pushes the bulb harder with each drive.

He pinches my nipple between his thumb and forefinger, groping the flesh as his harsh breaths fan over my heated skin, snarling and gnashing his teeth in barely restrained hunger.

The Curse is rearing its head, torn between fighting what's happening and soaking it in.

With each thrust, my screams ricochet off the walls of the cave. The echo turns into a symphony, harmonizing with Ordus' grunts and groans. Pleasure pools and spills from my core.

His hands are on me. Around me. Over me. I'm not sure. I can't think from the combination of him fucking me and the way the Curse is jerking around inside me. It's painful at the same time as it makes every sensation heightened.

Bright lights flash everywhere—maybe it's in my mind. Maybe it's real. I cry from the pure pleasure that ruptures through me, and it only climbs higher when this thick bulb pushes into me. I can't feel the sting of pain through all the euphoria, but all at once, it becomes too overwhelming.

"My mate," he rumbles. "My perfect mate."

I push his suckers away as he gives short thrusts, his knot inside me, pushing against the spot that makes me see stars.

Ordus roars as spurts of liquid heat coat my insides and drip out of the place where we're connected. The Curse thrashes against the walls of my body, frantic, feral, and I feel like I can't breathe or I'll explode. Tears gather in my eyes, and I try to blink them back. It all feels too much.

"I must return the mark." I can barely hear Ordus' heavy rasps over the live wire sparking in my veins, threatening to wrap around my heart and crush it so it stops beating. His cock pulses inside me, pumping me full of his seed.

"Will it hurt?" I force out, the sound almost animalistic from the darkness clawing at my throat.

"I'll be gentle."

A tear trickles down my face. "You're always gentle."

He kisses my wet cheek. "Only with you."

I drop my forehead to his, trying to swallow back the searing pain in my soul. "I'll be gentle with you too."

He lowers his lips to the left side of my chest, like where I put my mark on him. Teeth pierce skin, and the Curse comes alive. Agony like nothing I've ever known rushes through my veins. Blinding white light bursts behind my eyes. My soul twists and tears like I'm about to rip into a thousand pieces. I open my mouth on a silent scream.

Everything goes black.

33

ORDUS

I clutch the seaweed bag tighter, eyes darting around the water for threats. The fish within buck in their attempts to escape their fate of becoming my mate's dinner.

It has been ten days since Lazell made his ultimatum, eight since Cindi and I married.

There is no telling if the Curse is broken.

Game has not changed. I still must travel far to hunt. The earth below is nothing but sand, stone, and decay.

I don't dare travel to Krokant to see what state the land is in, whether there is absolutely nothing or if there is...more. I want to check my family's graves as well, but anything I do will mean that I am separated from Cindi for longer, and it is killing me.

My wife comes first. Always. If the Curse remains, then so be it. What's done is done. There is nothing I can do about it.

Tonight, we will flee, biding our time on the mainland until I can determine whether my kingdom has been saved. And if the Curse never lifts, I will protect Cindi any way I can, Vasz too.

I swim hard across the barren land, hating that Cindi is alone and vulnerable on the island. Vasz hasn't willingly left her side once, not unless I all but throw him out of the den.

A flash of color out of the corner of my eye stops me in my tracks. I frown, squinting against the murky waters to make out the hint of...green?

It can't be.

I swoop low to the floor and quicken my pace to get a better look. Sprouting from the sand are two shoots of bright green grass.

Grass.

Tentatively, I reach out and brush my finger along a shoot to make sure I'm not dreaming. Prickles rain across my skin when my nail hits it and it doesn't float away. This is the first sign of life I've seen in these parts in over twenty years.

It worked. The Curse is broken.

A smile splits across my face. My mate did it.

I race toward the island. I must tell my Cindi. Hopefully, she is awake so I can see her eyes brighten with delight. My family's lands are saved—their deaths weren't for nothing. If Yannig could see me now, he'd call me to the palace and insist on throwing a feast in my name, no one but the two of us in attendance. Chlaena would make decrees in my honor. My mother would be proud her outcast son has saved the lives of all krakens.

We did it—the ones my people see as vermin are the very reason they will continue to exist.

My nostrils flare as I close in on the island. A subtle wave of foreign scents are quickly approaching. Among them sits an unmistakable scent.

My knuckles crack. They're coming.

I jet the remaining distance and climb straight onto shore, speeding between the trees toward the hut. I smell her long before I see her. Our scents are mingled from the time we spent in the den this morning, seeing how many times I could make her climax. It's the most exhilarating thing to watch—and feeling her walls clamp down around me? A few times, I thought I was going to die.

Hearing my approach, she pops her head out from the hammock, and her entire face comes alight. Her brown eyes twinkle beneath the sun as the cool breeze carries her scent toward me. My eyes track the bite mark on her chest, and I release the barest purr.

Vasz huffs and resumes his chewing like I'm nothing more than an inconvenience.

My wife stumbles out of the hammock, and I whisk her off her feet, transferring her from my tentacles to my arms before she can so much as say hello. My lips are on hers the moment she's close enough, and she kisses me back like we've been doing it for thousands of years rather than mere days.

My tentacle wraps around her thighs. I shiver, tasting the remnants of my seed in the threads of her pores. It feels like if I blink too hard, it will all disappear.

I feared the worst after I bit her, but the worry was short-lived once she awoke, skin glowing like she'd had the best sleep in her life. Not once have I seen her sway in her steps or snooze in the middle of the day. She no longer sleeps longer than Vasz, and she moves faster, surer than I'm used to.

"The Curse is broken," I rasp against her lips, barely believing I can finally say those words. It feels right to have her in my arms like this.

This is what I prayed to the Goddess for. Not a mate, but a partner, someone who completes me. Someone who is smart, brave, and sees me for who I am.

Cindi's beautiful eyes round. "What? Really?"

I nod. "I saw grass growing not far from here." Soon, kelp and reefs will return. I'll make trips to the mainland to collect seeds to hurry the process along. "But they're coming. You must go to the den."

Vasz perks up and immediately sprints toward the beach, barking and growling and acting like he can take all krakens on.

"No." She shakes her hand, pushing against me as I head toward the tunnels into our cave.

"You must. It isn't safe," I growl.

We've discussed this before—the possibility of the krakens coming early before we can make our escape. She refuses to leave before giving it time to see if the Curse has been lifted.

"Ordus," she scolds. "They need to see that tattoo. They won't take your word for it."

I stop with a snarl. She has used this reasoning a great many times, and it's the truth. If we want to stay on the island, we will need to prove it to them.

"At the first sign of danger, you run," I say, staring at her so she knows this is my compromise—because I am capable of doing that. "Promise me."

She traces the mating scar on my chest. "I promise."

I hesitate before cupping her face, nuzzling my nose against hers. "I love you, Cindi."

Pressing her lips to mine, she breathes, "I love you too, Ordus."

A smile stretches across my lips. Cindi has broken every curse there is, and nothing makes me happier than knowing that, despite all odds, she still chose me.

"We need to go," she says, pulling back.

Grumbling under my breath, I snatch a machete off the ground, pass it to her, and follow Vasz to the beach. I set her down by the trees so she is at a safer distance from the water.

Vasz comes up by my side, a low warning growl in his throat. Then, one by one, krakens appear out of the water, just as sickly appearing as they were when they soiled my shore ten days ago. Females and males gather around. Only a few are civilians, most previously holding rank as hunters or sentries. In the middle stands the worst of them all.

"Ordus," Lazell starts, eyes flicking between me and my mate. When he dares look at Vasz, the mutt leaps forward, and he staggers back, hand partially raised in case Vasz carries through.

I bare my teeth at Lazell, but I do not bother correcting him. Cindi told me it is best we "send him on his way as soon as possible." There's no need for "small talk"—I'm not sure what that is, but I agree.

"You said eleven days," I speak in kraken tongue.

The corners of his eyes twitch. He notices my lack of correction too. "There is no need to delay the inevitable," he says simply, sneering at me and mine. I shift to block his queen out of view. "It was foolish to waste such precious time as we did."

I raise a single brow. "So you did not see the life growing along the floor during your swim here?" I address the entire crowd.

Many avert their gaze, guilty. Some appear struck, as if they cannot get their tongues to move to form their answer. If grass is appearing by my island, Krokant would be bursting. They'd be able to taste the quality of the water, the new shoots of life that spread beyond the small parcel.

A Counselor's jaw feathers, and I see it—her excitement. Not the morbid glee of spilling blood, but the elation of winning something grand. Of renewed purpose. She's seen it.

"No—" Lazell begins, attempting to shift my focus back on him.

"I pray the next words out of your mouth are not a lie. Swear it on the Goddess that you did not see. *Swear it* on Edea that the Curse remains."

Lazell sputters. "We have no guarantee the Curse has been permanently broken—"

"Swear it on the Goddess," I roar. Krakens flinch at the sound and bow their heads in respect. "My mate, *your queen*, ended the Curse. She was chosen by the Witch's daughter to bear the mark of the Curse." I point to Cindi. "That *human* is my destined bride, and you will all bow down in respect for her saving your brother, your sister, your daughter, son, mother, friend. *She* is the reason you live."

I nod my head at Cindi. Slowly, she turns around, moving her hair over her shoulder so all can see the tattoo glimmering blue in certain light, like the glowing algae in our cave or the threads within my skin. There is no denying it holds magic. My kind knows well enough that no human can replicate such a trick.

"The Witch's daughter inked the Curse into her skin so she may carry it and bring it to heel. If her blood is spilled by krakens, the Curse will return, and all hope is lost."

Chlaena was a military strategist. Yannig was a diplomat. My Cindi? She is a survivor, smart with her words and vicious. *Strong.* The perfect queen.

I am her weapon, and she is my voice.

For what do my subjects fear more than death? Being promised the certainty of life, only to be given a sure death, be it the Waste or hunger. To rot away into sand that will drift and disperse, forever forgotten.

To be given hope and lose it? That is a curse in and of itself, and Lazell, ever the wise Counselor, sees the threat as clear as the dawn.

Will the blood of one fill his gullet if it costs him the life of all? Will hatred feed his hunger if what I say is true?

To believe my lie, or to end in a massacre? Decisions, decisions.

I meet Lazell's eye and revel in his fury. His silence is all the answer I need.

"Kneel for your queen," I boom, daring anyone to defy me.

Sentries and Counselors cast nervous glances between each other as I stare down Lazell, their unspoken leader, waiting for his next move. His tentacles that usually mimic his surroundings are stiff at his sides, unmoving against the tides. He works his jaw, mulling over his options. Then he dips his head in the barest show of respect.

"Lower," I order.

He's tense as he does as I demand, curling his spine in a pathetic attempt at a bow.

"More."

Satisfaction oozes through me when he bends at his hips, bowing low enough for waves to splash against his face. One by one, the krakens follow Lazell's lead in a deep bow that, for once, makes me feel victorious.

I may be a king in name only, but today, I have true power. I've always longed for this feeling, yet it feels like nothing in comparison to having my mate look me in the eye and accept me, to feel her leave her mark on me and call me hers, as she is mine. That type of power could turn me into the type of male who could fill the sea with corpses.

That type of power is what my people should fear.

Cindi comes up behind me, placing her small hand on my back. "Is it over?" she whispers.

My tentacle immediately wraps around her, and I lift her into my arms, tucking her close to my chest. I nod, heading for our den. "Now I can put a cub in you without worry for your safety."

Her jaw drops. "You can *what?*"

"You needn't worry. I'll take care of you, my little mate."

"I don't doubt that for a second."

A smile stretches across my lips, one she matches. Cindi trusts me, and that's the greatest gift of all.

EPILOGUE

"Ordus. Ordus. Ordus."

He's not listening to me, holding on to Cindi as she stares at a...tomb? Boot? I don't know what the thing is called. She just yells at me whenever I get it wet.

"Ordus. Ordus. Ordus."

His face twitches, but he's still not responding. All his focus is on cradling Cindi—and not me, which is highly offensive.

The sun is out, the sand is between my toes, and the waves are calling me. No kraken has dared come near the Island in a long, long, long, long, long time. They are no threat. Why does Cindi and Ordus want to sit beneath the trees and do nothing? It's so boring.

I stomp my feet to get their attention.

More rejection.

Whimpering, I step forward to nudge Cindi's arm so she'll throw the stick, but one of Ordus' tentacles picks me up and moves me further away. He moves too quickly for me to bite him for such an insult.

Why would he deprive our Queen Mate of something she enjoys so much? She loves throwing the stick—which I find odd. It must be a human thing. I keep having to bring it back to her so she can chuck it again. It gets tiresome very quickly, but it is my duty to keep her happy. If I must catch the stick all afternoon to please her, then that is what I will do.

Ordus hasn't been letting me be around Cindi as much since her stomach became big and round—sometimes it moves like there's something trapped inside—another human thing, maybe? My child? Her scent has changed. There's a faint kraken smell to her. I don't like it.

She never goes out on her surfboard anymore.

She hates me.

She must.

Why else would she not throw the stick? Why else would she spend all her time with Ordus now? At night, he even banishes me from the den to do something to Cindi—I'm not sure what, but I'm pretty sure he abuses her in there, and I can do nothing to make it stop. All I can do is put myself between them and try to protect her from enduring such pain.

He doesn't even take me to the mainland anymore because the hunt is closer, and I don't get to see the loves of my life unless I swim out there alone.

He must hate me too.

I whimper, stomping my feet. The Goddess must hate me too if she has cursed me to an existence where I am ignored.

My ears perk up when she holds her hand out. "What have you got there, baby boy?"

Oh, she does love me.

Cindi loves me very much.

She called me baby boy.

Panting and wagging my tail, I ignore Ordus' scowl, picking up the stick to drop it into her hand. But it falls right back out of my mouth when something pushes her stomach from the inside. It's moving again. Why is it moving? Is my child hurt?

Without heeding Ordus' warning, I rush over to her, sniffing her belly. "Speak to me. Do you need help?" I say to her stomach, nuzzling my face right up to it to hear its response.

Cindi looks up at Ordus. "He's kicking again."

My eyes widen. Is the child hurting my human? Is this Ordus' fault?

He rumbles his approval and places his hand over her stomach, purring when he feels the baby move. Will he take her to the mainland by boat again? To be seen by the *dock tore* again—whatever that is?

Why is no one answering me—

Cindi scratches the spot right behind my ear that—oh yes. That's what I'm talking about. Right there. My back leg starts kicking, and every horror in my life vanishes.

"Ugh," she complains, disregarding my pouting when she stops petting me and tries moving to her feet with Ordus' help. "Yannig's pushing against my bladder. I need to pee."

I huff, skulking away toward the trees that have only gotten bigger and more colorful since the Curse was broken. Maybe I need to find a better stick.

No, I need to go to the mainland to get a coconut. It has been so long since I've gotten a new one. What if the coconuts have forgotten about me? What if I'll never be able to experience that type of love again? If I can just get one, everything will be alright again. There will be no more sadness, pain, loss. Cindi will be awed by my prowess and my ability to hunt them down for her. There is still much room in my cave for another.

Perhaps I will go to the mainland today to stock up.

But it is so far, and I do not want to go alone. I mustn't leave the island unprotected; what if someone tries to harm my child Cindi is keeping from me? What if *Ordus* does something to upset her? Who will be there to keep him in line?

I am so very busy. I do not have time for the things I enjoy. It's like the Goddess is punishing me for working so hard. Yes, I get the pats, and Cindi calls me a good boy, but the love of my life is still out there, waiting for me to bring her home.

I nose the ground, eyes darting to every fly that buzzes past.

Something hits the ground beside me. I yelp, skittering away from my attacker as I bark at it to show I am not scared. No, not at all.

The warning growl cuts off. Is that—*no*, it can't be. But how?

I glance up at the sky before dropping my gaze down at the beautiful, round, green fruit in front of me. *A coconut.* I sniff it just to be sure.

A coconut from the forbidden coconut that glows at night.

Oh, she's perfect. Ripe and green, untouched by harsh seawater. It's like a newborn coconut.

But how is this possible?

My tail wags harder and thumps against a tree. Another coconut falls from the sky.

Is this a blessing from the shark-doggopus Goddess? I am being rewarded for all my sacrifices. That must be it. Just as Cindi recognizes my brilliance, so does the Goddess.

My tail hits the tree several times, and another lands on top of the pile. Am I...am I magical? I simply thought it, and it appeared.

I'm a witch.

Yes, that must be it.

I snatch the coconut off the ground and sprint across the forest in search of Ordus, skittering to a stop when I find him tying something around a tree. My eyes narrow as I set a curse upon him to do everything I order.

There is only one king on this island.

And that king is me.

The End.

WANT MORE?

Want to see how life looks like for Cindi and Ordus' new family? Or maybe see the dildo get put to good use...

ABOUT THE AUTHOR

From an early age, romance author Avina St. Graves spent her days imagining fantasy worlds and dreamy fictional men, which spurred on from her introverted tendencies. In all her day dreaming, there seemed to be a reoccurring theme of morally grey female characters, love interests that belong in prison, and unnecessary trauma and bloodshed.

Much to everyone's misfortune, she now spends her days in a white collar job praying to every god known to man that she might be able to write full time and give the world more red flags to froth over.

(Update: Avina is now writing full time)